Praise for …

# Waterfall

"I love stories about strong, capable young women—and I love stories set in other countries. Mix in a little time travel and some colorful characters, and Lisa Bergren has stirred up an exciting and memorable tale that teen readers should thoroughly enjoy!"

**Melody Carlson,** author of the Diary of a Teenage Girl and TrueColors series

"As the mother of two teens and two preteens, I found *Waterfall* to be a gutsy but clean foray into the young adult genre for Lisa T. Bergren, who handles it with a grace and style all her own. Gabriella Betarrini yanked me out of my time and into a harrowing adventure as she battled knights—and love! I heartily enjoyed Gabriella's travel back into time, and I heartily look forward to *Cascade*, River of Time #2!"

**Ronie Kendig,** author of *Nightshade*

Praise for …

# Cascade

"A romantic tale that twists and turns with every page, *Cascade* is the ideal sequel to *Waterfall*. A riveting tale to the very end, this adventure follows Gabi back into the arms of the dashing Marcello as the events of history unfold around them in the present. Lisa T. Bergren leaves us with only one question: Can their love transcend time? Read this book—you won't regret it. I could hardly put it down!"

**Shannon Primicerio,** author of *The Divine Dance, God Called a Girl,* and the TrueLife Bible study series

The River of Time Series

*Waterfall*

*Cascade*

*Torrent*

# TORRENT

*The River of Time Series*

# LISA T. BERGREN

David C Cook
*transforming lives together*

TORRENT
Published by David C Cook
4050 Lee Vance View
Colorado Springs, CO 80918 U.S.A.

David C Cook Distribution Canada
55 Woodslee Avenue, Paris, Ontario, Canada N3L 3E5

David C Cook U.K., Kingsway Communications
Eastbourne, East Sussex BN23 6NT, England

David C Cook and the graphic circle C logo
are registered trademarks of Cook Communications Ministries.

The website addresses recommended throughout this book are offered as a
resource to you. These websites are not intended in any way to be or imply an
endorsement on the part of David C Cook, nor do we vouch for their content.

This story is a work of fiction. All characters and events are the product of the author's
imagination. Any resemblance to any person, living or dead, is coincidental.

LCCN 2011932486
ISBN 978-1-4347-6429-4
eISBN 978-0-7814-0783-0

© 2011 Lisa T. Bergren

The Team: Don Pape, Traci DePree, Amy Kiechlin
Konyndyk, Caitlyn York, Karen Athen.
Cover Design: Gearbox Studios

Printed in the United States of America

First Edition 2011

1 2 3 4 5 6 7 8 9 10

062911

Now this is not the end. It is not even the beginning of the end. But it is, perhaps, the end of the beginning.

—*Winston Churchill*

# Chapter One

We'd shaken the dust from the gowns the guys had left the three of us and slipped on our "medieval disguises," as I called them, but there wasn't a whole lot we could do for Dad.

"Yeah, that's not gonna work out so great," Lia said, staring up at Dad's T-shirt.

I looked him over, still not quite believing he was with us, alive. We'd buried him, laid flowers on his grave, and mourned him for seven—no, eight months now—and yet here he was, hands on hips, ready to take the lead in our family again. Like we'd never been gone. Which, for him, we hadn't been.

From his perspective, we'd grown up by a couple of years while he was at an afternoon's dig.

Such was the nature of time travel.

His brown eyes flicked from me to Lia and back again, like he couldn't quite believe his eyes either. In our luxurious gowns we looked more like women than teens, which had to be freaking him out all the more. He turned toward the walls of the Etruscan tomb.

"Adri, this is amazing," he said, reaching for the flashlight in his back pocket and taking in the frescoes, inch by inch.

He'd always been that way. Preferring archeology you could slice and dice, *control,* over teens who were so…unpredictable.

Mom wrapped her arms around him and leaned her cheek against his back, closing her eyes. "Yes, it is."

I held my breath and felt Lia still beside me, both of us staring at them. Mom and Dad. Together again. I swallowed hard around a lump in my throat and felt my eyes and nose begin to run.

He grinned over his shoulder at Mom. "What's gotten into you, Adri?" He caught sight of us. We probably looked like we were seeing a ghost again. Literally. "Girls?"

I couldn't bear to keep looking at him. Not if I was supposed to keep it together.

"I'll tell you. Soon, Ben," Mom said. "After we're out of here." She hadn't quite figured out a way to tell him that we'd gone back in time to rescue him, before he was killed in an accident. Way before the accident. It would be hard enough to get him to believe we were time travelers, that he wasn't living some sort of wild dream.

She leaned back and reluctantly let him go. "But first, we need to figure out what you can wear. Because Lia's right—*that* isn't gonna work." She looked him up and down. He was in his archeologist's uniform—a battered, old "I Left My Heart in Roma Antica" T-shirt, khaki cargo pants, and work boots. So handsome, with his broad shoulders and wavy hair—which I'd inherited, along with the big brown eyes and long lashes. *My dad. Here. With us.* I sniffed and swallowed hard, past the lump in my throat, trying to get my brain in gear. There were things to do, urgent things, if we were to keep him safe. And after losing him once, I wanted to do all I could not to lose him again.

"The boots might be okay," I said, assessing. "We could tell them they're Norman. As long as they don't look too closely."

"At least he isn't wearing sneakers," Lia said. She was crawling toward the entrance of the tomb, her bow hitched over her shoulder.

"You'll have to stash that flashlight, too," I said, following Lia. "That would totally freak them out." I reached down and picked up my broadsword, sliding it into the sheath on my back, then strapped onto my calf a leather dagger sheath, a seven-inch blade already in it.

"Adri," Dad said blankly, "our children are arming themselves."

"Trust me, it's a good thing," Mom said, picking up her staff.

"You're kidding, right? And what are you doing with *that?*"

I didn't wait for Mom's answer. I crawled after Lia to the tomb's entrance. It reminded me of an igloo, in a way, something Mom said she'd never quite seen in Etruscan tumuli architecture before. I tried to peek beyond Lia, see what season we'd landed in. How much time had passed? Did Marcello leave us our gowns three days...or three *years* ago?

Lia reached the end and peered outside, first in one direction, then the other.

"Go, Lia," I growled, feeling as if I might burst from the anticipation. It was like landing at some exotic airport and being in the very back of a packed jumbo jet, unable to get out. I well remembered the last time we'd arrived in Marcello's Toscana, how we'd run across them on the road to the castello, how he'd taken me in his arms and held me like he never wanted to let go...

"Lia, *go!*" I said.

She whipped backward and almost bumped her head into mine. "Hold on," she whispered, staring at me with wild eyes. "Enemy soldiers, nine o'clock."

I leaned my back against the side wall, sitting next to her, and glanced back at Mom and Dad, coming our way. I lifted a finger to my lips and then closed my eyes, listening to the men draw nearer outside. They were talking, laughing, clearly not on alert.

Lia eased her bow from her shoulder and slowly drew an arrow from the quiver at her back. There was little room for her to aim, but if we were discovered, it would at least buy us time. I slipped the dagger from my calf strap, rehearsing a likely scenario. She'd shoot the first man and come running out of the tomb, hopefully screaming, counting on surprise to work on our behalf. I'd follow behind and, with luck, cut down the second. I didn't know if there were more, but that'd at least get us outside, give us a chance at making the tree line.

Which was kinda important. Because if we didn't escape the tomb right away, and the men called for reinforcements, it might very well become our own grave. Who were they? Paratore men? Fiorentini? What had happened?

My eyes settled on the limestone wall across from me, and for the first time, I saw more frescoes. Winged figures. In a row. They caught my attention because Mom always liked finding "Etruscan angels." I patted her hand and nodded at them. I'd just noticed that interspersed among them were other figures—a Roman legionnaire, with his distinctive fringed helmet, and a Greek ruler, crowned with green laurel leaves, and what looked like a peasant—when I felt Lia tense beside me.

I could hear them more clearly now. Two of them, laughing and talking. Relaxed. Like they'd been on guard duty too long.

Enemy soldiers here in disputed territory, and in such a relaxed state, meant one of two things: either Castello Paratore or Castello Forelli was still in the wrong hands. Or both were.

I prayed that it was just Castello Paratore. That Marcello was nearby, not miles away in Siena or beyond. When we'd left, our guys had been about to retake this land again. But who knew how much time had gone by since then, what had transpired, how many battles had taken place…

*Marcello, Marcello…please be alive.*

I prayed that we wouldn't have to try and go back in time to save him as we had my dad. That he'd simply be here, waiting for me, opening his arms to me, kissing my cheeks and—

Lia sucked in her breath, and with one glance, I could see that they'd spotted her. They were moving from shock to suspicion, reaching for their swords, turning to call out—

She rolled out of the passageway—leaving me room to move at the same time—and shot the first man. I sent my dagger flying, but the second man saw it coming and ducked to the side. We both watched it sail past, as if it was moving in slow motion, handle over blade, until it stuck in the tree trunk five feet beyond him. He looked back to me and pulled his sword from his side scabbard, growling in fury.

Hurriedly I rolled outward too—easier than crawling in a gown—and pulled out my broadsword as I rose. Lia was aiming her arrow at the first of two other men now rushing in our direction. Above them I could see the crimson flag flying from the parapets of Castello Paratore and knew immediately that my nemesis again resided there. Cosmo Paratore. I swallowed bile at the thought of seeing him, remembering well the murderous rage in his green eyes.

But I had more pressing issues than Paratore. The knight approached me, studying my face as if I were a cobra, never looking away from me. He was about Marcello's size, far bigger than I, and he eased a massive sword in a figure eight at his side, as if warming up. "Could it be?" he asked. "The Ladies Betarrini have returned?"

I ignored his question, knowing he was only trying to distract me with banter. I had to be ready for his first strike, and thought through how he might lunge or turn and pull the full weight of that sword down toward my shoulder.

"Gabriella, look out!" Dad cried in English behind me.

I turned just in time and sucked in my breath. The arrow came so close to my belly that I felt the feathers brush the thick embroidered thread of my gown. Then I heard the grunt of my adversary as it plunged into his gut. His sword tipped, nearly out of his hand, and dipped into the ground between us. He stared down at the shaft of the arrow, which had pierced his chainmail.

I looked back to see another arrow flying in my direction, and I ducked and rolled, army crawling as best I could toward a boulder that would give me some sort of protection. I surveyed our battlefield, wondering just how bad our situation was. Lia had turned her attention to the sniper above us, and Mom turned to face the two men who attacked them, slowly turning her staff in her hand. Dad had picked up the dead knight's sword but looked around at us like we were in the middle of some sort of terrible dream.

"Dad!" I screamed, seeing a knight almost upon him. "At the ready!" It was the command he'd used a thousand times with me, training me to fence with a far lighter blade. Instantly he assumed the position, but I could tell he wasn't mentally prepared. I remembered the first time I'd met the strike of one of these heavy medieval swords—how the force of it had so surprised me, how it had reverberated in a teeth-crunching, breath-stealing echo down my arm to my very spine.

Dad had just braced his back leg and brought up his sword when his attacker reached him. He narrowly blocked the second strike, moving as if he were still in his dream world. I shook my head. It would be seconds before the knight got the upper hand and cut him down.

"No way," I muttered, pushing to my feet and running toward him. "I'm not losing him again." I screamed a battle cry, hoping to distract the knight, but he was focused on my dad, driving him backward, one step at a time. With each clang of the swords, I could see he was getting closer to Dad's neck.

I drove toward his attacker, holding my sword with both hands like a battering ram, ignoring two arrows that sang by me. But the Paratore knight caught sight of me coming and flung himself back from my father at the last second. He brought up his sword, nicking my arm. I cried out, feeling the warmth of blood as it flowed down my skin, beneath the wide sleeves of the gown.

My cry seemed to wake Dad from his stupor, and he lunged at the knight, driving him backward this time. Mom was there, then, clubbing the man from behind with her staff, sending him to his side and his sword skittering away. She reminded me again of some sort of freakin' Viking queen, with her staff at an angle, her blonde braid swinging, her legs askew, braced.

When the knight groaned and then rolled, reaching for a dagger at his waist, Mom clubbed him again, knocking him out cold.

*Yeah, that's my mom,* I thought in wonder and admiration.

Dad was looking from her to the unconscious knight, in shock again.

"Stay with us, Dad," I said, touching his arm. "These guys play for keeps."

"I see that," he muttered.

Lia sent another arrow flying through the brush above us.

"Did you get him?" I asked, searching the trees and bushes for the sniper again.

She shook her head. "I don't think so." She glanced toward me. "He might be headin' home."

My eyes moved to Castello Paratore and the hated crimson flag rolling in the cold breeze. For the moment no other guards seemed aware we were here. We'd taken down six of them. Probably the patrol assigned to keep watch over this hill. "We gotta get outta here," I said.

"Agreed," Lia said, rising.

Mom was already pulling the chainmail off of the tallest knight. I knew what she was after. His clothes for Dad.

"Whoa. *Mom,*" Lia said, eyebrows raised.

"Hush now and help me," Mom said, clearly in no mood for teasing. Lia bent to pull off his boots. Dad stood aside, still staring at us like he couldn't believe this was all real.

"Adri?" he muttered.

"Help me lift him, Benedetto," she said. "You need his shirt and trousers as well."

"Are we truly in such a state that we need to rob a poor dead fellow of his clothes?"

It had taken us a few days of being here to understand, to comprehend that we weren't in some ongoing nightmare. Why would he be any different? Again I caught myself way too entranced in watching Dad move, speak, think things through. We were on dangerous ground. If I didn't keep it together, we might all soon be dead. More of our enemies might show up any sec.

Hunched over, I moved toward the last of the tumuli—the mounded, round roofs of the Etruscan graves—and cautiously peered around a giant old oak. I could see the guards on the walls of Castello Paratore, her gates firmly closed. They seemed relaxed, not yet alerted to our arrival or the sounds of our battle. But then my eyes went to the hill above me, and I worried that the sniper was making his way to the castle right now, about to shout out his alarm.

We had a few minutes, at least. I hurried back, for the first time recognizing that it was winter. The trees and brush were barren. The question was, what winter? The winter following the autumn I left, making it now 1344? Or another year entirely? It was late afternoon; we'd soon be swallowed by the dark. It could be cold and wet in these high hills of Toscana. Higher up, farther east, it was even known to snow on occasion.

I hurried over to my family and the unconscious, bleeding knight, now in nothing but his filthy leggings, the medieval version of long johns. "Let's go," I urged. "Dad can change when we're someplace safe."

"And where is that?" Dad muttered, grasping his bundle of stolen clothing more firmly.

"I'm hoping ahead, outside the next castle." I reached down and picked up the fallen knight's dagger. I'd already taken the pearl-handled dagger out of the tree trunk and resheathed it in my calf strap. "Here," I said, handing it to Dad. "It's good to have a backup."

He took it from me, staring into my eyes as if I were some foreigner speaking a language he didn't know. As if the medieval Italian wasn't enough…his daughter was speaking a warrior dialect.

"Come on, Ben, trust us," Mom said, taking his hand. She held the staff on her opposite shoulder. I moved in front to take the lead. Lia dropped back to keep an eye on our rear flank.

"When did you learn to wield that, Adri?" Dad asked, after a few minutes of walking.

"The last time we were here."

"And why don't I remember that?"

"You weren't with us," Mom hedged.

"You've never been interested in sparring before. I thought you were a pacifist," Dad said to her.

"I was. Until my daughters were fighting for their lives."

He didn't respond to that; perhaps he was considering what he'd just witnessed. We entered the woods to the south, those once claimed as Forelli territory. Was it back in the hands of the Sienese? I shivered and rubbed my arms, feeling the chill of the late afternoon as we slipped beneath the shadows of the forest.

We paused near where Marcello had allowed me to change into a gown the first time I arrived. I remembered the way his eyes had crinkled up at the corner in a mass of laugh lines when I emerged wearing it backward. I remembered the feel of his hands, calm and efficient, as he helped me button it up the back. I remembered his expression, so warm and intrigued…

Trust me when I say I'd never captured a guy's attention from the start.

And no guy had ever so captured me.

Dad emerged, wearing his new clothes, wrinkling up his nose. "Do these guys ever shower?"

"Not as often as we'd like," Mom said with a smile. She reached up and straightened his collar. "You might not smell so great, but you look hot."

"Ewww, Mom," Lia said. "We're *right* here."

"Cut me some slack," Mom said under her breath to us so Dad couldn't hear. "I've been without him for a while."

"I know, I know," Lia said, groaning.

I smiled and pushed forward. I'd only been away from Marcello for what—a half a day?—but I thought I knew a little of what she felt. I couldn't wait to be reunited with Marcello. To have him beside me, taking my hand in his, meeting my dad…

The idea of that brought me up short. But just for a second—Dad *had* to love Marcello. He had to.

I pushed forward, reaching the riverbed, the reeds dry and crackling in the breeze, the brush nothing but spires of stalks awaiting spring's greening. After pausing a moment to listen and look for enemy patrols, I scurried across the rounded stones to the other side, my family right behind me. We watched for a few seconds, but no one seemed to be around.

The path eased onto the road, the road where, last time, I had run across Marcello. But not this time. Three birds flitted around the giant, barren oaks above us, craning their necks to watch. Other than that, there was no sound but the crunch of the rust-colored leaves beneath our feet.

I glanced back at Lia when we passed the boulder and trees where we'd taken shelter last time, worried that Marcello's troops were enemies. We paused there now, catching our breath. Lia watched the road in one direction, and I watched the other.

Dad looked like he belonged in medieval Tuscany, with his long curls that brushed the edge of his collarless shirt. His olive skin and dark eyes were meant for this place, all earthy and whole-some and alive. I couldn't help myself; I wrapped my arms around him and hugged him tight.

"Wow, what's this for?" he asked.

"I'm just glad you're here, Dad. With us."

"Adri?"

I glanced at Mom; she was tearing up. "Later, Ben. I'll tell you later."

"O-kay," he said slowly.

Lia looked over at us, her eyes filled with confusion. "Why aren't they after us yet, Gabs?"

I shook my head. "Maybe you got the sniper and they haven't found the guards at the tumuli yet."

"But when they do—"

"Yeah, I know; we need to keep moving." I turned and set the pace again for us, a soft, padding, steady clip. In half an hour we reached the crossroads, and ten minutes later I slowed, hunched down, and eased toward Castello Forelli, careful to remain hidden.

My breath caught when I saw the rebuilt walls and gates, the movement of guards at the top of the walls. Hoping, wishing, I half stood before Lia whispered harshly. "Gabi, *get down.*"

That was when I saw it. The long, white banner with the red cross on it, waving above Castello Forelli.

The Guelph cross.

Firenze's symbol. Not Siena's. Not Marcello's.

The question was now, if Firenze still held Castello Forelli, where would I find Marcello?

# Chapter Two

Lia pulled back on my arm, easing me farther into the brush, thoroughly hidden from the guards high above.

I thought about what it was like when we'd left—hours before for us but apparently much longer for those here. I had so hoped that our men were on the verge of recapturing Castello Paratore *and* Castello Forelli. They'd had an opening...there were so many of our guys in this valley between the castles. Castello Forelli had been in shambles, her gate and front wall decimated. And now she was whole, repaired, stronger than ever. How long had that taken?

"How long have we been gone?" I asked Lia.

She read the fear in my eyes. Had we been gone years, decades? It'd be difficult to find out the date here. There were no newspapers, no computers, no watches, no cell phones keeping track of it. But we had to find out before we were too far from the tomb and our time tunnel. And yet if we were caught in enemy territory...I shuddered at the memory of being thrown into the cage in Firenze and hauled upward, left to die. How much worse would our punishment be this time?

"What if we try to make it to Signora Giannini's?" Lia asked.

I frowned. It was maybe a few miles from here. But Siena was a good half day's journey. "If she's alive."

"If they *are* there, they'll hide us, let us stay overnight," Lia said.

She was right. We hardly had a choice but to go and see. I nodded once. "But let's head over those hills. We'd be idiots to keep to the roads."

"Good plan."

I turned toward Mom and Dad. "We'll go to a friend's cottage to learn what has become of the Forellis—"

"And find out the date," Lia put in.

"Do you think the Gianninis are still there? If this has become Fiorentini territory?" Mom asked. She'd come with us, once, to assist the young mother with her harvest while her husband was away fighting.

I shrugged. "Do you have a better idea?" I glanced at the sun that was obscured by gray clouds. "I don't think we can make Siena before nightfall."

"Someone's coming," Dad said.

For the first time, I heard the rumble of horses' hooves. "Patrol," I growled. We rushed backward, easing farther into the forest, and took positions behind rocks and trees. The twelve men galloped past on the road, their eyes casually scanning the forest. On duty, but not yet on alert. Their demeanor oozed the confidence of men who'd been in control for a while, not threatened in the least. And their captain was one I recognized: one of Lord Paratore's most trusted men. My eyes met Lia's, remembering how Paratore had captured her, threatened to torture her. How he'd nearly brought us down in Siena. How he'd threatened me when he captured me the next time, leered at me. If Lord Greco hadn't been in the mix…

A shiver ran down my back, and I looked around, feeling the chill of the woods overtake any sense of warmth. How far back had the Fiorentini pushed the Sienese? How long ago?

At the crossroads we heard them divide and glimpsed one group heading toward Castello Paratore. Where were the others?

"With good luck they'll bypass the tumuli on the road below," I said.

"With bad luck they won't," Lia returned, "and they'll find the dead knights we left behind."

*And then the hunt will be on,* I finished silently.

"We cannot be captured here," Mom said.

"Let's go, Gabi," Lia said, moving out.

I shook my head. Going to Signora Giannini's took us a couple miles deeper into enemy territory. It felt wrong. And yet we didn't really have an option. We needed someone who owed us, someone we could count on. We needed a friend. And the Gianninis were the closest thing we had.

We were about a quarter mile up the hill, having just found a deer path, when we heard the alarm bells of Castello Paratore.

Lia paused, glanced back at me, and then doubled her pace. They'd check the main roads first. But the bad part was that every enemy knight would now be on heightened alert, looking for us. Not *us*-us, necessarily. But anyone out of the ordinary. Anyone who would be capable of cutting down a patrol of knights. Luckily their first thought would not be a family, especially a family with three women dressed as nobility. Unless that sniper had escaped Lia's return fire and reported back…

One option would be to take to the road and pretend we were just travelers heading from one city to the other. But it'd be odd for us to be on the move without horses or luggage. And if just one person recognized us—

*Best to stick to the deer path,* I thought with a shudder. Besides, there were more places for us to hide in the woods, should they broaden their search. It would take us much longer to reach the Gianninis, but it'd be safer.

We reached the other side of the hills a couple of hours later. While my parents and I rested, Lia moved ahead of us, scouting the area. My stomach rumbled with hunger, and I knew we were all in some serious need of water. *Please let us spend the night with the Gianninis,* I found myself praying. *Please, please.* The sky was growing thick with gray clouds. The last thing we needed was to be caught out in the rain.

"So…why exactly did you want to come back here?" Dad asked, sitting on a mossy rock and picking a dried weed apart with his fingers. "Why not stay in *our* Toscana, where people aren't out to kill us?" He glowered over at me.

"So…right. This isn't the best situation," I admitted. "But it'll get better. I just need to find out where Marcello is."

"Who's Marcello?"

"The guy she's in love with," Mom said.

Dad's mouth dropped open and he looked over at her. In his mind I was still about fifteen years old, not almost eighteen. Not that three years would make a huge difference to a dad.

"So we're here because of some teenage infatuation—"

"Not infatuation, Dad. Love."

His mouth clamped shut.

"Lia, too," Mom said. "She's on the verge, anyway."

"I don't know if I'd call it *love* yet," I said, seeing the alarm in Dad's eyes.

"And that…that's okay with you?" Dad asked, staring at Mom.

She stared back at him, a rueful expression in her eyes. "They're pretty amazing young men, Ben. I think you'll like them."

"And…they couldn't find amazing young men back in our own time?"

"Probably," she said with a nod. "I mean, I've seen you staring, noticing. Our daughters have become young women."

"Yeah, about that. I can't figure out how—"

She reached out and caught his hand. "Sweetheart, the biggest thing I discovered, last time I was here, was that I didn't want to be anywhere without our girls. I discovered I'd been missing them for a long time. And I don't want to miss them again. Just like I don't want to miss you."

He dragged his eyes from Mom to me. "You could take us back?" he asked. "Leave us in our own time?"

"Maybe," I said carefully. I looked to Mom, wondering when she would explain.

"Ben…" she said, hesitating, her light brown eyebrows furrowed.

He remained still, waiting.

"The reason the girls are so different, so grown up, the reason you weren't with us the last time we came, is because we came *back* in time to save you."

"Save me."

"Save you." She bit her lip, obviously choosing her words. "About eight months ago"—she paused, choking up, then she cleared her throat and went on—"you were in a terrible accident. On a road near our excavation site. It was mid-December—we'd come during the girls' vacation—and it was raining."

He shook his head. "Did I get a concussion? Because I don't remember that. We've never come to Toscana in the winter—"

"You don't remember it because you haven't yet *lived* it." Remembering, she looked up to the gray clouds, and I saw that her skin was about the same color. "A farmer came around the bend in the narrow road, about the same time you did, and you swerved to miss him. You were killed instantly."

He straightened. "Killed," he said dully.

"We buried you, Dad," I said, my voice cracking. Tears immediately welled in my eyes.

"And then, the following summer, we found the new tumuli site, up on that hill," Mom said, gesturing back behind us. "And within Tomb Two, the girls discovered the time tunnel. They went back, came here, without me. Then returned. I went with them that second time. And then we knew we had to try a third trip—to try to save you."

"You came back for me," he said, his tone numb. "And it worked."

"Yes. But what I don't know is if we can ever go back now," Mom said. "We've seen that we're modifying history by being here. Castello Forelli—in our own time, it was in ruins. But when we returned for you, it was whole, a tourist attraction. So…buildings can be saved. History can be changed to some extent. But a life, once gone…Can that be changed too?"

"We could go back, to right before…" He couldn't seem to make himself say it. "Not even come to Tuscany that Christmas."

"If we can get to that year," I said. "There's a fair amount of luck involved."

"Or is your time done then, regardless of where you are?" Mom asked. "Will you meet some accident on a Colorado highway instead of a Tuscan road?"

"But the same logic could be applied here, Adri. If my time is up, then will I die here? Some arrow find my gut? A knight cut me down?"

I shuddered. "I hope not. But don't you think…Dad, *we* think we might have a better chance here, in this time, to see you *live*. Don't you see? We'll never have to face that horrible day in our lifetimes. Not if we're here in the fourteenth century."

He studied me, then Mom. "So, then, we just give up our lives as we know it? Everything we've worked so hard to accomplish, gain?"

"Would that be so terrible?" Mom asked in a whisper, reaching out to touch his thigh. "Benedetto…" she whispered, "you don't know what it was like, seeing you dead." She swallowed hard. "Living life without you. Pushing forward, knowing my best friend was gone forever." Her big eyes grew teary, and Dad wrapped a hand around the back of her neck. "This place, Ben, that time tunnel has given us a second chance. Maybe we're meant to be here, all together. Meant to discover life anew, as a family."

"I wasn't convinced at all either, Dad," Lia said, rejoining us. "But trust me, this place, this *time,* grows on you."

I smiled at her, then nodded in the direction she'd just walked from. "What'd you see?"

"We're about a quarter mile from the Gianninis'," she said, pointing northward. "Let's stay to the woods, though. There are Fiorentini patrols on the road."

We waited until it got darker before we dared leave the woods and head down to the Giannini cottage. I remembered the last time we had been there, when Signore Giannini had returned home so ill with the plague. I wondered again if they were all dead and gone by now. Or had he recovered, as Luca had, before any of the rest got it?

As the rain began to fall, we hurried down the back path, and I knocked on the door. Lia stood behind me, arrow drawn but hidden, in case an enemy answered.

Signore Giannini came to the door, and I took a breath of awe and relief. Friends, at last.

"M'ladies," he said with a gasp, looking as though he was going to pass out at the sight of me and Lia. His eyes moved beyond us, to our parents. *"Entrate, sbrigatevi,"* he added, drawing us in. *Come in, quickly.* He stared toward the empty road for a long moment before closing the door. "What are you doing here? It is not safe!"

Inside, Signora Giannini immediately set to bustling around us, handing us lengths of cloth to dry our hair, sending children to the fire to fetch us cups of warm stew. I introduced my father to the family, noting that the kids looked like they'd grown an inch or two. Had it been a year? Three?

"We have been away since the great battle," I said. "We escaped and went home for a time and came back to find Firenze had retaken these lands. Our friends at Castello Forelli are long gone. Pray, tell us what has transpired."

"Why did you not go directly to Siena?" he pressed with a grumble, as the children gave us our mugs of hearty stew. "It would've been far safer. And without horses? Guards? Do you not know what could happen to you—to us, for hiding you?"

I stared back at him. "Trust me when I say we had no other option."

"Siena owes you a great deal," he said with a slow nod. "And as a loyalist, I do too. We lost this edge of the border, and the castellos, but we held a great deal. Most credit the Ladies Betarrini and Lord Forelli and his men for accomplishing that."

My heart pounded at the sound of the Forelli name on his lips. "Lord Forelli—do you speak of Marcello?"

He nodded, once. "Lord Fortino has long languished in Firenze's prison."

I paused, absorbing his words. *Fortino in prison? Still? No. It's not possible…* "How long?" I asked.

"Since the battle ended, more than a year ago now."

I glanced at Lia and Mom. A year ago. It'd been autumn when we left. It was winter now, so I figured we'd returned about fifteen months later. Fifteen months! Had Marcello given up on me?

"Fortino still lives?"

He shook his head gently. "I have not heard a report in some time, but we hear very little in the country."

"Especially on this side of the border," his wife added.

I sighed. Fortino had been in such poor shape when we last saw him—beaten and bloody—how could he have survived more than a year in prison?

"Lord Marcello has been given the title in Lord Fortino's absence and made one of the Nine."

"One of the Nine?" Lia asked in wonder. "He's in Siena?"

"As we speak," Signore Giannini said. "He resides in Lord Rossi's palazzo." He stared at me, still clearly wondering why we hadn't gone there first.

"And the Rossis?" I asked. "What became of them?"

"Tried for treason and hanged at the city gates," he said with satisfaction. "Every last one of them."

I shuddered, thinking of Lady Romana, her father, and the rest of the family strung up from the gallows. They deserved it, for their treachery. How many Sienese had died trying to turn back an attack the Rossis had helped orchestrate? Hundreds? Thousands? But still, I had known them. Eaten with them, conversed with them…slept in their house. And poor Fortino. He'd almost married Romana, seemed to genuinely care for her. What damage had that heartache done to his battle for life?

We each had a few bites of stew, conscious that we were taking the family's only food, and filled up on water.

"You can sleep here tonight," Signore Giannini said. "But I must insist you be gone before daybreak."

"What would happen if we were discovered here?" Dad asked.

Our host looked at him as if he were crazy. "We had to swear our allegiance to Firenze in order to keep our farm. My family and I would die if they knew of our betrayal," he said. "And the man who found you would be very rich. The bounty for the Ladies Betarrini has been set for more than any other in my lifetime."

"A price on your heads," Dad muttered under his breath in English. "Just what we needed."

Lia smiled. "Don't worry," she said lowly. "We're used to it."

# Chapter Three

The Gianninis managed to borrow a neighbor's horse and gave us two of their own, too. Although one was an ancient nag with a sway back and another carried both me and Lia, we made good time; by noon we were about halfway to Siena.

As the forest thinned and the road widened, I got more and more excited about seeing Marcello. "He remains your own," Signora Giannini had said. "Long has he pined for you, even while he draws the eye of many eligible young women. Hurry to him," she said with a sideways squeeze of my shoulders. "He will be beside himself with joy."

I intended to. In fact I continually fought the urge to break our horse into a full-on gallop. We'd just turned the bend when we saw twenty-four men on horseback, coming our way. "Good guys?" Dad asked.

"They have to be, this far in," I said, hoping my tone conveyed more confidence than I felt. After all, it had been right about here that we'd once been ambushed on the road to Siena. "If they were Fiorentini, they'd hardly be so bold."

We pulled up and waited for the men. In minutes they were before us, their horses prancing on the muddy road. "State your name and business," demanded the captain, his brown eyes snapping from one of us to the next.

"We are the Betarrini family, on our way to see Lord Forelli," Dad said, just as we'd rehearsed it.

The younger man beside the captain let his mouth drop open, then abruptly closed it. They shared a glance and he nodded once. "It is they. I met them more than a year ago in the Rossi palazzo. At a ball." His eyes traveled up and down me, then across Lia, obviously thinking we didn't look nearly as hot as we had then. And we weren't riding sidesaddle, causing many men to crane their heads for another look.

"We shall escort you to Lord Forelli," the captain said. "While these roads have remained safe for some time, Marcello would have our heads if any harm came to you."

My eyes met his. "You know Marcello?"

He smiled, and I saw a cute gap between his front teeth. "Since we were boys," he said with a nod. "I am Captain Anselmo Palmucci. This is my brother, Alessio," he said, looking to the younger man beside him.

"I am Lady Gabriella Betarrini." I went on to introduce my sister and parents. Then we moved out, down the road, Captain Palmucci and his brother flanking me and my sister, while others protected my parents. An extra mount was found for my sister, and the men insisted my mother not travel on the old nag's sway back.

"Hardly appropriate," said Captain Palmucci, "for any of the Ladies Betarrini to travel on anything less than a fine mount." Arrangement were made to send the horses back to the Gianninis, and we moved out at a faster pace.

"We have been gone for some time," I said. "We gained word my father was alive—not dead, as we had presumed—and we were blessed to find him. Tell me, what has transpired for Siena in the last year?"

"We turned the Fiorentini back in the great battle, but, as I assume you know, we lost both Castello Forelli and Castello Paratore, as well as another outpost on our northwest border. Since then there have been skirmishes here and there but no further battle." He shrugged his shoulders. "They taunt us; we taunt them. But it is all bravado, an effort to keep the enemy in line."

"And...Lord Fortino Forelli? What word have you about him?"

Captain Palmucci hesitated and then looked at me from the corner of his eye. "He remains imprisoned. The Fiorentini have been most vile in their treatment of him, but as of a month ago, he still lived."

I swallowed hard. It took little for me to remember the cold, shivering nights of the cage, the people throwing rotten fruit at me as I entered the city. How much worse had Fortino suffered? How much more could he tolerate, given his once-weakened health? The last time we were here, such continuous trauma would have sent him into asthmatic fits.

"Marcello must have plans to free him," I said.

"He has tried every *diplomatic* road possible."

I stared hard at him. Diplomatic, right. But by now Marcello had to be thinking of something more Tough Guy. Like storming the city. The problem was that Firenze seemed to have twice the men Siena had. Hand to hand, our soldiers could be easily turned back. We needed a diversion to draw them out...or gain a way in.

I thought of Lord Greco, the man who had both imprisoned and freed me, and how his tat matched Marcello's—they were clearly a part of some sort of ancient brotherhood. My eyes slid over to Captain Palmucci. Was he one of them too?

"Tell me, Captain Palmucci," I said, "how is it that I met your brother at a ball in Siena, but not you?"

"I was otherwise occupied, working on Siena's behalf," he said with a sly smile. "If I hadn't been, nothing could have kept me from a celebration that boasted the Ladies Betarrini as guests."

I smiled. Man, I loved ancient Toscana. Every guy I met liked flirting with me. If I wasn't so into Marcello, I could definitely get used to being a popular girl—something that I'd never had a chance to do in Colorado, in my own time.

In a few hours we started to glimpse Siena—peeking through the valleys, then hidden behind hills, then visible again. Her high, red stone walls and tiled roofs served as the foundation for the white and black marble cathedral and bell tower. I fought the urge to break away from our orderly group and gallop up and into the city. I knew the way, didn't I? Through the winding streets to the great piazza, Il Campo, and above it, to the old Rossi palace?

I forced myself to wait, to not raise alarms at the gate. *Marcello, I'm here. Can you feel me?* So strong was our connection that I almost believed we shared some sort of sixth sense about each other. I knew it was silly, but I couldn't help wondering…

An hour later we finally entered the gates, and we could hear people shouting, spreading the news that the Ladies Betarrini had returned. By the time we reached Via di Banchi, we were mobbed, people shouting and reaching out to touch our skirts and our legs, to pat our horses. If it wasn't for our escorts, I thought we might very well have been stopped in place, unable to move.

Captain Palmucci and his brother led the way, ordering people out of the way, forcing their way forward and tugging on our horses to follow. Lia, Mom, and I smiled as we reached out to touch the people's hands, feeling very much like princesses receiving our public. Dad just stared in openmouthed wonder at the spectacle of it all. I was sure it all must have still seemed like a crazy dream to him. Hadn't it felt the same to us for days the first time we came here?

"It appears Lord Forelli has gained word of your arrival," Captain Palmucci said, all deadpan over his shoulder. I looked beyond him and grinned. Marcello was there with Luca and two other men in gold tunics, making his way to us.

When he neared, Captain Palmucci said, "M'lord, I found these fine folk on the road from Castello Forelli."

"I'm grateful to you, friend," Marcello said, barely pausing to clasp hands with him before coming alongside my mare. The people pushed backward, giving us a little room, a pocket of space. "M'lady," he said, reaching up to clasp my waist and covering my face with his eyes like he was kissing it all at once.

I leaned down to hold his shoulders, and he helped me to the ground. "Gabriella, how glad I am to see you. I so feared—"

"Shh," I said, reaching up to touch his lips. "I'm here now. And I was never far, not in my heart."

He pulled my fingers into his and then kissed them once, twice. I threw my arms around his neck, and he kissed me then, ignoring propriety. Longingly, pressing me close. The people cheered and laughed.

A man coughed beside me. And then I knew. *Dad.*

I looked up quickly to confirm my hunch. *Great. This could be...
awkward.*

"Dad...uh, *Father*, this is Lord Marcello Forelli."

Marcello's eyes widened in surprise as they moved from me to
my dad and back again. "Your...f-father?" My waist suddenly felt
cold at the absence of his warm hands.

"I shall explain later," I said hurriedly to him. "But yes. This is...
uh, Lord Benedetto Betarrini."

Marcello bowed deeply and then, keeping his head tucked in
deference, said, "M'lord, I am so pleased to make your acquaintance.
And I humbly ask for your forgiveness over my most forward manner with your daughter."

Dad frowned and crossed his arms, ridiculously proud of himself, totally milking the moment. If I wasn't so happy he was alive, I
would've killed him.

"I think I like this guy," he whispered to me at long last. Then
he reached out a hand to clasp Marcello's, and they looked into each
other's eyes, silently communicating.

*Oh, brother,* I thought, fighting the urge to roll my eyes. "Father,
have you made the acquaintance yet of Marcello's cousin, Luca Forelli?"

Okay, I was being totally evil, but I wanted the Protective Father
Heat off my back. Dad's eyes followed mine to Lia, who was standing with Luca and Mom. He immediately turned and went toward
them.

Marcello and I shared a small smile as he took my hand in his,
and we edged closer to each other again. "Ah, my love," he said, "how
I've missed you."

"Forgive me my absence, m'lord."

"All is well, now that you are once again home. Come," he said, placing my hand on his arm. We stepped forward, gliding over the cobblestones toward Palazzo Rossi, now called Palazzo Forelli.

The crowd parted before us, people pressing back into others to make way for us as we walked side by side. Women held their hands over their mouths, tearing up, and men smiled broadly. There was one thing the Italians loved more than family and God, and that was love. And I knew that in Siena, my love for Marcello, and his for me, had already been spoken of for months. Signora Giannini had hinted at it; Captain Palmucci's reaction to our presence had confirmed it. And now the people made it undeniable.

I glanced over my shoulder and saw that Luca and Lia were directly behind us, with Mom and Dad behind them. "Good to have you back, m'lady," Luca said, cocking his head and quirking a smile.

"Me? Or my sister, Sir Luca?"

He grinned down at Lia. "Both of you. Marcello and I have been lonely wolves pacing the den, looking for our She-Wolves."

I smiled up at Marcello, and he smiled too. "A fair assessment," he said.

"But it appears you have had much to occupy your attention, m'lord," I said. "I hear you've been made one of the Nine."

"Largely due to you."

"To me?"

"To you. Had it not been for your…diversion during the battle, it is likely that Siena would have suffered far greater casualties. They'd breached the gates and were only narrowly held back. Had the reinforcements that you detained arrived, Siena may well have been overcome."

"I was more concerned with drawing them away from *you* than the city," I said lowly.

"I understood that. But you accomplished both. The city found herself more grateful than ever to you, your sister, and mother. And after the treachery of Lord Rossi, the Nine found they were short a man. They graciously elected me."

"I always thought you were more the soldier than the politician."

"I don't know," he said, nodding toward the open, fortified door of the palazzo. "There seem to be advantages to both."

I smiled and entered, noting the fresh coat of whitewash on the plaster walls. We climbed the stairs and entered the main hall, where there were finely carved chairs and settees scattered about, as well as a blazing fire in the old stone hearth.

Marcello shared a word with a servant, who left, presumably to fetch refreshments. Seeing that I had moved to the flame, he asked, "Are you cold, beloved?"

"Only a chill from the road, m'lord."

He turned, and with a pull of his head, servants brought us chairs. In seconds we were settled on them, woolen blankets spread across our laps, trays of hard salami, soft cheese, and crusty bread delivered, goblets of watered wine poured. The servants disappeared, closing the doors behind them.

Only we six remained in the cavernous hall—my family, Luca, and Marcello.

"Was it quite difficult, returning?" Marcello asked, leaning forward.

"Nay," I said. "It only took us some time to locate my father."

His eyes moved over my parents, and then he shook his head. "'Tis a miracle."

"Indeed," Mom said, taking Dad's hand.

"That is why you left? To try and save him?" His eyes searched mine, and I saw the traces of torture within them, the waiting, the wondering.

I covered his hand with mine. "It was our only escape, the tunnel," I said. "But yes, the chance to save my father…we could do none else." I studied him, silently begging him to understand, to forgive me for leaving him again.

He gave me the small, tender smile I loved so, his eyes warm like melted chocolate. "So your story shall be that you were away, searching for your father in Normandy—"

"Britannia. Let's make it Britannia," Dad put in.

"Britannia," Marcello said easily. "We've told some that you originally hailed from that far north—in case rumors spread that English is your alternative language—but that you spent some time in Normandy. A bit farther apace will be a good thing. Already there are men in Normandy seeking you."

"Us?" Lia said blankly.

"On behalf of the Nine," Luca said. "We couldn't very well stop them. They were bent on finding the She-Wolves of Siena and rewarding them further. Once again, you are considered the saviors of the battle."

"In truth Siena seems a bit lost without you. The Nine are only somewhat sufficient in keeping the tongues of gossips busy. The people need something more intriguing than us to do that," Marcello said, raising his goblet in a silent toast to us.

"Even better if one of the Nine is in love with one of the Ladies Betarrini," Luca said with a grin.

Dad sat up a bit straighter in his chair.

"And his captain in love with another," Marcello said.

Luca cast a furtive eye in Dad's direction, and his smile faded a little.

It made me and Lia and Mom grin. It'd take some time, but we were confident that Dad would come to admire Marcello and Luca as we had. Any other outcome was impossible to consider.

"So when they find no trace of us in Normandy and return, will that cause difficulty?" Mom asked.

Marcello shrugged. "Normandy is a big land, is it not? And you are clearly merchants, constantly on the move. We can explain it away."

"Because you are one of the Nine now," I said, narrowing my eyes at him.

"That aids my authority to quell rumors," he admitted.

"But being one of the Nine does not make him God," Luca said. "We need to know what we should say to those who heard that Lord Betarrini was thought dead."

We all looked toward Dad. "I could be Lady Betarrini's second husband," he said.

"No," Mom said. "You are my first and only." She looked to the rest of us. "Can we not simply elaborate on what Gabi said? We thought him dead but then learned he was still alive?"

"We're merchants, yes?" I said. "What if his ship was lost at sea? But then he was found on a remote island? Surely that's happened many times…"

Marcello and Luca were nodding. "Yes, that could work."

"So, Dad, where were you shipwrecked?" I asked. "Tell us, so that we might all remember the same tale."

He smiled and leaned his elbows on his thighs, his hands clasped beneath his chin. "I believe it was somewhere far away, a place where few could ever verify my tale, and fewer would voyage to inquire."

The other men nodded again, pleased that he understood what they were after.

"It was an uninhabited isle off the coast of Africa, a few miles from where I had ventured to expand our trade in spices," Dad continued.

"Uninhabited," I said. "Most convenient."

"Indeed," he said. "And I awaited rescue for long months—"

"Before you were rescued and made the long journey home. I think that would make our timelines match up. We were reunited in Britannia and began our journey, just narrowly beating the snows in the mountains."

"Months and months on the island. Existing on nothing but coconuts and bananas," Dad said with a smile.

"Coconuts? Bananas?" Marcello asked.

"Coconuts," Dad said. "With a bark-like covering, hard shell, and inside, a sweet, white flesh and milk you can drink."

"Sounds like food of the gods," Luca said.

"It is, in a way."

"What of ba—?"

"*Bananas*. A tube-like fruit that also grows in clusters from palm-like trees. They ripen from green to yellow, and you peel them. The fruit inside is soft."

"So soft you can mash it and feed it to babies," I said.

"Wondrous," Marcello said. "So then you were reunited six months ago and began your journey here."

I nodded. "But we stayed in inns and in large cities, conscious to keep our identity hidden, in case there were any Fiorentini loyalists about."

"Making it impossible to track your journey, in case anyone decides to verify your story." He smiled at me and my family in admiration. "I must say, you are most excellent at spinning a tall tale."

"Only if it allows us to live a free and honest life here," Dad said, a tinge too sternly. *Okay, Dad, ease up on the whole honor front...*

Marcello's smile faded. "Of course."

"What of your brother, Marcello?" I asked carefully. "Is there any news of Fortino?"

"Too little." His big, brown eyes moved to the fire, as if he could see his brother's image in the flames. In the fifteen months he'd been here without me, he and Luca had filled out—become more men than the boys they had been. He shook his head a little, and his curly ponytail edged over one shoulder. I shifted in my seat, wishing we could be alone. I wanted to kiss away his sorrow, his fear.

He'd dealt with more than a year without me, wondering if I would ever return. He'd lost his father and seen his brother beaten and taken prisoner. He'd lost his home—not that this palace was too shabby—but it wasn't *home*. He was more a man of the woods than a man of the city. And to know your brother was hurting, maybe even dying—who could really relax and enjoy any part of their life with that going on in their head?

I leaned forward and took Marcello's hand. "So…how are we going to get him back?"

# Chapter Four

Mom spent all day in a room, hidden away, trying to teach Dad the dances we'd be expected to lead after the celebration feast tonight. Their distraction was welcome—giving me hours with Marcello and Lia hours with Luca. We took a stroll along the city wall, finding it too difficult to maneuver along the crowded streets full of well-wishers. Up top we had to contend only with grinning guards who raised playful eyebrows in our direction.

We paused at the highest point of the wall, where it descended to a valley and looked out for miles over brown, winter-dormant hills. "Gabriella," Marcello said, turning to me. He took my hand in both of his and stared into my eyes. "Tell me you won't leave again."

"I'll do all I can to never leave you again," I said, as much as I could promise.

He stared into my eyes, clearly understanding but wishing he could press for more.

"I don't know if leaving is even an option," I said. "If we go back, would my dad die en route? Would we lose him all over again?"

"You could halt your journey before his death," he said reluctantly. "As you did to bring him here."

"And what? Go back to freshman year with a seventeen-year-old's body? Run the risk of running into a younger version of myself?" I shuddered. "No way," I muttered in English.

"Freshman year?" he asked.

"A nightmare I don't wish to share," I said with a grin.

His eyes remained curious, but he didn't press. He probably didn't want to encourage me to think of the possibility of leaving. And I couldn't blame him. Had I been the one who had to survive a year without him, I would've been a total basket case. Zoned. A puddle of tears, all the time. No, that just would not work. Here, *here now* was where I belonged.

"If you are to stay, then I should speak to your father, without delay, of my intentions."

His intentions…about marriage? I shifted uneasily. "Uh, about that. Let us wait a couple of weeks, all right? My father…he has so much to absorb, understand about this new life. Should you speak to him too early—"

"He would say no to *me?*" he said, suddenly Prince Uppity Pants.

I smiled. He had a right to be a little miffed. If he lived in my time, Marcello would've been in the running for Sexiest Man Alive in *People*. Rich, powerful, and hotter than wasabi, he was a *force*. "In *Normandy*," I reminded him, "girls rarely consider marriage before eighteen. No, more like twenty-one, twenty-five."

He wrapped his burly arm around me, placing his hand at the small of my back and pulling me close. "And so how many days must I count before you reach your eighteenth birthday?"

I thought for a moment as he kissed my temple and then slowly worked his way down to my cheek with light, gentle, lingering presses of his lips. Who was I fooling? I was as eager to be with him—forever—as he was with me. Did I really have to wait until I was eighteen? And in this crazy time warp, when was my real birthday anyway? This was all so wild and crazy and foreign, why not bail on it all and follow my heart?

"How many days, Gabriella?" he growled, then found my lips with his. We kissed for a long moment.

"Too many," I said, my eyes still closed. I was memorizing the leathery, spicy smell of him, the feel of his arms around me, the way he made every inch of my skin alive with interest, pulling me, like a rising moon to the far horizon.

"Then I shall speak to your father about my intentions."

"Not yet," I said, edging slightly away. If we stayed together, making out, I'd be agreeing to an elopement within minutes. I already felt a little dizzy and flushed.

"We'll speak of it soon," he said. "And determine our best course."

"Agreed." We continued our walk, and I did the math for how long it'd be before I turned eighteen. I knew it'd be a factor for Mom and Dad. If we took into account that it was technically February here, it was really only about one month away. Never mind that we'd skipped some time in our back-and-forths. If this was the life we were going to assume, shouldn't we assume its date stamp too? If that was the case, I was going on nineteen, not eighteen. Yeah, I was picturing my parental units' faces too. It'd be a struggle, for sure.

"Let's get Fortino home first," I said, side-stepping it. "He should be with us to celebrate."

"*If* we can get Fortino home," Marcello said. He shook his head, a distinct ache in the movement. "It's been more than a month now

since we last had word of him. I have pursued every means of negotiation possible but…"

"But?"

"It is nothing," he said, looking away and then gathering me
up in his arms again. I heard his pounding heart as I nestled
against his chest. He didn't have to say anything more. I got it.
The only trade the Fiorentini would ever make was Fortino for a
Betarrini.

"You cannot steal inside Firenze's gates and rescue him as you
once did me?" I asked.

"It is possible that Lord Greco will aid us once more, but it puts
him at undue risk. It is he who has sent me reports that Fortino yet
lives. It's likely due to him that my brother lives at all."

"And you have held to a truce for all this time?"

"An uneasy truce," he allowed. I looked up into his face. "And
yet hours ago I received word that a small patrol of Fiorentini knights
were cut down around the tumuli between Castellos Paratore and
Forelli." A small smile edged his lips.

"A most unfortunate event," I said, matching his small smile.
"Perhaps it's time to extend some good will," I chanced. "Show them
that we are once again a city that is willing to offer a hand to our
neighbors. Squelch such violence. Reengage them so that we might
both prosper."

His eyes narrowed. "And how would we accomplish that?"

"With a visit, of course," I said, edging past him, unnerved by
his hard stare.

"I would simply approach the gates and they would welcome me
in?" Marcello said.

"Nay. That'd be far too dangerous. But what if it was a far grander spectacle? Something both Firenze and Siena had equal interest in? The Nine meeting with the grandi, sitting down at one table to dine, to move past the past, on to the future." I dared to look back at him.

"And what would draw them to such a table?"

"The Ladies Betarrini, emissaries of peace and goodwill."

He let out a big laugh over that one. "Last I knew, you had killed a good number of Fiorentini and injured more. There is not one man in that city that doesn't salivate at the thought of seeing you strung up just as the Rossis were here in Siena."

I swallowed hard as he paced past me to stand on my other side, staring out to the valley again with me.

"There is one man," I said.

He shook his head. "Rodolfo Greco has already risked far too much. And it's far too dangerous. It would never work."

"Then let us find another plan that shall," I said lowly. "I am willing to help in any way I can, beloved. For your brother. My friend. Anything."

But I could tell he already was thinking.

He turned and touched my cheek, so softly I felt more the warmth of his hand than his skin. "I shall find a way, Gabriella. To bring him home. You shall stay here, in the safety of Siena."

When I returned to my quarters, Giacinta and another maid, a young brunette named Savia, were awaiting me. Savia poured a bucket of steaming water into a wooden tub that was already half full, and Giacinta tossed in several sprigs of lavender. I smiled and moved past them to where they'd laid out a gown for me.

"Oh," I breathed. "It's magnificent." I reached to finger the exquisitely embroidered bodice on the luxurious golden silk. Off the shoulders and tight-fitted, the gown would cling to my torso and hips, then cascade in luxurious, generous folds of the skirt.

"He had it made for you as soon as he moved to Siena," Giacinta said, coming beside to admire it with me.

"So long ago." I smiled at her, but I could well imagine those lonely moments. The thought of Marcello pining for me sent a pang of ache through me.

"We must be about it, m'lady," Giacinta said, "if we're to have you ready in time."

I nodded, and we turned toward the tub and bathing screen. In short order the two maids helped me undress and turned their backs as I slipped beneath the blessedly warm waters. "Would you care for us to scrub you, m'lady?" Giacinta asked.

"Nay," I said, as ladylike as I could. Apparently I'd reached the status that required servants to wash me like a baby. "I shall see to it myself. Return in half an hour to see to my hair though, will you?"

She gave me a little curtsy, as did Savia behind her, then quietly closed the bedroom door.

I dunked myself under, letting the water infiltrate my oily, filthy hair. Then I reached for a chunk of the lavender-laced lard soap, scrubbing my head until I had a little layer of bubbles. If there was one thing the fourteenth century needed, it was some decent hair products. But it was what it was, so I continued the process of cleaning up my body, rinsing, and then I sat in the water while it cooled, which took only a few minutes. *Decent hair products and hot running water.* The Romans had had it…when did the Italians lose the technology? I smiled, imagining Dad coming up with the same thought. *Yeah, he won't be short of things to do.*

I rose and dried off with a rough towel, then wrapped it around me. I donned long underwear and had just begun to try to wrap my torso with a long cloth—the medieval version of a bra—when the maids gently knocked and then entered at my soft invitation.

Giacinta batted away my hands and undid my clumsy start at the cloth. "Nay, you shall ruin it. You must have a smooth line under such a gown!"

I closed my eyes and willed away my desire for modesty since that was clearly not on the top of anyone's list. And with underwear like this, how was it really possible? She began at the waist, tucking the edge in after two rounds, then quickly and efficiently wrapping the rest of the way up. "Mummified," I muttered as she tucked the end under my right armpit.

She ignored my mutterings in English and turned to the gown, lifting it with some effort. I'd picked it up myself—it weighed at least ten pounds with all the heavily embroidered fabric. Teaming up, she and Savia lifted it over my head and then let it fall. The top of the sleeves were tight, clinging to my upper arms, and at first I worried it was too tight, that it wouldn't fit. But they tugged it into place, and I saw that it was perfect, the sleeves gracefully billowing out at the elbow again.

Giacinta moved behind me and cinched the bodice closed—as tight as the arms, by the feel of it. But she quickly had the fifty or so loops and buttons closed. She stood back to admire me. "Oh my," she said, lifting a hand to her mouth. "You're truly a vision, m'lady."

Savia bobbed her head in fervent agreement. "A vision," she parroted. She bent to help me slip into matching tapestry slippers, and then they led me to a small dressing table.

I was glad that I recognized none of the furniture. Apparently Marcello had emptied the palazzo and started anew, wanting nothing that reminded him of the Rossis, their treachery, or their end. It was a bit creepy, really, living in their house. But hadn't Marcello lost enough in the battle? If he couldn't get his own home back, he, of all people, deserved such a prize as this fine palazzo on the piazza. I hoped I'd see the day the castello was restored to him too. In the meantime I'd help transform his memories here, from betrayal to love, from treachery to trust.

Giacinta swiftly combed out my mass of tangles, ignoring my wincing, then she began to create an intricate series of coils, incorporating strands of pearls and fine, gold thread. An hour later she finally was done, and she stepped aside so I could peer into the dim, cracked looking glass. "You are a wonder, Giacinta," I said, smiling over my shoulder at her before sneaking another peek. Only on the day of my presentation in Firenze had my hair been fancier. My usual style ran the braid or ponytail route, but this…well, this made me feel A Hundred Percent Girl. Which was fun, once in a while.

A knock sounded at the door, and the two maids shared a secretive glance. Marcello. It had to be. He'd come to escort me to the ball. Savia let him in, and he strode across the room as if he owned it. Which he pretty much did, of course. But that was part of what was different about him since I returned—that whole manly confidence thing he had going on. A sense of ownership, power. No wonder he had been chosen to be one of the Nine.

I tried to rise from my chair with the grace of some sort of beauty queen and walked toward him.

His hand moved to his chest. "M'lady, you are far more beautiful than I even imagined you would be in that gown."

"I am most grateful for it, m'lord. Thank you for such a fine, extravagant gift."

"There will be a hundred more for you, should you care to have them made," he said dismissively, his eyes only on my mine.

"I couldn't," I said. "It'd cost a fortune."

"You can. The coffers are full, Gabriella, and yours to use as you wish. And there's the additional account holding the gold the Nine gave to you and Evangelia before. You are one of the wealthiest women of the city, Gabriella."

I smiled. Because like, two months ago, I was begging Mom to borrow thirty bucks for a sweater.

Rich. I could get into that.

We took the secret tunnel down to the Palazzo Pubblico, where tonight's ball would take place. Two knights led the way, with me, Marcello, Lia, Luca, and my parents following behind, and two other guards behind them. We could hear the people laughing and singing in the palazzo above, their own party already started.

"The last time I was in a tunnel with you three," Luca said, "it felt far less promising."

"Oh, that was horrible," Lia said. "Don't even talk about it."

I sighed, remembering that terrible day, when he was so deathly ill, and the villa was being destroyed behind us. How enemy soldiers hunted us. How we had to go deeper into Firenze's territory in order to try to escape. How we had to separate. It really was some kinda crazy miracle that let us survive.

I thought about the questions that had clung to me ever since I first arrived in this time. Musings about God's reason for bringing us here in the first place. There had to be a rationale, some sort of mission for me to accomplish to warrant all that I'd been given—love, family, my dad's life, money. I mean, people didn't just land into that kind of luck, did they? Usually they deserved it, because they were worthy. Because God knew they'd do the right thing with all they'd been given.

I glanced back down the tunnel at Mom and Dad. They were archeologists, not medical doctors. They wouldn't be a huge help when the plague arrived. But they were smart, crazy smart. Maybe they could figure out a way to help. But then I thought of the Forellis' castle. How it once had been destroyed but, in present day, was whole. Our mucking around in the bogs of history had created that change—what would happen if we were able to treat and save all those who were to die in the plague? What would that change in the future? And was that a good thing?

"We're here," Marcello said as we emerged from the tunnel. He raised a brow and offered his arm. "Ready?"

I shook off my dark concerns. *Quit with the emo thoughts, Gabi,* I told myself. I was supposed to feel like a debutante on her presentation day. Or at least what I thought it might feel like to be a debutante at her first ball. In Colorado we didn't do much of that whole Southern belle thing. Which didn't mean we didn't think about it…every girl, deep inside, wants her moment on the floor. That moment when she feels like a princess. Noticed. Admired. Known.

We'd had the rock-star reception in the piazza when we'd returned to Siena before, as her victorious She-Wolves. But this, this, I thought, as the entire room hushed and all eyes turned to us, was my Serious Princess Moment.

On Marcello's arm I glided to the center. Lia and Luca, Mom and Dad, were right behind us. In the middle of the hall, Marcello brought me to a stop, and we stood in a line.

"Ladies and gentlemen," Marcello said loudly. "None is more glad than I to make this announcement. The Ladies Betarrini and Lord Benedetto Betarrini have returned to Siena."

The room erupted in applause, and I grinned back at faces I recognized—the Nine, their wives, other nobility. Marcello gently turned me, and we greeted those behind us. There were a couple hundred people in all, but everyone stared at me like they knew and loved me.

That was the overwhelming sentiment of the moment: love. Never had I felt that kind of goodwill in one place, from so many. I was so caught up in it, so adoring My Moment, this chance to be with Marcello again—possibly forever—that I drifted in a kind of zoned-out bliss from dinner to dancing. When it finally ended, I was reluctant to let it go.

At the tunnel entrance I hesitated.

Marcello glanced back at me. "Gabriella?"

"We should go back through the piazza," I said. We could hear that the city's people were in full-fledged party mode. We could smell the smoke from the bonfires. "Let's join them in their festivities."

Marcello shook his head. "It's far too dangerous. Come, you may greet your people during the light of day, should you still so desire it."

"They fought alongside us, Marcello," I said. "Many of our people gave their lives to our cause. Who are we to remain separate?"

"Remember your arrival? That was during the day, before the people were full of wine. Tonight they shall be relentless in their fervor."

"It may take us a while, but we'll get across Il Campo eventually. Come, love. This night has been far more amazing than I ever imagined. I'm not ready for it to end. Are you?"

He stared down into my eyes, as if searching my face for the right answer, and then he looked over at Luca.

"I'll call in a few more men," Luca said with a laugh. Lia had her game face on, and my parents seemed open to it.

I smiled, but Marcello frowned, as if second-guessing himself. "We will not take such risks often, Gabriella," he warned. "But Siena would be most grateful for the opportunity to greet her She-Wolves."

Six more of Marcello's knights, dressed in gold tunics, assembled behind the other four that had been with us all evening. "You three will be with Lord Forelli and Lady Gabriella," Luca said. "You three with me and Lady Lia. And you four shall surround the elder Betarrinis." He looked to Marcello for confirmation, and Marcello nodded once, affirming his plan.

They would essentially form a barrier around all of us, but I knew it was the best I was going to get. So I went with it. We moved out, and within minutes a cry went up, waving through the crowd in a repeated echo. "The Ladies Betarrini! She-Wolves! The She-Wolves!"

We were halfway through the piazza when circles of dancers and throngs of people stopped us. People were howling like they were wolves out during a full moon, laughing and cheering. Everyone we passed kept a respectful distance, but they reached out their hands for us to touch them, like we were bestowing magic or good will or something.

"She touched me!" screamed a woman.

"I've been touched!" yelled a man.

And so it went, over and over as we made our way forward.

A large man dared to step forward. "Begging your pardon, m'lord," he said, "but I wondered if the lady would be so kind as to consider a brief dance."

I wanted to dance. Not in the provincial, hoity-toity manner of the nobility within the Palazzo Pubblico, but in the earthy, celebratory way of the people outside, moving with so much joy, so much momentum, their breath clouded before their faces in the cold, dark night as they passed by.

Marcello kind of scoffed—which really bugged me—and was shaking his head, preparing to say no. "I would be most delighted," I said. I stepped forward and took the man's hand, and two men on fiddle-like instruments—*viellas,* if I remembered the term right—immediately began to play the song they'd been playing when we arrived.

"What is your name, sir?" I asked.

"Nanni Bencini," he said so bashfully I imagined he was blushing to his collar, though in the dark of night I couldn't see it. "M'lady, you've done me the greatest honor."

"Say no more, good man," I said. "Simply show me the ways of your dance."

Others filled in around us with Luca, Lia, and my parents on the far side of the circle, grinning my way. It seemed that all their dances were done in circles, reminding me of a bat mitzvah I'd gone to last year for a friend. I just hoped they wouldn't lift me up on some sort of rickety chair. That'd really make Marcello—who was already silently steaming behind me—go ballistic.

"Come, Marcello," I said, "Join us."

"I'll stay here and keep watch."

The other three knights on guard duty exchanged a look, but Marcello remained stubbornly focused on me.

*Whatever,* I thought, shrugging my shoulders and turning back to the circle. He really could be so irritatingly *decided* at times. Maybe this would help him loosen up. Give me a little more freedom. Because, well, I had a dad again. And I didn't need Marcello for some psycho father-figure-slash-boyfriend role. I needed him as my boyfriend. That was it.

On either side of me, men were showing me the dance steps, the women beside them doing the same. The musicians slowed the music so we could catch on to the steps, and then a man on the far side called out, "Get on with it!" and they immediately went to double time. We were off, kicking out our heels, tapping our toes, lifting our knees, and then galloping three paces to the right. Strong hands grasped mine, and then we were weaving, trying to keep to the dance steps while moving in and out of other lines of people. I laughed when I missed steps, and others laughed with me, instantly forgiving or perhaps too drunk to care.

I was concentrating so hard on the steps that it took me a while to figure out we'd joined with other circles of dancers. My family was separated, and yet the joy and goodwill among the people made it seem like they were all family to me—like the greatest family reunion ever. Like even if I didn't know all their names, I knew I belonged with them. Pulled, I lurched forward and laughed, catching up again, smiling as people came together in the center of our current circle and clapped.

At one point I was on the high side of the shell-shaped piazza, and I could see the entire mass of dancing people below me. They were singing a new song, each on the trail of the person ahead of them, interweaving. I ducked and went under the arms of a group waiting for ours to pass by, and then when we were at the center, it was our turn to pause and let a hundred others go under our arms.

Lia and Luca passed by me, Lia laughing, Luca looking like he might be regretting the whole thing. Lia called over her shoulder, "It's like a town-wide, medieval version of Twister!"

I laughed, and they were gone. We'd lost the guards somewhere in the mix. I hadn't seen my parents in fifteen minutes—they were likely on the other side of the square—and I'd changed partners thirty times because every time we moved into a tight circle, released our companions' hands, and yelled "*Vita!*" we turned and were claimed by a new group of people. I had no idea why we were shouting *Life!* to the sky, but I'd never really understood the whole Macarena phenomenon either. I just went with it. And it was super fun. The most fun I'd had at a dance, like, ever.

But I was feeling guilty about leaving Marcello behind. He'd probably be ticked off and scared out of his mind, even though we were in the heart of Siena, surrounded by her people, probably safer than we'd be anywhere else. But if I'd just gotten *him* back after a fifteen-month absence…

I craned my neck and tried to see where my current line of dance partners were heading, hopefully down toward where I'd left Marcello, or up near the top left of the sprawling arc, near an entrance, where I could duck out and wait for his arrival. That was close to the palazzo. Maybe he waited for me there anyway, hoping to grab us as we came by, like netting prize goldfish from a bowl teeming with others.

I barely paid attention as new men took my hands and pulled me down toward the center of the piazza again. I was looking for my sister, my parents, any of the Forelli knights, hoping to duck out—

That was when my companions tugged me to my knees, making me clunk one on the cobblestones. I winced and looked around in confusion, thinking this might be another dance move I'd yet to learn, but three earnest faces stared at me. "M'lady, we aim to free Lord Fortino Forelli."

I blinked several times, trying to make sense of his words. "Fortino? You can get to him?"

The one across from me nodded and looked me in the eye. "But we need you, m'lady. You and your sister."

My eyes narrowed. It didn't take much to remember what the Fiorentini wanted in exchange for Fortino last time.

Our heads.

"Lord Marcello and I," I said, "we've discussed this. He cannot see the way in through Firenze's gates, and he cannot abide the risk to either me or Lady Evangelia."

The one to my right nodded. "We mean you no harm. But here's our plan…we bring you to a city—"

"A neutral city," amended his friend.

"…in chains," resumed the first, "as if we're willing to hand you over to them, but as we make the exchange, our men attack, and we get you and Lord Fortino to safety."

"Away from Firenze, we believe we'll have a good chance at success," said the second.

*A good chance. With Lia and me at stake. Marcello will never go for it.*

I tried to rise, but the men held me down. "Forgive us, m'lady. We saw no other way to talk to you. Each of us owes Lord Fortino our lives. We served with him in the battle."

They'd served beside Fortino. Knew him. My friend. I shoved back a wave of fear and stared sternly at each of them. "Go to Lord Marcello with your plans. He will hear you out."

They glanced at one another, as if trying to decide how much to tell me.

The one in the middle shook his head. "We've gone to Lord Marcello before. And we doubt Lord Marcello will tolerate any plan that puts you or your sister in danger. Which we understand well. But the Fiorentini are so determined to have you in hand again, they will not give up on it until Fortino dies. The Nine have offered ransom after ransom—kingly ransoms—and they always receive the same answer."

We shared a long, hard, silent look.

"We see no other way," said the first man. "And time is running out, m'lady."

I looked at him sharply. "You have received recent word on Lord Fortino?"

"Indeed," he said simply. Gravely.

I considered him. I knew well how stubborn Marcello could be. And that he'd put my safety ahead of his brother's. Every time. I found his chivalry charming most times, but in a case like this? With Fortino edging ever closer to death's door? If there was an option, even a crazy idea? Shouldn't we at least consider it? I knew I couldn't live with myself if Fortino died and we hadn't tried every avenue to save him…

"Come to Lord Marcello's palazzo tomorrow at one," I said. "I shall aid you in your persuasion—to at least get Lord Marcello hear you out. But release me now, before he finds us here and demands that you are sent to Siena's prison in chains." The three shared a look and then immediately stood.

I did too. And saw Marcello four rows away from me, looking frantically in the other direction. "Quickly," I said, "take my hands and lead a dance line right over there, past Lord Marcello."

Two of the men did as I bid, gradually forcing smiles to their faces. We entered another line, which broke and cheered and let us in like we were long-lost family members, and we headed right toward Marcello and his men like a churning chain pulling up anchor.

"*Gabriella,*" Marcello said, half in relief, half in total agitation.

I laughed and fell into his arms, waving my companions and the rest off. The people cheered, and soon my parents circled close enough for us to grab them. Lia and Luca hurried up along the top edge of the piazza, no longer dancing. Luca ducked his head, knowing Marcello was fuming. "Forgive me, m'lord," he said.

"I warned you," Marcello said, his voice barely discernible over the music and laughter and singing. "I warned you all."

"Of what?" I asked, cocking a brow. "We danced, laughed, sang. What is so terrible about that?"

He clamped his lips shut and then took my hand, pulling me forward at a quick step, away from the others. In seconds we were in a relatively quiet alcove, away from the crowds. He paced before me for a full minute, running his hand through his hair, beginning to speak, stopping himself, pacing some more. Then finally, "Gabriella, do you have any idea how much I love you?"

His face was so full of pain and anguish, I melted in to a puddle of guilt and regret. "I think so," I said in a whisper.

"Do you know what it does to me when I think you might be in danger? And particularly when I can't get to you?"

I nodded carefully. It wouldn't do any good to tell him I felt safe here in the piazza. This was about his feelings.

"Can you…would you be so kind as to avoid putting me in that position in the future?"

"As best I can, my love," I said, forcing the words out.

His shoulders relaxed, and he pulled me into his arms, then held my face between his powerful hands, searching my eyes as if wishing he could read my mind, know everything in me, of me.

I lifted my chin, wanting his kiss, wanting his forgiveness, wanting to feel close to him again. After hesitating a moment, he obliged me. Then he took my hand and led me out of the alcove. I felt like All Kinds of Loser.

He was going to be seriously ticked at me tomorrow when the boys came calling. But what was I supposed to do? I wanted his brother freed as badly as he did. And if it was just me and Lia standing in the way of a family reunion, keeping him from saving Fortino…well, that simply had to be fixed.

One way or another.

# Chapter Five

The men arrived when we were mostly done with our noon meal the next day. A servant came to the table and leaned over Marcello's shoulder. "M'lord, there are three men here to see you. They say it is urgent."

I picked at a chicken bone on my wooden trencher, a medieval kind of platter, half-full of uneaten food, unable to look at him. Or my parents. They might know something was up.

"Who are they?"

"Signores Salvatori, Bastiani, and Bonaduce," he said.

Marcello paused, then carefully set his knife on the edge of his trencher. "Tell them to return again on the morrow, an hour later, so as to not disturb our sup."

"Very well, m'lord."

"Wait!" I cried. *Too loud, Gabs.* I sounded as jumpy as I felt. "Is it not wise for one of the Nine to listen to his people, even if he does not care to?"

Marcello paused and stared at me for a long moment. Then he said to the maid, "I'll be in the Great Hall in five minutes. Apparently m'lady wishes to take visitors."

I gave him a small smile. I knew he had done me an honor, giving in even when it wasn't my place to jump into the mix. *Way to go, Gabi. Sneaker. Betrayer. You should just tell him. Tell him, before it's too late.*

Lia, Luca, and I rose with him, but my parents stayed behind after accepting second portions of chicken and bread. "They don't make it like this anymore," my father whispered, lifting a woodstove-charred crust into the air.

I smiled. "They haven't for a while."

I placed my hand on Marcello's arm, and we moved toward the Great Hall. I was trying to figure out a way to tell him, warn him what was to come, but he obviously already knew that these guys were after Fortino's rescue. Was I really holding that big a secret? I had simply made sure they would be heard.

Marcello and Luca settled on chairs at the far end of the hall, and Lia and I moved to stand beside the tall shuttered windows that looked out at the piazza, cracked open for a bit of fresh air to ward off the smoke from the hearth. Lia and I stared down at the piazza as men finished packing up their tents and wooden crates from the market, heading home for their own noon meal and siesta.

That morning, I'd told her what was coming down.

And she'd agreed to take part. I didn't know what this place had done to my sister, but I liked it. Suddenly she was all Guts and Sass and Bring It. I guess that came with the territory.

Marcello nodded to the servant, and the man moved off to fetch the visitors. They returned quickly, and I could feel my stomach clench over what was to come. It was good Mom and Dad weren't here for this. That'd complicate it even more.

The men entered the hall, strode to the end, and bowed before Marcello and Luca, who remained seated. Totally the lord meeting his people. It was a little weird; I'd seen Marcello lead men into battle, but he'd never really assumed the lord title, with Fortino being the older of the two. Now, as one of the Nine and with Fortino gone so long, I supposed it was what was expected of him. But again, I felt a little like he'd grown up a bit without me in the year we'd been apart.

"I thought we'd concluded our business the last time you visited," Marcello said, frowning.

The main dude, Signore Salvatori, glanced my way and clasped his hands nervously in front of him. "We have further word, m'lord, of your brother."

Marcello leaned forward. "What word?"

"My sources tell me he fares much worse." He swallowed so hard I could see his Adam's apple bob up and down. "The Fiorentini took one of his eyes, and they threaten his other." He glanced our way. "They have learned, already, that the Ladies Betarrini have returned."

Marcello's frown deepened, as if their words were menacing swords.

"That did not take long," Luca said.

"We knew it wouldn't," Marcello grumbled. He glanced toward me.

Maybe that was why he was all agitated last night. He was worried there were already agents from Firenze within the city, out to get us. *Well, you're gonna love what's comin' next…*

"We have proposed, through our contacts, that we meet the Fiorentini in Sansicino. We are to bring the Ladies Betarrini, and they are to bring Lord Fortino."

Marcello rose so quietly, so slowly, but with such power in every inch of movement, a shiver of fear ran down my back. He stepped over to Salvatori, looking like he wanted to punch him out. "That was not your *place*," he ground out. "Such negotiations are only for the Nine to make, and"—he shook his finger in the man's face— "one we would never so foolishly dare. To say nothing of the fact that it would put the Ladies Betarrini in unprecedented danger, something I cannot condone."

"You might not, beloved," I said gently, stepping forward. I looked back at Lia and then reached out to tentatively take Marcello's hand. His face held a mixture of fury and fear. "But we would. Well we know the pain of a family divided," I rushed on, "a treasured member lost. And Fortino—we love him as a brother too. We cannot stand idly by when there is something to be done."

Marcello's eyes narrowed, and his gaze went from me to the men and back to me again. "You spoke with these men last night," he guessed.

"I did," I said, willing myself to not back down as a ripple of pain shot through his eyes. "Forgive me, m'lord, for not telling you of it sooner. But when they told me they had further news of Fortino, I knew you'd at least wish to hear them out."

"Don't you see?" said Signore Salvatori. "This is our opportunity. We've gone over plans, time and again, to steal into Firenze and try and free Lord Fortino. But there's never a good way out again. Since your daring rescue of Lady Betarrini, our sources tell me that Firenze's most prized prisoners are held behind several layers of protection. Our only chance is to draw them out, out to someplace where we have a fighting chance. And our only way to draw them out is to pretend to offer what they want most—the Ladies Betarrini."

"He has a point," Luca said, lifting a hand in Marcello's direction.

Marcello sighed and shook his head, dropping my hand to put both on his head. He closed his eyes. "It is not what Fortino would want." He looked at all of us. "Freeing Fortino would be a great honor for Siena. But what happens if we *all* die in the effort? Can you imagine what a blow that would be to our city?"

We were silent for a moment, absorbing the idea.

"No pain, no gain," Lia muttered, so quietly only I heard her.

"M'lord," I said, facing him. "Siena is a fine, strong city. Cities like this find their footing even after sustaining massive blows."

Marcello studied me, his eyes peering into mine as if to see whether I was really ready to do this. "It may indeed be our last opportunity to save him. But if I were to rescue him and lose you…" He swallowed hard and took my hands in his.

"And yet what if this is a door that God Himself has opened? A chance for you to bring home both a brother and a bride?" I said. If he needed to believe the Big Guy was in on it, I was up for it. And maybe He was. Maybe that was why I'd been brought here in the first place. Just for this. "Let us at least try to save him, Marcello."

Lia stepped to our side, and Luca to the other, so that we could confer in privacy. "If we don't do this, Fortino will surely die," Lia said, shaking her head. "And I cannot live with that, m'lord. To not try at all is a form of murder itself. If we are to die, let us do so trying to save your brother, trying to accomplish something honorable and true."

"Right," Luca said. "As is our normal practice."

He cocked a grin, and Marcello was drawn into a small smile himself. He shook his head. "Can we not settle into some semblance of peace for a while? Normalcy?" He eyed me, and I could almost read the question in his eyes. *You know, settle down, get married, have a couple of kids?*

"Come, beloved," I said. "Let us make plans to free your brother. As quickly as we can. Then we can see to your desire for peace and normalcy."

"Do you swear it? That you will settle into such things with me then?"

"Easily sworn," I said. "Because there's nothing I'd rather do than to live life with you, Marcello."

Dimly I could feel Lia freeze at my words. But I ignored her. We'd deal with saving Marcello's brother first. Then we'd figure out a way to convince my sis to sign away her forever to the republic of Siena.

While we awaited word from the Fiorentini, expected in a few days, Marcello invited us to come along with him on his official journey to visit San Galgano. The city was about fifteen miles south and east of Siena—a pretty safe area for us to go on an outing—and a good way to break everyone in to the whole idea of meeting with the Fiorentini in an effort to free Fortino. Especially Dad.

Maybe if Mom and Dad saw we could come and go and remain secure, they'd be down with our Supergirl plan to swoop in, scoop him up, and nurse him back to health in Siena.

Or yeah, maybe not.

Of course Marcello brought along a hundred of his nearest and dearest knights. You know, just to make sure we had company in case trouble came near.

Mom and Dad were excited. In all our years of visiting Tuscany, we'd never taken a day to journey out to the old abbey, which in this era was fairly new, of course. The day was crisp and cold but clear, the sunrise a pale yellow and tangerine to the east.

We rode together in a small group, the six of us—me, Marcello, Luca, Lia, Mom, and Dad—with the knights forming what amounted to protective groups on every side of us but twenty yards away. A group of servants traveled behind, hauling a mule train of supplies.

Since it was the middle of winter, the fields were nothing but furrows of overturned dirt. Smoke tendrils rose to the sky from small cottages and larger villas alike. I imagined households awaking to the day, breaking their fasts in cozy, warm little kitchens.

Dad was filling us in on the legend of San Galgano. "I have always wanted to see it for myself," he said excitedly. "I believe it to be the true basis of the Arthurian legend of Excalibur. Medieval troubadours must have spread the legend to England, where they picked up on it and made it famous."

"Truly, a man sunk a sword in a stone?" I asked.

"No way," Lia said, lapsing into English.

Mom raised a brow. "Stranger things have happened, no?" she asked, referring to our being here at all—all due to two hands on an ancient stone wall. I stared at her for a long moment. My mom had always been a facts-only kind of girl. I always had to make my case to get her to believe, and that case had to be full of provable facts.

It was the scientist in her. But our leap through time appeared to be changing her. Changing all of us.

"San Galgano performed many miracles afterward," Marcello said, making the sign of the cross from forehead to chest and across again, a note of defense in his tone. Luca did the same. "Why is it that you doubt this story?" he asked, blinking at me with concern in his handsome eyes.

I shifted, trying to get comfortable on my sidesaddle. Marcello had insisted we use them, given our official task in the visit. Then I shrugged. "I know not. In Normandy we are taught to suspect everything. Believe once proven. Don't you find the tale rather… wondrous?"

"That is exactly how I think of it. Wondrous. A miracle." He smiled at me, and I admired him anew. He truly was the most handsome guy I'd ever met. Strong chin. Prominent cheekbones. Large, warm eyes. He was attractive all the time—but when he smiled, man, I was lost.

"The Cistercian monks think of it as a miraculous land too," he went on with a wry smile. When he glanced back and spotted Dad giving him a steady stare, he hastily dropped it and looked forward again as if caught doing something terrible.

"What do you mean?" I asked, trying to distract them both.

"They own most of the valley ahead of us," he said. "Every principal building. Most of the industry. The people work for them."

"But it is a good valley, a prosperous valley," Luca added. "Her people are content."

As we neared, I could see why. It was beautiful country, with a strong river and many creeks, soil that was dark and rich, and heavy forests, even though much had already been cleared to make way for more farmable acreage.

"So why did San Galgano thrust his sword in the stone?" I asked.

Dad smiled. "He forswore everything he hated—wealth and war. Violence and lust." Did he glance at Marcello when he said that last word? *Oh, you did NOT, Dad! C'mon…* "An angel—"

"Archangel," Marcello gently corrected.

"*Archangel*," Dad repeated with a nod, "came to him and asked him to come here, to this place."

"The twelve apostles, too," Marcello said.

"Do you wish to tell this story, or may I, m'lord? Mayhap our version in Normandy is different than yours."

It was Marcello's turn to nod in deference. But he was smiling, and he gestured for Dad to go on.

"On Montesiepi he was told to build a church, and once there, he thrust his sword into the stone in an effort to create a rudimentary cross. He succeeded—only the end remained visible, which, indeed, looked like a cross."

"And then the pilgrims came," I guessed, "and the monks after them." I'd spent enough time in this country, in my own time, to know how it worked. If something holy happened, the people had to come check it out.

"Indeed," Dad said, clearly pleased with me.

When Marcello and Luca started chatting about something else, I leaned back over the rump of my horse, toward Dad. "So…do you think it's a hoax?" I asked.

He pursed his lips. "I, like you, would like to see it myself. But many have tried over the years to pull it from the stone and failed."

"I read that they tested the alloys around 2000," Mom whispered. "Completely consistent with an eleventh- or twelfth-century weapon."

Lia glanced at me with raised eyebrows. Her expression said, *Impressive.*

I hoped I had the chance to give the old sword a pull. Mayhap I was the true queen of England, and Excalibur would show it was so. I giggled under my breath. *Yeah, that's just what you need, Gabs. A whole other gig drawing some serious attention...*

The abbey rose from a wide basin surrounded by hills that would become miles of crops—sprouting wheat and grapevines full of leaves and fruit—come summer. She was all the more inspiring sitting as she was, alone in a field, with a terra cotta brick monastery sprouting off one side. Montesiepi was the high hill beyond her, and on top of it, we could see the round church built around the sacred stone.

The monks were already coming out to greet us.

"Lord Forelli," said a tall one—more handsome than most—standing in front of four others, "you have done us a great honor with your visit." They were all barefoot and dressed in the brown robes with white rope belts. I shivered at the thought. Especially on the cold stone of the abbey or monastery...

"It is our good pleasure," Marcello said. He dismounted and helped me down, then introduced us all. "I have brought you gifts of indigo and gold leaf for your scriptorium, Father."

"It is most welcome, m'lord. And a fine meal will soon be available to you on top of the mount. In the meantime, would your guests care to see the abbey?"

Marcello cast us a sly smile. "I think they would favor a visit, yes. And I know that they are quite intrigued with the sacred stone."

"Well then," said the tall monk, "let us be about it." He leaned down and whispered in another man's ear, and that one set off toward the path that led upward. *Probably needs to tell the kitchen staff to get on it,* I decided.

We moved into the grand abbey that reminded me of so many cathedrals we'd seen in France, with the pronounced ribbed arches and high, narrow domes. The columns were fluted, with elegantly carved capitals, and as we walked down the center aisle, I thought the setting would make for a fairy-tale kind of wedding. On either side of the main part of the church, high above, were small round windows, filled with the thinnest, creamiest stone that allowed filtered light to seep through swirls of brown. At the front, beyond the marble altar, was a large, carved crucifix backlit by a massive, round window and, below it, arched windows. On either side of the main area were long apses with arch after arch. It was lovely, really. Somehow light, in the midst of tons of stone. Ethereal. Holy.

After a brief turn through the public rooms of the monastery and scriptorium, we exited and began our climb up the hill. It felt good to be off my horse and stretching my legs. I fought to stay on Marcello's arm, as was expected, rather than dash ahead. At the top the tall monk led us into the small, round chapel.

"Such a strange shape for a church of this time period," I heard Mom whisper.

"Maybe the Pantheon served as inspiration," Dad returned.

"Or the Etruscan tombs all about," she said, smiling.

They were quiet then, knowing the monks would want silence. I went directly to the top of the boulder, which was raw and open, like it had exploded through the perfect travertine floor, and neared the oxidized, dark metal sword that emerged from it. I circled it, noting its rough texture—and the ancient form of it.

Marcello was kneeling on a small bench before an altar, praying. After a moment he rose, crossed himself, and backed away several steps before he turned and offered his arm to me. He gestured to the frescoes about the room. "Ambrogio," he said in my ear.

The freaky thing was, I knew the artist. Ambrogio Lorenzetti. I'd met him once, if not twice, at the parties in Siena. Out of the Sienese school of art, which I knew would generate some of the most famous paintings in all of Italia. I'd been dragged through the Uffizi—a dizzyingly full museum in Firenze—enough to know that much. But it wasn't until now, here, that I put two and two together. When I was staring at his frescoes, recently laid down on the wall.

Wait until Mom and Dad heard that—that I'd met Mr. Fresco. They'd freak.

We admired the domed roof, which was formed out of alternating layers of terra-cotta and white travertine, giving it a sort of muted candy-cane look, and then took turns saying a prayer at the small altar, which showcased an elaborately framed, gold-leafed, iconic painting of the warrior, relinquishing his sword to an archangel with massive wings. When I knelt, I didn't know what to say. Was I to pray to Galgano? The angel?

*God*, I silently said instead. *Thank You for bringing us here safely. Get us back to Siena without any trouble. And help me to figure out how to get Mom and Dad to buy in to our whole hairy plan. Amen.*

I rose, awkwardly making the sign of the cross, wondering if God was tugging at my heart to relinquish *my* sword, but I laughed it off. That was impossible. Not with what we had ahead of us.

As we exited, Marcello said quietly, "I have never seen you pray before." His eyes were full of hope, admiration. He took my arm, and we moved toward a small portico, where the monks had set out a table full of rustic, simple, but tons of food.

"Yes, well, it is different in Normandy."

"Prayer is prayer, regardless of where you are," he said. "No?"

"In some measure," I said.

As the group assembled, he led me to the corner of the portico, and for a moment we were hidden behind a large pillar. He wrapped his arms around me, standing behind me as we stared out over the valley. It felt good to be held by him. Warm. *We could get married down in the abbey and honeymoon someplace like this,* I mused. But, of course, without all the monks about. That wasn't exactly romantic.

He kissed the side of my head and then turned me, tucking a stray coil of hair over my ear as he liked to do. "Prayer *is* prayer, regardless of where you are. Is it that you feel need a priest to help show you the way?" He tucked another strand. "No woman has as many independent thoughts as my Gabriella. Tell me what you need, beloved, and I shall see you have it."

I laughed under my breath at his gentle jibe, even as I considered his offer. Maybe it'd help me to sort things out, to have a priest around. There was so much about faith I didn't know. So much I felt like I ought to know, but I felt like an idiot asking. I smiled. "You are kind to think of it. I believe I would like that—if he was the right sort of priest." My smile faded when I thought of the horrid little priest that had been at Castello Forelli when I arrived. That dude had had serious issues and clearly disliked me from the start. But I'd met others since then, others that seemed friendly and open.

"Then you shall help me find the right one. Castello Forelli needs a new chaplain."

I stared at him, waiting for him to notice what he said.

"I mean, Palazzo Forelli," he amended.

I looked to his hands and then up into his face again. "You miss it terribly, do you not?"

He sighed and looked to the valley. "Every moment of every day," he said.

"I know," I said. "I miss it too."

After a moment we knew we had to join the others and did so. The monks had baked fresh fig pudding and served it to us hot, with a delicious sugary sauce on top. It was spicy and nutty and gooey. I could've eaten ten bowls of it, but I had to stop after two. We broke the bread we brought and cut the hard cheese and dried meats and fruits.

Mom and Dad sat side by side, staring out the archway at the high green hills all about us.

"Tuscan bliss," Lia whispered, catching me staring their way. They'd always, always loved this country, with its unique valleys and hilltop villages, and after long days on a dig, they would often stand with their arms around each other's waists and stare out at the view.

"Just taking it in," Dad would always say.

"Tuscan bliss," Mom would add.

Over and over, always the same thing. And now they were back together, able to keep on saying it. Maybe until they were old and in rockers on some Tuscan porch. Lia and I shared a smile. Mom and Dad were back in their own little orbit. But this time we were in it too. We both felt it. Things had shifted, fundamentally, within our family dynamics. We still had the same kind of banter, but there was a sort of awareness that we had been missing before. And I loved it.

"M'lord, what news do you have of your brother?" asked our host gently, continuing his conversation with Marcello.

"He lives yet," Marcello said somberly, ignoring me entirely. "But I would covet your prayers for him, Father."

"And you shall have it, m'lord. Daily," he added, giving him an encouraging smile. "Not only for health, but for freedom."

"We shall soon fight for his freedom. Bring our names to the Lord daily in the next week, please. For protection. For wisdom. For strength."

I shared a look with Lia, wanting to kick Marcello under the table, to remind him my folks were listening and we had not yet told them of our plan…

"Again, 'tis yours for the asking."

Finally I let my eyes casually shift to Mom. She'd missed none of it, of course. While Dad was still in his Tuscan Bliss state, she'd heard enough, knew enough from her time here before. I looked away, but I was too late.

"Gabriella," she said lowly, "is there something that your father and I need to know?"

I sighed. "There is, Mom. A lot, actually. And…well…I don't think you're gonna like it."

# Chapter Six

So my folks...yeah. Not so down with the idea as we were. You know, putting our lives at stake, possibly being tortured, imprisoned, torn apart forever, killed—basically things that made every parent's Do Not Allow list.

Mom finally convinced Dad to let us go—"These men have risked so much to save our girls"—but there was one requirement: They insisted on coming along. Which was pretty much the last thing I wanted. Now I'd be concentrating as much on keeping them safe as on freeing Fortino. Mom was wicked good with her staff, and Dad was out of his dream-fog and decent with the sword, but the fact was, the more of us who went, the harder it would be to get us all back alive. I didn't like it. But I didn't have a lot of choices.

Several days later we headed out of Siena at sunrise—ungodly early—toward Sansicino, a high hill town to the east of Toscana, in the traitorous republic that had aided Firenze during the battle but now maintained a "neutral status."

*Yeah right, like you guys get to pretend you're just sitting it out...*

But it was what it was. I was so excited that we were finally on the move, on our way to rescue Fortino, that the first few hours of our ride slid by. As agreed with Firenze, we left with only twenty-four men, including Marcello and Luca, my dad, and the Three Amigos from the piazza, as I'd dubbed them—Signores Salvatori, Bastiani, and Bonaduce. The Fiorentini were to arrive with no more than that either. If they played by the rules.

Sansicino had been chosen because it was a hill town, on a mount so high that their "drawbridge" was basically a half-mile-long true bridge that led to the city gates. It made her amazingly defensible, and enemies could be seen from miles away. Our plan was basic: We'd make the exchange, then our guys would bust Lia and me loose, and we'd all rappel off the side of the castle to the hill below the wall and join up with our men—plus reinforcements. To say that that Marcello and Luca were amazed that my mom was willing to fling herself over the edge too would be an understatement. I practically had to give them CPR.

"Daring is in their blood," Luca said, admiring Lia, me, and our mom.

"You don't know the half of it," Dad put in. I laughed at him. We'd pretty much always been the good girls, in the background, all our years with him. But he'd recognized that we'd grown up and changed, and he'd grasped some of who we'd become since being here. And he clearly admired it.

Mom and I had packed a basket full of medical supplies, hoping the Fiorentini would allow us to see to Fortino's wounds even while the men were still in negotiation. I shuddered every time I thought of Fortino with an eye gone. But I hoped that would be the very worst we would have to deal with. I'd heard servants whispering of repeated floggings. That he'd almost died last year before Lord Greco stepped in and placed him in his own dungeon cell. But he'd recently been taken back to the city prison, and things had obviously gotten much, much worse.

What if we had taken longer to return? What if we never had? If the rumors were true, I could only picture Fortino dying. Cold, alone, tortured by infected wounds…It was such a terrible picture that I could hardly think of anything *but* freeing him. I remembered his smile, how close he had been to death when I first arrived, how he had been returned to us, almost as shockingly as my dad had been. In those days and weeks he had become a brother to me. And he'd fought for us, for Marcello, for Siena. We owed him. We all owed him.

"You know that it will mean another battle, if we take Fortino and escape," I said, for the hundredth time.

"I'm well aware of it, Gabriella," Marcello said, "as are the rest of the Nine. We are prepared to again defend ourselves—and our She-Wolves."

"I only want to know you're prepared."

He and Luca shared a small smile. "We are," Marcello said calmly.

"Are they gonna let us in on their plan?" Lia grumbled.

Both men stared forward, self-satisfied expressions on their faces.

"I don't think so," I said.

We spent the night at a villa tantalizingly close to Castello Forelli and then skirted her lands on our way up to Sansicino. It was raining like crazy, and we tried to keep oilskin capes over our heads and clothing to stay somewhat dry, but I was shivering. Seriously, my teeth were chattering and everything.

Georgii and Lutterius, who were twins—something of a novelty in this time—rode ahead, scouting for enemies that might be hidden about. They seemed more like big, friendly Labrador puppies than knights, and I worried for them. "What if they run into a trap?" I asked Luca.

He shrugged. "It is a scout's duty to be aware, to spot what others cannot."

For as much time as I'd been here, I still wasn't quite used to the medieval Tuscan man's way of thinking. It was so dang *harsh*. We might as well have been with a group of Special Ops guys assigned to ferret out rebels among the caves of Afghanistan. My hope was that we'd get over this hurdle and actually experience life like Marcello had imagined—settling down, finding peace. But was that a realistic hope while Castello Forelli remained in enemy hands?

*Not likely.*

I didn't know what Georgii and Lutterius hoped to see—we could barely see more than fifty feet ahead of us, given the fog and the pounding rain. Any prints on the road that might give them clues would surely be washed away. *Whatever.* I wasn't going to ask Marcello to call them back. I knew it'd be fruitless.

So we rode on through the rain and muck, with mud splattering up from the horses' hooves to their bellies—and our dresses. I fought the urge to whine, "When are we gonna get there?" But I really wanted to know.

When Marcello drew closer, he gave me an encouraging smile. "As fine as this weather is, you'll be glad to know we're only an hour from Sansicino's bridge."

I sighed in relief. "Very good, m'lord. At least we'll be able to change into dry clothing and sit by a warm fire."

"Indeed."

Men's shouting, muted by the rain, brought both of our heads forward. Someone was coming. Fast.

Marcello had just barked his warning and the men were on the move, taking defensive positions, when a man on a massive gray gelding rounded the bend of the road, spraying water and mud with every hoofbeat. Right behind him were Georgii and Lutterius, swords drawn, faces—normally alight with mischief—now filled with fury.

The men at the front had no time to meet his charge, only to stand and ready themselves for a strike. We were relatively confident, given our twenty-four to his one, but did he have companions close behind?

But he never drew his sword. He simply charged by our line of horses and yelled, "*Consiglia loro di cessare l'inseguimento,* Marcello!" as he did. *Tell them to cease their pursuit!*

Marcello looked after him, wheeling his horse around so that he was between me and the newcomer, as did Luca with Lia and Dad with Mom. But then he yelled, "Hold!" and lifted his fist in a sign that echoed the command.

The twins immediately peeled off to either side of us and brought their mounts to a stop. Everyone else maintained his position.

The man on the massive gelding pulled up on his reins, then slowly turned and looked at us all. He removed his own oiled hood and urged his skittish horse forward. He was a bit hard to make out through the pounding rain, but after a few steps Marcello laughed, then urged his horse toward the man. They met and clasped arms, speaking and turning to look our way.

Then I recognized him. Greco. It was Lord Rodolfo Greco.

Mr. Tall, Dark, and Handsome.

Dangerous as all get-out and just as confusing.

The man who had tracked me down. Brought me to Firenze, before the grandi. Slapped me before them. Then fed me. Bound me and put me in a cage. And then helped Marcello free me.

"Gabi, is that—?" Lia began.

"Yeah. It's him," I said, licking my lips. I wished I had a canteen of water. Of the nice metallic, Girl Scout variety. Not the repurposed animal skin that made me never want to drink again. I sighed. Dying of thirst while drowning in a sea of rain.

Rodolfo and Marcello turned to face me. "We'll rest here for a moment. Take shelter under those trees," Marcello said. We moved toward them, but finding relief from the rain under them was kind of fruitless. The old oaks were massive, so the limbs gave us some partial breaks, but they weren't the same as in the summer, when fully leafed.

"Lady Gabriella," Rodolfo said, nodding toward me. "Lady Evangelia," he added to my sister.

"Lord Greco," she said. Appropriately. But I couldn't seem to say anything. Dry throat, I thought. But in truth I wasn't yet ready to speak to the man.

When Marcello dropped to the mat of dead leaves and grass at his feet and then turned to me, I braced myself. It made sense, if we were breaking. He wanted me off the horse and closer to him. He studied me, concern in his eyes. "You are well?" he asked quietly.

"Well as I can be," I returned in kind. "Marcello, I know he helped you free me…but he is also the same man who captured me and dragged me into Firenze behind his horse."

The muscles in Marcello's cheek tensed. "What? Surely he did not—"

"He did."

Marcello stared into my eyes and then pulled me around to the other side of my mare, where we could speak more privately. "You never spoke of it."

"You never asked!" I sighed. "Marcello, there was hardly time for us. We were in constant battle, from the time you freed me to the time I left."

"And yet you said nothing as we made these plans to bring you here."

"It hardly seemed appropriate. You had greater things to be concerned about. And I…I didn't think it would be *him*. Here."

"What is greater than your welfare? Do you…can you not trust him, Gabriella? Based on my testimony?"

I closed my eyes. "I do not know, Marcello. You said yourself that he had to pretend a certain amount in order that the grandi would not know he was a Sienese sympathizer." I thought of the Rossis, of them all hanging from a rope, their necks at odd angles, feet dangling, and I shuddered. If Rodolfo was our friend, he was taking a grave risk indeed.

"We need to hear him out. And in the end, he did help us rescue you. Without him we would've never made it out of Firenze."

I nodded. "You're right, of course. It's only foolish, idle memories getting in my way."

"Not foolish," he said, lifting my chin. "It was terrible, what you endured."

"Stay with me. Please, Marcello—"

"Say no more, my love." He wrapped an arm around my waist and led me over to the rest of the group. Luca was regaling my parents with the tale of my rescue, and they looked at him, Lia, and Rodolfo in wide-eyed wonder. He paused in his tale when we neared, and Rodolfo stepped forward.

"M'lady," he said, ducking his head.

I dipped my head in response. "Lord Greco," was all I said. "Are you quite well?"

"Well enough. I am weary of the road and this relentless rain. What news do you bring?"

He cocked a brow and straightened. "*Relentless* is the correct term. But I must get back to my men before they become concerned. They believe I am in the cottage of an old friend, warming myself by the fire." He smiled. Even soaking wet, he was one of the most handsome men I'd ever seen. After Marcello, of course. There was a raw power in him that both drew and repelled me.

"You sneaked away?" Luca asked.

"Indeed. But I must leave shortly, or our plan will fall apart."

"Understood," Marcello said. "What must we know?"

"The grandi have charged me with bringing back the Ladies Betarrini. I assume you won't allow us to exit Sansicino, let alone enter Firenze's gates, with them in hand."

"Across my dead body," Marcello said.

"And mine," Luca echoed.

"As I knew it would be," Rodolfo said. He shook his head. "And yet Lord Fortino might not live through the night. I left him in the cottage of my friend, by the fire, but he is in dire shape," he said, sorrow and warning in his thickly lashed brown eyes.

"Can we go to him? See to him?" I asked. "We have supplies and—"

"Nay. 'Tis impossible. And my friend is doing what he can for him. But be forewarned, my friends. With him in your care, escape may prove impossible."

"We shall manage," Marcello said. "We have no choice but to try."

"And if you're caught?" Rodolfo pressed, wiping his face of rain and flinging it aside. "The men of Sansicino shall be obliged to imprison you, hand you all over to the Fiorentini for not honoring the agreement."

"We shall not be caught," Luca said.

But Marcello remained silent. He was clearly thinking about us with Fortino now. Two men would have to haul him in a blanket and be protected themselves—

"You assisted me in our escape," I said, "when I was little more than dead weight. We can do the same with Fortino."

"But you merely needed food, water. Rest. Fortino…"

"As you said, we have little choice."

Marcello stared at me for a long moment and then looked to Rodolfo. "We shall conduct our negotiations and attempt to escape the trade—but you obviously knew that."

"Offer a treasure for Fortino," Rodolfo said, as clear on how this was going to play out as Marcello himself seemed to be.

"The negotiations will drag on until nightfall, and when the opportunity is right—"

"You shall make your escape," Rodolfo finished for him. He looked around at all of us. "Stay clear of me. I shall look like nothing but your worst enemy and, in battle, be forced to cut down any within my reach."

"As you must," Marcello said. "Thank you for coming to us. For all you've done to keep Fortino alive…" His voice broke, and he looked away, blinking rapidly, then took a deep breath. "I would very much like to say farewell to him, if I cannot save him."

"I shall do my very best to see that you can." Rodolfo clasped Marcello's hand, and they looked into each other's eyes as old friends. "You know that this will incite yet another great battle between our two cities."

Marcello slowly smiled. "Mayhap I'll retrieve the castle that was stolen from me when it's done."

"I do not know if you will want it back." Rodolfo smiled in return. "I hear she again has a most terrible neighbor."

Cosmo Paratore, he meant. I shivered at the thought of the man who had threatened Lia so. The man who wanted to kill me. The man whose ears I'd ordered cut from his head.

I hoped he stayed in Firenze, where he belonged.

# Chapter Seven

We processed up the long, stone bridge, built atop a series of progressively taller arches, to the gates of Sansicino. The rain had stopped and the clouds cleared, leaving everything fresh and dripping, glistening in the peach light of the late afternoon sun.

There was no sign of the Fiorentini. Were they here already?

"While we negotiate," Marcello said, "you and your mother shall see to Fortino?"

"Of course," I said.

"Keep in mind, as you bind his wounds, that he will endure a fair amount of jostling—"

"I know, Marcello. We'll do our best to bind him well."

He reached out his palm, and I laid my fingers in it, staring into his eyes. "Keep close to me, Gabriella."

"There is no place I'd rather be."

Okay, so if it was a movie and my sister and I were watching it, we might have burst out laughing. Totally corny. But I swear, when you're in love, you enter this state where such things sound exactly right. So right, they make you want to weep. Just looking at him, knowing how much I loved him and how much he loved me, made me want to cry.

But even I dimly recognized my love-fest was getting ridiculous. Not that I could help myself. I only wanted more of it. I found myself praying for one more month, one more week, one more day with Marcello.

*Don't let us die today, God. Let us wake tomorrow—both of us. Together.*

The guards watched our approach. "State your name and business," shouted one.

I almost laughed out loud. *Dude. Like you don't know who we are. The town isn't that big…and this has to be all that your people have been talking about for days.*

"I am Lord Marcello Forelli," my man managed to respond with nothing but a tone of respect. "We are here to meet with the delegates from Firenze, as was arranged."

The guard looked over the rest of us, his eyes lingering over Lia and me. Then he turned and shouted to someone below him to open the gates. The gates creaked open, inch by inch.

And we moved in.

When the last of our group was in, we were immediately surrounded, with four men to every one of ours.

We looked around in stunned amazement. When the Sansicinians had demanded we limit our numbers, we didn't expect an attack. In all negotiations between the Fiorentini and Sienese, Marcello had never seen anything like it—I could tell by the surprise on his face.

I couldn't bear to look back at Mom and Dad. They were probably freaking. I was freaking.

"Lord Forelli," said a short nobleman with a pointed beard. "I am Lord Ascoli." He edged past the front group of soldiers, choosing to stay seated on his horse rather than look up at Marcello. *Short-man syndrome,* I decided. "Forgive the uncommon *welcome,* but we have greeted our Fiorentini friends in equal manner. So that this process might go as peaceably as possible, I ask that you and your men relinquish your weapons."

The muscles in Marcello's cheek tensed, and he paused before responding. "As a defender of this city, surely you recognize that it is unwise for a knight to ever relinquish his sword, especially when he is about to encounter his enemy."

Lord Ascoli gave him a small smile, and his narrow eyes flicked over to me and Lia. "It has not escaped us that this coming trade requires certain precautions. After all, you once went to great lengths to free your lady from Firenze. You only just now welcomed her back to Siena after a significant time apart. Even with a great love for your brother, what one feels for a woman…" He admired me openly then, and I struggled to remain still. His eyes returned to Marcello. "As administrator of this exchange, I must ensure that both parties do as they have promised. Please hand over your weapons. They shall be returned to you when you depart."

"How do I know that the Fiorentini have been treated in the same manner?" Marcello bit out. "After all, you allowed them passage through your territory during the last battle. You may very well be siding with them and only feigning your neutral stance as mediator."

Lord Ascoli's mouth twitched, and then he turned aside and lifted his arm. "Please join us in the piazza."

We resumed our march inward, and I cast a worried glance back to Lia and my parents. If our men were forced to give up their weapons, would our plan work at all? How would we fight our way to the walls? As the gates shut behind us, I couldn't fight the sinking feeling that we had entered a trap that would be far more difficult to escape than we imagined.

I knew that our men would sneak closer to the cliffs at the base of the town come nightfall, but they could not breach the gates, storm the town. We had to go to *them,* over the wall, in order to find freedom.

The town was designed like most of the other Tuscan hill towns I'd been in. Narrow cobblestone streets, tiny limestone houses that were two or three stories high on either side. Red-tile roofs. Not the orderly, machine-processed kind of tile that we had back in Colorado or California, but hand-pressed, sun-dried tiles that varied in hue from brick to burnt orange. I looked across those tiles to my right, noting how the streets descended beneath us in three rows before hitting the cliff wall. Atop that wall were soldiers, patrolling, prepared.

We had expected to encounter them. But this, before the negotiations even began…I looked to Marcello, and with one glance, I knew he shared my concern.

The road ended at a town square—small compared to Siena's and Firenze's—a rectangular piazza with a church on one side, a small public building on the other, and four palazzos forming the other edges.

About twenty knights warily rose as one from the steps of the church, where they were surrounded by a hundred of Sansicino's men. Among them was Lord Greco. Not one of them wore a sword at his belt.

"So you see, m'lord," said Ascoli, pulling to a stop, "the men of Firenze have indeed been asked to do the same as we have asked of you. We are determined to see this through as we promised. As a point of honor, please do as has been requested of you."

Marcello's jaw clenched, and then he gave Lord Ascoli a hard stare. "Where is my brother? The Fiorentini have seen that we have the Ladies Betarrini. But I have yet to see that they have Lord Fortino among them."

"Relinquish your swords, and we shall take you to him."

"You shall bring him out here," Marcello ground out, "or we shall assume this is a trap and draw our swords against you."

Lord Ascoli raised one brow. "Your brother is in poor condition. Moving him might prove perilous."

"From what I understand, my brother might not survive the night. I will not condemn these women and my men without even knowing if he is truly here."

Lord Ascoli gave him a cold stare, and then he turned to lift his chin to two guards. They immediately jogged across the piazza to the public building, which was heavily guarded, and disappeared through the door. Our horses shifted beneath us, agitated by the tension they sensed among us. No one exchanged a word. I noticed, for the first time, that townspeople lined the square in pockets, observing, pointing, whispering.

After several long minutes the knights emerged with two others, each carrying the corners of a blanket with a heavy form inside. They paused beneath the building's portico.

"Send one over to confirm it is Lord Fortino, and that he yet lives," said Ascoli. "But the rest of you shall remain here."

"I will go," said my mother.

Marcello glanced at her in surprise and then nodded, seeing she was already untying the basket of medical supplies from her saddle.

Dad dismounted and helped Mom down from her horse. She gave Dad a small smile of encouragement and then strode across the piazza like she owned it, well aware that every eye was on her. She knelt beside the man on the blanket, her skirts billowing up beneath her. I could see that she was checking his pulse. She leaned down as if she was trying to hear what he was saying. Then she looked over her shoulder and nodded at Marcello.

It was him. Fortino was here. And alive.

"Call her back," Lord Ascoli said.

"Allow her to stay and do what she can for him," Marcello returned. "If he dies, this deal is void."

"Very well," the small man said, waving his hand dismissively. "Now relinquish your weapons, and we shall make the exchange. You can leave our town before nightfall and reach Siena tomorrow."

"I wish to discuss other options."

"That does not surprise me," Lord Ascoli said. "But be warned that there is little that you can offer that shall dissuade our friends of Firenze from their mission."

"There is a great deal for them to consider," Marcello insisted. "And we would be most grateful to you, our mediator, to see it through. Your work will be well rewarded."

Lord Ascoli's pointy beard lifted. "I see. Well then, shall we adjourn to the Great Hall?" He lifted his hand toward the public building. "We can sit down as gentlemen and discuss it in all manner of civility."

*Yeah, buddy. Money talks, doesn't it?*

"Agreed," Marcello said.

But our host did not move. "M'lord," Ascoli said, like a tired parent to a child trying to get away with something. "We shall take your weapons now."

Marcello grimaced. Maybe he'd hoped they'd forgotten that particular demand. After a moment of hesitation, he gently slid his sword from its saddle scabbard and reluctantly handed it to the closest knight. He nodded over his shoulder, instructing the men to do the same.

Lia and I remained still, hoping they'd forget that we were likely armed beneath our oilskin capes, but Lord Greco spoke up. "Do not forget the Ladies Betarrini. They might prove to be the most perilous opponents of all."

The Fiorentini laughed, and I sighed. *So much for that idea...*

They took my sword but either didn't think to look or didn't dare to search for the dagger strapped to my calf. They searched the men, but after I gave them my sword and Lia gave them her bow and arrows, they seemed to be satisfied. Marcello noticed it too and wiped away his smile as if he were merely rubbing his face in agitation.

"Dismount, friends," Lord Ascoli said. "My men shall see that your horses are watered and given a bucket of oats."

The men followed Marcello's lead and handed over their reins to the Sansicinians. Marcello and Luca helped Lia and me dismount. "Stay close," Marcello said, offering his arm.

"Always and forever," I returned.

We entered the public building and then walked down a long hall to the far side. There, two massive doors opened up into a white-walled room decorated with frescoes of battle scenes and religious occasions—pretty much what you saw in every town with any kind of money at their disposal. Dad was immediately drawn to the frescoes, but I saw Mom was still with Fortino to the right of the door. I hurried over to them as the men moved to banquet tables full of fruit, meat, cheese, and bread. Servants poured goblets of watered wine.

Marcello followed me to his brother and paused when a young, portly priest, dressed in the traditional brown robe and belt, nodded and took a step backward. I looked at him. Why did Marcello pause? Did he know the priest?

But he was already kneeling, across from my mother. I took to my knees beside him, forcing myself to look at Fortino. Fortino's head was wrapped in bandages, which covered his missing eye. He was terribly gaunt again—had they starved him?—and his skin was the same color it had been when we almost lost him before, a horrible, bluish gray. And the smell...I almost gagged. The odor of rotting flesh told me he was riddled with infection.

"He will not survive a journey," Mom said sorrowfully, under her breath, to Marcello. Her blue eyes met his brown ones, and she shook her head, as if in pain for him.

Marcello clasped his brother's hand in his own and brought it to his chest.

"Fortino," Marcello said lowly, "we are here, brother."

Fortino opened his eye as if it took everything in him to do so. "You...you should not have come."

"We had no choice. We had to try."

"I am dead already." He looked to me and then closed his eye in pain.

I glanced at Mom, silently asking her for her assessment, as she finished pressing into his belly.

"I think he's bleeding inside," she said bitterly, in English. "His belly is distended but hard as a rock. They have beaten him relentlessly," she continued, switching to Italian. "You must not let them take Gabi." Maybe seeing Fortino made it all the more real to her. It was one thing to hear of being thrown into a cage and being exposed to the elements. But to see the effects of a physical beating? Her face was stricken—half out of rage over Fortino, half out of panic for me. And Dad was right behind her.

"I will fight it with everything in me," Marcello promised them.

"M'lord," said Ascoli, coming closer. "Shall we begin?"

"In a moment."

Clearly irritated, the small man reluctantly turned away, edging past Luca, Lia, and my father, who had joined our circle.

"Fortino," Marcello said gently, squeezing his hand.

Fortino stirred, as if he might have fallen asleep for a moment. His good eye blinked open. "You have been a fine brother, Marcello. The best any man could ever ask for."

Marcello stared at him for a moment and swallowed hard, acknowledging his farewell. "As have you," he said at last.

"Honor our father's name."

"With everything in me," Marcello pledged. He swallowed hard. "I shall miss you, brother."

A tiny smile lifted Fortino's lips, and he looked to me. "Find distraction in Gabriella. She was always meant for you."

"Well I know it," Marcello said, smiling too.

But then Fortino was asleep—unconscious?—closing his eye. Marcello hesitated and then leaned forward to put his ear to his brother's mouth, listening. "He yet lives," he whispered. In an instant his expression turned from agonizing grief to fierce determination. He rose and assisted me up too, then paused to whisper something in Luca's ear.

With that we proceeded over to a long table.

"You shall be expected to stand behind my chair," he said in my ear.

I nodded, shoving down a wave of aggravation. *So the boys will sit down and chat for hours, and the women are expected to stand?* But I'd promised to stay by his side…so I went and did as was expected. Everyone was seated, and yet there was one open chair. But did they offer it to me? No way.

Yeah, not everything in Medieval-ville was cool. Women's rights were a ways off. A long ways off.

My eyes followed the direction of Lord Ascoli's gesture.

The guards opened the tall doors, and through them strode Lord Cosmo Paratore.

I stared at him, openmouthed for a second, panic stalling my heart and then sending it into a rapid *thud-thud-thud.*

Marcello saw him then and abruptly stood, taking a half step between me and the man who surely wanted to see me dead. "Lord Ascoli," Marcello sputtered. "How could you invite such—such— *vermin* inside your city walls?" He said it to our host, but he looked to Lord Greco, who was sitting back and casually eating a date. Was Greco putting on an act? Or had he known?

"Cease your theatrics, Marcello," Cosmo Paratore said, sitting down and gesturing toward Marcello's empty chair. "Come, let us speak of what is to be done, once and for all."

Marcello put his fists on the table and leaned menacingly toward the man, with an unwavering stare. "Order the release of my brother as well as my rightful property. Retreat to the border that was established by our grandfathers. *That* is what can be done."

Cosmo arched a brow and reached for a date; then, for the first time, he allowed his eyes to go to me. He'd let his hair grow long, covering his damaged ears. The ears I'd ordered cut from his head. His green eyes were bright with interest. He pursed his lips. "I notice that in your demands you do not plead for your lady's hand, her safety," he said, biting into the date.

Marcello faltered, embarrassed. It wasn't part of the plan. I knew that. I knew it. But it still stung. Just as Paratore hoped it would. He knew something was up. As did Ascoli. My heart settled into a triple-time beat. We were in trouble. Big trouble.

"We are here," Marcello said belatedly, "solely to negotiate Fortino's release, one way or another." He paused, took a breath, then sat down and looked toward Lord Greco. Like a man now, not a boy begging for a chance. "I am prepared to offer Firenze a chest full of gold in exchange for my brother," Marcello said. "And our mediator ten percent for his trouble." He glanced at Lord Ascoli. The man gave him a regal nod, barely hiding his smile.

"Unacceptable," said Paratore, beside Rodolfo.

"It was made clear that we would exchange Lord Fortino Forelli only for the Ladies Betarrini," said another short lord. I tried to remember his name. He was one of the grandi I'd met in Firenze.

"Surely you don't believe I will hand them over to you. My brother is barely alive, so poorly has he been treated!" Marcello growled.

Lord *Barbato*, I finally remembered. He was short and scruffy, with a beard that was closely trimmed over a rounded chin. I remembered that I thought of him as a terrier the first time we met in Firenze. All high energy and ego. It was easier to focus on him than my enemy, Cosmo Paratore.

"Fortino's imprisonment has long spared your people further battle," Barbato said simply. "The people's fury was assuaged by punishment meted out to him."

"The people?" Marcello challenged. "Or her governors?"

"Both," Barbato returned easily.

Marcello took a deep breath and placed his hands on the table, palms down, as if steeling himself. "Such is the terrible price some of us must pay," he said carefully. "Fortino knew it as well as I. But you've extracted his worth and more. To take home my gold, enough gold to feed a thousand families for a year, is more than fair in exchange for allowing us to take him home to die. The Ladies Betarrini are no longer a part of this bargain."

Lord Barbato considered him, then looked down the table. All of them slowly shook their heads, including Lord Greco. Cosmo Paratore simply wore a small smile directed at me that said *You are sooo in trouble.* His confidence sent a shiver of fear down my back. Were our hosts truly neutral? Or were they on the side of the Firenze, ultimately?

Barbato looked back to Marcello. "We must adhere to the original terms that brought us to this table. We cannot return to Firenze with anything less."

Lord Ascoli, at the head of the table, cleared his throat. "The original terms, Lord Forelli. Your brother in exchange for Lady Gabriella and Lady Evangelia Betarrini."

Marcello let out a scoffing sound. "It would be one thing if you were offering my brother, well and whole. If he had been treated as a nobleman ought in this past year." He lowered his voice. "But you have brought me little more than his corpse."

I winced, hoping his lowered voice wouldn't carry over to Fortino, still over at the edge of the hall with my family. But I suspected it was nothing Fortino himself wouldn't have said in order to negotiate more powerfully. He'd know Marcello said such things not to be unkind, but to further their joint cause.

The men of Firenze shared a look. Lord Barbato glanced at Paratore and Greco and then gave Ascoli a nod. *Some sort of prearranged signal.* I tensed.

"They understand your frustration," said Lord Ascoli soothingly. "And therefore shall only require Lady Gabriella in exchange for Lord Fortino." By his tone you would have thought he was offering a case of Turkish apricots in exchange for a case of plain old apples. Like it was a huge favor, taking me off Marcello's hands.

It took one look at Paratore to make my stomach turn. He was grinning.

"We could have demanded all three of the Ladies Betarrini," said Lord Barbato, casting an eye toward my mom. That put Dad over the edge. He took a step forward, his face hardening. "But we knew that would have been too much," Barbato went on. "We are reasonable people. Don't forget, we were once your friends."

*Yeah, those days are seriously over.*

"We recognize that it is a great sacrifice to give us Lady Gabriella," he continued with a nod in my direction, "which is precisely what is required to consider this exchange at all. Firenze's people will not abide by us merely *giving* you Lord Fortino. An eye for an eye, you know."

"You've literally taken an eye and more," Marcello ground out. "Even one of these fine women is far too great a price in exchange for what remains of my brother, and you know it."

"Take your brother home, where he can breathe his last in Siena," urged Lord Greco.

"His last," Paratore echoed in a whisper, tracing the edge of his goblet.

"To take him *home*," Marcello said to Greco, "I'd have to take him to Castello Forelli."

Lord Barbato hesitated. "We are prepared to offer you Castello Forelli as well as Lord Fortino in exchange for Lady Gabriella."

Marcello stilled.

*Seriously? In exchange for me?* I groaned, inwardly. *These guys want me bad.* Far more than we expected. Not that I was flattered. There was only one reason they wanted me—to humiliate Marcello and Siena. And any way you cut it, that couldn't be good news.

Marcello flicked his fingers away. "Keep Castello Forelli. I now have a much finer home in the palazzo vacated by the traitor."

*Way to go! Throw 'em off—make 'em think we don't care about Castello Forelli.*

Lord Barbato leaned forward on the table, hands clasped before him. "It is clear to us that you have great feelings for Lady Gabriella."

Marcello studied him for a moment, then glanced back at me and offered his hand. I looked down at him and slipped my fingers into his. "'Tis no secret that the lady holds my heart," he said to them.

"So is it that you fear that Lady Gabriella will be tortured as your brother has been?"

"That is but *part* of my trepidation about releasing her to you, but yes." He was milking the conversation, drawing them out, getting us closer to nightfall, closer to the point when we'd have a chance to make a run for it.

"We are noblemen," Paratore said, waving in either direction along the table. "She shall be treated with respect."

I almost laughed out loud. It took everything in me to pretend I was every inch a medieval lady who knew her place.

"I released her from a *cage* the last time I was in Firenze," Marcello bit out, returning his focus to them. "Your *noblemen* left her to die in it—you, Lord Barbato, and you, Lord Greco—without water and food. She suffered through nights in the cold. Untold humiliation. You believe I will take you at your word when you tell me she shall be treated with *respect?*"

The Fiorentini were silent for a moment.

"There is a perfect solution," Lord Barbato said carefully.

"And what is that?"

Barbato glanced down the table at Rodolfo. "Lord Greco has generously offered to take Lady Gabriella's hand in marriage."

We froze. All except Dad. "*Scusa un'attimo*—" he demanded, striding forward. *Now, see here...*

"*Ben!*" Mom called.

But it was too late. I groaned inwardly; Dad had tolerated the fake potential prisoner exchange deal, but once we started talkin' marriage… he was undone. Two burly guards grabbed hold of Dad's arms and, with a nod from Lord Ascoli, escorted Dad out. "I've heard quite enough!" he shouted over his shoulder. "Only I may grant Gabriella's hand in marriage to anyone! She is not some sort of chattel to be bartered off—"

The doors shut behind him, and his shouts were muffled. Mom was standing by the doors, a hand over her mouth. *Great, now we're gonna have to free Dad from some sort of cell…*

Lord Barbato cocked a brow and glanced at his cohorts. "The Normans. You would think they knew the ways of war by now."

Paratore laughed and said, "Lady Gabriella is hardly the virgin daughter of nobility, awaiting her groom—"

Marcello shoved back his chair and stood so suddenly it fell over, almost knocking me over with it. Luca and his men were only a half second behind, the others gathering behind us.

The Fiorentini rose too, and the Sansicinian guards behind both sides, and then it was a total glare-fest for a long, tense moment. Like the second before two hockey teams gave in to their pent-up anger and just went at it.

"Gentlemen, gentlemen," soothed Lord Ascoli. "I'm certain Lord Paratore did not mean to question Lady Gabriella's, ahh, *purity*. He merely refers to the fact that she has been as fierce an opponent on the battlefield as any man. Hardly the sort of woman we are used to encountering."

Marcello glanced at me, silently inquiring if I was all right, if he could let this assault to my honor go. I knew my face had to be about the color of a tomato by now. Out of all the things I'd dealt with in ancient Toscana, I never thought a hundred men would be in the room when the subject of my virginity came up.

I waved at him. *Let it go. Please, please, let it go.*

He shook his head and reluctantly resumed his seat.

"Lord Forelli," Rodolfo said, after a moment, "I know it would take great sacrifice from both you and Lady Gabriella. But under my roof, upon my arm, no harm would come to her. She would be treated as a lady. Mayhap it would even be the first step toward lasting peace between our provinces again."

Marcello stared at him for a long moment, tapping his thumb on the table. I was trying to figure it out too. Was it a way for Greco to make sure I stayed safe, in case I *had* to go to Firenze? Or was he merely helping us extend the conversation, the time, to get us closer to nightfall, so that we could attempt our escape?

I knew what they were after. Potential headlines from grocery-store news rags back home came flying through my brain—*She-Wolf Dumps Siena for Firenze! Who Would You Choose? Lord Marcello or Lord Greco? Readers Respond Inside...*

"Your price is still too dear," Marcello said.

"Come now, m'lord," said Ascoli. "If you truly love her, demonstrate it. Ensure her safety, her health, her future, by allowing Lord Greco to marry her. It is the ultimate form of self-sacrifice. And as he said, it may be the first step in bringing our provinces closer together again."

Marcello shifted in his seat and glanced up at me. "I would give my very life for Lady Gabriella. The question is her happiness. If I hold her heart as clearly as she does mine, it would eviscerate us to remain apart. But I leave it to her to decide."

I frowned down at him. *What? Great, put it on me.*

I lifted a hand to my chest. "'Tis a great deal to ask, m'lords. A lady cannot come to such a decision lightly."

Lord Paratore snorted. "You've made hundreds of decisions in an instant upon the battlefield. Why is this any different?"

"'Tis one thing to decide to move and save one's life. Another to commit one's future." I glanced at Rodolfo, but he avoided meeting my gaze.

"Give us an hour to discuss it," Marcello said.

"Please, take more than that," Lord Ascoli said. He flicked two fingers toward a group of knights at his right, and suddenly the room was full of movement. Every one of us was guarded by two of our hosts, as were the Fiorentini.

"What are you doing?" Marcello said, pulling against the iron grip of the knights on either side of him.

"Ensuring this deal is completed, as I pledged," Lord Ascoli said. "Mayhap a night in the dungeon shall convince Lady Gabriella that marriage is a winsome prospect, regardless of her groom."

"You dare not," Marcello growled.

"Indeed I do," said Lord Ascoli, lifting his brows. "We shall resume our discussion on the morrow. As we break our fast, Lady Gabriella shall tell us what she has decided."

He knew. Somehow he'd figured out our plan. Had our men been discovered, seen stealing toward the hill town? Had Greco sold us out?

"And if my brother dies this very night?" Marcello said. "Then there is nothing to discuss."

"You are correct. If Lord Fortino dies, our discussion is complete," Ascoli said. "I shall send you home with his corpse to bury in honor beside Castello Forelli. And I shall send Lady Gabriella to Firenze. Her fate remains in her own hands, just as long as Lord Fortino tarries between this world and the next."

# Chapter Eight

They pushed me forward, and I stumbled into the center of the small cell. I turned to rush the door as they locked me in. "Please," I begged. "Do not do this. Lord Marcello, he shall see you well paid if you will only assist me—"

The guards eyed each other but ignored me, turning to stand on either side of the door as sentries. I clenched the rough, hand-forged metal rods in my palms and fingers and leaned my forehead against them. What had I been thinking? Talking Marcello into this? My parents? My sister? Now we were all in danger.

I'd pictured us battling our way out, hand-to-hand combat. In danger that way. Not in danger because we'd been outsmarted.

"Gabriella," said a familiar voice.

I lifted my head and peered through the dark.

It was Dad, two cells away.

"I'm here," he said simply.

I turned to go over to the side of my iron cage and clung to the bars there. "I'm so, so sorry, Dad. I didn't know this was how it would come down," I said.

"I know that." He hesitated. "So I take it you're here because you didn't agree to marry Bachelor Number Two."

I laughed under my breath and said in English, "They're totally using me to pressure Marcello. Lord Ascoli wishes for me to 'consider my options.' Some *options,* huh? I can choose to rot in her prisons or give in and become Rodolfo's wife."

Dad's eyes shifted to the guards. "Is it a way for him to protect you?" he asked in English, casting a sidelong glance at the guards, as if they might interpret what he was saying.

"I…I think so. It's all so complicated," I said, putting a hand on my forehead.

"Does our friend—" he said, avoiding using Rodolfo's name, "—does he have feelings for you, Gabi?"

I looked at him in confusion, then shook my head. "I don't think so. He has some sort of old pact with Marcello. He knows that Marcello is the one I love."

"That does not mean that he doesn't—"

Footsteps on the stone stairs brought both our heads around. Men came down, ducking their heads beneath the low clearance, and I saw in a moment that they carried Fortino between them.

"Oh!" I cried, then switched to Italian. "Nay! Leave him in the hall, where he will be warm!"

They ignored me, dumping Fortino at the front of the cell between me and Dad and locking it up tight as if he might jump up and make a break for it. Fortino groaned but then was still.

"You can reach through the bars to do your rites," said the knight to a priest who stood to the side. I hadn't noticed him arrive with the others. The same dude from upstairs, about Marcello's age and round-faced. The weird little ring of hair and shaved crown wasn't really working for him, either. Not that it did for most of the holy men I'd spotted.

He kneeled and reached through the bars to feel for Fortino's pulse.

"Does he live?" I asked in a hoarse whisper.

"By a thread," he returned. He looked up at me, sorrow in his eyes. "He is dear to you, too?"

I nodded, too choked up to dare answer, and sank to my knees in the corner, as close as I could get to Fortino. I shook my head slowly. "Why, Father? Why would God let such a good man die in this terrible way?"

He waited until I met his gaze. "This is not of God. But God allows men to make their own choices. Women, too," he added with a nod.

I stared down at Fortino. "He'd finally regained his health, after battling for a decade to do so. He hoped to be married…" My voice broke then, aching with the sorrows that Fortino had endured.

"To Lady Rossi," the priest said softly.

That brought my tears to a stop and my head up. My eyes searched his. Had he known Fortino when he was well? Could he be an ally? But then, their coming nuptials had hardly been a secret…

Fortino moaned, whimpering in his unconsciousness. I closed my eyes and thought about all he had endured. The flogging, the beatings that had left him bleeding inside…the taking of his eye. Lord Barbato had wanted him here, to remind me of how bad it could get, of what might be ahead of me if I chose the noble route, refusing Greco's offer.

I stared as the priest began a soft prayer in Latin and opened a small pouch and set a corked vial of oil, a wooden cross, a bit of dry bread, and a small bottle of wine on the stone floor. "Through this holy unction and His own most tender mercy, may the Lord pardon whatever sins or faults you have committed, brother…"

"Extreme Unction," Dad said lowly, as the priest reached for the vial of oil and uncorked it.

I glanced up at Dad in surprise, so lost in thought I'd forgotten he was there. *What must he be thinking?* I knew that at this point, he likely was back in the This-is-a-Nightmare-Somebody-Wake-Me-Up stage. We weren't Catholic, but we'd spent enough time in Italia to know about Extreme Unction. *The last rites.*

The priest thought Fortino was about to breathe his last. Which really shouldn't have shocked me. I'd been thinking about it ever since we first saw him, since Marcello basically said good-bye. But being here, now, on the cold stone floor, hearing the ancient words, it was all of a sudden *real.*

"No, no, no," I moaned. "It can't be time," I said in English.

The priest paused in his litany, seeming to understand me, even though he didn't speak the language. How many other mourners had he comforted?

"It shall be a relief for Lord Fortino," he said gently. "His battle has been long and is finally at an end. In heaven he shall have his reward."

"Reward?" I scoffed. "All Fortino ever wanted was health. Love. Laughter."

"And he shall have all three ahead of him," the priest said gently. He turned back to Fortino and let the vial of oil flow to his fingertip, then traced the sign of the cross on Fortino's feet. "*Quidquid deliquisti…*"

I fell onto one hip and leaned against the bars, watching the priest perform the rites, translating the few bits of Latin I knew in my head, no fight left in me. It *would* be a release, of sorts, for Fortino to let go, give in. He'd fought for so long…

"By touch," the priest said, anointing Fortino's hands. "By taste," he said, touching his lips. "By smell, by hearing, and by sight," he added, bushing over my friend's nose, ears and tenderly making the sign of the cross over his one good eyelid.

A chill ran down my back as Fortino stirred, coughed feebly, and then stilled. Through it all, the priest continued his recitation, moving into the Lord's Prayer. But was he speaking more quickly now? Was he worried Fortino would die before he was done? Did the rite not count if he did?

A guard brought down a torch and lit several huge, dripping candles along the far wall, then departed. I hadn't realized that it had been really quite dark. In the flickering light I stared at Fortino's profile, so like Marcello's. What if it was Marcello, instead, that I was saying good-bye to? The tears began to flow down my cheeks again.

"You were close, Gabi?" Dad asked quietly.

"He's been…like a brother," I said, gasping for breath between my tears.

The priest finished his litany, placed a bit of bread on Fortino's tongue, a tiny sip of wine, closed it and watched him swallow. He made the sign of the cross in the air above Fortino, whispering in prayer and then rose, crossing himself. But he didn't go far. He simply moved to the far wall of the passage and ducked his head. Praying? Asking God to welcome one of His children home?

I looked up, the stone ceiling of my cell swimming behind my tears, and I rubbed my eyes with my palms.

"How is it possible, Gabi?" Dad asked tenderly in English. "How could you be in so deep with these people in such a short time?"

"Give it another week, Dad. It's not all like this," I returned. "And yet, this is part of it too. This deep, dark grief—it kind of shakes you up, makes you appreciate life, love more. It opens your heart."

"With all the gentleness of a crowbar," he said. "And being thrown in jail? That wasn't ever something I thought I'd be doing as a dad."

I shot him a guilty smile. "Dude. It's not often a father and daughter get to spend jail time together back home. It's way cooler than a Daddy-daughter dance, don't you think?"

He smiled back at me. "If you were looking for some Daddy-daughter time, I could think of about a hundred better ways to spend it, dance or no."

I shook my head. "I'm sorry, Dad. Sorry I got you into this."

"Seems to me like it chose you. Us, now. But tell me, Gabs. Why…how do you know you're *supposed* to be here?"

I looked up at the ceiling again and then with a groan, rose, so I could face him, and keep an eye on Fortino, too. "It's like…what do you want most when you are as tired as you could be?"

"My bed."

I nodded. "And what do you want most when you are super hungry?"

"Food. Any food. The fastest food possible."

"More than that," I pressed, wanting him to see that I was after something different. "Think of *Survivor*. All those endless days of rice. What do they want most?"

"To win the feast challenge."

"Right," I said. "Steaks, hamburgers, icy drinks, fruit, vegetables." I reached through the bars and opened and closed my fists, figuring out how to translate what I was feeling. "I think I was kind of asleep for a while, coasting through life. Eating an all-rice diet. Having enough food, but not *food*. Do you know what I mean? This, this"—I sadly glanced down at Fortino, who was breathing so shallowly I could barely see his chest rise and fall—"life here, is full, even if there's grief. There's joy, too, in the midst of it. It's *life* like I've never experienced before. It's like I only was experiencing it at twenty percent, and now I'm at a hundred." I looked over to Dad. "Does that make sense?"

He stared back at me. "I understand." He paused. "Your mother's right."

"About what?"

"You've grown up. Become a woman. Thinking adult thoughts."

I returned his tender smile.

"Gabi, I'm sorry that we haven't been around much in these last years, I mean, before I…"

*Before you died.* I nodded.

"We were so wrapped up in our work, and once you girls became so good at taking care of yourselves…"

I shook my head and moved away, turning my back to him. "Dad, can we have this talk later?" I asked, lifting a hand. I couldn't really deal with it right then. Not on top of everything with Fortino. If he kept talking, I knew I'd be weeping, wanting nothing but a hug from him that I couldn't get.

"Sure," he said quietly. "I just want you to know, regardless of what comes, that I'm proud of you. And I love you, Gabriella."

I nodded quickly, not trusting myself to speak. The knot in my throat was already the size of an orange.

"I trust you," he said. "To make the best decision you can."

That really got me. Dad always talked about making the best decision you could at the time and not beating yourself up about it later. It was part of his *it is what it is* mantra. Him telling me he trusted me to do that, now, when he knew the decisions ahead of me…well, I was both touched and totally irritated.

The irritation won out, and I returned to the bars nearest him. "But Dad…I need you to tell me what to do here. If things"—I paused and eyed the guards and the priest, who was still nodding and muttering in prayer—"don't go as planned. What am I to do? Marry a man I don't love? Or spend the rest of my life in a prison like this?"

His look hardened. "We will see you freed, Gabi. From what I already know of Marcello, he will not rest until that is accomplished. And I will be with him."

"As long as he lives—and you live. You died on me once before…"

"Hey now, quit the negative talk, Gabriella. At the ready!"

I automatically took half a step, as was our routine when sparring, and then smiled. He wanted me to prepare *within*. For what was coming our way. He smiled back at me.

"Yes!" Fortino said.

We both looked at him in surprise, and I hurried to the corner and kneeled again. "Fortino?"

"Gabriella, do you see them?" he asked in wonder, his speech forceful and lucid, his eye wide and staring upward.

I looked too, searching the stones above him. But saw nothing but moss and a big, fat spider.

"Do you hear them? The singing. *Oh*, such a song I've never heard. They're beautiful, Gabriella. Beautiful," he said, practically groaning in his wonder.

I was crying again, finally realizing that he was seeing what I could not.

"*Le porte sono aperte*," the priest said, kneeling by Fortino's head again. *The gates are opened*. I'd kinda forgotten the holy man was even there.

"Tell me, Fortino," I said. "What is it that you see?"

"Do not ask it," admonished the priest. "God will show you, too, when it is your—"

"Angels," Fortino said, as if he heard no one but me. "Gabriella, are they not the most wondrous creatures you've ever seen? Their wings…their *wings*…"

He reached out and moved his fingers as if he were stroking the edge of something. His face was alight. Glowing.

That was the only way I could describe it. Total and complete glory in every inch of his body, as if he was being lifted to heaven right before my very eyes. As if he was already a part of it.

The room felt electric. Every hair on my body was standing up. I felt flushed, hot, weirdly filled, while at the same time surrounded, warmed.

And at the same time I could feel the chill of Fortino's withdrawal. "Fortino," I said, choking on my tears. "Not yet."

But he didn't answer. Only smiled, his one eye filled with a vision I could not see, only felt.

I wept. Because it was the end.

Because Marcello wasn't here to see it.

Because Fortino was experiencing something so enticing and perfect and I felt a part of it, and yet, not.

And then he took a breath.

His last one.

# Chapter Nine

The guards came and collected his body and departed, the priest following behind. I cried and paced, long after he was gone, unable to stay still. I got lost in plans to go to the Etruscan tomb with Lia and Mom and Dad and return earlier than before, to save Fortino. To wade into battle, help prevent Fortino's capture, to regain Castello Forelli, to spare Marcello my long absence. But in cascading back and forth like a ping-pong ball between paddles of time, would we get lost somewhere in between? Would our luck truly hold?

And what had we just witnessed? Had there truly been angels in the cell with Fortino? Could he see them because he had some sort of inside track? Because of the priest's prayers? Or had he just been hallucinating, his body giving out? But his eyes had been so different, his face glowing so much that it had practically lit the room...

Dad stared over at me. "I wonder...when I died...I wonder if I saw anything like that."

"Yeah," I said. "I don't know. But doesn't everyone? You know, 'go to the light' and all?"

"Maybe," he said distractedly. "Maybe."

I kept pacing while Dad settled down and after a while snored softly in the corner of his cell. *Really, Dad? Really?* Who could sleep at a time like this? Didn't he know that Fortino's death had most likely unlocked some freaky gears of change? Was the deal off the table, as Marcello said? Or would the Sansicinians release Dad and send me off with Greco, like Ascoli said? Why wasn't anyone coming?

I clasped the rough bars and leaned my forehead against them, welcoming the shock of their frigid temperatures as if the cold might numb and slow my crazy, rambling thoughts. The rhythmic sound of Dad's gentle snore comforted me after a while—he was here, with me; I wasn't alone—and it made me realize how tired I was too. I finally gave in and sank down into the far corner of the cell, pulling my knees close to my chest in an effort to keep warm and leaning my head against the rough stones of the wall. I was so tired of trying to figure out what came next, of trying to rethink and outwit the past. So weary after all the tears I'd cried over Fortino.

*Sleep, Gabi. Sleep, sleep, sleep—*

What felt like seconds later, rough hands awakened me, pulling me to my feet and then lifting me. But judging from my stiffness, it had been hours. A hand clasped over my mouth, muffling my scream.

Dad heard my cries anyway. "Gabi? Gabi! Gabriella!" he cried. "Stop! You have no claim upon her! With Fortino gone, there is no trade to be made!" But the men carried me upstairs with as much care as they would take with a sack of potatoes. In a small room they set me upright.

Lord Ascoli was there, as were Greco and Barbato.

Paratore hovered in the corner, smirking. "With Fortino's demise your time in Sansicino has ended. Have you decided, m'lady? Will it be Lord Greco or Firenze's dungeons that you shall brave?" He hid a smile behind his hand.

"My father was right. Fortino is dead. You must now release me! There is no more negotiation."

"That, my dear, is not an option," Barbato said. "Firenze needs her prize. And we aim to give it to her, regardless of our lack of agreement with your Sienese lord."

"I am far more than a pawn in your game," I grit out, throwing back my shoulders and lifting my chin. "Cross me, cross Marcello now, and you shall live to regret it."

"Come now. It is hardly a harsh sentence to marry Lord Greco," said Lord Barbato, appraising Rodolfo. "You may protest as much as you wish in order to preserve your honor, but I imagine you will soon succumb to his charms, just as so many of our eligible daughters have at home."

"Then he can marry one of them," I spat, staring at Rodolfo, trying to get a read on him. What was he thinking? Was this all an elaborate setup to help me escape?

"As Rodolfo suggested," Lord Barbato went on, "it would be a first step toward meaningful peace between our provinces. Your 'sacrifice' would benefit many."

"There shall be no peace. Lord Marcello will lead the Sienese in an attack."

"I think not. Marcello knows that as soon as the first arrow flies, your neck shall be cut."

I stared back into his small eyes. "And if I choose the dungeon?"

"A most enticing idea," Paratore put in. "I know the perfect one."

Barbato paused and considered me. "You do not wish to take that route, m'lady. Many more of your beloved Sienese shall die. You know as well as we do that they would undoubtedly fight, and die for, their She-Wolf."

"As would a great number of Fiorentini," I said tiredly. Death, so much death. I'd just told my dad it made me hunger for life. And at this point I was starving for life. Fortino's face had been so full of it, right before he died. It was time for life, love, peace. I ached for it.

I shook my head. *Whatever.* I just wanted to move. Escape this sense of claustrophobia. Be on my way...*somewhere.* Outta here. Perhaps on the road, out of this hilltop fortress, Marcello and his men could rescue me. Or I might find my opening to escape—I still had the dagger. I.stilled and looked at Lord Ascoli. "What of Marcello and his men, my parents, my sister?"

"The Fiorentini will depart now, with you as their promised prize. In an hour I shall release the Sienese, who have been divided and are held in various parts of the city. Lord Fortino's body"—he paused to make the sign of the cross from forehead to chest and across, as did the others—"is already in the finest casket our woodworkers make." He said it like he was the big man, generous and all.

*Wow. Can you be any more proud of yourself?* I fought the urge to roll my eyes and closed them instead, as if the mention of Fortino's name brought me to tears again. *Think, Gabi. Think!*

"In addition, Lord Forelli shall receive his castello back, a most dear concession on behalf of Firenze," Barbato said. "Even though he declared otherwise, we know it shall help assuage his angst over losing you."

I couldn't help myself; I smiled inwardly at the thought of Marcello back where he belonged. Home. And out of the creepy palazzo where none of us could escape the memories of the Rossis, no matter how many layers of whitewash they put on the plaster.

Once he and his men had control of the castello again, it'd be hard to roust them from it. It was a serious win for Siena, even if Marcello had denied it. He wanted it; he just didn't want the Fiorentini to know how dearly he wanted it. Not that he'd ever trade it for me—I knew that. But if I could win it for him as part of this crazy gamble…

"I think you shall find life at my side not entirely disagreeable," Rodolfo said gently. His eyes totally said *trust me*. I wanted to, but I remembered that I didn't like him much when he was playing Captain Firenze. I only really liked him when he was playing Covert Friend. Was that what he was doing now?

"M'lady," he said, reaching out his hand and falling to one knee. "Upon my life, you shall be safe with me. You would do me and Firenze a great honor in becoming my bride."

And if Marcello trusted him…

And if I was to escape, these dudes had to let their guard down…

Slowly I reached out my hand to place it in his. "I accept, on behalf of all the women who will not have to bury a husband, a son, a friend, be they citizens of Firenze or Siena."

Not that I was really going to do it. You know, marry him. But Lord Ascoli clapped excitedly, and Lord Barbato smiled broadly. Paratore, of course, continued to grumble. He was probably ticked I hadn't chosen the whole Dungeon Doorway.

Rodolfo did not let my eyes go as he rose and covered my hand with his other. "Stay at my side, and I shall see no harm comes to you," he said, looking down at me tenderly.

I slipped my hand from his and shifted, overcome by the sense of betrayal I was feeling. Hadn't Marcello asked the very same of me just the day before? But what could I do? I could arrive in Firenze in chains again, dragged behind a horse—*yeah, been there, done that*— or I could arrive atop one. It would be far easier for me to make a break for it if they didn't *think* I was going to try. And if I wasn't exhausted. Marcello would understand. I had to play the part. If I was to survive.

Because the last thing I wanted was to end up in that stupid birdcage again.

They hustled me out to the courtyard, where the Fiorentini were already mounted and ready. The knights grinned when they saw me on Lord Greco's arm, but they all kept silent. Wherever they were keeping the Sienese men at bay, they apparently didn't wish to make them aware of their victory in claiming me. At least not until we had gained enough ground between us. Then, I was sure, the taunting would begin.

Rodolfo swept my wool cape around my shoulders, fastening it under my chin as if he were already the attentive husband. Then he led me to a beautiful white mare outfitted with one of those aggravating sidesaddles. They made riding twice as hard—and it was nearly impossible to hold my own reins. Which was by design, of course. *Keep the She-Wolf on her leash and all.*

He bent and took hold of my waist in his hands and lifted me up to it, then settled my slippered feet into the stirrups. All the while, he cast me small, lingering glances with his gorgeous, smoky-hot eyes, making me shift in the saddle, feeling uncomfortably warm. What was that about? Was he playing the role of entranced fiancé? I didn't know; I just knew that it was making me feel some kind of uncomfortable. And disgusted with myself for kind of liking it.

He took hold of the edge of my skirt and settled it to the side, totally covering my feet again, and a few men near us chuckled, as if he'd looked up my skirt instead. *Oh brother*, I thought. Stupid boys were stupid boys, no matter the era.

They quieted when Lord Greco frowned in their direction, and it was my turn to smile. He mounted his gray gelding beside me, and we all headed out, two by two, down the street and out the open gates, then across the long, descending bridge.

Beneath fading stars I could see the very beginning of the sunrise, the color of a dark, red rose. My breath clouded before my face. "It is beautiful, is it not?" I murmured, using the excuse of looking to the east as my chance to scan for any sign of Marcello's men. Could they see me, in the faint light of day? Know I needed help?

"You enjoy sunrises, m'lady? Or the color of roses?"

I stole a glance at him, surprised that he had come to the same conclusion on the color. But Rodolfo had that habit—surprising me, as if he had some sort of inner knowledge of my thoughts.

"Both," I said with a small smile that I thought would appear flirty. The guys behind me would eat that up. Talk about it around the campfire that night. Spread the rumor when we reached Firenze. That there really was something between us besides politics. And maybe, just maybe, that would help me stay alive to better pick my opportunity to escape—when it didn't require a dip in the icy Arno

River and dodging arrows, etc. *That,* I could do without. And the cage. There was a lot in Firenze, when I thought about it, that I could add to my Most Dreaded List.

"As my bride, m'lady," he said, reaching out a hand, "I shall fill your rooms with roses and kiss you awake at sunrise."

I was glad it was still pretty dark as a burning blush climbed my neck. Did he know I was only pretending to go for this? And his words were a little...forward, right? Whether we were engaged or not? Well, maybe if they had come from Marcello, I would feel differently...

He lifted his hand again, waiting, and I saw it then. A tiny piece of parchment, peeking between his fingers.

I took his warm hand and looked into his eyes. "I shall look forward to it, m'lord," I said. *Now that,* I thought, *will give the boys something to talk about.*

Slowly I slid my hand from his, and with it, the piece of parchment. For the first time, I was glad I wasn't holding the reins, which were tied to Lord Greco's.

I was dying to read the note, but first, there wasn't enough light, and second, the dudes behind me would totally see. I had to wait. Forced myself to wait. My palm grew sweaty waiting as we finally finished crossing the bridge and started down the western road. But when we were deep into the eastern woods of the Chianti region and reached the first crossroads that would lead north to Firenze, the men pulled up and circled.

Paratore was departing, speaking in low tones with Lords Barbato and Greco. With one last sneer in my direction, he wheeled his horse around and headed east, with two men on either side of him. Back home. To Castello Paratore, most likely. Perhaps to be ready as Marcello neared.

"So," said the captain, "you still believe it is safest for us to travel to Roma?"

I frowned. What was this? *Roma?* Why would we go to Rome?

Rodolfo looked at each of the men but refused to look at me. "Marcello and his men shall expect us to ride toward home. They will be sorely disappointed to not intercept us on the road to Firenze. Once my nuptials with Lady Gabriella are complete, we can travel without fear."

My heart stopped for a sec and then beat twice as hard, making me actually bring a hand to my chest. I stared hard at him, but he still didn't look my way. Lord Barbato smiled over at me. "I have arranged every detail with our friends in Roma," he said. "It shall be a day you will remember forever."

Right. Like I was worried I wouldn't have a wedding straight out of the latest issue of *Brides* magazine.

They'd planned it all out. Known, from the start, that it was me they wanted. And they'd come up with a way to ensure it would happen.

As the sun climbed in the sky, my heart sank lower and lower. None of Marcello's men charged after us. They were probably as many miles north now as we were south. I wondered, briefly, why they just hadn't made sure we got hitched in Sansicino, but then I knew why:

Had word reached Marcello, there would have been no way that our men would have left without battle, weapons or not. This way, with only the word that I was gone, Marcello would be driven to pursuit rather than upheaval inside Ascoli's precious city walls. Ascoli had neatly washed his hands of all of us and undoubtedly kept a sweet Fiorentini finder's fee for my capture.

Even now the priest rode with us. Why not do the whole outdoor wedding thing here?

Then it came to me. The people of medieval Tuscany would only recognize a wedding performed in a church. It was something holy to them. Required. No vineyard or oceanside weddings in Italia in this day and age. No way.

It was shortly before noon when Rodolfo shouted out to his captain and the men allowed their horses to head toward a meager stream beside the road. I didn't miss the fact that two rear scouts had just returned, wearing expressions of confidence and ease, and that two others were sent out to take their place.

I was led by Lord Greco and two men, who all turned their backs when I went behind a tree to relieve myself. I stayed there a moment, finally unfolding the note, which by that time had become a damp ball in my palm.

*Your deepest desires shall be met. Trust me. —R*

I read it, over and over again. His handwriting was elegant, almost like calligraphy. But that was not what so captured me. It was the promise. My deepest desire was to be with Marcello, forever, of course. He was promising to get me to him, to safety. Right?

But what was this turn toward Roma? And while I could excuse the words as simply code, something that the Fiorentini would dismiss as a love note, I saw as having different levels, different meanings.

*No, I won't go there. He's reassuring me. Roma is south of Siena, farther away from Firenze than ever. He intends to use our location to help me escape.*

I hoped. I refused to believe anything else. That he would actually use me to betray his friend or his pledge as one of the brotherhood. If he were willing to do that, would it have not been far easier to let me die in the cage?

I emerged from my hidden perch, and Rodolfo led me to the stream, where he scooped cold water with a small wooden bowl and let it flow over my hands. I rubbed my face, loving the wet on my dusty skin, and then when I blinked my eyes open, he was offering me a handkerchief to dry. So thoughtful…so ahead of me at every moment.

We broke bread and ate the hard pecorino cheese in silence, while the men chatted and laughed around us. What was there to say? Only one question came to my mind. "How long shall it take us to reach Roma?"

"Two days," he said casually, "if we can keep this pace." He was sprawled out on his side on a blanket, leaning on one arm, facing me as if we were out on a romantic picnic and had been hanging out together a lot.

Two days. Two nights on the road.

"Fig?" he asked, offering me a dried orb.

"Grazie," I said, reaching for it.

He held on, teasing me, and I laughed in confusion. He smiled, making him look more the Roman god than ever.

Okay, so he was cute. Like movie-star cute. And his interest was flattering, but I loved Marcello. Right? Right. But I found myself kind of overwhelmed with all the attention—what was the deal, anyway? I'd never had a boyfriend in my life, and here, the guys seemed to line up…

The two guards nearest us moved away, as if to give us a moment of privacy. I shoved the fig into my mouth, knowing it was too big for one bite but wanting a measure of distance and distraction from Rodolfo.

He turned and lowered himself onto his back, putting his hands behind his head, as if he knew I didn't want him to make any move. He was just playing with me, toying, flirting, like every other Italian male.

He stared up into the trees. "So tell me, Gabriella. What is it that you long for most?"

I hesitated and swallowed my fig. *Huh?* "What do you mean?"

"Is it a grand palazzo? Fine gowns? Children? What would bring you happiness?"

My eyes shifted to the trickling river. Come spring, it would be ten times as wide and just as deep. On and on it went, rushing toward the distant horizon. Like time. Like life. Sometimes gently falling from one pool into the other, other times fast and cascading, and still other times narrowing into a funnel, a torrent of knots and waves.

I returned my gaze to my hot-as-all-get-out captor. *Marcello's friend,* I reminded myself, centering my thoughts on Marcello. I looked up to the wide, barren branches of the oak above us and then closed my eyes as I felt the tiny bit of warmth from the sun on my face. "What most of us want, I think. Love. Family. Friends. Laughter." I smiled and dared to look at him again. "Adventure."

He laughed and nodded. "Hardly a surprise."

I looked up again, my eyes trailing from the old trunk of the tree to where it split into several limbs. "Wisdom. I want to become one of those old women everyone seeks out because she's figured it out."

"Figured it out?" he asked, confused by my contemporary phrase.

"Learned. From my mistakes, as well as my good decisions, so that I make better and better choices. So I can more clearly see the path best taken."

He nodded, covering me in a gaze that made me feel as known and appreciated as Marcello made me feel.

Which was...decidedly awkward. I rose. "Should we not be on our way?"

He rose too, looking at me quizzically. "Indeed we should." He had a piece of dried grass in his hands, and he picked it apart, methodically. "Do you not wish to know what I long for most?"

My resolve was crumbling. I looked up at him, seeing the sorrow and the longing in his big eyes. "What is it for which you long, Rodolfo?" I asked softly. Why was I feeling so defensive, tensing in preparation for his answer? He was my friend. Marcello's. He simply needed someone to confide in.

"Peace," he said, shaking his head and looking to his men, packing their things on their horses. "Between Siena and Firenze and beyond." He took a step toward me, seemingly lost in thought. But I took a step back, toward the tree.

"Like you, wisdom, but to assist my people." He shook his head again. "There are people, Gabriella, peasants. But peasants with dreams bigger than any nobleman I know." His dark eyes lit up with excitement, and he clenched his fist before his face with a smile of excitement. "I long to have the time to help them take a step toward those dreams. And another. And yet another." He took a second step toward me, as if to emphasize what he was saying. And I did too, bumping into the broad trunk of the oak tree behind me.

He stared down at me, and I dared to look up into his eyes. I had to know now. If I could trust him, truly trust him. "What else?" I asked.

He stilled, staring down at me so intently that he breathed in short huffs, as if he was holding his breath for a second at a time. He shook his head again. "Do not tempt me, Gabriella," he whispered. "I am doing all I can." He leaned closer and truly—it was like someone else was controlling my body—I lifted my face closer to his.

His eyes searched mine. And then he leaned in to kiss me, entwining his fingers into my hair, his other hand around my waist, pulling me to him.

I gave in.

Traitorous, two-timing, skanky wench that I was, I couldn't help myself. Seriously, I just didn't have it in me. He had me totally, completely confused.

And his kiss was far too sweet. I wanted it to be like poison on my lips, sour, killing. But it was far from that. Oh, so far from that…

Dimly, I heard the men cheering, and I pushed Rodolfo away, gasping for air like he'd taken it all from me. Like I could reclaim who I'd been seconds before, reverse the flow of the river, of time. And once again be only one thing: Marcello's own.

Which was far better than being this.

His betrayer.

# Chapter Ten

I awakened the following morning feeling like I seriously had a Scarlet A sewn to the bodice of my gown. It didn't help that Rodolfo was just a few feet away, even if he slept with his back to me.

Every man in camp was well aware that I'd allowed Lord Greco to kiss me; the fact that I'd shoved him away after would be quickly forgotten. They considered me Greco's. Traitor to Marcello. In their eyes, the battle was over.

*You deserve it,* I told myself. *Loser.*

I doubted Marcello had ever even looked at another girl once I returned to him, let alone kissed one. I doubted he'd even glanced their way. Not since Romana was gone. Not since we'd exchanged the *L* word. He was that kind of loyal, that kind of faithful. That kind of loving. My love. My one, true love.

*If a two-timing, treasonous jerk-o-rama of a girl can actually have one, true love…*

I wearily made my way among the sleeping forms to the creek bed, ignoring the two guards who hastily rose and hovered behind me.

At the riverbed I sighed, crouched, and splashed my face. I rubbed it as if I could wipe away the nightmare I'd begun the day before, staring at the dark sky above, still lit with stars, though they faded with the approaching light of day.

I cupped my hands beneath a small flow of water and waited for them to fill.

"Sometimes we are more harsh with ourselves than we are with others," a man's voice said, surprising me so that I ended up splashing my dress more than my face.

I squinted in the dim light, and the priest was laughing. The priest from the dungeon, who had administered Fortino's last rites.

"Oh, 'tis you. I confess, Father, I didn't even see you there," I said. But then I'd been totally distracted with thoughts of Rodolfo and my own stupidity.

He laughed again, crouched on the other side of the stream, and looked up. "Yes, 'tis my common experience. Being somewhat invisible. I doubt you know much of what I speak, being a She-Wolf and all. Everyone seems to take note of your every move, do they not?"

I cocked my head and stared over at him. "What is your name, Father?"

"Tomas. Father Tomas. Or just Tomas."

"Just Tomas?" I repeated. I knew few priests in ancient Tuscany who didn't demand the full respect of the title.

He hesitated, dipped his fingers into the water and watched them drip into the stream. "I was excommunicated two years past."

I let that sink in a moment. *I think excommunicated means cut off from the Church. Even…condemned.*

"You no longer serve the Church?"

"I serve my God," he said, poking a stick into the water and watching water divide on either side. "But no, my Church no longer allows me to serve in her name."

"But you...with Fortino, you..."

"Performed the rite of Extreme Unction." He cast me a small smile that I could just barely make out in the dim light. "God heard it. He is bigger than the Church. You saw it yourself—Fortino was on his way home to the Maker."

*Ah, so it was a power thing.* Tomas was some sort of rebel not up for supporting the concept that the Church was All That. The High Church boys didn't like that sort of thing. Especially in this era. I remembered that much of my medieval history lessons. We were only a couple hundred years away from the Reformation, when Luther would kick into gear and the Church would totally divide. Become Catholic and Protestant. I knew some kids back home who went to a mega-church, who didn't think Catholics were even Christian. It was still ugly, five hundred years after the fact.

Religion. I thought it was all stupid. It was enough to be on The Path, right? Getting closer to God? Wasn't the Christian faith kind of like an ice cream store, with a bunch of different flavors? You had your Baptists, your Lutherans, your Episcopalians, your nondenoms, your Catholics. They were all after Jesus as their head Dude, right? What did it matter?

After witnessing Fortino's death, his vision, I was more than a little freaked out by the faith thing. But I wanted more of it. To know a little more of the Big Guy before I was on my own deathbed. And hopefully be greeted through those opening gates that Fortino saw when it was my turn to go. Which might be sooner than later in this place....

"What did you do?" I asked Tomas. "To get...dismissed?"

"Excommunicated?" he returned without flinching.

"Yes, excommunicated. And Rodolfo, Lord Greco—he knows?"

"He knows." He dropped his voice. "But Lord Barbato does not." He stared at the water for a moment and then held my gaze. "I killed a man."

I paused, trying to get it in my head that this big, roly-poly man, just a little older than I, was a killer. Murderer. But then, who was I to talk? I'd done the same in battle. Over and over again. "Why?" I asked.

"Because he was about to kill a woman. His wife."

I think I blinked a few times. I'd heard it on the news. On shows like *Dateline*.

I finally found my voice again. "Why were you not hanged?"

"The villagers knew the man to be a tyrant. They knew I acted only because I had no other choice."

"And did you?"

He repositioned his stick in the water. It was getting lighter out. I could make out more of his face as he looked at me. "I could have given up my own life. But I did not," he said, with just a tinge of shame, dropping his gaze.

So that was what he had meant, about us being more harsh with ourselves than others. He'd wrestled with his own guilt.

"The woman...was she grateful?"

"Nay," he said. "She cursed me." He shrugged. "She no longer had a man. Someone to put a roof over her head, bring her food as well as a beating."

I paused, trying to absorb such an idea. He saved her, and she cursed him for it? But I remembered Signora Giannini, battling to make it without her husband. He was no abuser, but it was hard in these times to make it alone. Especially as a woman. I thought of the old woman outside of Firenze who'd saved me and Lia. It was the same thing with her, scraping by, watching the crop rot on the vines.

"I've run over the memory, time and time again. But trust me, Gabriella, when I say to let it go, move on. Endeavor to make a better choice next time if you can, especially if you made a choice in error. And if you didn't…" He shrugged again. "If God confirms you're in the right, embrace it. Let it change you and the course of your stream. Your future."

He rose and, with surprisingly light steps over the largest of the stones, crossed toward the men and horses. I saw that Rodolfo was up, stretching, and I quickly looked back to the water. I watched where the water wound around stones and reconnected below. That was what Tomas was talking about. The stream as life.

Had I made a decision that would forever divide me from Marcello? Or was it merely a stone in the river, a temporary obstacle, something to get past?

After taking a drink, I forced myself to rise and join the Fiorentini. If Marcello and his men hadn't overtaken us in the night, I doubted they would. Clearly they'd headed north toward Firenze, as expected. Why would they suspect that we would head south?

"Did you manage to sleep?" Rodolfo asked as I neared, cocking his head in an endearingly caring and attentive manner.

"For a few hours," I said. I gave him a small smile. After all, the kiss wasn't entirely his fault, and I'd all but ignored him all afternoon and evening yesterday. "'Tis better than none at all."

"Indeed." He bent, took a loaf of crusty bread from his sack, and offered me half. We stood together, choking down dry pieces for several minutes as the men removed saddles—left on in the night in case we had to flee—rubbed down the horses' flanks and then replaced them.

"No freedom for long for them," I said. I bit my cheek, knowing he'd probably think I was referring to myself too.

Maybe I was.

"Gabriella," he said quietly, tossing the rest of his loaf to the brush and facing me. He wiped his lush lips with the back of his hand and finished chewing. "Forgive me for yesterday."

I looked over his shoulder. The nearest man was more than twenty feet from us. "'Twas as much my fault as your own," I said. "You did what you had to." *You know, to continue this charade.* At least I hoped that was what it had been. That it'd all been in my head—

He searched my eyes and then looked away, to the rising sun, then back to me, searching my face. My heart was pounding. *What is wrong with me?*

"I've tried to forget it. Getting to know you, the first time. Coming to see why Marcello admired you so. But I fail, every time. I know your heart belongs to him, my brother. And I barely slept this past night, given my self-recriminations."

*But might there not be a spot in your heart for me, too?* his big, brown eyes silently asked me. So it was as I feared; there was something real, something living, growing between us, tying us together.

It hadn't all been a show for him, as it hadn't been for me. I had to end it. Cut from this direction of the river. Fast.

"I am meant for one man, Rodolfo," I whispered. "And that is Marcello."

The men were looking our way, then sharing raised eyebrows and smiles, thinking it was yet another romantic moment. It was good they thought that. It would help us keep up appearances a while longer.

"I mistreated you while you were in my care last," he said with a sigh, as if that explained my allegiance.

"Nay. I know that you did what you had to do, to preserve your role. Had you not, had they figured it out…Rodolfo, I wouldn't be standing here today. I owe you my life, several times over."

He was still for a moment, considering my words, and then he nodded, kicking his toe into the loose dirt as if he was trying to kick free the stone in the ground. "Since he has not yet arrived, I assume Marcello is a good bit behind us."

"As do I," I admitted.

"Do you have it within you?" he asked, leaning closer to my ear. "To continue this farce, even straight to an altar? We shall need every hour we can give him. And our companions…Gabriella, they have one goal."

I looked at him until he met my eyes. "As far as an altar. But no vows," I whispered fiercely. "I shall never exchange vows with anyone other than Marcello." It felt good to take a stand for what I knew was right, true. But there was a breath of tearing, too. A moment of thinking, *I can't believe I'm turning this guy down.* I didn't like it. It shamed me, acknowledging it. But there it was.

He blinked his long lashes, then nodded. "I shall see you to free-dom before that. Now we will straighten and you shall allow me to embrace you. As if you are falling for my charms. As many other women in Firenze have."

I didn't doubt it. He was reminding me that he was Mr. Hot-o-rama when I didn't need the reminder. But I'd probably hurt his pride. So I did as he'd instructed.

He straightened, gave me a lingering smile, and touched my chin with the knuckle of his forefinger, looking into my eyes. After a breath he gently placed his hands on either side of my face, then closed his eyes and kissed my forehead. Then he pulled me into a warm embrace, so warm, that I felt the chill of the morning anew when he released me.

When he offered his arm, I took it, allowing him to lead me to my mare.

He was a good man. A fine man.

Almost as good as Marcello. But he was not Marcello.

*Not him,* I reminded myself sternly.

# Chapter Eleven

We rode into Roma the following day, and I had a hard time getting my bearings. More of the ancient Roman wall was still standing, and of course, most of the buildings weren't anything like what survived into modern times. Many of the hills were covered by rubble, and grass and trees were making serious headway in reclaiming the earth as its own. Most of the commerce and people seemed to be centered near the Forum and Coliseum.

"You have been to Roma before?" Rodolfo asked me, studying my face.

"It's been some time," I returned. *Like, almost seven hundred years.*

"She is not as she once was," he said. "Since the papacy was moved, really."

The pope, not in Rome? Vaguely, I remembered that the popes had resided in France for a time. We'd visited the sprawling Palais des Papes in Avignon when I was about ten. Was it during these years that the Church had considered France safer than Italy? At the time we visited Avignon, I had a hard time getting a grip on the fact that they feared for their lives. Having been here, now, I got it.

Lord Barbato neared us on his high-stepping mount. "We shall go directly to Palazzo Vivaro," he said. "All is prepared."

Rodolfo nodded, and the nobleman moved on ahead of us.

I didn't know what I was thinking. Had I really thought we'd settle in, spend a few days, hit a couple of parties, do some sightseeing, and *then* get to this marriage business? But all at once, I realized that they intended for this marriage to happen right away.

*Tonight.*

I looked to Rodolfo. "Might we convince them to wait until the morrow?" I whispered. The knight in front of me glanced back; he'd obviously heard.

"Come now, beloved," Rodolfo pretended to chide me gently, having noted the knight's attention too. "There is no need to hesitate. You shall find I am the most gentle of husbands."

The knight in front of me chuckled. *Okay, whatever. Pretend* that *is the reason; that I'm afraid of my wedding night.* "It is only that I wished to have my parents with me when I exchanged my vows," I said.

"Unfortunately that is impossible," Rodolfo said sadly. "When all is complete, mayhap your parents can come and visit us in Firenze. They are welcome anytime, Gabriella. Your family shall be my family."

I looked into his eyes. He seemed to be reassuring me. Telling me he was *that* trustworthy—like family. Or was he suggesting something else?

I was so confused. So. Confused.

"Very well, m'lord," I said quietly. The other knight in front of us turned back to look at me. He was probably wondering where my fight had gone. I hardly sounded like a She-Wolf.

We wound through several small neighborhoods, past herds of goats and sheep, until I finally saw something I recognized—the old Roman Forum. Although a few of the structures had been placed upright again, no reparations had been made. Only the massive, triumphal arches on either end—and a few remnants of the old temples—remained vertical. Brush and trees and long, dry grasses grew among the white stone columns and capitals. A barber had set up shop under one of the arches, now half as tall as I knew it truly was, so deep was the dirt and brush. I gawked at it as we rode past. And I got a pang in my chest, remembering Dad's "I Left My Heart in Roma Antica" shirt. He'd bought it, just over there.... *Dad, Mom, Lia, where are you?*

"You enjoy the old relics?" Rodolfo asked, squinting at me as if he were trying to figure out my fascination.

I shifted, startled by his interruption in my reverie. "I do."

"Mayhap we can walk down here on the morrow," he said. "We shall spend our first night together there." He nodded upward, and I forced myself to not look so surprised at his words—*our first night together*—in case the nosy knights were again paying too close attention.

*He's playing the part,* I told myself. *Only playing a part.*

But the light in his dark eyes unnerved me. I could trust him, right? He wasn't just playing me? Herding me into a corner I could not escape? Thinking he could convince me that I had feelings for him once I was, you know, his *wife*?

My eyes drifted to where he pointed, above the old marketplace, in the direction of the Coliseum, not yet visible. A sprawling, white stone palace had been erected, with an elaborate portico bordered by massive urns on the western edge, facing the Forum, just to one side of Trajan's Market. We'd have a view of all of it, and from the other side of the palazzo, I wagered we'd glimpse the Coliseum, too. Long, dark green flags drifted in the wind—the nobleman's colors?

"Lord Vivaro has tapped into what remains of the old Roman aqueduct," Rodolfo said, nodding toward the fountain on one end of the portico. "Some have told me that he even has rebuilt something that echoes of the ancient bathhouses, with a caldarium and frigidarium."

I shivered at the thought of a cold bath on a winter's day. And then I shivered a second time at the thought of being trapped up there in the palazzo. Now that we were in the city, I'd look for an opportunity to escape, but I needed a distraction, something that would give me a ten- or twenty-minute lead. Anything less than that, and I'd likely be recaptured and hauled back. I scoured my mind for memories of places in Roma I could count on to be here now. The remains of the old Roman palaces on the Palatine, and the Pantheon...The Etruscan ruins were south—in the opposite direction of where I wished to go—and yet there was little to the north.

Outside the city were the old catacombs. I might be able to make it there and hide through the night. I thought they might be somewhat in the right direction, if I wanted to get back to Siena. But I shuddered at the thought of spending the night among the old limestone tombs with countless skeletons still on their shallow beds. The thought of it had once made me giggle in excitement, exploring with Lia a few years ago; now it made me Seriously Freak Out.

Okay, so the catacombs were a last resort. Hopefully I could make my way to the palazzo stables, swipe a fresh mount, and put some serious miles between me and the Bad Boys—with luck, maybe even before they realized I was gone.

I still had the dagger strapped to my calf. If all this came down and I had to give it up, I'd be super frustrated. But so far, it would have been much worse to pull it out. It was like having an old Colt revolver in a sea of enemies armed with Uzis. It'd only work in just the right place at just the right time.

But if I got all the way to the crowded palazzo, would it just become five times more difficult to escape? Or might I find an opening as I was being prepared for my evening nuptials with one or two servants? I remembered well the day in Rodolfo's palazzo, when a score of maids were sent to bathe, scrub, and decorate me like a refurbished Christmas tree. If that many were with me this time...

My panic mounted as we entered a side street and began climbing the hill. I knew Lord Vivaro's palazzo wasn't far, given the increased amount of traffic. It was obvious that our host was vastly wealthy, and a great deal of commerce was rolling through. Trains of mules passed us, some with empty packs, others with new loads. I kept gazing at side streets, wondering if *this* was my last opportunity or *that* was...but I'd have to cut my reins, so thoroughly were they tied to Rodolfo's, and then what was I to do? Ride sidesaddle without reins? Impossible.

"Do not look so frightened," Rodolfo said, so quietly I almost missed it. I turned to him. Was I that obvious? "All will be well, m'lady," he said, reaching for my hand.

I placed my sweaty hand in his, and he squeezed it, looking into my eyes. "At this time on the morrow, you will feel much different," he said.

I'd told him I could make it as far as the altar, but not the vows. He was remembering that, right?

After one more bend in the road, the grand Palazzo Vivaro came into full view. Across the street a massive complex, a block wide, had been set up. Probably Vivaro's own little city of industry. Cloth in many different colors covered stalls, but not in the manner of the simple merchants of Siena. These were taller, wider stalls and offered far more exotic goods. Rodolfo followed my gaze. "Fabric from the Orient, tapestries from Denmark, spices from Africa, gold, silver—whatever you might wish for, Lord Vivaro can obtain it for you in Roma."

I nodded, impressed. Lord Vivaro came out of the merchant complex, catching sight of us. He was of medium build, with a massive beard, a playful turban, and merchant's robe. I knew it was him from the way everyone treated him with deference, how he was swarmed and had to cut away, ignoring his posse, to reach us. "He enjoys playing the role of the exotic merchant," Rodolfo said with a smile, leaning toward me. "But he was born here in Roma."

Our host threw his arms out so broadly, with such a wide smile, that I had no choice but to grant him a small smile in return. "And so! You've brought us our Vestal Virgin, the greatest prize of all," he said—to Lord Greco? Lord Barbato? It was impossible to tell as he covered me in a look of pure admiration.

"A She-Wolf of Siena was the best we could do," Lord Barbato said flatly.

"Ah, m'lady," Lord Vivaro said, "you are as fine as the stories have told. You honor me by being here." He took my hand without asking, bent, and kissed my knuckles, staring at me the whole time.

When he straightened, he kept my hand in his. "If only the other half of the matched set had been delivered with her…"

*Lia.* I pulled my hand from his, but he only smiled up at me, unperturbed.

The noblemen of Firenze had dismounted, and Rodolfo politely waited until Lord Vivaro stepped aside, so he could assist me down to the ground. When my feet reached the dirt road, Lord Vivaro smiled and clasped his hands together before him. "A most handsome couple," he said.

"Enough, Vivaro," Lord Barbato said in agitation. "We assume the chapel has been prepared? The guests await us?"

I looked at him in surprise. I shifted in panic but then felt the low, steady pressure of Rodolfo's hand on my lower hip, holding me in place.

"Nay!" cried Vivaro with a playful frown. "Nay, nay, *nay*. This is to be my finest hour, as host to the union between Lord Greco and Lady Betarrini!" He threw a hand into the air. "If you wished them married so quickly, you could've had your own priest perform the ceremony." He flicked a hand toward Father Tomas in the rear of our entourage.

Barbato leaned toward him and said, "You know we need the proper people here to witness it."

"And they shall be here, in but three hours' time," Vivaro said with a cat-like smile. "Imagine it…just as the sun sets across the Forum, these two shall become one." He clasped his hands together to his chest, as girly as a middle-school cheerleader with her first crush.

"Three hours?" groused Lord Greco, as if he were as agitated as Barbato at the wait.

"Come now, m'lord," said Vivaro, taking my arm and ushering us up the palazzo's front steps, while speaking past my shoulders to Rodolfo. "I had no idea at what hour you would arrive. Is this not perfect? Just enough time to bathe, don new clothing—my gift, with which I hope you will be most pleased, my darling," he said to me, before returning his gaze to Rodolfo, "—and meet your bride upon my portico. It shall be most ideal. They shall talk of it for ages."

"And if the Sienese come?" Lord Barbato said tiredly, pinching his nose. "Even now, they are likely on their way."

"That is not my responsibility," Vivaro said, with a curved hand to his chest. "I am to see to the fanfare, you are to see to the rest. Is that not what we agreed?"

Lord Barbato faced him, looking down on him. "We agreed that the fifteen lords mentioned, along with their wives, would be here, waiting, when we arrived."

Vivaro giggled at him. "One does not keep such a room full of power waiting for hours. Even you know such things, Lord Barbato." His smile faded. "These are my allies, my comrades. I will not trifle with their time."

Barbato lifted his chin, studying his host for a long moment. "Very well," he said.

"Very well!" cried our host with glee. "Very well!" he repeated almost to himself, and giggled.

*Nutcase,* I decided. *Not all there.*

We reached the top of the stairs and entered under a portico, thirty feet tall, with columns that had surely been salvaged from the Forum herself. "She's magnificent, is she not?" asked Vivaro, seeing me admiring them. "It's taken me over ten years, but I think you'll appreciate my building efforts." He snapped his fingers, and five women, dressed in Roman togas, came my way.

*Playing the role,* I remembered Rodolfo saying. I had a sinking feeling the whole night was going to be like some freakish costume party. "When in Rome," I muttered, stepping forward as the servants gestured for me to follow them.

I had three hours. The sooner I could be away from the men, the more opportunities I might find to escape. If I could escape right away, could I gain a three-hour lead? And if Lord Barbato was correct, if the Sienese had figured out we'd moved south rather than north, then could I meet them somewhere along the road?

For the first time in the last three days, I felt a twinge of hope.

I turned and glanced over my shoulder at Rodolfo, and he gave me a small smile, studying me with those big model-worthy eyes as if he already knew what I planned. Following my gaze, the servant girls giggled. "He is quite handsome, m'lady," said one.

"Yes," I returned, remembering the maids in Rodolfo's palace, the first time I put on a wedding gown in his presence. I fought to pay attention to the way we were going, mapping out the palazzo in my head, knowing I'd need to remember if I was to escape, but my mind kept going back to that afternoon, when he'd been in the massive, ornately decorated room with me. When he'd circled me, admiring me from all sides. Then, how he confessed on the way here that he'd tried to forget me, but failed. That there was something more…

I shook my head. *Concentrate, Gabi. Let it go. You have to stop this silly little sidetrack. Marcello holds your heart. Marcello. Rodolfo knows it.*

I looked back over my shoulder, trying to remember what I'd just seen—or rather what I'd just not seen—so I'd recognize the hall, and I spotted him. A massive, black-skinned guard with a turban, bare chest, and white balloon pants, as well as a massive, curving sword at his side. *Yet another character in Vivaro's play*, I thought. A slave—a eunuch?—out of Arabia. But the dude was all business, glaring back at me with black eyes as if I were a bug he'd like to flick off his sleeve.

So. I'd have to ditch the girls. And the dude. I could do it. *I think.* I had three hours. Probably two hours, forty-five minutes, now.

We were finally there. With a shy grin, the head girl reached for the door handle and pushed it, holding it open for me.

I couldn't hide my awe. Before me was a sprawling room, a throwback to ancient Roman times. Fountains trickled. Palms waved in massive pots. Piles of fruit sat on massive platters. Twenty more women, all in togas and barefooted, sat about on pillows and elegant lounges, eating, laughing. And it was *warm,* the first room that felt warm, wall to wall, since I'd left my own time. We'd seen a pretty big plume of wood smoke emerging from the palace when we arrived; but here, in this room, not one fire was lit.

The girls caught sight of me and began to rise and move toward me, smiling in greeting. They were all lovely, some of the prettiest girls I'd seen in one place. It was like landing in an NFL cheerleader camp. Or rather, the Roman Centurion Cheerleader Camp. In the center of each of the other three walls of the room, three more black guards were stationed, dressed as the one behind me had been. I glanced over my shoulder and saw that Numero Uno had been joined by a second. I sighed.

I hadn't found an escape route.

I'd entered a circus-like, posh prison.

A Roman version of a harem. Something for Vivaro to showcase.

That was what he was. The ringmaster in a new kind of circus.

And I was his prize tiger.

*She-Wolf*, I corrected myself. And somehow I still had to sniff out a way to escape.

# Chapter Twelve

The girls surrounded me, shielding me from view of the guards—who, from what I glimpsed, gazed at us in boredom—and assisted me with undressing, as quickly and methodically as a mother with a toddler. In seconds they were down to my underclothes. I held my breath, freaked that they'd find my dagger. But thankfully they allowed me to keep my remaining clothing for a bit, ushering me forward while still retaining my human shield. It was then that I realized why the room was so warm with no fires blazing, how they all were surviving without shoes on their feet. Beneath the floor was radiant heat, warm to my toes.

Radiant heat. Tubes of hot water coursing underneath the tiles so the heat would filter upward. My rich friends in Boulder with the big houses and wide-planked floors had it too. And if I remembered right, such luxury in this time period demanded that somewhere in the belly of this palace there had to be a sweltering furnace room, with servants sweating like pigs, feeding massive flames to heat the water that was coming through here.

The hostess opened another set of doors, and I left the giggling mass behind me. Only Main Girl and a second, as well as the original guard, came with me. I gasped again. Before me was an enclosed pool, intricately tiled, with a wide fall of steaming water pouring in one end and exiting through a doorway on the other end. On all sides were more elegant columns holding up the ceiling. Candles along either wall gave the massive room a spa-like feel and filled the air with the scent of beeswax.

"It is quite beautiful, no?" asked Main Girl.

*Uh, yeah.* "Quite," I mused.

"Please," she said, gesturing toward the pool. "Take your ease."

I hesitated. How was I to take a swim and hold on to my knife? They clearly assumed I'd finish my undressing and enter naked. After all, this was a Roman bath. Once, when I was traveling in Turkey with the fam, Lia, Mom, and I had ventured into a bathhouse—and then rushed out when we discovered that women were hanging out in the nude. My eyes traveled to the end of the pool, where I saw piles of cloth—towels?—a table, and jars filled with salts and oils. A massage-type of arrangement, probably my next stop.

"May I…may I have a moment?"

Main Girl's pretty eyebrows knitted together in confusion. "You wish for us to go?"

"Please. There is much on my mind." I smiled at her like I would to Lia, when I wanted her to understand something, wordlessly. "In hours I shall become a married woman. Might I have a few minutes alone?"

"Of course," she said with a knowing smile. She made a *chit-chit* sound, and the others immediately followed her out. The guard closed the two, tall doors, both at once, giving me a look that said, *Don't try anything—I'm right outside.*

I was alone in the bathhouse. I turned and rushed along one edge, noting that, as suspected, there were no windows. But there was another set of doors on the far end. I ran across the tiled floor, warm in here, too, past the massage table, and grabbed hold of the handle. Cautiously I turned it and peeked out.

Another guard stood in front of it, burly arms crossed. Two others stood behind him. The guy in front frowned at me and shook his head back and forth in warning, then he lifted his chin as if to say, *Get on back in there where you belong.*

*Dang it,* I thought, pulling the door shut in frustration. *Those guys are everywhere.* Now I knew why Main Girl wasn't concerned in giving me a little Alone Time. She was confident I couldn't escape. I blew the air out of my cheeks, racking my brain, trying to think of a way I could hold on to the dagger. Without it…I shuddered. My eyes went back to the first set of doors. When Main Girl and Guard Number One came through, they needed to see me in the pool, not standing there looking guilty.

Quickly I ditched the rest of my underclothes and unstrapped the dagger. I wrapped it in the center of my lace-trimmed pantaloon thingies, leaving the valuable trim in view. I'd plead for them to allow me to keep them, a gift. It was really my only option. Because from what I remembered of Roman bathhouses, I was likely to be buck-naked for a little while.

I sighed and slipped into the warm water, frustrated that precious minutes were slipping by. At this rate my three hours would evaporate like the steam all around me. I dived under and swam the length of the blue-and-green-tiled pool in a fanciful mosaic of dolphins and whales and fish. I let the hot waterfall at one end pour over my shoulders and hair, praying that God would show me some way out of this place. And fast.

Main Girl appeared in my line of vision again, to one side, and she gestured for me to swim to the far end. Two more servants appeared, standing on either side of the table. They picked up a lush cloth, holding it from each side, waiting for me.

I did as she bid and swam to the other end, hoping the guards had the decency to look away, eunuchs or not. But the servants stepped down into the pool, ignoring the water seeping up their skirts, and shielded me as I rose, quickly wrapping the rough towel around me while I was still in the water. I was led to a submerged chair to one side.

One girl set to work on my hair, rubbing it with lavender-scented soap, allowing me to rinse and then carefully, elaborately working orange-scented oil into the ends. The other took her turn, scrubbing my shoulders and arms with coarse sea salt, washing them off, and then rubbing more of the orange oil into my skin. Hair Girl had me rinse, worked in a milder orange soap, and had me rinse again.

They left to retrieve two new towels, and after a brief turn on the massage table—appropriately private from any male eyes—I was wrapped and led into the next room.

I almost forgot. *How could you forget, Gabi? Man, talk about your epic failures…*

I turned and glanced to where I'd left my dagger and under-clothes. But they were gone. I froze, my eyes shifting to Main Girl. Did she wonder why I was looking for the disgustingly dirty, road-worn items? They'd definitely seen better days. Had they been set aside? Or had my sad plan merely failed, the dagger discovered and disposed of?

I turned away, hoping she wouldn't see any of those questions in my eyes.

The three guards separated, one entering the massive bathhouse room, the other two going through the next set of doors. This was a much smaller room, with water that was just barely warm. I stepped down into the small pool—about the size of a deep Jacuzzi—and, after rinsing the salts and soaps and oils, out the other side.

The next set of doors opened, and I gasped at the dancing tendrils of steam and water dripping down the solid marble walls. My hostess hurriedly closed the doors behind me, and I moved to a marble perch. The atmosphere was horrible in the room, like a tomb lit only by red-hot stones. Main Girl took a ladle and dipped it in an urn, then spread the water across a line of lava stones, which immediately sizzled, releasing more steam into the air. We were in there for about ten minutes, choking on the hot, thick air before she looked at me. "Exit once the steam ceases." She nodded once and disappeared through the next set of doors, leaving me behind.

It took about three minutes for the steam to almost clear. But that was close enough for me. I had to get out of there before I collapsed. Suddenly I was feeling the distance between me and my lunch. How many hours ago had that been?

The next room was a frigidarium, exactly as I had feared. *Just get it over with, Gabi,* I told myself, eyeing Main Girl, with my prize again tucked beneath her arm. *How does she not feel the dagger?* I'd done my best to hide it, but the fabric was thin, and the dagger was no dainty little thing.

I plunged into the cold, deep pool, which was deeper than I was tall, and hurried to the other side, just three feet away, and up the steps, shivering. Main Girl wrapped me in yet another rough towel, and I was led into the last room, a larger pool room that was about the same temperature as the original bath house. I dipped into the shallow pool, letting my chattering teeth come to a rest as I swam to the end, about ten feet away.

"It is done?" I asked her as the servant girls wrapped me in still more towels and led me into a small dressing room with a fire at one corner and a window at the other. I could see that the sun was getting low in the sky. I licked my lips and eyed my precious bundle under her arm. No guards were present in the room. Would I have to make my escape in nothing but a towel? That wouldn't work out so hot.

"Your baths are done," she said, following my gaze to the pantaloons under her arm.

But then more troops arrived, and my hair was combed out, woven, and wrapped around my head, creating a sort of twisty, Roman-inspired updo, somehow miraculously secured with pins. *Good luck with that,* I mused, knowing how difficult my hair could be and how likely it was that it'd start sprouting, busting loose as soon as it could. Apparently Roman brides didn't wear their hair down, like the Tuscans. But when the girls were done and a delicate gold band was set across my forehead like a crown, it seemed reasonably secure.

My skin was rubbed with more oil, and dots of intense orange oil were dabbed at the base of my throat and my ears, on the insides of my elbows, and behind my knees, making me smell like I was in the middle of a flowering orange grove. My nails were buffed and oiled. My teeth brushed with a stick that tasted like coal and then another that tasted of mint. I rinsed and spit into a bowl and wondered where I could get more if I was to stay in this time. There was hardly a lineup of options at the local Walgreen's, and my mouth hadn't felt this good in a long time....

When they wrapped me in a long toga, I almost laughed. This really was Lord Vivaro's show in every measure, regardless of what Barbato might've thought. But the toga wasn't of simple white cloth; it was of a soft, thick silk with a very fine weave. *Bridal toga,* I mused with a smile, fingering the material. Out of all the places I thought I might land in Italia and all the scenarios I might encounter, this nod to ancient Rome definitely had not been on the list.

A servant bent and slipped a ring on one toe, then sandals on my feet, wrapping the straps up and over my ankles. She tied them at my calf and then scurried away. The others melted away too, leaving only me, Main Girl, and the first guard.

Main Girl came behind me and secured behind my neck an elegant, ancient necklace with amber stones set in copper that had turned an oxidized green. She then handed me a set of matching amber earrings, with three orbs in progressively larger sizes.

She smiled as I paused to admire them. "They are a gift from Lord Greco," she said. "Procured by Lord Vivaro, of course. They once belonged to a very fine Roman lady. And amber is good luck for a marriage. Often you can find the stones with a ladybug or beetle stuck inside, for all eternity."

I glanced at her. Bug jewelry was not my idea of cool, but *whatever...*

"It symbolizes the eternal nature of love," she explained with a small, quizzical nod. "When two lives are fused into one."

I thought of Rodolfo, of exchanging such vows with him. And then I thought of Marcello. I shook my head. No, it was Marcello, definitely Marcello; he'd had my heart from the start. Any other thought of any other man just felt wrong, no matter how intriguing and handsome Rodolfo might be.

Marcello was my man. If I was to get hitched, the only one that felt right.

"You have an hour," Main Girl said. "Please, eat. Rest. For tonight there shall be little of that." She had a knowing look in her eye. She turned to go but paused at the table that held my bundle and looked back at me, as if she knew exactly what was inside. Maybe she'd even peeked. But then she turned and left the room, with Guard Boy following her.

I didn't bother to look. I knew he was right outside.

Hurriedly I stuffed three black olives in my mouth and went to my bundle. As soon as I lifted it, I knew. She'd outsmarted me. Kept me calm by bringing it along. But the dagger was long gone.

Feeling kind of nauseated, I forced myself to gnaw on some hard cheese, thinking, thinking, thinking of how I might escape in the next hour.

My eyes moved to the window on the far side of the room. I hurried over to it and opened the shutters wider, shivering as the cold air moved into the warm room. I leaned out and saw that the covered portico was beneath me, facing the Forum, and judging by what I could see at the corner, I was three stories above the ground. But what interested me most was the six-inch ledge at the base of my window. I leaned farther out.

If I could get out *there* and scoot along to an empty room, could I get away?

I hurried over to the doors and casually opened one. "I will attempt to sleep for a time," I said regally. "See that I am not disturbed."

The big, black man blinked and then nodded once, as if I was by far the most aggravating chick he'd ever had to deal with. I closed the doors and leaned my forehead against them for a moment. *Please, Lord. Please make a way for me.*

I took a small cloth and wrapped a round of unleavened bread, cheese, and olives up in it and tied it to the belt of my toga. I glanced around, looking for anything more I might keep warm in, but there was nothing. *Maybe I'll find something in another room,* I decided.

I had to hurry.

I went to the window again and looked out, deciding I'd head to the nearest corner to my right, with just three windows between me and my goal. I didn't know what was around that corner, how exposed I might be, but if I could make it all the way around the face of that wall of the palazzo, it'd be good. The more distance I could put between me and this room before it was discovered I was gone, the better.

# Chapter Thirteen

The knock at my door made me jump in surprise. Hurriedly, I closed the shutters and went to the door and cautiously opened it a crack. Rodolfo. With the guard behind him.

His lips parted, and his eyes widened in wonder. He shook his head a little. "M'lady…you are exquisite."

I fought the urge to stare back at him. Because he appeared more the Roman god than ever, all six feet of him, his olive skin glistening with oils beneath his white toga, tied at the waist. A ring of greenery around his hair. And the smell of him—perfumes of sandalwood and spice…

I let out a scoffing sound and turned, forcing myself to walk away, flipping my hand in the air. "It appears as if Vivaro has dressed us both for this performance—you as the triumphant hero and me, your conquest." I paused at the fruit bowl and lifted a tiny apple to take a bite, hearing the door shut behind him and feeling his approach more than hearing it. He was silent. Stealthy. How did he do that?

He put his broad hands on my shoulders and then dragged them downward, terribly, beautifully, painfully slowly, across several inches until they rested on my upper arms, skin against skin.

I could feel the warmth of his chest behind me, and I closed my eyes, trying to summon the strength to move away, to break this trance I seemed to be in. But he was pulling me closer, silently asking my permission. Letting his left hand run down the length of my arm, entwining his fingers with mine, wrapping both our arms in front of my waist. I could feel his breath past my ear. Felt him hold it a moment, then pick up speed, full of desire. His lips, soft and warm, pressed into my temple, then moved down toward my jaw. Each kiss sent delicious shivers down my spine, down my arms. "Gabriella," he moaned, each word a warm *huff* upon my skin. He leaned his face against mine, heavy, as if weak. "Forgive me, I cannot help myself. I want you. Want you for my own. Be my wife. Be mine."

I closed my eyes in pain at his words and then turned, half wanting to break away, half wanting to reach up and invite him in for a kiss, an unbridled kiss. To give in to the madness, the desire, forget what was behind me. To stop fighting. I was so tired. So very tired of fighting, fighting, fighting. Would it not be easier in some way? To give in to this marriage? Maybe they were right. Maybe it'd force Siena to establish peace again with Firenze. Bring peace to the land…

And then what? Where did that leave my family? And Marcello? *Marcello.*

I leaned in to him, resting my face against his chest, feeling the *ba-dump* of his heartbeat, thinking. And he wrapped his arms around me and remained still, waiting, giving me time to think, stroking my back, my arms, holding his breath as if he wanted to say more and then thought better of it.

To be held by him felt good. Undeniably good. I'd have to be an ice queen to deny it. But it wasn't the feeling of utter peace, total *centeredness* that I felt when Marcello held me. Slowly I drew away and looked up into his eyes. And within a second he knew. I saw flashes of pain, regret, guilt, sorrow in quick succession beneath his thick lashes. He lifted his finger to his lips, and then he touched mine and shook his head. *Don't say anything.*

He lifted my chin and softly kissed me, lightly. There was no demand in it, only invitation. *Just one more try,* I thought. To see if I'd lean in. Kiss him back. But I gently pulled away. As our lips parted, I looked into his eyes, knowing the sorrow in my own. "If Marcello had not claimed my heart first, it might have worked," I said regretfully.

"Might we not leave it to God?" He gestured around the room, the muscles in his cheeks tightening and a hint of bitterness entering his tone. "After all, we are here. And there is little chance for me to help you escape."

"Nay," I said quietly, understanding more and more. "Those opportunities are well past us." Had he really wanted to help me—really and truly—he would've done it by now. Before we reached Rome. But deep down, if he was honest with himself, he really hadn't wanted it. I knew that now.

"He'll come for you," Rodolfo said nonchalantly, lifting an orange and pulling a dagger from the rope at his waist to cut off a portion of peel, then slice out some flesh and place it in his mouth. "Before our vows are exchanged," he said with derision, pointing at me with the knife, "Marcello will arrive."

I shook my head. "He hasn't had enough time."

Rodolfo chewed and swallowed, then shrugged. "I say it again. Let us leave it to God. If he arrives in time, you're meant for him. If not..." A smile pushed back some of his anger. "You have gambled in the past. Why not now?"

"Because the stakes are too high. Are they not?"

He considered me for a long moment, and his smile faded. "Indeed," he said with a grave nod. His eyes met mine again. "Lord Vivaro shall be here within the hour to fetch you. Forgive me, m'lady. I have failed you in more ways than one."

"You did what you felt you must."

He hesitated, as if wrestling with the desire to cross the space between us and kiss me until I admitted I was just a tiny bit in love with him too.

But he didn't. He didn't.

Instead he turned and walked from the room without a backward glance, closing the door behind him like a sleeping baby was behind it.

I stared hard at the door, wondering just what had come down. A full minute later I finally moved numbly to the fruit bowl to grab a piece for the road. And discovered Rodolfo's knife. I picked it up and glanced toward the door.

It hadn't been left by accident. He was helping me. Giving me the tiniest bit of an opening, if I really wanted it. Was he thinking I'd try to fight my way out through the giant guards outside and all of Vivaro's and Barbato's men? Did he really think I'd try? Or did he simply want to erase the guilt over his deception toward me, toward Marcello, in this and yet... "Still end up with the girl," I muttered, finishing my thought aloud. "Sorry, handsome. But I think I've somehow *always* been promised to another."

I moved out to the ledge and almost lost my balance right away. I panted like I was in labor, trying to catch my breath and calm down my fluttering heart.

Yeah, it looked easier than it was. The ledge was six inches deep—a tad wider at the window wells. I discovered that having the length of a dollar bill was just not enough of a foundation, once a girl was out on it, ten feet above a portico. It was like being on top of a ladder on top of a crate. That tall.

And the portico roof beneath me was slightly pitched. If I fell, would I be able to stop rolling before I fell off the edge on the far side?

I tried to distract myself, to think of how wide a balance beam was and take comfort in the fact that I had a building behind me, even if my toes were sticking out over nothingness. But then I had totally flunked out of gymnastics. Lia was the graceful one. Me? Notsomuch. And the sandals? Not exactly rock-climbing soles.

Stubbornly I moved on. At least on this part of the building, I was shielded from the view of people below. I could hear them gathering. Laughing. Playfully shouting. Getting ready for a wedding. My wedding.

Thoughts of that got me to the first window. I dared to peek in and glimpsed a man inside, carefully combing his hair with an ivory comb while staring at himself in a looking glass. I straightened and waited for a moment, trying to ignore the goose bumps forming on my bare arms in the breeze, and counted to sixty before I looked again.

He was gone.

With a sigh of relief I moved past the window, knowing if I exited that room, I'd be right beside Mr. Big Black and Mean. I had to get farther away. Much farther away. And it was cold in the evening breeze, maybe fifty degrees, and there I was, out in a silk toga. I had to move to stay warm.

The volume was increasing below, I decided, as I edged onward. It sounded to me that Lord Vivaro had invited far more than what Barbato had wanted there. He'd turned it into a serious party. But then that fit the image of the guy. Were they all told to wear togas?

I'd reached the next window. After a second to gather my courage, I peeked in. The shutters were mostly closed, but I could see a young couple making out—totally making out—and I smiled. I'd be past their window in a flash. And they were into each other wayyyy more than they were into the view. I moved on.

*And now, ladies and gentlemen, I give you Window Three.* I peeked in. It was empty. I quickly looked ahead at what I'd face next; the edge of Lord Vivaro's palazzo was but four feet from his neighbor's. Without the portico covering beneath me, I'd be thirty feet above the ground once I turned the corner. I glanced back at the room. Edging the shutters aside, I decided to jump in for a moment, catch my breath, and warm up a bit. I shakily climbed down into the room and stood against the far wall, panting, closing my eyes.

*Lord, is there a better way? Show me. I need Your help. Show me. Protect me. Free me. Amen.*

The prayer came easily. I decided that people in total Freak Out Mode were like that: Good pray-ers.

I continued to draw deep breaths like a deep-sea diver preparing for a twenty-foot plunge without a tank and rubbed my arms, willing them to warm up. It was risky, staying here. I had to get farther away while I had the chance.

But it was a total act of will to get back out on that ledge. I moved out, caught my balance, and looked out to the Forum, glad it was mostly deserted at this hour. The sun was already getting lower in the sky. *Get going, Gabi. Go!*

I didn't stop until I'd turned the corner and foolishly looked down to the alley, three stories below. Servants moved in and out of a door, dumping dirty water and refuse on a pile. Thirty feet would be a long way to fall. *I'm going to break both my legs…or become a quadriplegic…*

*Move, Gabi,* I told myself. I didn't have time to pause, and the last thing I needed was to be caught here, in the middle of a full melt-down. *Move, move, move,* I chanted silently, edging right, fighting the urge to move left and back around the corner, over the portico, where the fall would be much shorter. The only thing that eased my mind was that I could literally almost reach the neighboring build-ing. Even though I couldn't touch it, the sensation of its presence steadied me. It was far more comforting than staring out to the great expanse of the Forum.

After a while of shuffling along, I dared to look up and to my right, thinking I should've hit another window well by then.

I pulled up short at what I saw.

The bad news was that on this side of the building, there were no other windows. And it would be impossible for me to escape the front side of the palazzo. The guests at the front would be admiring the palazzo as they arrived, wondering if anyone they knew might be visible in the widows…Someone would be sure to see me.

I studied the columns at the corners, wondering if I could get a good enough grip to slide down to the next level, but quickly dismissed it. They were far too large to get a good grip on. But then I looked across at the neighboring palazzo. It was smaller than Lord Vivaro's by half but almost as tall. And up ahead, there were three windows on this side of the building facing me.

I edged closer and looked down and into the windows, their shutters shut tight, with only a hint of light inside. *Trying to keep the cold out,* I thought, feeling the goose bumps roll down my chilled arms. I moved on, trying to get a glimpse of anyone, anything in the other two windows.

I got nothing.

I looked left, back from where I came. Then right, toward the front face of the palazzo. And down, where a kitchen boy dumped some fat and grease on a pile and then moved toward the Forum edge of the property to peek around the corner, up at all the guests. Even from over here on this side of the building, the party was getting louder, with more high-pitched laughter and shouting. How long would it be before they discovered I was missing?

I looked back to the neighboring building. Chances were, the shutters were as flimsy as Lord Vivaro's, and I could crash through them without a whole lot of effort. They were slightly lower than where I was, which was helpful. But what would I find inside? Would they turn me over right away to Lord Vivaro? He had to have a pretty far reach. My only chance was to crash through, regain my balance, and run on through the palazzo before anyone realized who I was and tried to nab me.

I took a deep breath, tried to balance on one foot as I lifted my right foot up to quickly grab my dagger. I'm talking Seriously Risky Gymnastic Business. I thought if I had it in hand, I might feel stronger, more ready. But it proved impossible, given my position, and I gave up.

I refocused on the window across from me.

*Four feet? I can do that.*

*But from a standing position? You're going to miss. Fall to your death.*

I stared at the window across from me. Nobody was in the alley now, for the first time in a while....

Before I could think about it another second, I leaped, shoulder-first.

# Chapter Fourteen

I remember the sensation of total freefall, with a forward edge, for too long a time. The catch of one leg on a stone ledge. The sound of splintering wood. Rolling, rolling. Something cutting my arm. The sound of breaking pottery. And then I was still.

Gradually I became aware of cold stone tiles beneath me.

The sound of an old man coughing. Wheezing.

Mentally I ran through my body from fingers to toes, squeezing and stretching, checking for broken bones, checking to see if I could move at all. It wasn't every day I tried my hand at death-defying leaps. But I'd made it. All seemed in order.

When I heard the cough again, fully realized I wasn't alone, I sat up quickly, reaching for Rodolfo's dagger as I rose quickly to my feet.

*Whoa, dizzy,* I thought, fighting to look like I was anything but. My vision gradually settled and centered on an old man, covered in blankets, sitting by a small, crackling fire.

He was smiling, smiling so much that his eyes lit up, but he was gasping for breath. "We…we…have…a door," he joked.

I'd probably surprised him into his wheezing attack, and instantly I felt a flood of guilt.

I lowered my dagger and lifted my free hand. "Forgive me, m'lord. If I'd had a choice…"

He continued to smile and cocked a gray brow. "A-apparently."

"You are the master of this house?" I asked gently, to which he nodded. "Are there others here?"

"J-just s-servants," he managed. He covered his mouth with a fist, fighting to not dissolve in another fit of coughing.

One of those servants might be on their way now, if they'd heard me crash my way in. But then these big palazzos, with their stone floors, weren't like homes in modern days. My assault might've just sounded like a *thump* to them…which might make them think the old man had fallen. My eyes went to the now-broken shutters—I couldn't shut them, they'd have to be replaced—to the table I'd over-turned and broken pottery across the floor.

We both heard the *slap-slap-slap* of sandals on the marble floor in the hall.

"Q-quick, h-hide," the old man said.

I scanned the room and saw that the only decent hiding place or escape was a narrow door beside the hallway door. I hurried over, well aware that I rushed to a place that would be but five feet from where the newcomer would enter. I'd just slipped behind the second door—which appeared to be a narrow staircase leading to the roof—when I heard the first door open. "M'lord, what has happened here?" cried a young woman.

"I—I fell," the old man said.

"Through the *window?*" asked the girl, obviously looking over at the shutters.

"I g-grabbed at them, t-trying to break my fall. But failed."

It was a flimsy excuse, but if he was lord of the house, no servant would argue with him. "Are you hurt, m'lord? Should I fetch the physician?"

"Nay, nay," he gasped. "I s-simply need a moment to myself. Let me be. Return in half an hour."

"As you wish, m'lord," she said. "I'll send a boy to clean up the mess and bring you fresh water."

"Good, good."

I could almost see her bow, her retreat. And then she was gone again. But I waited until the boy arrived, did as he was told to do, and disappeared again.

"You can come out now."

Tentatively I opened the door.

He smiled at me, already much improved. "Do you wish to tell me who you are?"

"I am a woman being forced to marry a man I do not love."

He cocked a brow and pursed his lips, considering. "There have been many before you who have endured the same. Many who will follow."

"But I do not wish to be one of them," I said. I went to the door and cracked it open to peer down the hall.

"You are Lady Betarrini."

I looked back at him. "I am."

A slow smile spread across his face again. "Lord Vivaro will be most distraught over your disappearance."

"Indeed he will," I agreed.

"Fortunately for you, I find my neighbor most tiresome. And there have been few occasions in which I have even favored Firenze over Siena."

It was my turn to smile. "Then I believe we might become good friends."

He leaned forward, and I stepped across the room to take his hand. "We already are, m'lady. I am Lord Zinicola."

"It is an honor, m'lord," I said with a small laugh. "Someday, I shall send you funds to reimburse you for damages."

"There is little need," he said, waving me off. "I am an old man who could die any day, with no children and more money than I need. Your arrival is the most interesting thing to happen to me in years."

I smiled. "While I would love to stay and get to know you further, I must make haste. Would you be so kind as to tell me how I might escape to safety?"

"I'll do much better than that," he said. "I shall see to it myself."

*Seeing to it himself* meant instructing a trusted manservant, Carsius, who was about fifty years old, to do it for him. Lord Zinicola tottered over to me, placed his finely embroidered wool cape over my arm, and reached for his sword and scabbard, which he handed over to me too.

"Nay, m'lord. I couldn't."

He waved me off and pushed the sword into my hands. "From what I hear, you wield it with far more skill than I ever hoped to." He gave in to a coughing fit. Then, "Put it to good use, girl. Find your freedom."

I bent and gave him a quick kiss on the cheek, feeling more hope with a sword in my hands than I had in days, and then I was rushed down a back staircase that ended in the stables. Carsius clearly wasn't as keen on this misadventure as Lord Zinicola was, but he did his duty with regal, methodical movements.

"Here, m'lady," he said, gesturing to a shallow cart already hitched to a horse. "Lie down in the middle. I shall surround you with sacks of grain and drive you to safety. We must make haste. Already they search for you."

"All right," I said, climbing into the cart's bed and lying down, already glad for the protective, warm layer of the cape. It would protect me from the cold and help disguise my toga once I was on my own.

Carsius was halfway through the process of packing me in when we heard a shout near the stable doors. We shared a long look, and he picked up the pace. He'd just placed the last sack atop me, leaving me in a sort of grain-coffin, when someone arrived. "Oh, Carsius, 'tis you," said a man. "I fear my lord has a favorite guest missing."

"Missing, you say? Most unfortunate." I was surprised at how calm he sounded. "I'd assist you in your search, but I am about my own lord's business, hauling this grain to the poorhouse before sundown."

"Very well. If you see a woman in a long toga as you travel, will you kindly inform us?"

"Surely every woman in a toga is already at your lord's palazzo."

"Not this one." The man apparently left, and I heard the creak of leather as Carsius took his seat in the saddle. I dared to take a dusty breath. It was good I wasn't an allergic sort of girl, because this kind of setup would've sent me into a major fit. I felt the cart lurch and heard the wheels crunch as we turned and headed out the stable gates. Carsius paused outside, presumably to shut them again, and I listened so hard I could hear my heart pound in my ears.

That was when they neared. Rodolfo. Lord Barbato. And Lord Vivaro.

"You've allowed her to escape, you fool," Barbato said in a hiss.

"I did nothing of the sort. She was under guard at every moment," Vivaro protested.

"There must have been *one* moment in which she was not," Rodolfo said.

"There is simply no way she could have escaped the palazzo," Vivaro said, "unless she sprouted wings and flew away. Besides, she is a girl alone, without funds—how far can she get?"

"You do not know the legends of the She-Wolves of Siena very well, do you?" Rodolfo ground out, sounding every bit the frustrated groom with a runaway bride. "We trusted you, m'lord. Trusted you to ensure that this would be a safe place to bring her, to see the deed done."

The wagon lurched forward again, and I strained to hear the rest.

"I shall make it right and find her. I am as distraught as you are, m'lord. This was to be the feast of the year at the palazzo…"

Their voices faded into the crunch of gravel and stone beneath the wooden wheels of the cart. They had not even bothered to stop us. Were we one of many still on this street? How long until they stopped everyone to search for contraband, like toga-attired brides?

I shifted, gingerly rolling my right shoulder, which had taken the brunt of my fall into Lord Zinicola's quarters. I was going to have a nasty bruise across it, but it didn't feel broken or dislocated. Still, it was my right, and that was my sword arm…and my crazy leap had strained my hamstring again, this time in the opposite leg. I could feel it tensing up. *Not good for a girl on the move,* I thought. A girl alone.

A girl who, if she were discovered, would need to fight her way out.

We traveled for a time, and I fought not to groan in pain every time the cart bumped, an effort that after a while sent tears streaming down the sides of my face. Maybe my shoulder was hurt worse than I thought and the adrenaline of my escape had masked it a bit. I ran through various potential diagnoses I'd find on WebMD.com. *Dislocation?* I might be able to snap it back into place by slamming it against a wall or tree. Hadn't I seen that in the movies before? *Broken collarbone?* A friend had one of those once. She'd just had to wear her arm in sling for six weeks. But it'd be tough to do that and handle a sword. The worst-case scenario would be if I'd actually broken the shoulder at the joint. I pictured myself in a year or two, with an arm frozen in place. There just was no way to heal an injury like that in this day and age.

*C'mon, Gabi, it's not that bad. You're giving in to hypochondria. Feeling sorry for yourself! You're free! Concentrate on that!*

*For the moment,* returned my Negative Voice.

*Until I'm back with Marcello,* I thought, pushing back Miss Negatori.

With a bump we finally left the wretched stones and I heard the crunch of gravel and dirt. While there was an occasional wrenching on this road too, at least it wasn't as often as it had been on the old Roman roads.

*We're getting farther away, exiting the city.* I smiled, wondering when I might be able to sit up and where Carsius was thinking of cutting me loose. It was driving me crazy, not knowing where we were, not being able to see. I heard horses coming then. Six? Eight?

"*Aho! Tirare su le redini!*" shouted a man behind us. *You there! Pull up!*

I braced as Carsius gradually brought his horse to a stop.

The horses rode up alongside us. Two on either side, I thought. If Carsius was up for taking on one, could I possibly bring down three? I had some serious doubts.

"Lord Vivaro has offered a king's bounty for the capture and return of a woman."

"Oh?" said Carsius drily. "I have not known Lord Vivaro to be all that interested in women."

The men laughed at that. "Even so, this was a treasured guest, due to marry another this very night. He would pay dearly for her return. Have you seen her? She is reportedly quite beautiful, with dark hair wound about her head. And dressed in a toga?"

"A toga," repeated Carsius, all deadpan in his voice. "She should not be difficult to find."

The man paused. "She is fairly adept in the arts of escape and war. 'Tis Lady Gabriella Betarrini."

"The She-Wolf of Siena?"

"One and the same. Have you seen her?"

"Nay. But I shall be looking for her now. Mayhap with the ransom, I could purchase a small cottage and take my old age in ease. What is the She-Wolf doing here, in Roma?"

The newcomer paused. "Would you mind if we search your cargo?"

Carsius let out a scoffing laugh. "You think a woman such as Lady Betarrini would be huddled beneath my bags of grain? Nay, she is on a fine, white steed, making her way toward Siena as we speak. It shall be the latest story they tell of her. But if you wish to tarry, by all means, dig through my cargo."

I almost gasped at his audacious words, although they were perfectly delivered. I tensed, clenching the hilt of my sword, thinking through each move that would bring me fastest to my feet, given the encumbrances of a skirt and the heavy bags of grain—

"Where are you headed, old man?" said the man, gruffly.

"North. Delivering these to the poorhouse."

"If you spot the lady, and come to us with word, we shall capture her and cut you in for the reward. Agreed? Come to us rather than any of the others. Understood?"

"Indeed, sir."

They set off, and I sighed in relief. But his words, *rather than any others,* echoed in my mind. There would be a number of men out looking for me tonight, intent on capturing the elusive bride of Lord Greco.

Fan-freakin'-tastic. Just what I needed—a bunch of mercenaries, plus Rodolfo and crew, out on the hunt for me.

# Chapter Fifteen

We pulled up about twenty minutes later. I helped Carsius shove the last bag from me and sat up. He glanced around warily, in all directions. "This is as far as I can take you, m'lady, and still get back before the dark becomes too deep." He offered a hand to help me rise and then climb down.

We were on a hill, in a small grove of Roman pines, and the rubble beneath my feet told me this was once a villa, although precious little remained. The sunset, a deep, rich mix of peach and gold, filtered through the trees to us.

"I am most indebted to you, Carsius," I said. "You honored me by hiding me and foregoing the bounty hunter's reward. I shall see you rewarded when I reach Siena."

He gave me a small smile and nodded once. "'Tis my honor to serve my master, m'lady. No further compensation is needed." He bent to unhitch the brown gelding from the wagon and brought the animal around toward me. "Besides, Lord Vivaro perturbs me as much as he does my master. It pleases us both to toy with him this night."

I grinned with him, but his smile faded fast as his eyebrows lowered and his tone intensified. "You must keep off the main road to Siena," he said. "I saw four more groups of mercenaries about. Cover as much ground as you can at night. Sleep during the day. In two or three days you'll reach Siena. You can find your way?"

"I can find it," I said. I felt like a homing pigeon about to be set free. There was no way I *couldn't* find it. I strapped on the sword and scabbard.

Carsius held out the reins of the gelding to me, and I frowned. "Oh, friend," I said, "you must take him back."

"Nay, on the highway I can say I was robbed of my mount, and once inside the city walls, it will be easier for me to steal back to the palazzo on foot. 'Tis m'lord's wishes for you to be on this fine mount and given this," he said, reaching into the back of the wagon. He handed me a sack filled with supplies and a skin full of liquid.

"You have been most gracious," I said, blinking back grateful tears.

He shrugged and gave me one last nod. "Go with God, m'lady. 'Tis an honor to have met the woman behind the legend."

"Go with God," I returned. "And do not believe all you hear."

He lifted a brow, glancing at the sword at my side, and I laughed, caught acting the part of She-Wolf even as I denied it. And then he headed off, down the small road. Rome was several miles distant, and I knew he did not wish to be caught outside the walls come nightfall. *Protect him, God. Keep my protector safe.*

I pulled the gelding deeper into the trees and watched as the sun continued to sink, even as I scoured the horizon in all directions for the men of which Carsius had spoken. I could see a small merchant train ahead of Carsius on the main road to Roma, and to the west a group of four men on horses who could very well be one of the mercenary groups. Italia seemed to be filled with men out to make an extra buck or two. With wealthy lords who employed their own forces of knights, men came from as far as Germany to fight for them. *Germania,* I'd heard them call it.

As the sun disappeared, so did any trace of heat, and I pulled Lord Zinicola's cape closer. It was a dark brown with black embroidery so thick, it made the fabric stiff. I pulled the hood up and over my hair, still miraculously atop my head. And then I looked northward, to where I knew Marcello must be. Had he laid claim to the castello? Or was he on his way south, toward me, even now?

Never had I wanted to see him more. Why was that? Because I feared he thought I had married Rodolfo? Because I'd let Rodolfo kiss me? Or because the whole thing had just confirmed, more than ever, that I was crazy about Marcello?

I shivered, longing for the warmth of his arms around me. Was it only a week ago that we had stood on the portico of San Galgano and watched the sunset? I closed my eyes and remembered him kissing my hair, the heat of his body as he held me, the feeling of never wanting to be apart. He'd been so freaked when he thought I might be in danger the night of the dance in Siena. How was he coping right now?

When the birds ceased their song and the insects of the night began their tune, I cautiously moved out and down the other side of the hill, along a small path I'd picked out as the sun set. From there, by the light of a quarter moon, I made it to a smaller road heading north, a good few miles west of the old Roman road that connected Roma to Siena. It was sound advice for me to steer clear of it, but my only hesitation was that if Marcello and company were heading south to free me, I'd likely miss them.

I wished I knew this country as well as I knew Toscana. Unfortunately most of my experience had been on the A1, the major highway of my own day. That didn't exactly offer me any great clues as to where I was, other than major landmarks. But I knew enough to hope I might make Orvieto by sunrise, or close to it. If I could do that, I'd be halfway there.

Once I was fairly confident that the road was pretty well maintained, I urged my gelding into a trot, moving along at a quick pace. My eyes were drawn by every movement in the nearby forest, creatures of the night. Now and again, I passed a country villa or cottage, or caught the scent of wood smoke, letting me know that I wasn't entirely alone. After a while I allowed my horse to ease his pace, and opened my sack of food from Lord Zinicola. I couldn't see the contents, so I merely reached in and took whatever I touched first. *Dipping for dinner,* I thought to myself.

Dried apricots were first. Beneath them was a layer of almonds. I ate only six of those, reserving the rest for the next day, considering them quick protein. Beneath that was an oatcake. I bit into it, and smiled in pleasure. It was more cookie than bread, with dried berries and nuts embedded in the rich, moist dough. I forced myself to only eat half, saving the rest, and then tied the bag back up and reached for my skin of water, pulling my horse to a stop.

I uncorked the top and tipped the dried skin back. The water, fresh and clean and obviously drawn from the old Roman spring, tasted sweet in my mouth. Apparently Lord Zinicola had better access to drinking skins than Marcello. I'd have to send for a few of these, too, along with the tooth-cleaning supplies, *once I'm outta here.* I took another long gulp, recorked the top, and tied it back onto my saddle.

That was when I noticed the gelding's ears. They were pricked forward, alert.

I was not alone.

I grabbed the reins and wheeled the horse in a small circle, searching the hills for any sign of company. My eyes hurt, I was looking so hard. Nothing.

But just as I was about to head out, I saw the dim outline of a man astride a horse, ahead of me on the road. I froze.

"Be at peace, m'lady," he called. "'Tis I, Tomas."

Tomas? Father Tomas? As in Rodolfo's priest?

Was this a trick?

"Do not flee. I mean you no harm."

"Come ahead," I said, wagering he could see me no better than I could see him. I reached for my dagger and clenched it between my teeth so I could quietly pull out the sword. While I doubted Tomas would do me harm, he had traveled in dangerous company. I scanned the horizon to my right and then my left, wondering if Rodolfo's men would surround me.

If they did, they'd have to kill me.

Because I was becoming no man's bride this night.

Tomas neared, riding at an easy pace, and when he got closer, I saw that he rode bareback. "You are a difficult woman to find," he said.

I slipped the dagger back into my waistband. "That is by design."

"Lord Greco has released me. He said he'd had a vision and thought there might be a pilgrim on the road in need of care."

I grinned. "He did, did he?"

"Far be it from me to not abide by a vision," Tomas said, obviously in on the stretch-of-truth too. "I set off immediately. But when I had gone a fair piece, I knew I must have missed you, that you must be taking a route more difficult than the Roman road. The arduous route. The pilgrim's route."

I smiled again. "Indeed. I seem to frequently take the most difficult path possible, whether I want to or not. Does that make me a pilgrim?"

We moved off, riding side by side. "Some would say it is so," Tomas said. "That suffering brings one closer to God. That He allows us to suffer until we've learned what we must."

I thought about that a moment. "Do you believe it?"

"I believe it is always possible to draw closer to our Lord, whether it be during times of suffering or during times of celebration. It is all life, and all of life comes from God." He paused. "You can sheathe your sword, m'lady. I mean you no harm."

I wished I could see him clearly. "You are not the bait, the means to lull me into a sense of peace so I do not keep watch for others?"

"Oh, you should fear others, but not Rodolfo's men. They remain in the city, scouring every corner for a potential hiding place."

"And the mercenaries about?"

"Sent by Lords Barbato and Vivaro. They were most distraught with your departure. We must outrun them."

I smiled, feeling pretty proud of myself for my escape, even if I had wrenched my shoulder. I sheathed my sword. "So, Tomas—tell me of what transpired when it became known I was gone."

"Our host fainted, in time, and was carried to his quarters with much fanfare."

I laughed. It was one way out of the mess—pretend to faint, and hope the men who were angry with you would just disappear.

"Later he demanded that the party go on, even if there was no wedding—"

"Appeasing his guests."

"Indeed. No one likely left that party wanting—they were privy to the greatest scandal of the year, Lady Betarrini's escape, as well as the feast of all feasts at Lord Vivaro's."

We rode in silence for a time.

Then I dared, "Do you think I grieved Rodolfo's heart, Tomas?"

He considered my words. "He was torn, but I am confident you are both on the right path."

I paused. "Thank you."

"You understand that the only thing that will keep you safe is to marry Lord Forelli, as soon as possible," he said.

"Why?"

"It is my assumption," he said, "that Lord Forelli, being a shrewd man, has sent his men to regain his rightful property. But according to the agreement made at Sansicino, you must become Lord Rodolfo's bride in exchange for it."

"Marcello did not agree to those terms. And Fortino's death…" My voice broke, and I swallowed hard. "His death certainly made it all void, regardless of whether or not Marcello has regained his rightful property."

"It matters not. Lord Barbato and Lord Ascoli will assure any who ask that *that* was the agreement. When it comes to pass that only one part of the bargain was honored, they'll come for you *and* the castello."

I shrugged, even if he couldn't see me. "They're going to come for us anyway. It's inevitable."

"True enough. And you may be captured. But you could be captured as the bride of Marcello, or the potential bride of Rodolfo. Which would you prefer?"

I thought about it. "I really don't prefer either option, Father. I wish to enter matrimony when I wish, how I wish."

"Which is all well and good. But I don't think you understand me. M'lady, if you are captured again, there shall be no party. You will be hauled before a priest in Roma or Firenze, an arrow at your throat, and forced to exchange vows with Lord Rodolfo. Then four lords of the grandi will ensure that those vows are properly consummated."

My eyes widened.

"It is not a matter of morals as much as it is of politics. And you see, m'lady, you have pressed the lords of Firenze to great lengths. If captured, you will be held by the surest means possible—consummated vows. Or they will see you dead."

I swallowed hard. "And…if I was Marcello's wife?"

"It would give you reasonable protection. At best they would hand you over immediately in exchange for prisoners that they want. At worst…" He shook his head.

"That was not what transpired for Fortino."

"Nay, but he did not comply with any of their demands. From beginning to end, he refused every request. And as a lady of Siena, the wife of one of the Nine—to hold you then would be to invite far more than Siena's faithful to attack Firenze's walls."

I let that sink in. But I was thinking of his words, *He did not comply with any of their demands.* Tomas thought I might be different from Fortino.

I might be. I might cave as soon as one of them *thought* about torturing me. But maybe not. Maybe I'd hold strong, stay true to the cause. And yet I couldn't make it through what he'd endured, if I was honest with myself. The floggings? The taking of an eye? And I didn't think I had it in me to be killed rather than marry Rodolfo. I'd give in to that, choose life over death, even if I had to be with a man I didn't love as I did Marcello.

For a moment I thought again of Rodolfo, of his kiss. I shook my head and blinked, trying to wake from my silly daydream. *You are meant for one man, Gabi. One.*

But why did I keep thinking about Rodolfo, keep wondering what it would have been like to share just one more kiss?

No. *No.* If I was going to stay in ancient Toscana, it had to be Marcello that I married. And it had to be soon. Just in case...

But how on earth was I going to convince my parents?

Tomas pulled up, and I went a few paces farther before I realized I'd left him behind. I circled my horse around, trying to see his face in the dark, but could only see his upheld hand, as if he was telling me to shush.

I couldn't hear anything. I glanced to the east and saw that the sun was beginning to rise.

But that was when I saw my gelding's ears again prick forward and heard it myself.

*We've got company. A lot of company.*

I turned, and Tomas pulled alongside me.

"Do you have a weapon, Father?"

"None but the Lord."

*Great,* I thought. I was all for God watching after us, but what I needed at that moment, judging from what was coming our way, was an armory. And men to utilize the weapons inside.

"Ride hard, Father. And stay with me."

"Every step, m'lady."

We surged into motion, trying to see the road ahead, help our horses avoid holes and branches. But it proved easier to let them have some free rein, trying to pay attention to their signals that told us to prepare for them to slow or dodge or pulse forward. The animals seemed to understand that we did not want to be caught by those behind us. Maybe Father Tomas's prayers were working.

I struggled to keep my seat and was glad I had a regular saddle beneath me. I had no idea how Tomas was managing, bareback. *That truly is a miracle.*

As the sun illuminated the eastern hills and my gelding found a stretch of sure road and cast himself headlong down it, I dared to glance under my right armpit.

A group of twelve men was riding in, fast, from our right flank. My heart exploded inside me. It was almost painful. But it got worse. I glanced under my left arm next, and I seriously thought I was having a heart attack. An identical group was coming in from the other direction. I leaned down, trying to make myself more aerodynamic, to coax every second of lead we could get. But Father Tomas was not as fast. He was slipping behind me, his weight and lack of a saddle holding him back.

"Go ahead, m'lady! They will not kill a priest!"

I did as he said, eight paces ahead of him, then nine. But I wasn't so sure. An excommunicated priest, once in Lord Greco's employ? Hanging out with the escaped Lady Betarrini? He'd be tried for treason, tortured, killed. No one would speak for him. Not the Church, which had disowned him. Nor Lord Greco, who continued to hide his true sympathies, his true feelings.

I groaned inside. *God, a little help here?*

We veered to the right and followed an old trail, still heading due north. A moment later I glimpsed the U-shaped indigo span of Lago di Vico. My heart sank as I realized I'd drifted east during the night's journey, as well as northward. *No wonder they found us.*

The trail followed the edge of an old limestone canyon, with a steep drop on one side, forcing us closer to those troops chasing us from the right flank. I urged my horse forward, willed him to give me everything he had, well aware that our pursuers were drawing nearer with every stride. But I could see that none drew arrows.

They intended to take me alive.

Which was both good and bad news.

Terror at what Father Tomas had described rang through me. I was no longer paying attention to him, solely focused on reaching safety. *There's no way, no way I'm letting them haul me back to Roma. No way I'm marrying Rodolfo tonight and sharing my bridal chambers with four Old Dude observers.*

No. Way.

I heard a man cry out and looked back to see Tomas sitting ramrod straight, his face a mass of pain. An arrow was sticking through his shoulder. *Oh, God, no!*

I started to pull up on my reins, but Tomas saw what I was doing and waved me on. "Go, m'lady, go!"

But I was conflicted. I'd left men behind before. In the battle so many had died, protecting me, keeping others from reaching me—Giovanni, Pietro…Could I bear the burden of yet another man's life?

The priest's face grew more alarmed. And angry. "Go! Off with you! Now!"

Deciding then, I dug my heels into the horse's flanks, and we were once again rolling at full speed. But I'd lost some precious seconds. The knights who chased me were so close, I could make out the color of their eyes. They wore the deep green colors of Lord Vivaro's crest, and I knew they had but one goal: to bring me back, to right the wrong done against their master.

The front man, closest to me, appeared to be their captain. With sandy hair and blue eyes, he had that rugged, stalwart, determined, Germanic look about him. And all that determination was focused on me.

I finally outpaced them, reaching the place they would intersect my path and be forced to follow, now just ten or twelve strides behind. I leaned down again, as low as I could, feeling the churning motion of my mount, seeking to become one with him, making his burden easier. In a few minutes I had widened the distance between us to fifteen strides. Then twenty.

I dared to hope, hope that I could outrun them for good. But the ravine continued to wind its way along a tiny stream at the bottom, apparently a winter and spring runoff that fed the lake in the distance. And the canyon was deep. Like the arroyos we had at home in Colorado, with steep cliffs of clay-like dirt eaten away by sudden rains and swelling, temporary rivers below. The cliff was probably fifty feet high and a good seventy-five-degree angle. I'd never attempted to go down anything close to it on horseback.

*But if I leaned back…*

I'd still likely fall, break my neck.

*My only chance is to outrun them.* I leaned down again, letting the horse move, move with everything he had in him. After a minute, maybe two—when I couldn't stand it any longer—I looked again at my pursuers and smiled.

Only half were still behind me, and they were now thirty or forty strides behind. It was working. I was outrunning them!

I smiled and had my first thoughts about getting to safety and then, somehow, stealing back to their camp at night and helping Tomas gain his freedom. They'd not be kind to the fat priest. They'd ask him why he was with me, claim he had assisted my escape. Maybe even toss him in prison. I couldn't let that happen. And the arrow—I had to help him get rid of that arrow—

I gasped and pulled up on the reins, finally figuring out why the rest of the men weren't behind me. I hadn't outrun half. They had split off and met the road again, beyond the shallow hills. Cutting me off.

My gelding came to a stop, kicking up a cloud of dust. I wheeled him around, and we took a few steps up the hill, thinking my only chance was to cut between them, escape right down the center.

But then six men crested the hill.

I pulled abruptly up on the reins again and my horse whinnied, letting me know his frustration. But he was a finely trained mount. Lord Zinicola had seen to it that I had the best. A horse I could trust.

They spread out in a semicircle, two deep, making sure there was no escape for me. And they slowed to a walk, casually moving forward. Three men surrounded Father Tomas, who slumped over, now their prisoner. *How bad is the blood loss?*

"Come, m'lady," said the young, blond captain, drawing my attention again. He smiled, and his blue eyes glittered with pleasure. "You have given us a fine chase, like any wild mare. But 'tis time to return home. To submit to the bit and reins."

The other men laughed as I wheeled around and eyed the ravine at my back.

"I am no wild mare," I grit out, my gelding dancing beneath me, nervous at their approach. "And I shall not be tamed by any *bit* or *reins*." I gave their lineup one last look, confirming what I already knew.

There was only one way out.

"Nay," said the captain with a smile of admiration. "You are no mare, but the true She-Wolf of Siena. As vital and intriguing as the legends boast."

They edged forward, now just ten paces away. A few were dismounting. They'd come after me and grab my reins and then it'd be Game Over.

"You haven't seen nothin' yet," I muttered in English.

Then, just as the first man reached for them, I ripped the gelding's reins to my right and kicked his flanks as hard as I could.

# Chapter Sixteen

We pretty much flew over the edge.

I leaned back, as far as I could, knowing I'd have to rely on the strength of my legs and my mediocre sense of balance if I was to have half a chance. I released the reins, needing both my arms outstretched. I took a breath before we finally touched ground for the first time.

The combination of momentum and gravity threatened to immediately unseat me. I folded forward, only narrowly holding on, squeezing with every ounce of strength I had in me. The gelding slid and then gathered himself to leap again, and we sailed another nine or ten feet before he hit the ground a second time. I got my first twinge of hope—*we just might make it*—as he leaped a third time. It was upon that third landing that I finally lost my grip and fell to one side, so fast that I was off his right flank and rolling down the embankment before I fully understood what was happening.

Over and over I went, growing dizzy, swallowing dirt, feeling clods of it brush through my hair, go up my nose…When I finally came to a stop, I paused, took a coughing, sputtering breath, and then leaped to my feet. *Whoa, too fast.* The canyon tilted and whirled like nature's carnival ride until I took several breaths. My vision came into focus.

And what I saw terrified me.

My gelding was on the far side of the trickle of a stream, limping badly.

Two men had tried to follow me over the edge, but both had fallen. One lay still, face down on the canyon wall. The other was making his way toward me, taking big, sliding, dusty leaps down the rest of the way. I scanned the rim, high above, and saw the backs of men as they raced down the canyon road, no doubt looking for an alternate route down to me, or at least to surround me once I came up again.

*This is not looking good, Gabs. Not good at all.*

The knight was getting closer. I turned and ran toward my horse, toward the scabbard that held my sword, but my action spooked him, and he skittered off again. Forcing myself to slow down, I walked toward him, cooing to him, trying to ignore that the dude on the other side was now just twenty feet away. I kept looking over my shoulder in this exaggerated slow move—literally doing my own slow-motion action sequence—so I wouldn't scare the horse, but I only had seconds before the dude reached me.

I concentrated on the horse, easing over to him as the man caught his attention too. I could see his foreleg was bleeding; his riding days were definitely over. *I'll have to get out of here on foot, right after I take care of this—*

I grabbed the sword and pulled it out just as the gelding decided he'd had enough and limped away again. I turned and met the surprised knight with a strike that he barely blocked.

He was my height, panting, as dirty as I probably was, and held my sword against his, above his head. Our faces were maybe a foot apart, our arms above us, like some sort of Death-by-Tango move. "I do not wish to harm you, m'lady," he panted.

"Good. Then don't," I panted in return, in English.

I dodged, turned, and brought my sword around, which he again parried. After two more strikes I became dimly aware of shouting and laughter above us. The men were now on either side of the canyon and were watching us as if we were gladiators in the Coliseum. But my opponent wasn't going for the kill—he was clearly going for the capture. Again and again, I brought my sword toward him, but all he did was meet each one with his own to block it. With each strike there were groans and gasps and shouts above us. They were like a bunch of construction workers on lunch break watching one of the toughest moments of my life come down before them.

"Take care! She has a dagger!" cried one of the knights, as I quietly slipped it from the rope at my waist. It was a miracle it hadn't dropped away when I fell—or that I hadn't stabbed myself as I rolled. I clamped my lips shut, concentrating on the guy in front of me. I knew it wouldn't be long until Mr. Blond Captain grew tired of such games and sent still more men down to fetch me.

This had to end. Fast.

And yet we were both getting more tired by the second. Sword fighting was like doing power aerobics with a thirty-pound weight in my hands. We circled each other, swords lowered, with me considering how I might escape or end it and him likely considering how to grab me without hurting me. That had to be what was holding him back. He was clearly stronger. *Don't hurt the merchandise,* I could almost hear Lord Vivaro saying....

So if I couldn't beat him by strength or skill, I had to outsmart him.

Or outrun him.

"Come, m'lady," he said warily, noting my hesitation. "Surely you see that there is no way out."

I paused. There was *always* some way out.

"What is to become of me?" I asked in a whisper, begging him to think he was my confidante, my protector in some odd fashion.

The hardness around the edges of his eyes eased. "It shall be a trying two days for you. And then it will be well. You shall be Lady Greco de Firenze, the envy of many."

"I am so weary," I said forlornly, as if I might suddenly dissolve into sobs. "So very weary." It was an easy act for me, because I was so tired. But when his sword lowered and he reached out his hand for mine, adrenaline surged through me. I whirled and struck, as if on automatic cycle.

I hit him with the flat of my blade at the back of the head, hoping to merely render him unconscious. I didn't ever want to kill another who wasn't out for my blood. There'd already been so much death.

His companions up top audibly drew a breath—it was like an amphitheater of sound down below—and my opponent stared at me in shock—his eyes saying, *How could you do that?* Then he fell to his knees and to his stomach like a floppy, dead fish, face down in the crusty sand of the riverbed.

I bent, turned his head so he could breathe, felt for a pulse—*he'll live*—and then surged into a run down the canyon. My only hope was that those in pursuit above would hit an obstacle, keeping them from tracking me, or maybe I'd hit a second ravine that branched off this one so I could ditch them altogether.

I didn't know how many more man-to-woman combat scenarios I could survive. I concentrated on the path before me, jumping from rock to rock rather than sinking into the fine, crusty, sandy dust of the riverbed. I knew that some of the knights had gone ahead to try and find a way down, cut me off, now that I had chosen a direction for escape. The others followed along at their leisure, taunting me, yelling down at me.

"Give in, She-Wolf!"

"You make something so simple, so difficult!"

"You are trapped! There is no way out!"

"Return to your proper place—this is hardly suitable!"

But their taunts only made me more determined. I ran faster, harder, smarter, and was pleased when they had to up their pace on either side to keep up with me. The taunting eased as the canyon widened and deepened and they grew farther from me. I could feel their fear—that I really might find a way out of this trap—and that fear fed my momentum.

I turned a corner in the arroyo and then another, choosing to stick with the deepest canyon each time, wanting to keep the barrier of height from my potential captors as long as possible.

I ran for a mile, maybe two, wondering where this arroyo might end, when I might finally lose the knights and climb my way to freedom, when I saw them.

Three knights, casually moving my way.

I stopped. Stood tall. Hoped I didn't look scared enough to pee my pants.

The blond captain was dead center, his mount's hooves splashing in the shallow remains of the river. Two fearsome knights followed slightly behind, flanking him on either side.

I couldn't imagine turning, outrunning them over the last miles I'd just covered. On foot? No way.

*This is it,* I thought. *It's over.*

*But I'm not going down without a fight.*

I wanted my last stand to be epic. To fight in a manner that would be a credit to female knights for years to come. But…uh, yeah. It really didn't come down that way.

From twenty feet away, Blondie casually dismounted. He didn't even draw his sword. He just strode toward me, and his demeanor told me that he was clearly here to end this.

*At the ready,* said my father's voice in my head.

I lifted my sword, dropped one foot back. If they wanted me, they would have to take me kicking and screaming.

I wished they were here, my family. Lia, picking off these guys—and those arriving above—with arrows. Mom, standing beside me, ready to take on her share with that rockin' staff. Dad…Well, maybe he would be better with his sword right now. I'd take him too. I'd take any of them. Because right then, I felt desperately, feverishly alone.

Blondie was still striding toward me, not pausing, not drawing his sword. It scared me—his total and complete confidence—and then I steeled myself, knowing that was exactly what he was after. Off his steed he was taller than I'd thought, a good three inches taller than I. And as broad and strong as Marcello and Rodolfo.

I bit my lip and lashed out at him with my sword when he came into range.

But he anticipated my move. Bent backward, watching the blade pass his chest by an inch, as if that was exactly what he had planned.

I turned, letting the momentum of the sword carry me, as I took a step back and then brought it down, two-handed toward his head.

He blocked my strike by grabbing my arm with both of his.

I'd never encountered such a move. I stood there, staring into his eyes in shock. *He'd never drawn his sword.*

"It ends here, She-Wolf," he said.

I was reaching for my dagger when I felt an iron hand grab my wrist and shake it loose. Massive arms engulfed me from behind and separated me from my sword.

One of the huge knights dragged me along—my feet barely touching the ground—and didn't even react as I hit and kicked and scratched and even bit him. We finally came to a stop, and I looked up.

Blondie was already on his mount and looked tiredly down at us. "Hand her to me," he said with a sigh, as if he was asking for a pack of mints or a map.

Burly Knight tossed me up, halfway, and Blondie hauled me the rest of the way up and over the horse, so I was sitting directly in front of him, basically in his lap. "Ah no, She-Wolf," he said in my ear, reading my mind. "You shall not have access to my back at any point in time." He wrapped his arms around me and pulled me closer, as if he owned me.

Which he pretty much did at that moment.

*Yeah, soak it up, Jerk. You think you have me...*I shoved down a surge of fury and frustration. It'd be better if I could get out, escape up top, away from this cursed canyon. It was a death trap.

We rode out the way they had come, to a place in the arroyo that broadened, flattened, and made for easy entry...or exit. Blondie and the rest of the men were largely silent, which unnerved me more than taunting and bantering. And I was soon stiff, trying not to lean into Sir Blondie's massive chest behind me. Would we ride all the way back to Roma this way? I hoped not.

*Marcello. I need you!*

I chastised myself for my stupid hopes of rescue. *How many times does he have to save you, Gabi?*

*Well, if he wants me here, if he wants me as his own, he had better step up to the plate...because I'm seriously afraid I've just struck out for the third time.*

We paused at the top of the canyon, and I could see half the men heading toward us, the others waiting on the opposite side. At the sight of me in their captain's arms, they cheered, their call coming down the arroyo like the blast from a trumpet.

Captain Blondie laughed. I felt the rumble in his chest, behind me.

"Take your ease, m'lady. Your flight is over. You've done your best to preserve your will, your honor. And now you must bend to the forces of the gods. For they've surely thrown in their shoulders against you."

I considered that for a while. The scattered remains of the Roman gods, a decimated faith, against Father Tomas's God, who'd lasted a couple thousand years, the God I thought I was coming to know. Which was right? Who had more power? Or was it all a matter of our own imaginations, a yearning for something bigger, greater than we, especially when we felt weak?

We moved forward.

"Be at ease," the knight said again in my ear. "You cannot travel the miles we have ahead of us in such a manner."

"I shall have your name," I said regally.

"I beg your pardon, m'lady," he said, the same smile in his tone. "'Tis Captain Albertus Ruisi."

"You look like men I knew in Normandy," I said, after a while, baiting him.

"Many say I resemble my father, who was from Germania."

As I had guessed. *Keep him talking.* I relaxed a bit, but not totally. I wanted him to think I was giving in, giving up. I felt his arm tighten around my waist as I eased back, against him. "Did he come to Roma as a mercenary?"

"Nay," he said, like a secret in my ear. "He came as a priest."

I fought the urge to turn and stare at him.

We rounded a bend, and I saw Father Tomas, still bent over, maybe even unconscious, while still on his mount. "They are as fallible as any other man," he said.

The others rode to meet us, leaving Father Tomas behind. His horse stirred and took a few steps after them, pulling the reins from the priest's hands. But then he stopped.

"Please," I said. "Captain Ruisi, allow me to go to him."

He apparently followed my gaze, looking over my shoulder. "The priest? He is of no concern to us."

"Mayhap not to you. But he is God's concern."

I could feel his stomach muscles tense at the base of his chest plate, right behind me. A long moment ticked by.

"You can see to him when we make camp this night. Should he live that long."

"And if he doesn't?"

"Did you not just say that he was God's concern? If that proves true, he will live until we make camp this night. If not, we shall leave him for the wild to reclaim."

*Awesome,* I thought. *This dude has serious daddy issues.*

*Can You make this a tad easier, Lord?* I prayed. *Uhh, hello? If You're there?* My doubts about God's presence—about Him being little more than a figment of our imaginations—came crashing in. But I quickly decided I'd rather believe in Him than not. I needed Him. Needed Him bad, especially right now. *Be with Tomas. Help him…make it, Father,* I finished awkwardly.

Captain Ruisi gestured for a couple of men to bring the semiconscious priest along, and we moved south, toward Roma. Twenty-three knights. A half-dead priest. And one filthy, dirty girl.

We camped that night along the edges of the huge, sprawling Lago di Bracciano, perilously close to Rome. Captain Ruisi offered me the opportunity to bathe, promising me protection and privacy. But yeah, I wasn't feeling super trusting, so I did my best to wash my face and arms, conscious that I was dripping dirty water down the front of my Roman toga bridal gown. Not that I cared. But the boys in town were going to find it ridiculously amusing if I didn't cut loose before I got there. The guys here with me already thought it highly entertaining.

They glanced at me and laughed, some spitting out their pent-up guffaws behind their hands and others not bothering to hide their amusement at all. I approached them as regally as I could, well aware that my hair was coming down around my shoulders and that I had spots of dirt all over me. It was all I could do not to dive into the lake, frigid cold as it was. Every bit of dirt chafed at me, making me itch. I didn't need my enemies' laughter to tell me I looked like a train wreck.

When I returned from the water's edge, I saw that they'd finally taken Father Tomas down from his horse. "Is he—?" I began, terrified that I was too late.

"Nay," Captain Ruisi said. "But not long for this world."

"Please," I asked yet again. "May I...?"

He studied me a moment and then waved me on, as if whether or not this man lived was the last thing he cared about. As if the battle was over and his death would put a firm stamp of victory on it.

I hurried over to the priest, so terribly still, alone. The others kept far away, as if death might be catching. "Father Tomas," I whispered, shaking him a little by the shoulder.

There was no answer. How much blood had he lost through the day? In the late afternoon he'd grown too weak to even hold on, so knights had strapped him to his steed. The light of the bonfire nearby lit up half his face, leaving the other half in utter darkness. Listening to his breathing, I knew that was where he was—hovering between light and dark, life and death.

But he was breathing. Alive.

"I need a knife," I said. I lifted my head and looked to Captain Ruisi, conscious that one by one, the men looked to him too, all thinking, *There's No Way….*

He returned my stubborn gaze.

"Water. Bandages. And another blade, set in the center of that fire," I added.

A tiny smirk lifted the edges of his thin lips. "You think you can save him?"

"I can try."

He stared back at me for a breath, then two, before he nodded once, lifted his hand and flicked two fingers, setting several men into motion.

One of the hulking knights came over to me, paused a moment, and then handed me my own dagger from his belt. He stood there, at the ready, watching me as I bent, cut away the shoulder of the priest's robe—as well as the shaft of the arrow. Then he reached for the dagger again, and I gave it up without comment.

The other men arrived with my requests—water and bandages. Another man was stirring the fire, moving aside a half-burned log, placing a sword in the center of the white-hot coals.

I moved to place my knee between the arrow and Father Tomas's neck, wanting him still for what was to come next. I held the end of the arrow that had the head. The shaft was narrow, about the width of a pencil, really. I'd broken a few pencils in my lifetime. Could this be any more difficult?

I didn't wait any longer. If Father Tomas was to have half a chance, I had to free him of the arrow, and quickly. I twisted to get a better angle, grabbed hold of the arrow shaft with both hands, and snapped the head off as cleanly and quickly as I could.

Father Tomas moaned, frowned, beneath me, but he did not move. I was thankful for his unconsciousness. But I had to move very, very quickly.

I rolled him to his side, sitting in the dirt behind him. Then, grabbing hold of the other end of the arrow, its feathers tickling my wrist, I put a filthy, sandaled foot against his back, tried to get the straightest angle, and yanked.

It emerged far more easily than I had thought it would. But immediately, bright blood began running down the wide, white expanse of his shoulder. "Bandages!" I barked. "Water, and the blade!"

A man handed me a wad of cloth, and I stretched it over his shoulder, trying to staunch the blood on both sides at once. It was like pressing in on either side of a pierced water mattress. "The sword!" I cried. "I need the sword, wrapped in a cloth!"

They brought it to me, dropping it twice en route, it was so hot.

I studied it and wondered if I had it in me—what was next.

I knew the fastest, surest method to stop a wound from bleeding was searing it. And Father Tomas had lost so much blood already… But I was anxious, anxious that his heart could not withstand the pain yet to come. It reminded me of the night they'd pulled the stitches from my belly. The night they'd had to cauterize it…I still had the puckered scar to show for it. It made me shaky, remembering it.

Captain Ruisi was there, then. "Must I do it, She-Wolf?" he taunted. "Are you not all that the storytellers have said? Or be you only a woman?"

I glared at him, even if there was the glint of teasing in his eye. Perhaps he was not as eager to see a priest die on his duty as he pretended. He handed me a thick cloth with which to grab the glowing sword at my knees. It literally was red-hot, fading to black, and then slightly less red a moment later, as if the heat lived within it.

I took the cloth, folded it twice, then in half again. I reached for the sword and in a second could feel the heat radiating through. I had to move fast.

I eyed Father Tomas's wound at his back, kneeled against his side, wiped away the blood to better see the hole, pinched the skin together, then with my other hand, held the flat of the blade against it.

He moaned, shifted, but I was ready for it, moving with him as the disgusting scent of burning flesh wafted to my nostrils. I lifted the sword, when I could not tolerate it a second longer, and rolled him to his back, atop a portion of cloth. One side down, one more to go...

With a swipe of the bloody cloth in my hand, I eyed the hole at the front of his shoulder, about the size of a dime, pinched the skin together again, and seared it shut, this time using the tip of the blade. I closed my eyes, wincing at the sound of the flesh sizzling again, forcing myself to count, *a thousand one, a thousand two,* trying to get five seconds before I released him.

*There.* It was done. I turned and flung the sword away as if it were a poisonous snake. But the fire snake had done its duty. The wound at Father Tomas's shoulder smoldered, as if I'd just stamped out a tiny fire.

I stared at it, watched a tiny tendril of smoke rise from his charred flesh like a signal fire. I followed the curving line up, looking up toward the stars, bright even though they were accompanied by a rising, waxing moon.

*Oh, God,* I said to Him silently. *What have I become? Who am I?*

I searched within, trying to find something I remembered, something familiar, something beyond this young woman who was running running running, who was fighting off her enemies, who was performing triage medicine in the wilds of Italia in medieval times.

I had returned through the time tunnel, to this place, this time, sure that this was where I was meant to be.

But at that moment I wasn't sure at all. I choked back the tears, willing myself not to cry, but knew I was losing the battle. I rose and took a few steps away into the darkness, aware that Captain Ruisi and another were right behind me, giving me a moment and yet not giving me half a chance to slip away into the dark.

Turned away from them, face to the pitch black of the Roman hills, I let the tears fall, trying to keep my breathing from betraying my weeping as the tears poured down my face.

"M'lady?" asked Captain Ruisi.

I raised one arm, not turning, and he was silent. He knew. But I didn't care. Couldn't care. I was so far from home, so far from family, so far from Marcello…so far from *me,* that at that moment,

I thought the very stars might envelop me, enfold me, take over…
make me disappear.

I was having a panic attack.

I knew the symptoms…increased heart rate, wild thoughts, a
sense of being totally overwhelmed. I laughed then, and lifted a hand
to my brow. A panic attack? I could handle that. It was just something else to manage, get through. Tomorrow would be another day;
I would find another morning, another sunrise to give me hope, to
help me remember. I laughed again, the sound hollow to my own
ears. But even the action of it, the contraction of the muscles in my
belly, the force of air from my throat, reminded me that I was very
much here, very much alive.

Even if I felt like I was slowly disappearing.

# Chapter Seventeen

If I thought the first approach to the eternal city was difficult, it wasn't half as tough as this one. I glanced back, beyond my captor, to Father Tomas, who was staring back at me, clearly as agonized for me as he was in agony. Captain Ruisi's arms tightened around me, as if I was about to leap from our mount. "Relax, Blondie," I muttered in English. "Where am I gonna go?" I let out a humorless, desperate laugh.

I straightened again, and Captain Ruisi's arms loosened, holding the reins.

Apparently word had spread about my escape, and so, as Vivaro's knights paraded me back to his sprawling palazzo, people gathered to point and applaud and whisper behind their hands. Some women stared at me without smiling or averted their eyes, as if they felt a little of my pain. Others laughed, reminding me of kids at school who enjoyed the after-school brawl or abusing the underclassman— dumping-the-puny-freshman-into-the-garbage-can kind of thing. Mean kids. Now mean grown-ups. The kids ran alongside us like we were bringing a carnival to town, arms raised, laughing, shouting.

I had to speak to Rodolfo. Plead with him to find a way out for us. It was my only hope, since these people were never going to leave me alone. There would not be another opportunity to escape. People dropped what they were doing to follow us to the palazzo, eager to see how my arrival would play out. The last blocks leading up to Lord Vivaro's were agonizing. I felt like time was slowing, as if I were slogging through wet sand, waist deep.

A woman screeched and came at me, waving her fingers and speaking in a nonsensical language. Was she crazy?

Captain Ruisi kicked at her. "Off with you!" he barked.

I watched her run to the nearest building, clinging to it as if it might save her, looking back at us if we were chasing her. And there was a part of me that understood her.

*Okay, I'm losing it. I'm really losing it.*

We turned the corner and entered the final street, Lord Vivaro's street.

As we passed Lord Zinicola's, I saw that he and Carsius were out front, watching as we passed, saying nothing, though their sad eyes really said it all. I couldn't bear to look at them for long. They'd sacrificed so much, tried so hard to help me. And what had I done with their gifts? Blown it, big time. Gone and gotten myself captured and hauled back.

A fine legend I turned out to be.

When we finally reached Palazzo Vivaro, with its wide travertine steps cascading down to the street, I saw Rodolfo first, looking somberly in my direction. And then I saw Lord Barbato's chin, raised in triumph as I approached. But it was Lord Vivaro that I heard first, crying out in shock at the sight of me. "Oh, by the blood of Mars!" he cried, skittering down the stairs with his hands clasped together and shaking his head in horror. "What have you done to my beautiful bride?"

"We did nothing to her, m'lord," Captain Ruisi said, dismounting. "We merely pursued the She-Wolf until she could run no farther. And that was farther than we expected." He reached up for me and, when I hesitated, grabbed hold of my arm and roughly hauled me down.

A woman gasped.

"Is that really necessary?" Rodolfo asked sternly, now just a few steps above us.

"'Tis, m'lord," the captain said, turning toward him. "She cannot be trusted. At every moment you must guard your bride from fleeing. Even unto her death."

Lord Vivaro clasped one fist to his mouth and raised both of his eyebrows in exaggerated fashion, clearly loving every minute of the drama.

"Unto her death?" Rodolfo asked the captain.

Captain Ruisi cocked his blond head and met his gaze. "If you'd seen what I'd seen, you wouldn't question me."

Rodolfo stepped forward and took hold of my arm. "I understand."

"Rodolfo, I must speak to you alone—" I begged.

"The time for speaking is long over," he said angrily, staring down at me.

"Indeed," said Barbato, looking over Rodolfo's shoulder like an evil little messenger. Delight lit up his eyes. "The only words required of you this night shall be your vows." He dragged his eyes from me to the crowd, scanning it as if looking for enemies. "Quickly, let us get her inside."

He turned and walked up the steps, and Rodolfo followed him, hauling me along too.

"Nay, you shall not take her to the cathedral in that!" Lord Vivaro cried, trailing us like a fat cat following a tray of fish. "At least let me put her in a clean gown!"

"'Tis most appropriate, don't you think?" Rodolfo asked his host over his shoulder. "She-wolves are wild, untamed. Could a bride look more untamed than this?" he asked, giving me a wry up-and-down. Was he joking? Playing the part? Or was that a serious tinge of fury in his eyes?

"You have a point, m'lord. But I have a certain role to play in Roma."

"And Lady Betarrini robbed you of that role, Lord Vivaro," Rodolfo returned. He paused and faced the panting, fat man. "I am most sorry for your disappointment. But I sincerely hope that the private nature of the wedding ceremony shall ease your pain. The only Romans in attendance shall be the fifteen you have arranged to join us. That is enough! All of Roma shall clamor for your story, wanting every detail."

Lord Vivaro paused, studied me and then Rodolfo. "As you wish, m'lord."

So Rodolfo had something on him. I'd never seen Vivaro shut up before, and there it was. Barbato had taken Captain Ruisi a few paces away to speak to him. Their backs were to us.

"M'lord, may I have but a cup of water to drink?" I asked Rodolfo.

He studied me, then ushered me over to a carved marble fountain at the end of the hall. There, a cherub spit an unending stream of water. I cupped my hands beneath it and shakily took a sip. My back was to the rest of the room. "Surely you do not intend to see this ceremony through," I whispered.

He paused a moment, then leaned down and said in my ear, "I most certainly do."

The water slipped through my fingers, my makeshift cup forgotten. I stared at the carved face of the cherub before me and then forced myself to look Rodolfo in the eye. "M'lord," I said, gripping my silk skirt with damp fingers, twisting it.

"Lord Greco!" Barbato interrupted. He called him forward with a flick of two fingers. "There is the matter of your priest..."

Rodolfo glanced back at me and gave me a small, wicked smile. "Wash your face, She-Wolf. Take down the rest of your hair, in the manner of a noblewoman of Toscana. That, Barbato shall allow." He stepped away then to speak to Captain Ruisi and Lord Barbato, each keeping an eye on me as if I might slip away at any moment.

I tore my eyes away from Rodolfo's back, trying to make sense of his words. I watched the men join together in a small circle, nodding, gesturing, deciding my fate.

I felt a gentle touch at my arm and saw the beautiful Main Girl at my elbow. To her credit she did not gasp in dismay at the sad state of my filthy, torn silk toga. She only gave me a gentle, tiny smile and reached up to finish pulling down the few tendrils of my hair that remained in her elaborate up-do. "We have but a moment," she muttered. Another girl appeared and dipped a cloth in the fountain and reached up to wash dirt I'd missed from my face. A third arrived, and they eased me to a seat on the edge of the fountain. Trying to make me presentable, the best they could. Sweeping my eyelids with a coal stick. Dabbing my lips with a shiny ointment.

"Enough," growled Lord Barbato, edging past Main Girl. "She had her opportunity to be presented as a respectable bride." He took my arm and yanked me to stand before him.

He was shorter than I. I stared back into his eyes. "I did not ask to be a bride at all," I said.

"Yes, well, it has always been about more than your desires, has it not?"

I couldn't argue that. Ever since I got to ancient Toscana, I'd fought. For those I loved. For what was rightfully theirs. For what I'd wanted, hoped for. For love. For peace. For life. But it was always just out of reach.

Was this what God had brought me here to learn? That I could strive, push for what I wanted, but that eventually it was out of my hands?

"'Tis time," Rodolfo said, stepping toward me in the immaculate costume of a medieval nobleman—a crisp, billowing white shirt, a heavily embroidered tunic that reached mid-thigh, leggings in a fine silk weave, and new boots. How had he changed so fast? He'd been *right there* just a moment ago. And now here he was again, all GQ Groom of the Middle Ages.

"Rodolfo," I faltered.

"Shh. Truly you look more fetching even than that day in Firenze in all your finery."

I frowned in confusion. He thought I was worried I didn't look good enough for him?

He reached for a coil of my hair and rubbed it between his thumb and forefinger, then scanned my face. "Half Roman empress, half nymph of the wood. Lady Gabriella Betarrini."

"Soon Lady Gabriella Greco," Main Girl said as she handed him a white cape.

He gave me a sad smile. "It has a good sound to it, does it not?" He stretched it out and wrapped it around me. I wanted to throw it aside, but I could not deny the warmth of the soft fabric.

*Gabriella Betarrini. Gabriella Greco. Gabriella Forelli.* I rubbed my temples. *Marcello Forelli. Marcello, Marcello. I am sorry, so sorry. I can't see my way out—*

"Take my arm," Rodolfo said, "it soon shall be done."

"And that means—"

"I mean it shall soon be done."

Numbly I placed my hand on the back of his, and we paraded down the steps out front, like a prince with his pauper bride. Beside two white horses, he bent to take my waist in his hands and lifted me to the one in back. A sidesaddle, tied to the horse in front. He placed my filthy feet—once in delicate white sandals, now black with dirt—into one stirrup and then the next, his touch firm but gentle, slightly lingering. I searched his every move, every glance for a hint that he intended to stop this somehow. To free me.

But I got nothing.

"Must I bind your hands around the mare's neck?" he asked me. "'Tis what Lord Barbato has demanded."

I looked from him to the awful, thin lord beyond him, on a brown gelding. Then to Captain Ruisi, Lord Vivaro, and the bazillion knights all around us. I gave him a humorless smile. "If I were skilled enough to escape all of these, I would be worthy indeed of the legends."

"Oh, you are worthy, m'lady," he said with a smile. "Far more than you imagine."

He turned his back, mounting his steed before me, and ignored Lord Barbato's protests. "Captain," he said with a nod.

We set out, down the hill and through the streets, eventually reaching the Tiber River and crossing it. Dimly I took in my surroundings, continually trying to get my bearings in a city I knew… but didn't. Every time I thought I had found my way, my place, I was lost again. But then I saw St. John's. *San Giovanni in Laterano,* the cathedral of Rome.

It was about where I remembered, near the remains of the old Triclinium Leoninum, with its ancient mosaics my parents had always liked, and near a partially rebuilt palazzo. But the only other recognizable monuments for me were the obelisk, from Egypt, now lying on its side in a field to our right, and a glimpse of the pretty cloisters that Lia liked to sketch, to the other side of the big church. The basilica itself? It looked nothing like the one we knew in our own time, with its massive white facade and statues of popes and saints, so like St. Pete's.

It was about the length of twenty mall stores and three stories high. I glanced around, still trying to figure out if I was where I thought I was, looking for any possibility of escape. But Rodolfo was right there, gently taking me from my saddle and gripping my forearm, abandoning any sense of the normal lord-lady stuff and giving me no chance to make a dash for it. Did he really want this? Me to marry him when I had no choice?

He ignored my quizzical look and pulled me forward, up the steps, toward bronze doors that I recognized.

"Have you been to San Giovanni before?" he asked when I paused, looking up at the massive doors, twenty feet high and decorated with stars. I thought I remembered Dad saying they came from the first century.

"In another lifetime," I mused.

Two of Lord Vivaro's knights opened the fifteen-foot-high doors. The rest of the knights lined the stairs, in guarded formation. I knew there were some others that had gone to the back, to the sides, along the cloisters. There was no way they would allow me to escape.

"Rodolfo, I can't—"

"Do not say it, Gabriella."

"But this…" I said, feeling my heart really begin to pick up a pace of panic, "—you don't understand. I cannot—"

"You shall," he whispered.

I glanced up at him in confusion. What did *that* mean?

The modern-day basilica, which would one day dwarf this cathedral, had lots of natural light and massive sculptures lining the walls. But the medieval version was a big, dark building and felt more like a cave than a church. Fat candles dripped along the edges, onto the mosaic stones below, the beeswax scent melding with such intense incense that I felt I couldn't breathe. The remains of the sunset filtered through tiny windows, high up and to my left, smoke dancing and clouding before them.

Before us stood several men in long robes and hoods, as if part of a secret society. I realized then that Lord Barbato and Lord Vivaro wore identical robes and hoods. The two lords strode forward on either side of us. For what reason? To hide themselves? Because they

weren't totally proud of what was about to come down—forcing me
to marry Lord Greco?

*Well, they can't. Can't force me. I'll wait them out. They won't kill
me. They wouldn't dare.*

I paused, the truth of it sinking in. *Yes, they would. I've put them
through enough. Embarrassed them enough.* Here, in this towering
church that felt like a yawning chasm with only our small group
within, I felt the truth of it echo through my mind, my heart. It was
to end here, once and for all. They'd have me as bride, or they'd have
my head. And either way, Firenze came out as conqueror.

I bit my lip. There had to be a way to stop it. Had to be a way.

I looked to the priest when we reached him, over to the men
presiding—many of them hidden beneath the shadows of their long
hoods—and back again. The priest was some kind of bigwig. A cardinal, maybe? Or a bishop? I wasn't really sure. But I racked my
brain for the right title. I had to speak to him, beg him for mercy,
protection. He looked a little Spanish, with olive skin and a red,
wide-brimmed, tasseled hat and robe. He looked back at me as if I'd
interrupted his hot game of cribbage or something. Like this was the
last thing he wanted to do today.

*Okay, so I'm not gonna get any help from the holy man.* But I had to
try anyway. "Your Eminence," I said, gambling on a title that would
convey lots of honor and respect.

He peered at me in surprise, as if he did not expect me to speak
at all. The men around me got all jumpy.

"These men force me to these vows," I said, shaking my head
and pulling away from Rodolfo. "I do not wish to do this. I stand
against it."

"*Gabriella,*" Rodolfo said, taking new hold of my arm and yanking me closer again.

Captain Ruisi slipped behind me, and I felt a cold blade beneath my throat. "She is done speaking. Carry on, Your Eminence."

"Yes, be on with it," Lord Barbato demanded.

The small cardinal dude stared at me for a moment from behind the bouncing tassels on the brim of his red hat. Then Rodolfo shifted his grip on my right arm again, even as Ruisi's arm wrapped around me from behind, holding the blade at my throat. The priest turned tiredly toward the altar, made the sign of the cross and began to chant in Latin.

It was done. Over.

I was getting hitched.

Whether I wanted to or not.

# Chapter Eighteen

*This can't be happening.*

The cardinal turned to me and shook a silver baton-thingy at me and then Rodolfo, chanting words from a gigantic, open, hand-lettered liturgy book. Behind him an altar boy swung a censer, streaming sweet-smelling incense left and then right. Having trouble dealing, I zoned out, ignoring the words, watching as the puffs of gray smoke rose and danced in the fading light, up past the gold-laden Christ figure on a cross behind the altar. I stared at Him, remembering the first crucifix I'd seen when I first came to ancient Toscana. The tiny one at Castello Forelli in my room.

I'd prayed to God then, asking if He would tell me why I was here. What I was to do.

And the only answer I'd gotten, ever since, was to be with Marcello. To love Marcello Forelli. Be with him. Forever.

I'd even been given my dearest desire—my family, here with me, making it possible. How could I be giving in? Now? After all we'd been through? The way had been made! I only had to escape this trap....

I straightened and lifted my chin. Captain Ruisi shifted behind me, and I felt the edge of his blade at my throat. But I didn't think he wanted to use it. Not really.

Rodolfo dared to glance in my direction, obviously feeling me tense.

The cardinal continued his litany, and with each Latin word, I knew that it was here that I would take my stand. For life. For love. The cardinal turned the page, read another sentence, and then looked to Rodolfo. He had apparently just asked if he was vowing to have and to hold and all that stuff. My Latin was pretty sketchy. But I tensed.

Rodolfo looked down at me and stared into my eyes.

I silently begged him not to do it. Not to utter words I couldn't echo.

"Lord Greco," growled Barbato.

But Rodolfo's sad, brown eyes were on me, his hand now holding mine, caressing it. "I cannot," he said at last.

Then he glanced behind me, at Ruisi. "Release her. At once."

Captain Ruisi hesitated and then did as he said, taking a step backward.

"M-m'lord?" the cardinal sputtered.

But Rodolfo's eyes never left mine. He lifted my hand to his lips. "I cannot," he said again, looking toward the cardinal as if the matter was done. But he still held my hand.

Barbato and Vivaro were in a full-on tizzy. "What is this?" Lord Barbato blustered, coming near. "You most certainly shall! You gave me your word!"

"But she will not give me hers," he said sadly, glancing at me one more time. "Out of respect for her valor and courage—this woman has fought for Toscana and nearly given her life, time and time again, for it. That alone should give her the right to marry whom she wishes." He paused, and his voice went lower, more emotional, even as he smiled. "And it's clear to me that her heart beats for one man alone. And sadly that is not me."

"Nay," said a voice behind us and to our left. "I pray 'tis for me." It was a voice I knew well.

*Marcello.*

My eyes widened, and I turned full around, even as Captain Ruisi drew his sword. It was almost as if I didn't care. I tried to edge past him, to better see in the dim light, but Rodolfo drew me back.

Marcello was striding toward us, pulling his hood off, drawing a sword from beneath his cape.

Rodolfo and Lord Barbato reached for theirs, too, but then Lia, Luca, Mom, and Dad pulled their hoods back, all displaying weapons. "I would not do that," Luca said, easily striking away Barbato's impotent sword. "You don't want to see the Betarrinis angry. It is most unpleasant."

Lia moved forward, arrow drawn, to cover the noblemen Lord Vivaro had invited to the ceremony—or at least, those who'd managed to arrive. Marcello, Luca, and my family had obviously removed a few of them and borrowed their hooded capes.

I pushed Captain Ruisi's dagger away and fell into Marcello's arms. "You're here. You're here," I said. I couldn't manage much more through my tears, as I inhaled his scent of wood smoke and leather and spice. How had I forgotten the power of his embrace, the total *rightness* of it? I shoved away the guilt of being held by Rodolfo.

He pressed my lips to his for a quick kiss, his hand holding the back of my head. "You and your infernal need to rush toward your bridal day," he teased. "I keep telling you *I* wish to marry you. Let us see it done in Siena. Properly. In a gown that is *clean*."

"Let us make our escape and speak of marriage later, shall we?" Dad asked from a few feet away.

I moved over to him, where he was waving a sword at several men now on their knees. He embraced me with one arm, and Mom wrapped a free arm around me too. "You guys shouldn't have come," I said. Not meaning it at all, of course, but seriously scared now, for all of us.

"You are fools," Lord Barbato bit out. "You shall never escape this basilica. Every entrance is covered by Lord Vivaro's men."

I glanced at Lord Vivaro, who looked most pleased with this latest development—he'd have quite a story to tell at parties—but he was careful to nod fiercely after Barbato's comment. "You might have entered in disguise, but you shall not escape. Every entrance is covered," he said gravely. "Please, allow Lord Greco to complete his nuptials with Lady Gabriella, and we shall all retire to my palazzo as friends." He threw his hands wide and smiled.

Lia let out a low growl and moved her arrow to the base of his fat throat. "What do you think, Gabi? Would you like to see these nuptials through?"

"Not this day," I said.

"How about on the morrow?" Marcello asked, smiling and lifting my hand to his lips. "If I am your groom?"

"Hold that eHarmony thought," Lia whispered in English. "We gotta get out of here." She turned her attention to Marcello. "If their men outside gain word that all is not well in here, it shall be a blood-bath, church or not." I stared at her for a sec. My lil' sis was growing up. Seriously. Suddenly she was every inch the medieval warrioress. I wished I felt some of the strength she was oozing. With the appearance of my family, I was suddenly tired, so tired. Wanting to let my guard down and crumbling.

"Surrender," Barbato demanded with a small smile. "Or die trying to depart."

"You are hardly in the position to demand anything," Marcello said in a harsh tone. He leaned closer. "By the way, I have my castle back. Your displaced troops are with Paratore. And now I have my lady."

Barbato stared back at him, hatred in his eyes. "It shall never stand."

"Tie them up against the columns," Marcello said to my family, before returning his attention to Barbato. "It shall stand. As far as Siena is concerned, my brother paid a far greater price than was warranted, a blood price for Castello Forelli."

"And so keep your castle," Barbato said dismissively, as Dad dragged him backward toward a massive granite column. "You shall not retake your lady. She belongs to us now. I will see her wed to a nobleman of Firenze—either Lord Greco or another—" he said, casting a venomous look in Rodolfo's direction, "—or I shall see her dead."

"If any further harm comes to Lady Gabriella, I shall see *you* dead, m'lord," Marcello said, shaking his finger at Barbato. The veins in his neck bulged.

"You wouldn't dare," Barbato said, lifting his chin in defiance.

Marcello lifted his sword, his face a mass of fury. But I grabbed his arm and stepped between them. "Nay, love. He's not worth it.

Kill him, and there will simply be another Fiorentini ready to take his place."

Marcello sighed. "Although it'd be most satisfying."

I gave him a little smile. "Agreed."

Luca returned, and his eyes moved between Marcello, Barbato, and me as if he was thinking, *What'd I miss?* "All exits are guarded."

We paused, as a group, trying to think it through.

"There is another way," said a voice from behind the curve of a massive, green granite column. He moved forward, lurching in his gait, and I saw that it was Father Tomas, pain etched in his broad, white face.

"Tomas!" I cried, rushing toward him. I came under his arm, giving him some support.

"This way," he said, pointing to the altar.

I frowned at him in confusion but walked with him. Marcello came over to us. "Allow me, Gabriella." He nodded to Tomas. "He is your friend?"

"He is," I said, but I was eyeing Rodolfo as we passed him. Did he want out? Wish to come with us, leave Firenze behind? What would he endure there, when he returned, having betrayed Lord Barbato?

"'Twas but an idle dream, m'lady, you and I," he said with a gentle smile, but his eyes bore a measure of pain. "'Tis your truest path, to be with Lord Marcello." His brown gaze shifted to his old friend. "By your life?"

"By my life," Marcello returned, fist to his chest. "Gabriella shall reach safety." He paused. "Come with us, Rodolfo. I'd see you well rewarded in Siena."

"Go with him, traitor," Barbato called out from ten feet away. "I shall see you hanged!"

Rodolfo looked over at him with tired eyes and then back to Marcello. "I cannot. Firenze holds my heart, as it has all along. The only treasonous act I've committed is refusing to claim a woman's heart." His eyes flicked to me, then back to Marcello. He lowered his voice to a whisper. "I do not believe my brothers in Firenze shall hold that against me. Not for long, anyway."

"My debt to you has doubled," Marcello said, clasping his arm.

"There are no debts between brothers," Rodolfo said.

The two men shared a long look, then we turned and Marcello helped Father Tomas to a staircase, directly behind the altar, then down the steep steps. We weren't far behind—me, Mom and Dad, Lia and Luca. The last thing I saw of Rodolfo was a glimpse of the broad expanse of his back as he strode down the center of St. John's, Lords Barbato and Vivaro yelling after him, while Captain Ruisi, the cardinal, and five other men struggled to get free.

I hoped Rodolfo would find love someday. I hoped he'd be safe.

The temperature dived with each step we took down into an ancient grotto. We gaped for a moment at the ancient face of rock—the two crypts, ornately carved of purple granite, and a line of limestone crypts. The graves of popes? Kings? Saints? But then Luca was tearing down the stairs behind us. "Our escape has been discovered. We must be off."

Marcello turned toward Father Tomas. "Where?"

"That way," said the priest, panting, looking a ghastly shade of gray.

We all looked toward a door with a big lock on it. Another tunnel.

"Where does it lead?" Marcello asked.

"Does it matter? 'Tis the only way!"

"You do not know," Marcello said.

Father Tomas shrugged. "I had only heard of it from another who once served here. The clerics who serve here like to have a way out, should they be threatened."

"Sounds like an escape route to me," Luca said, glancing upward. We could hear the shouts of men.

Lia moved to the staircase, our shield, and drew an arrow. "I can give you a few minutes' lead."

"I'll stay with her," Dad said, giving Luca no opportunity. Luca turned, a knowing smile on his face. If Dad was protective over me, he was twice as protective over my little sis. Dad pulled out his sword, standing behind her.

Luca took Tomas's arm over his shoulder to help him walk. "Do not fret, Father. This group has good experience hauling ill men through long, dark tunnels."

I laughed under my breath. It was good, so good to be with all of them again. Together, I felt like we could do anything—face any enemy, make any escape.

I heard the *thrum* of Lia's bowstring. A man cried out behind us, then rolled halfway down the steps, dead.

"Go!" Lia cried.

Marcello struck the iron lock, again and again, with the hilt of his sword, until it finally broke loose. He swung open the heavy door and then glanced back.

"Here," Mom said, handing him a lit candle. She must've grabbed it from the altar upstairs. *Always thinking, my mom, planning ahead…*

Marcello took it gratefully, lit a torch at the end of the tunnel, broke off the candle and handed it back to Mom to light hers, as he tossed aside the gold candlestick. "Let it be said that the only thing we took from a church was a bride and some beeswax." With a wink he took my hand in his, and we ran down the tunnel, with Luca hauling Tomas behind us, followed by Mom, then, finally, Dad and Lia. About fifty meters in, we came to another door.

"See if you can bar it once we're on the other side!" Marcello called, rushing headlong down the tunnel. We knew that if Lia had given up her post, knights were surely already making their way in after us. A good archer might be able to pick off those of us at the back, even in the dark. The shaft was that straight.

We rushed through the doorway. I took half a breath when we heard the clang of it shut behind Lia and Dad.

"You do not know how glad I am to be with you again, Gabriella," Marcello said over his shoulder, between pants.

"Only half as glad as I, m'lord," I said. I grinned, feeling crazy—like we were running through a field of daisies, instead of for our lives. That insanely *invincible* kind of thing. Except on steroids. We ran for ten, then fifteen minutes, at a distinctly downward angle, until we abruptly met a closed door. We only narrowly stopped in time, so fast were we going. It had to be dark on the other side—there was no illuminated edge.

Marcello traced the frame of the door with the torch and then cursed under his breath, wiping his upper lip of sweat.

"What?"

"I can't find a latch. It may be locked on the other side," he said, giving it a shove with his shoulder. But it didn't budge.

Luca and Father Tomas limped into our circle of light. We could see Mom's bouncing torch, fifty feet beyond them. Luca unlooped Tomas's arm from around his shoulders and led him to a seat, ten feet back into the tunnel. "Shall we?" he asked Marcello.

"I supposed we must," my man said with a grin. He drew me back to Father Tomas, then pulled a sword from a sheath on his back. "I believe this is yours, m'lady," he said.

I was almost as glad to have my broadsword back in my hands as I was to be with my people. I instantly felt stronger, more capable of taking on what was ahead. Whatever. I was happily buying the lie. Mom, Dad, and Lia arrived, and we heard the clang of the heavy door behind us. Mom glanced at me and hurriedly stomped out her torch. Not that it mattered much—Marcello still had his. We all moved to the edges of the tunnel, knowing an archer would try to send his first arrow down the center.

Marcello handed me the torch. Lia and I stood behind our guys, who stood shoulder to shoulder.

Judging from the noise behind us, we'd only have one chance at this. *Please, God, please, God, please, God…*

"One, two, three," Marcello said. They ran toward the iron door at the end, and struck it together, Marcello with his left shoulder, Luca with his right.

The door immediately collapsed outward, with them on top of it.

Lia and I ran past them, all tough and SWAT-like, into a tiny piazza with a well at the center, searching in all directions for knights who would attack. But we only saw a tiny old woman, a cured ham in her hands. Her toothless mouth dropped open as she stared at us. But Marcello and Luca were already on the move. Clutching his shoulder as if it pained him, Marcello took my hand as Father Tomas, Mom, and Dad emerged. Luca resumed his position under Tomas's arm, and Marcello looked back at him. "Do you know where we are?" he asked the priest, glancing about the piazza. All around us were two-story houses, making it impossible to guess our location.

He shook his head. "I am a man of Firenze and the countryside. I've spent precious little time in Roma."

"We must get to Piazza Vesuvius," Marcello demanded of the little old woman. "How far is that?"

She drew up to her full height of perhaps four feet, ten inches, and gave him a Don't-You-Be-Impolite-With-Me look. In Italia, no young man spoke to older women in such a manner. I heard him groan, and he left my side to look down each of the four ways out of the piazza, seeking a landmark.

"*La chiedo scusa, ma siamo in pericolo,*" I tried. *I beg your pardon. But we are in danger...* "Can you tell us how to get to the Piazza Vesuvius, please?"

She gave Marcello another grandmotherly look of reproach and then glanced at me, in my crazy toga gown and hair down, sword in hand. "*Amdiamoci.*" *That way,* she said in a tone that said *enough with the crazy, rude kids these days,* hooking a thumb over her shoulder, toward one cobblestone street. She narrowly stepped aside to watch us all head out in a rush.

Dimly I wondered how long it would take her to connect the news of the second escape of Lady Betarrini from a forced wedding ceremony with the people she'd seen this night. I shivered as we reached the end of the street and saw the Tiber River. With one glance Marcello had his bearings, and after tucking my sword in his second sheath, he abruptly pulled me left.

We hurried as fast as we could, walking single file—except for Luca and Tomas—down the road that bordered the river. *How far?* I wondered. But I dared not ask. We were staying silent, trying not to attract any more attention than necessary.

But the bells behind us were ringing in alarm, and I kept getting curious looks at my dirty toga and hair—I was drawing entirely too much attention.

"We have to find you new clothes," Marcello said.

"A decoy," I returned. "Let us find a woman about my height, with dark hair. You have gold with you?"

He smiled back into my eyes, figuring out my plan. "I do. You intend to spend it?"

"I hope to." We hurried along, but few women were out at this hour, and those that we met were too short, too fat, too thin…until we met one that looked about right. "*Perdonami,*" I said. *Excuse me.* I touched her arm, and she glanced at me in such alarm and dis- taste, I took a breath in surprise. It was then I realized that everyone on the street believed I was a prostitute.

Marcello took over. "*Ho una proposta per lei.*" *I have a deal for you.* "I'll give you two gold florins if you trade your gown for my lady's costume."

She laughed as if he were crazy and looked me up and down, then back to him. "Her costume is worth nothing to me."

"But it is worth a great deal to us. Please, sell us your dress. Exchange it with my lady, and I shall pay you."

"Nay. If my neighbors, my friends were to see me in such a dress—"

"Three florins."

A gold florin had to be enough to feed a large family for what? A month? A year?

"Five," she dared.

"Four," he said, nudging her into a shop, me right behind. "But you must swear you'll wear the toga until morning."

"For four florins? I'd wear about anything," she quipped, looking back at him in the doorway.

Marcello smiled and told Luca and Lia to take the others to the stables and wait for us there, and then he followed us in. He slipped a coin over the merchant's counter, lifting a finger to his lips, and held a curtain aside to the narrow back storeroom, urging me to hurry. He let it drop closed behind me. In the gap between the curtain and door casing, I could see his back as he turned to guard us.

The girl turned to me and I hurriedly unhooked a line of twenty buttons down the dress, then untied the rope at my waist, smiling as I saw that it had left a line of white where it had protected the dirt-stained cloth. *I really was the dirtiest bride on record....*

"What happened to you, m'lady?" she whispered, as we traded gowns.

"'Tis better for you if you do not know. All you shall say, if you are discovered, is that you were paid handsomely for your old dress. No one shall blame you for accepting such an offer."

She smiled, curiosity alive in her eyes, as she turned and slipped on the toga, while I did the same with her gown, nearly gagging at the scent of BO. I concentrated on breathing through my mouth, not my nose. *Not that she's getting a precious, laundry-fresh dress, herself...* She'd have to burn it when she got home. With four gold coins she could purchase five new dresses and still have a total stash left over.

While she buttoned me up, I wound my hair into a knot and took the carved pins she offered me. When I turned back around, I smiled at the sight of her hair down around her shoulders. "Frightfully similar," I said.

"It's an honor to resemble Lady Betarrini," she guessed in a whisper.

"Remember," I said, shaking my head in warning, but smiling a little, "I never said so. And we were gone before you could sound an alarm."

"Like poof! Phantoms, or wolves," she said with another smile.

"Come," Marcello said, reaching through for my arm. "We must be on our way." He nodded to our friend and the merchant, and we left the store. It was then I noticed the neatly wrapped package beneath his arm. With my hand on his as we paraded down the street, we appeared the average Roman merchant and lady, returning home after a market stop. I froze as I saw a patrol of twelve Roman knights cantering around the corner ahead of us, but Marcello urged me on. "Continue to walk, Gabriella," he said lowly, smiling and leaning closer to kiss my temple. "We belong here. I am staring at you, showing the world how in love with you I am," he coached. "And you are watching the guards approach with interest, as if there's nothing to hide...."

I dragged my eyes from the cobblestones at my feet.

"Interesting, the commotion," he whispered, as the knights neared, "first the bells, now the soldiers, searching." He looked up with me then, to watch as the knights rode by, checking us out, then dismissing us, exactly as he had planned.

"Next time I get to be the girl in love, too distracted to watch," I complained.

He laughed, and we picked up our pace. After we passed two more streets, we turned left and then directly right, into an alley that stank of manure. *The stables must be ahead.*

We emerged on the small square, with feeding and watering troughs on either end, and I saw that my parents, Lia, Luca, and Tomas were all mounted. "Up you go," Marcello said, lifting me to my mount and handing me the reins as I slipped my feet into the stirrups. The saddle had a scabbard, and I slid my sword into it, hiding it quickly under my skirts as the stable master came outside. He was chewing on a loaf of bread, watching us go.

"For your silence," Marcello said, flipping a coin into the air toward him.

He caught it, eyed Marcello, and smiled a close-lipped smile.

# Chapter Nineteen

"All we must do is make it to the city walls," Marcello said, leading our line out.

*No problem,* I thought. The city walls were still a mile or two distant, and now other bells were ringing. How long until word reached every citizen that we had escaped? Lord Vivaro had to be as mad as the Red Queen in *Alice in Wonderland,* and Lord Barbato...well, I could seriously see him mouthing the words *heads will roll,* at that very instant.

*Yeah, good luck, losers.* In the company of my homies, I'd wager my chances any day. Even with Dad—so new to this time and their rough ways—and Father Tomas, weak from blood loss, together, we were strong.

And it was different from escaping Firenze that fateful night; most of Roma's citizens took idle interest in us but really didn't care one way or another if we lived or died. And they wouldn't likely risk their own necks to capture us—we were Firenze's enemies, not theirs.

Unless word of a reward spread. I sighed. If there was one thing Lords Barbato and Vivaro had, it was a seemingly endless supply of money. To throw lavish parties. Rebuild Roman baths. Hire mercenaries. And, surely, offer rewards. Lord Barbato knew he could ill afford our escape from Roma. Once we were gone, we'd be ten times as difficult to capture. And his dreams about making me the conquered bride of Firenze? Yeah, that was already down the drain.

But he'd have a better chance of killing us than capturing us. After what I'd been through, there was no way they were taking me alive again. And I guessed my family and friends felt the same way. What was better? To fight to the death? Or to be put to the stake after all kinds of humiliation or torture?

Death, every time. Not that I was up for the whole dying thing. I wanted to live. I'd be willing to fight to the death in order to live—in freedom, with Marcello, with my family. I suddenly understood all the campaign talk from home, of fighting for what you believed in, fighting for rights, fighting for freedom, fighting, paradoxically, for peace.

*Peace* sounded like a delicious dream to me right then, sucking me inward, backward, toward the utter weariness at my core. We were drawing long looks from those still on the street, our band of men and women, so many of us in matching robes and capes, stolen from the lords of Roma. But we ignored them, trotting down one street and then the next. Marcello paused up ahead, circled his horse, and silently waved us back. We turned and all made it into an alley before a Roman patrol of a couple dozen men passed. Marcello dismounted and sneaked to the corner to find out what they were up to; he returned and reported they were pausing to speak to those on the streets, asking questions. Looking for us. Trying to pick up our trail.

"Must make haste, now," he said under his breath. It'd only be minutes—maybe even seconds—before they crossed one of the streets from which we'd come, and someone tipped them off, told them we'd been seen.

We rode at a fast clip, under a raised, crumbling aqueduct and past the countless brick arches of Emperor Caracalla's old public bathhouse. *Almost there,* I thought, knowing the wall wasn't far. The knights of Roma would not pursue us beyond the wall, and Lord Barbato's and Vivaro's mercenaries made up only a fraction of their number. If we could make the wall, we'd break from most of the men who hunted us.

We turned the corner, glimpsed the repaired wall that marked the main entrance to the eternal city, had just taken a breath of hope, glory, when I saw them.

Men closing ranks, on horseback, fifty strong. Blocking our exit. Preparing to hunt us down. But they still hadn't seen us.

"This way," Marcello growled. We followed him into Caracalla's old structure—once a sprawling, public bathhouse that could handle a thousand customers at once—ducking under lower doorways, marveling at the massive rooms they led to. When we were into the third room, Marcello turned to Luca and lifted his chin. "Take Lia with you. I'll take Gabriella. We'll leave two horses here and make the Romans think we're here somewhere, so they'll scour every rabbit hole in the place."

I slid over to his mount and wrapped an arm around his waist. He reached for my sword from the saddle of my horse. "You may need this," he said grimly.

Our freed mounts whinnied and hurried into the next room, which was roofless. The floor bloomed with winter grass, and they waded into it like they'd found a field all their own. We rushed on, hit a dead end, and doubled back, then moved to a new segment of the old bathhouse's ruins. The complex was massive, one of Roma's hot spots back in the Empire's heyday. But as Marcello turned one corner and then the next, I felt like we were going in circles. We'd left the central structure with its towering hundred-foot walls and entered a complex maze to one side.

Then, all at once, we were out, and I took a deep breath, glimpsing stars just beginning to glitter overhead. Marcello abruptly turned and waited for the rest of our party to catch up, then led us back into the bathhouse. "Scouts," he grunted as explanation.

We walked down another massive, crumbling hallway, and I grimaced at the sound of horse hooves against the mosaic tiles, imagining the sound echoing down to those who now ran through these old halls, swords in hands, shouting, *Hey, they're over here!*

My eyes went down every dark passageway, and I squinted, trying to see if there was an enemy coming our way. A couple times, squatters, Roma's homeless, rose, making me catch my breath—once an old man, then an entire family. But they only stood to see who we were, what we were up to, alarmed by our after-dark intrusion.

We paused and then dipped down through a trough where a column must have fallen and been removed, and then another. I looked back, trying to see the three horses behind Luca and Lia, but it was getting too dark. *Stay with us, Mom and Dad!* I wanted to call.

Marcello abruptly stopped and stayed deadly still, staring to our left, just past the wall, beyond where I could see. From what I *could* see, we'd emerged a third of the way back, on the city wall side of the complex. *How'd he get us here through that maze?* I wondered in admiration. Maybe he'd played here as a child.

Satisfied, or maybe seeing some knights move away, he edged forward, peeking left. "You look to our right," he said quietly.

I did as he asked, staring so hard down the dark road that I began to see things in the dark. Over and over he paused when I tensed. Over and over I said, "*Non c'importa.*" *It's nothing.* When the rest of our party was out of the bathhouse complex, we moved down the road to our left, the city wall on our right side. We were heading toward Circus Maximus and the next gate, still a quarter mile distant. We rode hard, half-expecting troops to come after us. But after another couple minutes I dared to believe that Marcello had done it—that he'd fooled them into thinking that we were still inside the complex, hiding away.

He unexpectedly veered left and rode into the old arena, where the road began to slope down and we could clearly see a scary, dual-towered, double-walled gate, opening and closing. We were still in shadow so we were certain they could not see us. There were four knights along the wall at the top of the gate, two on each round tower and four on the ground. "These gates are never guarded," Marcello muttered to Luca, pulling our horse to a stop and waving at the knights in disgust. "They search for us."

"We could ride until we find a portion of the wall that's fallen down," Luca said.

"I don't remember many such sections on this side of the city, do you?"

Luca thought about it a moment and then shook his head. "On the other side, it's mostly down. This side?"

His eyes said *notsomuch.*

"We must be away," Marcello said grimly, as the others pulled in closer. "If we are discovered—we'll have more than we can handle.

Here," he said, gesturing toward the gate again, "we know the number we must battle. Are you willing?"

He eyed them all, and in the dark we could see their bobbing heads. "Gabriella?" he asked over his shoulder.

In answer I dropped to the ground beside his horse, as Lia had done from Luca's. "Go, m'lord. I shall follow." He'd be twice as effective if I wasn't on the horse with him. And Lia needed more room to wield her bow and arrow.

"How many can you take down?" I asked her.

"Two, before they know we're here," she said, eying the towers. Two riders had come in, hard, from the direction of the bathhouses, paused, then moved on, apparently gathering reports.

"That'll leave ten," Mom said.

"And I'll have time to take down two more, once they know we're approaching," Lia added.

"Which leaves eight," Dad said.

"It's as good as done, then," Luca said with sarcastic enthusiasm. "Shall we?"

Marcello moved ahead, watched for a moment, and then waved us onward. Lia and I crept forward, through knee-high grass, bent over. On foot we wanted to be farther ahead. The horses would pass us when they saw the first two guards fall, then they would hold the gates until we were through.

We were a hundred yards away, then fifty. The knights appeared to be watching for horses on the road, to their left and right, rather than anyone in the grass before them. It looked funny to see guards facing the city rather than any who might be approaching from beyond—guarding the exit more than the entrance. Lia licked her finger and lifted it, testing for breezes. "They'd kill us if they had the chance, right?" she asked, aiming at the first one.

"Without a second's hesitation," I said, knowing well why she hesitated. "It's us or them. And if we don't get out of here fast, it's likely to be us."

"That's what I thought you'd say," she said, letting the first arrow fly and, without stopping, drawing another and releasing it. We rose and ran toward the gate, yelling like banshees. The men, startled, looked scared, and then, as we entered the farthest reaches of their torchlight, about thirty yards away, they laughed and pointed, thinking it was merely two crazy women. No Roman man in his right mind would ever admit to fear of a woman, be they She-Wolves or not....

Three strode toward us, grinning in anticipation.

But their smiles faded as Lia bent to aim again and I kept coming, just as the four on horseback came charging past me. *Four.*

It gradually registered with me that one was missing. *Where is Tomas?* I paused just as I met the first knight, who had dodged Luca's strike. He kept coming toward me. Distracted, I belatedly raised my sword just in time to meet his, and then turned to bring my sword around in an arcing strike; I put everything I had into it. He deflected it easily and advanced on me.

I frowned in surprise. *I must be more tired than I thought.* It'd been a few days since I'd slept, really slept...since before Sansicino. And now, at the very worst time, I was feeling it.

I met his strike, ducked another, deflected the last.

And then Dad was there. "I've got this," he said through clenched teeth. "Go, Gabi."

Dad. My dad. Saving me. I took a few steps back, sword dragging along the ground, suddenly weighing a thousand pounds, and I panted, wondering at what exactly had transpired. In the last two weeks we'd gone back in time, saved my father before he died, brought him back nearly seven hundred years, and now he was saving me. It was enough to make my head burst.

I glanced back. Father Tomas neared, but only because his horse was following us. Somewhat. He got close enough, and I could see he was slumped over in the saddle, unconscious. I forced myself to run toward him, took the reins from his slack hands, pulled his boot from the nearest stirrup and mounted behind him. I looked over his shoulder and quickly felt for a pulse.

*Alive, he's alive, Lord. Help me save him. Save us all.*

I saw that Marcello had opened the gate, while Mom, Dad, Luca, and Lia still battled the last four knights. I glanced right and saw a patrol of Roman guards charging down the road toward us. I kicked Father Tomas's gelding with my heels and held on to him, knowing that to do so meant I couldn't defend us on the way through. It was either Father Tomas or the sword. And we'd never be this far if it wasn't for the priest. I wasn't leaving him behind.

Marcello saw me coming and opened the gate wider.

I pulled right, narrowly missing Luca as he took a blow and took several staggering steps backward. I then tugged left, just missing getting hit by Mom's staff as I passed. And then I was passing Marcello. "Patrol, approaching fast!" I cried, pushing through.

I steeled myself for the strike of an arrow in my back and did not pause until I was out of the reach of any torchlight. Only then, when I felt nothing, heard nothing, saw nothing, did I pull our galloping horse to a stop and wheel him around. The gates were still partially open, and in that span of about four feet, I could see glimpses of my loved ones still battling their attackers. I saw Marcello's guy go down, saw Marcello leap over the body and then disappear.

*Come on. Come on!* That patrol had to be almost on top of them by now. They hadn't been that far away. *Come on!*

I willed them to come through the gates.

*Please, Lord, please, help them. Release them. Free them!*

Lia emerged first, running with a limp, her right hand on her left shoulder. Luca charged through behind her, on his horse. He shouted to her, and she turned and lifted her right arm. Never pausing, he grabbed it, and she swung through the air in a crazy arc, landing squarely on the back of his horse. He continued to push the horse forward, toward me, toward the safety of the darkness. But I was looking past him, waiting for Mom, Dad.

And Marcello.

I slid from my horse's back.

I could hear the roar of men's cries. The patrol. My eyes filled with tears. I couldn't breathe. I was in full-blown panic. But I could not stop myself. I had no resources, no walls left. I let out a sob and ran past Luca and Lia. I had to go to them. Help them. Save them.

"M'lady!" Luca cried. I heard his grunt as he jumped from his horse before they'd come to a full stop. But I did not turn.

"M'lady!"

"Gabi! No! Stop!" Lia cried.

But I could see them now, my parents, Marcello, in a small circle, each meeting strike after strike, through the four-foot gap of the gate. I had to get to them. Help them.

I found my momentum, my last bit of strength, truly in a wolf-like fury at seeing my loved ones in such danger. *There is no way… No… Way…*

Luca tackled me, then. We rolled in the soft, sandy, dried grass, over and over before we came to a stop. I gasped for breath, the wind knocked out of me.

"We'll go!" he cried, already on his knees, then his feet. "But you stay here! It is what Marcello wanted!"

They ran on, he and Lia, and I turned, still wondering if my lungs would ever again draw breath. I saw Lia kneel, aim, and an arrow sail through the gate. Then another, on Luca's far side as he ran, the perspective almost making it look as though she had struck him instead.

I finally took a ragged breath, choked by my tears and panic, and then another, sounding more the asthmatic than any warrior. I forced myself to my feet as Luca and then Lia disappeared behind the gates again.

Held my breath while I couldn't see any of them for a second, two, three…

Sobbed again and ran forward, dragging my sword like a drunken knight, madly seeking one, just one of my people in the four-foot gap. But all I saw were Roman soldiers, Roman soldiers, Roman soldiers…

I paused, wondering if my loved ones were gone, dead.

A chill ran down my back.

*What good is freedom if not one of the people I love is with me?*

# Chapter Twenty

I was running again, a foreign cry in my throat—had I morphed into a real wolf now?—charging toward the gate. Twenty feet away, fifteen, ten, when I was again waylaid.

An arm encircled my waist and hauled me backward, kicking and screaming.

Gradually I understood the voice behind me was one of a friend, calming, soothing, desperately trying to reach me. "M'lady, 'tis I, Georgii."

"And I, Lutterius," said another.

I looked up through my tears, and gradually focused on the first, and then his twin brother—the funny scouts that had led the way to Sansicino. Georgii looked into my eyes, as if knowing my thoughts exactly. "Let us see to it, m'lady."

"Remain here," said his brother.

He gruffly handed me to a third man as they charged forward, swords raised. My heart pulsed painfully as twenty of our men joined them.

My eyes rose to a silver-haired, older knight I recognized. Captain Pezzati. "M'lady," he said, giving me that heart-softening smile, "your trial is at an end. We are here." He gestured behind him, and for the first time, I saw that we were not alone.

Behind him was row after row of knights, Siena's finest, on horseback, on foot, carrying torches, flags, shields, swords, bows.

A hundred, no, a *thousand* strong.

I gasped and fell to my knees, my hands over my mouth, trying to catch my breath as my tears began anew.

The man bent, caught me by my waist, and lifted me to a standing position. He slowly turned toward the men, and they cheered. "Lift your sword!" Captain Pezzati said in my ear. "Marcello's men need you now. To know that you are well. Whole."

It was about the last thing I wanted to do—to raise my thirty-pound sword when my whole body felt about as strong as a giant wet noodle.

But I did it. For my family. For Marcello and Luca.

And to be honest, even with the captain beside me, helping to hold my noodle-like elbow up, tears streamed down my cheeks as I stared across the men, lifting my sword higher and higher. It was what I saw beyond the Sienese knights in uniform that brought on the waterworks. Not only was the paid guard here. Hundreds of citizens followed behind.

"She-Wolf! She-Wolf! She-Wolf!"

I turned and was vaguely aware that Captain Pezzati continued to hold me upright, like a ventriloquist with a doll come to life.

I dragged my eyes to the gate and saw movement. Was that—?

And then I saw them striding through, their horses lost. I recognized them by silhouette. Mom, with Lia. Dad. Luca.

Marcello and the twins.

How had all my loved ones escaped?

"Whoa," said the captain beside me as I tried to move, faltered. I pushed his hands away as if my weakness was his fault. I stumbled forward, rose, and limped through the mushy grass toward them, knowing the guy was right behind me.

Mom and Lia reached me first, and we fell into a tearful embrace. Dad came next, wrapping us all with his long arms. I stood there a moment, despite the circumstances, caught in the sensation of being enveloped, entwined with the three people I'd loved longest.

Then Luca was there, shyly taking Lia's hand. She stepped away, a little bashful, letting Luca wrap his arm around her shoulders as they walked toward the men. The men cheered anew and then hushed as the Roman guards began filing out, taking formation before the wall. Hundreds poured out, like dry sand from a funnel.

I turned to face Marcello and the twins, then I stepped forward, and he was sweeping me into his arms, lifting me, cradling my neck, leaning down to kiss me soundly. The men exploded in cheers. Even my dad was laughing, in that unique way that was his, what I had so missed when he was gone....

But my eyes were on Marcello as he carried me, striding toward the men, who fell into tighter formation. I lifted my hand to his cheek and smiled. "You have no idea how good it is to be in your arms, Marcello. How much I missed you."

"Did it feel like half your heart was gone?"

"Yes." I nodded.

"Hmm. I might have experienced that. And more." He set me on my feet in front of the men, but his eyes were still on me. "Except my *whole* heart was gone." He looked up to the twins, on horseback. "See Lady Gabriella and her family, as well as the priest, to the back of our troops. Guard them yourselves, and bring twelve with you to make sure no one gets to them."

"Consider it done, m'lord," said Georgii. He offered his arm to me, and reluctantly I let him lead me through the sea of men that split before us. I glanced back for one more view of Marcello before the men blocked him from my sight again. I noticed that Lutterius, who followed behind, looked as though he was being punished, cut out of the action.

"Come now, 'tis not that bad, Lutterius," I said. "Many, many people wish to kill us. I'd wager you'll have to wield your sword to save us again before sunup." I giggled, recognizing that I was punchy, silly, but unable to stop myself.

"Pay her no heed," Lia said, rolling her eyes. "She has endured much."

"'Twould be an honor to defend you, m'lady," Georgii said. "We failed you once; we shall not fail you again."

"You did not fail us," I said tiredly. "We were merely outwitted in Sansicino. For a moment." I raised a finger as well as an eyebrow. "*That* is what *I* shall not let happen again."

"Until it does," Lia said with a laugh.

I giggled with her. She shook her head, and we finally reached the last group of men. Several huddled around Father Tomas, and they rose as we neared.

I fell to my knees on the blanket that was spread beneath Tomas and felt for his pulse as the men cheered behind us, responding to something Marcello was yelling a hundred yards away. He was revving them up, getting them psyched—for what? To take on the remnant of Rome? I glanced over my shoulder, and Dad looked down at me. "Let him handle it," he said lowly in English. "He knows what he's doing."

I held his gaze a moment and smiled. So he liked him. Respected him. A little.

I turned back to Tomas and leaned down, listening at his mouth to hear how he was breathing, but I had to rely on the rise and fall of his chest instead to know that he was still alive. It was far too noisy to hear. Mom kneeled on the other side of him. "See anything?" I asked as I pointed. "His wound was that side, that shoulder."

"Some blood," she said. "Arrow wound?"

"Yes. It went clean through." I reached under my skirt for my dagger, then remembered it had been taken at Lord Vivaro's. "Do you have a knife?"

She smiled and reached for her own, strapped to her calf. "Some girl taught me to carry one here. 'Tis quite handy." She set it in my open palm and I went over to Father Tomas's head and began cutting away the fabric of his brown robe. Once I had a flap cut out, I gently tugged on it and winced as it stuck to his skin, lifting it upward like a tent. Blood immediately began to spread again. "Dang," I said. "I cauterized it, but his robe…it's stuck in it. Fused with it, almost. We're going to need to get it off of him."

"Let's see how his back is first," she said. Luca helped us lift him to a sitting position, and I quickly cut one shoulder from his robe, exposing the entire front and back.

"Well, that's an entirely new fashion for a priest," Luca quipped, eyebrows raised.

I gave him a smile but then gently edged the fabric away, wincing as if it was my own skin tearing with the movement. "Can someone fetch us water? And clean bandages?"

"I could sew him up," Lia said, hovering over us.

"You've done that once," I said, remembering the giant whip-stitches she'd sewn into my side. "I think your surgical days are over."

"Fine," she said, sniffing. "But don't say I didn't offer."

The men cheered again. Then we heard the Romans, doing the same.

"Come on, Marcello," I muttered to myself as I stared at the amount of fabric still stuck in Father Tomas's wound. "Tell 'em we have no fight with them, and let's go home."

"He's lost a great deal of blood," Mom said doubtfully.

"He is my friend. And I will not lose anyone I love this night."

"Well, *okay*," she said.

I closed my eyes, and I pinched the bridge of my nose. "I'm sorry." I looked at Tomas from the side, hunched over, chin on chest. "This man, Mom…he has more to teach me. I feel it, deep inside me. He's already taught me some things that will stay with me forever. I don't want to lose him—not just for me. But for all of us. He's *supposed* to be with us. Just as clearly as we're supposed to be here, in this time. Does that make sense?"

Her eyes met mine across the broad expanse of his back. "I think it does."

"Good. Then…I'm so tired, I can hardly see straight. Can you see to him? See him through this night?"

"We will," Dad said, crouching beside me. He touched my shoulder. "Why don't you lie down, Gabi, before you fall over?"

"I think...I think that might..."

*Be a good idea...*

So it was fairly uncool for a battle hero, the symbol of a province, the source of Siena's pride, to basically pass out.

But there it was—I did.

Flat out, cold.

I knew it, remembered it all, as I came to, feeling my shoulder and hamstring ache with every bounce of the stretcher I was on, suspended between two horses. I looked up, saw my sister on the horse behind me, his nose over my calves as he walked, and lay back, groaning. I was basically suspended on a stretcher that hung from the rump of one horse and hung at an angle to attach beneath the neck of Lia's. I'd seen it once or twice in battle.

My head ached as if it were splitting open.

"Wh-what happened?" I forced myself to raise my head and squint at Lia, a brilliant blur of light with the sun right behind her.

"Fainted, passed out, dissolved," Lia said, teasing me.

"M-Marcello?" I tried to look up and over my shoulder, but realized then that I was strapped in. Probably so I wouldn't fall off.

"Nay, 'tis me, m'lady," Luca's voice said. He was on the front horse. He paused. "Marcello's on his way. I see him now."

"What about the b-battle?"

"The Romans gave it up. Retreated behind their wall again." I looked to my right and saw Georgii and knew before I looked to the left that Lutterius would be on my other side, fulfilling their promise to guard us. "They weren't intent on a fight, not truly," Georgii said.

"Good," I said. "I've had my fill of battles."

"Once they lost you, they lost their fight," said Lutterius. "It was always about you, m'lady. And 'twasn't even their claim to make. They were merely puppets, working for Lord Vivaro…"

"Yes, well," I said, "I am glad it came to a peaceful end. If you'd be so kind as to assist me, I can now rise." I struggled beneath the ropes, instantly feeling claustrophobic when they felt as though they were growing tighter.

It brought back too many memories, of being captured, hauled away, imprisoned…

"Hold on!" Lia cried, bringing her horse to a stop. "Gabriella, stop!"

I was frantic, beside myself, *out* of myself, trying to claw my way to freedom, kicking, crying.

"Gabi, wait!" Mom said sternly, now beside me, edging past Georgii.

I stilled at her voice, panting. I could feel my nostrils flaring, like a cornered, lassoed wolf. She set to my ropes, easily untying one, then the other.

I flung them aside, stepped off the stretcher, and stumbled. The stretcher was higher off the ground than I thought. Lutterius grabbed my arm, intending to help me, but I brushed him off and took several strides away, my hands at the sides of my head.

I was angry, furious, trembling I was so mad…and yet it wasn't at them…

I cried out then. Screamed at the sky, releasing all the pent-up fear and frustration and fury inside me. And then I screamed again. I don't know how long I went on before I realized that our entire army stood still, waiting for me to stop, wondering what was wrong with me. I glanced up at them and then away, to the hills. Was that Orvieto, high on the cliffs? I glimpsed Marcello on horseback, racing toward me.

He knew, then. I was awake. And losing it.

I panted, hyperventilating, thinking of the men who had been just west of here, coming after me, encircling me, closing in.

I stumbled away, in the direction of a group of trees in the middle of a field, ignoring my family's calls, remembering Captain Ruisi striding toward me, batting away my strikes, so easily tossing them aside, taking hold, taking me…

And then he was there, grabbing me again.

I screamed and kicked, fighting his hold, but he held strong, unmoving. Kissing me. Whispering to me. "Gabriella, Gabriella, 'tis me. Your own. Beloved, come back to me. You are safe. You are well. Gabriella…"

I stilled, but I went on weeping, crying as hard as the day I learned Dad died.

But it was Marcello who held me, not Captain Ruisi.

I slowly understood. It was like one had morphed into the other. Blond hair became brown. Blue eyes, chocolate.

"Mar-Marcello," I sobbed.

His grip eased as he sensed me relax, and I turned and buried my face in his chest, weeping. "I…I was so frightened," I explained. "The ropes—it brought back…"

"Memories," he finished for me, his tone tight, even as his hand stroked my head, my face, my back. "'Tis all right, beloved. All right. All will be well in time. Shh, now. Shh."

"They threatened…I thought…you and I…"

"Would never be together again," he said.

I nodded. A ridiculous, embarrassing sob left my throat, and he pulled me closer instead of pushing me away. He picked me up in his arms then and carried me the rest of the way to the grove of oak trees. He sat down on a fallen log and cradled me close, held me tight, until there were no more tears to wipe away.

This was how out of it I was: I didn't even care that I was red-faced, swollen, and snot-nosed from my sob-fest. All I cared about was him, his arms, holding me. Here, I felt safe, for the first time in what felt like years.

"Hold me like this forever," I begged, sounding like a forlorn, lost little girl, but unable to stop my pathetic pleading.

"I'd like to," he said tenderly, running his hand through my hair and tucking a tendril behind my ear, "but there is the fact that we're still a day's journey from home." He gave me a rueful smile. "Would you have us abide in this tiny grove forever? When we are yet in Umbria, not Toscana?"

I closed my eyes and sniffed, so weary again that I thought I might nod off right there. "Wherever you are is home to me, Marcello," I mumbled.

He bent and reverently kissed my eyelids, first one and then the other, and I left them closed, wanting to remember the feel of his lips upon them. "And my home is with you, Gabriella," he whispered.

I felt him stiffen, and I opened my eyes as he raised me to a sitting position.

My parents.

"She has come to herself again," Marcello said, awkwardly trying to set me on my feet from his lap.

"We are grateful to you, m'lord," Mom said, but her eyes—intense with fear—were on me. Dad frowned beside her. "We can see to her now."

"As you wish, m'lady," Marcello said.

He took my hand and set it in Mom's. Dad's arm came around my waist.

"I shall not be far, Gabriella," Marcello said. "And this night you shall rest in my mother's chambers in Castello Forelli. With a few days' rest, all will be well. You have been most sorely taxed. Far more has been demanded of you than any woman I know. It ends this day."

He bowed his head and then eased away. He was promising safety. Recuperation time.

Exactly what I was so desperate for.

But why was I feeling like something else entirely had just come down?

# Chapter Twenty-one

I awakened in Lady Forelli's chambers. I sat up and blinked my eyes several times, wondering if I was still dreaming. There were parts of the room that I recognized as that of Castello Forelli—the gray-white stone blocks, the wood of the window casings—but I'd never been in these quarters before. Maybe they'd sealed it off after Marcello's mother died; maybe it was too painful for Marcello's dad to have anyone in it.

I was in the middle of an enormous bed with four elaborately carved posts. Beneath me was some sort of feather layer—it was, by far, the most comfortable mattress I'd been on since I'd arrived. Most were straw ticks, stiff and a bit itchy. On top of me was another down-stuffed blanket, and a wool one on top of that. I pulled them up to my chin, feeling the chill of the massive room, even with a fire burning low in a corner fireplace.

On the far wall was a tapestry, twenty feet wide, twelve feet high, depicting lords and ladies on a picnic, but the intricate threads in colors of gray, blue, and white made the warm scene feel cold to me. The only other decoration on the walls was a crucifix, in silver.

I saw that someone had left me a pitcher of water and a pewter mug. I sat up and poured a glass, gulped it down and then another, my throat parched. Then I pulled on a dressing gown around me—*who changed me last night?*—and slipped my feet into ballet-like slippers. I went to the window and unlatched the three sets of latches on the shutters, then opened it wide. I was looking south, toward Roma. But all I could see was fog clinging to the brown and green hills below me. I peered over the edge—I was on the second floor, at the back of the castle. Knights loitered below me, on duty, trying to keep moving, stay warm. They were clearly bored.

*Bored is good,* I thought numbly. I'd had it with the fighting-for-our-lives thing. Maybe we were through it. Forever. Maybe we could settle into regular medieval life now. Embrace life while not having to battle for it every other day. *Yeah, that'd be nice.*

The door opened, and Giacinta came through with a tray in her hands. "Oh, m'lady!" she said in surprise, as if she didn't expect to see me at all, let alone up and about. "You're awake!"

"I am," I said with a smile. *Why's she* so excited? *Because we are all back, home in the castle?*

She scurried over to me. "Please, m'lady, come away from the window. You'll catch a chill." She took my hand and led me to a wide, ornate chair by the fire before throwing a log on the glowing coals, covering my lap with a blanket, and returning to the window to close it up tight.

"'Tis good to see you, Giacinta," I said. "I've thought of you often."

"As it is to see you, m'lady," she returned.

"Was it quite trying, your time away?"

"We managed." She studied me. "The entire valley is celebrating our lord and lady's rightful return, regardless of our somber weather. But when you didn't awake, we were so concerned—"

"Wait. What do you mean by such words?"

Her eyes widened. "Why, m'lady, you fell back into your deep slumber on your way to the castello and did not wake yesterday. Your mother said you were fiercely exhausted."

I nodded and accepted a mug of warm porridge from her. I ached from head to toe. Like I'd been in a car accident. Giacinta bustled around, making my bed and fetching a gown from a massive armoire at the far end of the room.

"Your sister slept by your side that first night, but she said you thrashed about too much to do it again." Her delicate eyebrows lifted and knit together. "Your dreams must have been most vivid."

I tried to remember them but could not. But maybe that was why I was so fuzzy-headed. Besides sleeping so long, I had probably been wrestling with nightmares.

"Is everyone well?" I asked. "All those who arrived with us?"

"Indeed. I heard in the kitchen that Father Tomas is sitting up and feeling much better."

I smiled. "That is good news. And what of…Castello Paratore?" I had to force myself to ask it. "Firenze? Do they move against us?"

She shook her head in surprise. "They have made no move to try to reclaim Castello Forelli. Mayhap they have accepted that Lord Fortino's sacrifice"—she paused to cross herself somberly—"was a steep enough price to pay." She drew more fully upright. "With all of Siena behind Lord Marcello, they dare not attack us again. Still, Lord Marcello is taking all necessary precautions. There is no cause for you to fret, m'lady."

"I see. Thank you, Giacinta."

She bobbed her head. "Would you like me to fetch a tub and hot water so you can take a proper bath? I did what I could while you slept—"

"That would be lovely," I said.

"I'll see to it right away," she said, with another quick bob. And then she was gone.

I forced myself to eat the rest of the porridge, knowing I'd feel better if I did, even if I didn't feel hungry. A few minutes later a soft knock sounded at my door, and Mom peeked in. "Ah, Gabi. I'm so glad you are awake."

I forced a smile—not wanting her to know I'd hoped she was Marcello—and waited for her to approach. She was in a fine gown I recognized as one of Lady Forelli's. I'd almost worn it once myself. She looked regal, stately, and she gave me a big hug and kiss before sitting in the chair beside me. "Brr, it's cold in here," she said.

I unfolded the blanket on my lap, sharing it with her. "Here," I said.

She smiled and tucked it on the far side of her lap, then lifted her hands to the crackling fire. "That feels good."

"It does," I said.

"How are you feeling?" she asked, turning to stroke my hair with her left hand and look into my eyes.

"Like I was run over by a semi."

She nodded. "I understand. I endured about a tenth of what you did and am feeling the same way. But then I have twenty years on you. I'll fetch some foxglove tea for you in a bit. You ate something?"

"Some oatmeal," I said.

"Good girl. In a few days, with proper rest, I bet you'll feel yourself again."

*Myself again.* Who was that exactly? What was that? I was so terribly weary. Weary was the only word for it. It was far different than tired. It was a bone-deep-ache kind of whupped.

"Gabi, your dad and I want to talk to you, when you're feeling a little better."

"About what?" I could feel the tension start to take hold in my neck.

"About the future. Your future. And ours. On the road…coming back here…"

"I lost it," I said numbly.

She nodded and turned to stare into the fire as I was doing. "It's understandable, Gabs. You've been through so much. But it—"

"Scared you," I finished for her. I knew what she meant. It had scared me, too. Left me in this numb place.

"Yes," she said, daring to look at me again. I glanced at her and saw there were tears in her big, blue eyes. Normally that'd make me tear up too—I'd inherited my dad's Kleenex response to Hallmark commercials—but it was like I was watching us from the corner of the room. Observing. Not feeling.

"I know you think you want to stay here, but—"

"I do want to stay here." I knew that. Regardless of what else seemed to be adrift in my mind right now, my heart had only one goal—to be with Marcello.

"R-right," she said. "It's only that your father and I would like to see you in a safe place. A place of peace." She shook her head. "We don't want to see you like you were, you know…"

"Freaking out."

"We don't want to see that again. We're worried about you, Gabriella. Seriously worried."

I nodded and took a deep breath. I wanted to deny it, to tell her it was fine, just a really, *really* bad moment for me. But it wasn't the truth. In that moment, as I walked toward the oak trees, as I struggled with Marcello's arms around me—I had literally thought he was Captain Ruisi capturing me again. *Psychotic* and *break* would be a couple of keywords I'd type into WebMD.com, if I was back home. *Panic* and *attack* would be two others.

"I understand, Mom. Give me a few days, though?"

"You've got 'em, kiddo. We're here for you. If you need to talk…"

"Thanks," I said after a moment's hesitation. I loved my mom, and she loved me. But I couldn't remember the last time she'd tossed out the classic "If You Ever Need to Talk" opener. Was that a symbol of our new relationship, here in old Toscana? Or because she was really, really freaked out about me?

I pushed the thought away. It was too much to think about, yet. It only made me want to crawl back into bed and sleep through the afternoon. There was one thing that kept me from it. "Have you seen Marcello?"

"He is out with Luca and the other knights, securing the perimeters, reestablishing boundaries between Castello Paratore and Castello Forelli."

I looked at her quickly. "It is safe?"

"It seems so. At the moment, anyway. Marcello said he'd be back by supper. It was good for him to go—he spent all of yesterday pacing the hall outside your room."

I smiled sadly. That was a pathetic way for anyone to spend the day. But I could picture him doing just that, fretting about me. "Giacinta seemed to think that Firenze has chosen to honor our move back into Castello Forelli."

"It seems so."

I heard the hesitation behind her words. "Or…"

"Or they only want us to think that."

I sighed. Meaning, of course, that they wanted to lull us into a relaxed state so we wouldn't be ready when they attacked.

Giacinta walked back through the door, leading six servants, carrying a tub between them and bucket upon bucket of steaming water. They emptied eight buckets into the wooden tub and left two for me to rinse with.

"I'll leave you now and be back in an hour with that foxglove tea," Mom said.

"'Kay."

I thanked the servants then and bolted the door before slipping into the steaming water, so hot that I had to get in gingerly, inch by inch, getting used to it. But the extreme heat felt good to me, as if I was scalding off the memories I wished to forget. And the water was easing the tension from my neck and the pain from my body.

I glanced down at my right shoulder and winced. A massive green and blue bruise covered it like a cap sleeve. From when I dived into Lord Zinicola's quarters, I assumed. There were others. On my arms and legs—some as wide as five inches. I had no idea where I'd gotten many of them. Running. Fleeing. Fighting.

I took a deep breath and went under the water, feeling the heat seep through my greasy hair and down to my scalp, over my face, into my ears.

And for a moment I relished the sound of nothing but the pulse of my heart in my own ears, reminding me that I was alive.

I wanted to wait for Marcello on the castle wall, for him to see me as soon as he was within view. But the knights would hear nothing of it, since Marcello had given them strict orders to keep me entirely out of sight. I supposed it was wise; I was a bit of a flag waving in the wind to our enemies. But I wanted to see him the second he was back. So I paced the courtyard until Lia emerged from the Great Hall, set up a couple of targets on sheaves of wheat, and handed me a bow and arrow. "Here," she said. "You can work out some of that tension that's about to drive us all crazy."

I looked at the bow in my hand. "You know I'm lousy with these," I said.

"Right. Let's change that." She strode off halfway across the courtyard and waited for me to join her.

With a sigh I trudged toward her.

"Sheesh," she said. "You'd think I was making you do all the dirty dishes in the castle. C'mon. It's fun."

"Fun for you. You could do it with your eyes closed."

"Well, let's see if you can do it with your eyes open."

I smiled with her, her teasing challenge seeming to awaken something inside me. *She knows me, my sister. Better than almost anyone.*

Mom and Dad came out then and wanted in. So we paused and set up more targets on sheaves while they fetched more bows and arrows from the armory.

"Great. Now I'm going to get bested by three family members," I whined. They'd all played around with a bow and arrow set for hours every day last summer after we'd get back from the dig. I'd elected to hole up in my room and catch up on texts and emails from friends until Dad called me down for a round of sparring. It was how Lia had gotten so good. What if she hadn't? And what if Dad hadn't encouraged me to fence? I shivered at the thought. We probably would all be dead many times over if my family hadn't been so intrigued with the ancient arts of war and hunting.

They ignored my whining and settled arrows on their bowstrings, then took aim. With another exasperated sigh, I did the same.

"On three," Lia said. "One…two…three."

Mom's went slightly left, missing the target. Dad's hit the third ring. Mine went high and broke against the stones of the castle wall. Lia's hit dead center, of course.

The knights on duty roared and cheered and laughed at our efforts.

"Who invited the peanut gallery?" Mom asked, already tucking another arrow nock on her string.

"Ahh, gives 'em a little something to keep them occupied," Dad said. "Let them have their fun."

I bent and retrieved an arrow from the massive bucket Lia had brought out and set up my next shot. If the last had gone high, then I needed to aim slightly below the target. We let another round fly. And this time mine went low, but stuck in the target, in the bottom.

The men laughed as if I'd hit someone in the heel, and I turned, hands on hips, and stared up at them. "Should you not be on the watch for men of Firenze sneaking our way? What if Lord Forelli is in danger?"

They instantly sobered and moved off, back to their positions, with chastened looks as they murmured, "Yes, m'lady." I felt a little guilty as I turned back, and Dad gave me a Was-That-Really-Necessary?

look. But I ignored it and took another arrow as my family all prepared their third shot.

Lia's was dead center. Mom and Dad both were closer to center. But mine went right. Even after twenty more, I only was able to stick four. "Good thing you're the archer in the family," I said to Lia, walking with her to hang up the bows in the armory.

"We all have something we're good at," she said with a shrug. "Does it bother you so much?"

"Well, it doesn't *bother* me. But I'd like to be a little better at it. Your skills, after all, have proven pretty useful out there."

*Okay, so it does bug me a little,* I admitted to myself. I wanted to be better at it than Lia, deep down. Or at least decent. Wasn't it a big sister's place to be adequate, if not the leader?

"How about a little round of sparring?" Dad asked me, setting his bow on a hook beside mine.

I smiled. "Rain check? I'd love to, but I'm suddenly totally tired again."

He nodded, his eyes hooded with concern for me. "It's best you rest, then. Can I walk you to your room?"

"Sure," I said. But inside, I was groaning. First Mom, now Dad. Even though we weren't scheduled to talk-talk for a few days, they clearly had a lot on their minds that couldn't wait.

*I should be happy,* I said to myself. After all, I had my dad back. He was here, with me, wanting to help me. I should be willing to listen to him read the numbers from the New York Stock Exchange, if that was what he wanted to share.

We split off from Lia and Mom, who headed to Fortino's den for a game of chess. A pang of loss struck me then. Fortino, who

had worked so hard to live, now dead. "Where did they bury him?"
I asked Dad.

"Bury? Oh, you mean Lord Fortino?"

I nodded.

He hesitated. "There's a plot in back of the castle, on a hill. Marcello buried him as soon as we returned…for obvious reasons. Marcello
wished to wait for you, but we had no idea how long you'd be out."

I grimaced. I could only imagine Marcello's pain.

"I want to see the site. Visit his grave," I said. Fortino was gone.
Being here, in his castle, where I'd first known him, brought it home
in a fresh, painful way.

Dad paused. "Maybe if Marcello is completely sure it'll be all
right…"

"We'll be safe," I muttered. We reached the back of the castle and
entered one of the turrets to climb the stairs.

Why did it seem like there were a hundred stairs instead of fifteen?

We reached the top, and I paused at my door. "Thanks for bringing me back, Dad. Or are you going to come in and tuck me in?"

He smiled, and I was reminded of how Italian he really looked.
Out of all of us, he was the one who looked like he really belonged
here. "You can probably handle it," he said, still smiling. But then he
grew more serious. "He loves you, you know."

*Marcello.* "I know."

"I mean, really loves you. I've seen it myself, now." He put his
chin in his hand, looked up, and then stared at me again. "It's pretty
complicated for a first love, isn't it?"

I stilled over his words. *First love.* As in…there would be a second?
Or was I just being overly sensitive? "Tell me about it," I said, not really

ready to get into it—if we were going to get into something at all. I studied him. "But you have to just go with what you've been given, right?"

How many times had he said that to me or Lia when we complained about the shape of our nails or the size of ears or our height?
Things we couldn't change. *You gotta go with what you've been given.*

He returned my thoughtful gaze and then seemed to decide to
let go of something—or maybe just put it off until later. "Get some
rest, Gabs."

"I will." I opened the door and was halfway through when I turned
and peeked around the corner. He was striding away, had almost reached
the stairs. "Dad?"

"Yes?"

"I'm glad you're here."

He paused and then gave me a small smile. "I am too."

"Can you come get me? If Marcello returns early?"

"I can," he said, "but I'd bet that when he hears you're up and
about, he'll be to your quarters before I get a chance."

I smiled and slowly shut the door.

I awakened to the feeling of Marcello's lips tenderly kissing my lids.
"Marcello," I whispered, wanting to feel his presence, smell the scent
of horses and leather and pine and cinnamon on him for a moment
longer before I dared to open my eyes.

"Gabriella," he whispered back. He leaned away, holding one of
my hands, and my eyes fluttered open.

We sat there for a long moment, just staring at each other. It was silly, really. But we couldn't stop ourselves. It was as if we both wanted to be certain that what we were seeing was real. That we could believe our eyes. He really was crazy-handsome. Totally studly in the leather chest armor, a loose coil of hair curling over one side of his face. He'd obviously run right up from the courtyard.

"It suits you, this room," he said, nodding beyond me, then staring at me again. "You look like a princess."

I shifted. "It's not odd, to have me in your mother's quarters?"

"It's not odd in that the intended lady of this castle is in her rightful place."

I smiled, acknowledging What He Was Saying.

"You are well?" he asked, tucking my hair behind my ear.

"Better than I was," I said, a little embarrassed over what had happened out there, among the oaks. "Forgive me, Marcello. I wasn't myself—"

"I know that, Gabriella," he said, now holding my hand in both of his. He slipped off the edge of the bed and kneeled beside it, placing his forehead on my fingers.

I paused. "Marcello?" What was wrong? I held my breath over his hesitation.

"Can you ever forgive me, Gabriella?" he begged, looking up at me, eyes wide and sorrowful. "I failed you. Failed you in letting them take you."

"Oh, Marcello," I said, rolling over and touching the top of his head as he bowed it again. "'Twasn't your fault, beloved. Try as you might, you cannot be everywhere at once."

"But I was to be your protector. I *am* your protector," he said, shaking his head.

I sighed and leaned back, feeling so tired that I thought I might pass out again. What was wrong with me? Mono? Some sort of Time Travel virus? Seriously. I felt sick.

"Marcello, I insisted on going. You cannot take responsibility for those things you do not control. And you need to know that, as your lady, I have my own mind. If you wish to control me…" I shook my head on the pillow and looked up to the ceiling. I didn't have the strength for this conversation. *Not now.* For the first time I noticed the ceiling was not only painted a deep blue, but decorated with thousands of delicate, golden stars. "Did your mother like stars?"

He glanced up with me. "She loved them. Once, when she was away to Siena, my father hired a fresco artist to do that, surprising her upon her return."

I smiled at the romantic gesture. Dimly I remembered a constellation chart in Fortino's den. His mother's work?

"She'd spend night after night up on the top of the wall with all torches doused so she could see better. On the best nights Father would take her to the hills, and they would lie on a blanket and watch as the stars drifted across the night sky." He gave me a tender smile. "I come from a line of men who fall for women with their eyes on the far horizon."

"My good fortune, that."

He paused. "Do you feel up to joining us in the Hall for supper? Or should I send a servant up with a tray?"

I hated feeling like the Weakling Upstairs, but I really doubted my own strength at that point. *Maybe I really do have mono…*

"A tray, then?" he guessed. I could see the shadows of fear in his eyes, despite his best efforts.

"Only if you'll join me."

He brightened. "I shall return in an hour."

We ate, mostly in silence, sitting side by side in front of the fire. I'd drifted off again while he was gone and was feeling half awake. And there was an odd awareness that he and I had never been alone together to eat. It felt strangely…intimate. And that reaction made it feel odder still. What was this? We couldn't have a meal together and talk? It was almost as if we had so much to talk about that neither of us could figure out where to begin.

"Marcello," I said quietly, when we'd picked the last of the roasted chicken from the bones and sopped up the sauce with our bread. Cook, just back to the castle today, had outdone herself. "On the morrow, might you take me to Fortino's grave?"

He abruptly rose and set his trencher on a side table and reached for mine. Then he went to the window and opened it, as if he was suddenly too hot. He stared out for a long time. I'd upset him. The thought of losing Lia as he had lost Fortino…I rose and went to him, wrapping my arms around his waist and settling my forehead between his shoulder blades. "Will you take me there?" I repeated gently.

"I shall. If you must."

"I must. Fortino…he meant much to me. I am so sorry, Marcello."

He placed his hands on mine and took a long, deep breath. In it I could hear just a bit of the overwhelming exhaustion I felt inside.

"You are weary too," I said.

"I am," he admitted.

I settled my cheek against his back. "We are far too young to feel like old people."

He laughed. "Indeed." He turned and cradled the side of my face. "But it shall pass. There is much ahead of us, Gabriella. Fortino…he would wish for us to embrace *life*."

*Life?* He was tired, yes. But he wasn't feeling this sick kind of tired that I was. Still he was being so sweet…

He studied me. "When shall you tell me what transpired in Roma?" he asked.

"In time," I said, shifting away. In retrospect, what was so terrible about it? Indulgent Roman baths? Being pampered, dressed in costume? I felt silly, guilty over giving in to feeling like I'd been through So Much. But I couldn't help it. It felt like a lot. There'd been my harrowing escape, sure. The chase, the capture. The fear that I was about to be made to marry, whether I wanted to or not. The horrific plan to verify that the marriage was consummated… Then our escape from Rome. It just was too much—too much for my brain and heart to take in.

Marcello took my hand before I was too far away. "Rodolfo… did he…? Did he not honor our agreement?"

He wondered if something had happened between us. If that was at the heart of what was going on inside me. For the first time I wondered if it *was* a part of it. I remembered our kiss in the woods. Our embrace in Palazzo Vivaro. I'd allowed it. Betrayed Marcello.

"Can we speak of it later?" I asked, staring at the tile floor, unable to meet his gaze.

He stilled, guessing there was more there—much more—then let go of my fingers. I felt the chill of the air flowing through the window then, on my palm, where his warm hand had been a second before. "Certainly, m'lady." He touched my chin and waited for me to look at him. "But we *shall* speak of it, in time."

I gave him the tiniest of nods, and, after a breath, he turned and strode toward the door. He paused there, his back to me, clearly wanting to say something. "Do you love him, Gabriella?" he finally asked, staring up at the door frame.

His words sent a shock through me. For the first time since awaking at Castello Forelli, I *felt* awake. "Love? Rodolfo?"

He waited, deadly still.

"Nay," I said, striding over to him. I put a hand on his shoulder. "Marcello, look at me."

Reluctantly he turned.

"If there is one thing I know to be true, it's this: I love but one man. And that man is *you*."

His eyes narrowed in pain and confusion. "Then what is it, Gabriella?" he asked. "What are you not telling me?" He took my hand in his and put it to his chest, covering it with his own. "What are you keeping from me that pains you so that you wish to sleep the day away?"

"I know not," I said to him. "Truly." I lifted my free hand to my temple. "Mayhap it's that I'm trying to pull together so much in my mind, my heart, in so short of a time. It's a great deal to absorb, Marcello. Even without the trauma of the last few days…

weeks. Every time I've been here, with you, I've experienced battle, disappointment. Death."

He nodded, holding his hands over mine, still on his chest. "But you've also experienced love. Extreme loyalty. Friendship."

*Yes, but...*

"I understand," he said at last. "Even for me, 'tis been a great deal. I need to remember that you went from the war, to this. Whereas I had more than a year, without you, adjusting, resting." He gave me a sad smile and tucked my stupidly stubborn hair behind my ear. "And for a girl of *Normandy*...such circumstances must be sorely trying indeed."

I returned his smile. "Normandy is far more tame," I said. "At least in some regards."

"I am praying that in the coming days, we shall know an era of peace. That is if Rodolfo can maintain his position among the grandi, and me with the Nine—together we might build bridges again, instead of this incessant fighting."

"'Twould be good," I said. If a bit weird. I pictured Rodolfo coming to visit. Marcello inviting him. *Sure, dude. Come by the house. Don't worry if you made moves on my girl. We'll hang out!*

I had to tell him. All of it. Rodolfo had ultimately been faithful to him, to me. But there had been that undercurrent of wanting something far different....

# Chapter Twenty-two

So, apparently, I'd come to the end of my record sleep-a-thon. Because even though my body was trying to pull me back into Slumberville, my mind was Awake, with a capital *A*. For hours I'd thought of nothing but Marcello, Rodolfo, Dad, Mom, Lia, the past, the future, tossing and turning. The more I thought, the harder I worked at trying to figure it out, the worse it seemed to get.

I stared at Lady Forelli's stars until I longed to see the real thing.

I finally threw off the covers and rubbed my arms against the chill. I carried a candle over to a trunk, rifled through it, and found the one I was seeking—a simple brown gown made of a sturdy wool. No adornment, nothing too fancy. But of an older fashion, and therefore higher at the neck and shoulder, warmer. I tossed it over my head, managed to reach a few buttons, then called it good. I grabbed a hooded cape and wrapped it around my shoulders, pulled on my tapestry slippers—wishing they had Ugg boots—and then long gloves.

I needed to walk. Outside. Move. See the stars.

Thinking of Lady Forelli, I blew out my candle. I knew the rest of the castle was likely illuminated anyway, with enough torches lit to guide the knights, should attack occur.

I cracked open my door to the hall, wincing as it squeaked, since I was next door to the quarters Marcello had taken—Lord Forelli's. I assumed he was sleeping, and he needed it.

After several breaths I assumed he'd not heard me. Otherwise, he'd be racing to his door, sword drawn. He was in that kind of protective mood. Then I tiptoed past his door, down the hall, entered the turret stairs, and circled downward to the bottom. I exited through the door, startling a sleepy knight on guard outside it.

*Marcello, really? Isn't that a bit of overkill?* We were inside the castle, after all.

He stood straighter and gave me a curious look. "M'lady? Is there something I can get you?"

"Nay," I said, giving him my most charming smile. "I simply couldn't sleep. I suppose that after sleeping so many days away, I'm quite finished." I raised my shoulders in a shrug. "I'm here to walk, get some fresh air."

He gave me a polite nod, but I knew he'd be following my every move. How long had I been under guard without knowing it? I supposed it was all right. Understandable. It just…rubbed me wrong. Felt a bit like the ropes on the stretcher a few days ago. Too close to the sort of imprisonment I'd experienced of late, elsewhere.

I walked to the center of the courtyard, looking up. But the moon was half full now, bright in the clear winter sky, and the stars dim. I sighed, frustrated, wanting one of those moonless, brilliant star nights where there was practically more white than black. And then I started to walk, fast. Power walking, of sorts. Trying to drive out all the frustration and confusion building inside me again like a silent scream. I walked the whole perimeter of the castle, which took about ten minutes. I wished I could be outside, in the woods, running through the trees.

I was attracting the attention of every guard on watch, but I ignored them. I wanted to break into a run, circling and circling the inside of the wall, but knew that they'd think I really was like a caged wolf. The last thing Marcello needed was more people thinking I was losing it. So I tucked my hands behind me and slowed my stride to a stroll, keeping my head down, thinking, thinking, thinking.

I was on my fourth round, just passing the kitchen and stables, when I saw him waiting in the center of the courtyard. I paused and then approached him. "Can't sleep?" I said.

"Not if you can't," Marcello said, staring with such deep compassion in his eyes that I held my breath. He lifted a bow toward me and said, "Lia told me you tried your hand at it yesterday."

"Tried," I said. "And failed. Most miserably."

"Then you must try again," he said, giving me a gentle smile of encouragement. I had never seen a bow and arrow in his hands, but I had no doubt that he was as expert with them as he was with the sword. "I find it settles me, if I cannot find a suitable sparring partner. Mayhap it shall be the same for you."

I nodded and stepped forward. He'd lit several more torches. I knew the guards watched, but I was mostly aware of Marcello. He stepped behind me, gently correcting my stance as I nocked the arrow and pulled back the bowstring.

"Most overshoot. Aim lower than you think you need to."

I let it fly, and it stuck to the top of the wheat sheaf.

"There you are," he said.

I laughed under my breath, positioned another arrow on the string, and aimed.

"Tell me, Gabriella, what it is that keeps you from sleep," he whispered.

I let the second loose, and it still was high, but a couple inches down from the first. I reached for another arrow and prepared for my next strike. "He kissed me, Marcello."

His hand stiffened at my waist. Then, "Did you return it?"

"For a moment."

He took several breaths. "Take your shot, m'lady," he said then.

I squinted, aiming, but my eyes were filling with tears. I let it go, and it hit the outer ring of the target.

"So now we are getting closer to the heart of the matter," Marcello said.

I nocked the next arrow as if I were a robot, automatically continuing my task regardless of what was going on. I aimed at the center of the ring, dark and red and representing—at the moment—every frustration I had. "I do not love him," I said hoarsely. I let it fly, and it struck the second ring.

I paused, and Marcello bent to retrieve the next arrow for me. I put my hand on it but did not take it from him, waiting until he met my gaze. "I was moved by his friendship. His loyalty to you."

Marcello let out a scoffing laugh. "Rodolfo is quite handsome. Powerful and wealthy. Winsome."

"No more than you, m'lord," I said. "I was under a great deal of duress. And when he… Marcello, you need to believe me… I allowed it, for a moment. But I was confused."

"And that was it?" he asked, his tone deadly.

"One more time. He tried to draw me in, convince me to leave it to God. To attend that first ceremony at Lord Vivaro's. See if you showed up in time."

He paused for one breath, then two. "So he loves you."

I dared to face him. His eyes went back and forth, searching mine, and I nodded. "He never said the words. Mayhap it was but a passing fancy—"

"Nay, I saw it in his face," Marcello said lowly, stroking my cheek with the back of his knuckles. "You are no man's passing fancy, Gabriella. You have a way...a way of stealing hearts. You and your sister. Mayhap it's your Norman upbringing. But every man and woman around you recognizes you as different. Unique. Other. And that makes us all want to know you more."

I paused, considering his words. "To be fair, Rodolfo was playing the role. Doing what was expected of him."

Marcello stepped slightly away so he could look me fully in the face. "Surely you are not that naive."

"Is he not one of your oldest friends?" I asked in irritation. "A brother?"

"That brotherhood ended when he attempted to draw you away from me. I just didn't know it, when I saw him last." He turned and strode away, but I raced past him and put a hand to his chest.

"Nay. Was it not he who made it possible for you to take on the robes and hoods of the noblemen at San Giovanni's?" I was guessing, but it only made sense.

His pause told me I was right.

"If he was truly willing to sever your friendship, to walk away from you in order to have me, would he have made the way for you? Would it not have made far more sense to keep you out?"

"I would've found my way in via another entrance, without him," he ground out.

"But you didn't have to, did you, Marcello?"

"He wanted you to choose, Gabriella. He knew we were there, that I would hear it if you willingly accepted the vows."

He looked away, took a deep breath, and then let it out slowly. Too slowly. "So after you rejected him, he did not make any further untoward advances?"

I wasn't sure what *untoward advances* meant, but I could guess from his tone. "Nay, Marcello, nay. He knew he had lost. That my heart beat for one alone." I reached out and rested my hand against his chest. "You."

I took the arrow from his hand, turned, and aimed at the center of the target, now an additional ten paces away. "Ever after, I tried to escape. At one point I went out on a ledge, three stories up and made my way around the corner—"

I went on to tell him of my leap to the other palazzo, the old servant helping me escape, Tomas's arrival, and then of Vivaro's men closing in.

Marcello stared at my arrow, stuck in the center of the target, and then turned back to me. "By sunup Captain Ruisi had cornered you and the priest."

"And by nightfall, I was back in Roma."

He kicked the toe of his boot against the hard-packed mud of the courtyard. "And then they took you to San Giovanni, where we found you."

"Yes."

He studied me. "I must know, Gabriella. You had a knife at your throat, so I would understand." He reached out and touched my cheek. "Truly I would." He took a breath. "But…were you ready to accept it? Had we not been there, would you have become…his?"

I shook my head. "Nay. *Nay*. Rodolfo knew it. He could see it in my eyes, the answer I was prepared to give, regardless of the threat. That is why he demanded my release." I reached for his hand. "Why does it matter? He stepped aside, made a way for us. Gave us the only edge he had the freedom to give. Is it not enough?"

He didn't answer. He simply reached for my bow, took an arrow from the basket, and aimed. He let go of the bowstring, and the arrow sailed across, hitting the center so close to mine that it cracked. "Not until I know he does not wish to claim what is mine," he said, looking at me over his shoulder.

"But I *am* yours," I said, putting a hand at his waist. "If there was anything good that came of those days in Sansicino and Roma, 'twas that." I drew closer, so I could whisper in his ear. "That. That I'm yours, Marcello. Always and forever. That is why I'm here." I reached around and put a hand on his chest, and he covered it with his hand. "Always and forever," I repeated. "It's why God brought me here, to this time, this place. Because I am meant for you, and you for me."

He dropped the bow and turned in my arms, taking my face in both of his trembling hands. "And there is nothing in your heart for Rodolfo?"

"Oh, Marcello," I said, looking into his eyes. "I care for Rodolfo. But I *love* you. You have my heart. What must I do to make you believe that?"

Slowly, never dropping his gaze from mine, he dropped to one knee before me. His intense expression made my heart pound. "Marry me, m'lady. Marry me as soon as we can obtain your father's blessing."

*And Mom's. That might take a while. Oh, and there's the small matter of convincing them all to live here forever...*

I pushed the hesitation out of my mind, not wanting him to sense any of it. He'd misunderstand. I smiled down at him, at the earnest, hopeful, little-boy look in his eyes, and tears rolled down my face. And I was glad for them, glad to be *feeling* again. Alive inside. "Yes, Marcello," I said. "If we can convince my family, I shall marry you."

He rose, grinning, and lifted me up in the air, twirling me and laughing. I could hear the low, approving laughter of the guards. If it weren't for the hour, I knew they would likely be cheering.

Gradually he let me drop, and I felt the strength of his arms and chest anew. There, in that moment, I remembered a bit of my own strength, my own power. But I was most acutely aware of Marcello, as he seemed to be of me. He bent and kissed me, gently at first, then more hungrily, pulling me closer. Abruptly he broke off, stepped away, his face flushed. I knew mine was as well. He lifted a hand toward me as we circled each other. "We must convince your father soon," he said.

"My father *and* mother," I said, looking at him with as much passion as he was looking at me. "And Lia. *Very* soon," I said. I edged closer and lifted my lips to him. He kissed me then, restrained. Deliciously restrained.

Then he took my hand, led me to the turret, up the stairs, down the hallway and into my room. I had hopes of more kissing, drawing closer to him in the privacy of my quarters, tossing aside restraint, but he put his hands on my shoulders and looked into my eyes with a grin. "God help me, Gabriella, I cannot take but another second of being close to you. Not if I wish to maintain your honor." He raised an eyebrow. "Stay here, She-Wolf. I must run to the well and dive in."

With that, he turned and left me, firmly shutting the door.

And I giggled. Then laughed. Laughed so hard I cried, until my stomach muscles hurt. I fell on my back, atop the bed, and stared at the stars above me.

*Oh, yeah, I'm back.*

*I. Am. Back.*

*I'm engaged.* I supposed that I had been technically engaged to Rodolfo, too, but that had been like a sentence—this was like a delicious, secret promise, filled with hope. I paced the room, thinking of a wedding, of looking into Marcello's eyes and promising him forever, of kisses that didn't have to end with separation…

And then I stopped cold.

*Mom and Dad are gonna SO freak.*

*And yeah, not in a good way.*

The only thing that got me going again, the only thing that got me appropriately sober to face my family, was that I had to dress for my trek to Fortino's gravesite. I was feeling kinda manic, alternately up so high I could barely stand still as Giacinta buttoned up the back

of my tight-fitting bodice, and so low that I wanted to sink to my
knees on the floor and weep at the thought of saying a final farewell
to Fortino. It didn't help that I was pulling on a beautiful, white
gown. In medieval society, apparently everyone dressed in white for
funerals, symbolic of the afterlife, and blue for weddings. But of
course I was totally thinking *Brides* magazine.

I'd been thinking of my wedding day for a few years now. What
girl didn't? I'd always imagined it as a small ceremony, with us barefoot on the beach in someplace like Hawaii. But it'd probably have
to be different here, marrying Marcello. The whole *Sound of Music,*
massive church gig in Siena…

"M'lady?" Giacinta asked.

"Hmm?"

She paused, and I gathered this wasn't the first time she'd spoken
to me. I buckled down, trying hard to concentrate.

"Father Tomas," Giacinta said, "he asked after you."

I nodded, shoving away a pang of guilt for pretty much forget-
ting about him in the last forty-eight hours.

"He's a kind man," she mused, tackling the next set of buttons at
my back. "The nicest sort of priest."

"Indeed. I like him very well."

"The men told me you saved him, back in Roma."

I paused, trying to remember. It was honestly fuzzy in my memory, from the time of our escape at San Giovanni to my breakdown
on the road.

Giacinta led me to a seat where she could begin work on my hair.
She pulled apart a section and began to comb it, then twisted it into
a coil that she wrapped into the next. I didn't truly care. I trusted

her—she'd done miracles with my hair before. "They say that he was done for this world, slumped over, bleeding to death in the saddle when you made it through the gates."

"They exaggerate."

She paused. "You did not go back for him?"

It was my turn to pause. I remembered the sound of it. Clashing swords. The cries of men. The dancing light of torches. The Roman guard, riding hard, toward us…

"Oh, m'lady," she said, laying a gentle hand on my shoulder. "Forgive me. I've upset you."

"Nay," I said. "'Tis all right. We got through. Escaped. That is what is important." I heard the waver in my own voice. Did she?

"Truly," she said agreeably. But she was pretending, suddenly chirpy in her chatter about her toddler daughter, Cook's return to work at the castello, and what was transpiring over at Lord Paratore's.

"Giacinta," I said coolly, "do you know if Lord Paratore is actually in residence across the valley?"

"He is, m'lady," she said grimly.

Our old nemesis, so close, and with a hundred reasons to try to bring us down. Was my dream of peace, of happily ever after on Marcello's arm just that—a mere dream?

There were a few years left before plague would decimate this valley and the ancient cities of Italia—all of Europe, really. We needed times of peace, prosperity to prepare. To shore up food, supplies. So that we could withdraw, close the gates, and do our best to weather the storm. Because after all this, there was no way I would lose Marcello to the Black Plague. No way.

All I had to do was to convince my parents and sister to weather it with us.

*Uh yeah, that...* I thought, feeling another pang of doubt, panic. But first I had to see Marcello through his mourning.

# Chapter Twenty-three

We walked up from the castle into the winter-brown hills and, even with a wool cape around my shoulders and Marcello beside me, I shivered in the damp cold. The charcoal gray skies rumbled, a storm ready to break in minutes. We followed Father Tomas. My family trailed behind, giving us a little space. The hundred men on guard—seventy-five between us and Castello Paratore, twenty-five on the other—notsomuch. Clearly their goal was to make sure we got in, got out, without incident.

Marcello held his arm firm beneath mine, but one glance at him told me that tears were streaming down his cheeks.

Fortino had been his last living family member. What would it feel like for me, if Mom and Dad were gone and I was burying Lia? Was I mean, making him come back here?

I could not imagine it, trading places with him. I glanced back at them, Lia on Luca's arm, Mom on Dad's, just to reassure myself that they were truly all there, with me.

I fought the urge to ditch the formality and come under Marcello's arm, wrap my own about his waist, to support him in the way I knew I'd want it. But this had to go his way, for him, now. Still, I kept stealing glances at him to make certain.

We climbed higher up the dirt path, up the hill, and for the first time I recognized that far more guarded us than I'd thought. There were hundreds of armed Sienese knights protecting us. Forming a living barrier between us and Paratore, to our north. But they were paying their respects again with us as much as paying attention to their duties. Wanting to say good-bye to Fortino. To silently say thanks. For sacrifice. For courage. For believing in what made the republic uniquely theirs.

Tears flowed down my cheeks anew, and I wiped my face again and again with a white handkerchief. At the top of the hill, we came to a stop, and I looked around again, amazed at the numbers. The funeral had already happened. Today they were here to be *present*, for Marcello, for me. Out of respect for Fortino. And somehow that was twice as moving.

Father Tomas stood at the far end of the mound of dirt that covered Fortino's grave. He bent, with a grunt, and grabbed a handful of dark, rich earth, letting some of it sift through his fingers. Then he took a pinch with his left hand, let most of it fall away, and eyed us. "Fortino began as little more than a speck, no greater than this," he said, flicking the rest away in the breeze. "And his body shall be reclaimed in time by this hill, this earth." He waited until we looked back at him. "But his soul shall live forever. In heaven he has already found freedom and peace and the healing that he so longed for in his last days on earth. Father," he said, lifting his face to the sky, "we trust that You have received this son into Your kingdom. Amen."

"Amen," we repeated after him. With one glance at Marcello's face, I knew he had never heard such a thing from a holy man. It was much too personal, far too informal. I was scared that Marcello might lose it. *I* was about to lose it. But he seemed to gain strength from Tomas's words instead. Perhaps it was the words of peace, healing, wholeness that helped him most. Because that was what Fortino had longed for, long before those last hours in the Sansicino cell.

Tomas said a few more words in Latin, picked up another fistful of dirt, and let it filter down over the mound, as if he was deep in thought. He took a final fistful, strode over to us, and picked up Marcello's hand. Tomas looked into Marcello's eyes with pure compassion. Marcello tried to steady himself as he returned the gaze. But when Tomas poured the crumbling dirt in his hand, Marcello's tears began anew—and of course mine followed. "The body decomposes, becomes dirt," the priest said in a whisper, "but what God created inside your brother lives. You shall see him again. Yes?"

Marcello nodded. "Yes," he said, through choking tears.

The priest went back to the top of the grave, closed his eyes, and made the sign of the cross, then stepped back. Then we all turned to leave.

And it struck me anew that Fortino was gone. Never coming back.

I glanced up, over to Castello Paratore, its crimson flags waving in the wind. They seemed to embody Fortino's suffering, his demise, his death.

*Oh yeah,* I thought. *They have to go. They simply have to go.*

We were a parade of people as we left the gravesite. I passed the simple stones that marked the graves of Marcello's mother and father. Under the branches of three scrub oaks, I saw for the first time a stone monument with the statues of two nobles side by side, man and woman, lying on their backs.

I'd only seen such a monument in the high churches of England, France, and Italy. "Who is buried there?" I asked Marcello, pointing toward it.

He rubbed the last of the tears from his eyes and searched to see where I pointed. "My great-great grandparents. They loved each other very much and insisted that they share a tomb; they died within days of each other."

I considered that. "How long has your family been here, Marcello, in this part of Toscana?"

He thought about it a moment. "More than two hundred years. Our land once stretched all the way to Firenze, but we could not hold such a vast property for long. My grandfather was the one who established the borders we now maintain, except for that which we share with Castello Paratore."

We walked in silence. Two hundred years. Being the daughter of Etruscan archeologists, I was kinda used to the idea of ancient history. But *personal* ancient history? I didn't know many back home in Colorado who'd had family there for more than two generations, let alone two centuries. I felt Marcello's connection to this land and the castello in a new way. When you lived in a spot so beautiful, a spot that had seen old generations die and new ones born, you fought for it. It was yours in more than a name-on-a-mortgage-document sort of way. It was yours because it had been claimed by your own, years before.

I spotted Mom and Dad ahead, speaking to an older man with a terrible hump in his back. "Who is that?" I asked, gesturing with my chin. I'd never seen him before.

Marcello looked down the hill. "Ah, yes. Signore Cavo. He's a dealer in ancient artifacts. I imagine they shall get on quite well."

It figured. Mom and Dad seemed to have an inner sense, a gift for finding those who shared their passion.

I thought of the beautiful amber and copper jewelry that Rodolfo had given me. Perhaps the merchant could get them back to him. The faster I could get rid of anything that reminded me of that day, the better.

Through a go-between. I doubted Marcello would be cool with me hanging out with Rodolfo at all. At least for a while.

We walked along outside the castle wall, and my eyes traced the line where new stones had been placed against the old. The Fiorentini had done a good job rebuilding the castle; it was hardly a patch job. You had to really look to see where they'd replaced stones. I remembered that terrible night, when we came back to see the front destroyed, the wall torn down. What did it feel like to Marcello, to once more be home? He'd never complained, never spoken of worry, just waited for his opportunity to regain what was rightfully his.

We entered the gates, and inside the Great Hall, Cook and the other servants had created a feast, setting it before us on a massive banquet table. There were fat chickens, slow roasted on spits; piles of loaves of bread; fish; oranges from Seville; and mince pies. It didn't take me long to figure out that this was some delayed funeral celebration. Apparently they'd been waiting for me.

Servants circulated, refilling goblets of wine, and soon, people were singing and telling stories of Fortino. One man stood up and told of hunting with him when they were boys, regaling us with tales of his superior marksmanship. Another told a joke that had always been Fortino's favorite. I wondered if this was what an Irish wake was like—the goodwill, the laughter.

Marcello rose, raised his goblet, and waited for all hundred guests in the room to do the same. When every eye was on him, he said, "Fortino was the finest brother that I could have ever asked for. He was not only a brother to me, but a fine friend, and I shall mourn his loss forever. But I choose this day to celebrate his memory. To celebrate his loyalty and sharp mind, his generosity and care. I choose to celebrate that, even when he was so near death, he enjoyed a period of renewed health, vitality because this woman entered our lives." He gestured to me.

The room erupted in "hear, hears" and then settled.

I smiled at the people, nodding once, pleased that I had been able to help Fortino, at least for a time, but then thinking Marcello would go on to speak about his brother.

But he was looking intently at me, and my heart stilled. *Oh, no. Not yet! Not here! Don't say it! Not in the middle of all these people—*

He looked to Dad. "We mourn the passing of my brother. But my brother knew that your daughters were some of the finest women to ever pass through our gates."

I could see Dad slowly rising to his feet in the corner of the room, and yet I could not bear to meet his gaze. Marcello walked over to him, utterly confident, never fearing—apparently never considering—that Dad might turn him down. Mom stepped forward, sliding her hand through Dad's arm.

"Lord and Lady Betarrini, I am deeply in love with your daughter, Lady Gabriella."

Dad's brow lowered. Mom looked concerned. *Oh no. No, no, no—*

Marcello saw it too and hesitated.

But then everyone else was coming to their feet, faces full of anticipation and hope. There was no way through but through. Quickly I moved to Marcello and took his hand. He smiled down at me and lifted it to his lips to kiss it. The action seemed to strengthen him. "Lord and Lady Betarrini, I humbly ask for your blessing over my coming nuptials. I hope to make your daughter, Gabriella, my bride, as soon as possible."

The people erupted, applauding and coming over to us, dividing us from my parents, thumping Marcello on the back, kissing both my cheeks. It took about ten minutes for the crowd to abate and people to flow out into the courtyard for dancing and singing. I was a little surprised at the festive mood—who knew funerals could be such fun? I'd never been to a medieval funeral feast; I only knew we were already at capacity at Castello Forelli.

Marcello stiffened when my parents were finally able to approach us again, chins high, shoulders back. They did not offer congratulations and hugs. Lia and Luca were to one side of them, their expressions screaming *You Are SO Busted.*

"Family meeting," Dad said in English, staring right into my eyes.

Inside I was thinking, *What? Now?* But I knew better than to debate it. I took Marcello's hand and squeezed it. "We can go to the library," I said. It was the only room in the castle that was likely unoccupied.

Dad led the way—out the door, across the courtyard, and into the wing that stirred sweet, warm thoughts of Fortino whenever I entered. But as we all filed in—Mom, Dad, Marcello, me, Luca, and Lia—it was about as cold as a room could be. Logs had been laid in the corner fireplace, ready to be lit.

Luca closed the door and stood to one side of it, arms folded.

"How could you?" my dad said, striding over to Marcello and poking him in the chest.

"*Dad*," I said, holding tight to Marcello's hand, angry at my father's aggression.

But Marcello took it. I'd never seen anyone attack him so—or him be so docile in response. He was showing deference, respect. Could Dad not see that?

"You should have asked for our blessing in *private*," Dad ground out, almost nose to nose with Marcello. "She is underage," he added, casting a furious finger in my direction.

"I beg your pardon, sir," Marcello said, eyes to the floor. "Forgive me for not coming to you and Lady Betarrini alone. I only thought…" He paused, took a deep breath and then lifted his other hand, palm up. "My only defense is that it was Gabriella I met first, long before I met Lia, her mother, and now you, sir. From the start"—he lifted my hand in his and looked into my eyes—"she claimed my heart. Like no other. I know that for her—for you all, sir—this seems rather sudden. As though it's happened within weeks. But you must understand; for me, Gabriella has carried my heart for almost two *years*. I feel as if I've been engaged to her for the past year and a half, when she promised she would return to me. And here, sir, here in *Toscana*, Gabriella *is* of age. Many women who are fifteen or sixteen marry."

"It's true," Mom said softly. She slid a hand over Dad's shoulder. Her affirmation echoed of support. I looked to her in wonder, as did Dad.

"You're in favor of this?" Dad asked, exasperation in every line of his face.

"I wish we had had the opportunity to speak of it before, Ben. But yes, I suppose there's an inevitable aspect to it."

Dad shook his head and then paced, hands on hips. "We have yet to even speak of how long we're to be here," he said, throwing out one hand. "Do you not all see that her marriage also commits us to life here *forever?*"

"And yet if we return, we do not know if *we* shall be together," Mom said, staring into his eyes.

Dad resumed his pacing, his fingers pinching his scalp as if he might be able to pry wisdom out of it.

Lia met my gaze. *You okay with this?* I silently asked her.

She smiled and glanced at Luca, then shrugged, as if to say, *How could I leave him?* And then she glanced at Dad. We were all worried—worried that if we went back, he'd disappear or ultimately meet his death again. We had no idea how much sway we had with history, with destiny. Sure, Castello Forelli had been rebuilt, whole. But was that really because of us? Or because of events that had transpired when we were here, therefore changing the future? Would such changes go as far as changing life itself?

There was only way to be sure that we would be together: We had to stay here.

I stared at the stones of the floor, waiting for Dad to come to the same conclusion. If Lia and I were both on board, and Mom was somewhat supportive, then he had to come along for the ride. The question was…would he go for this whole marriage thing?

He stood there, staring at the logs in the fireplace, hands on his hips now. Thinking.

He turned and looked at Mom, Lia, me. "A large portion of your desire to remain here is to save me," he said quietly. "But what if," he asked, each word tinged with misery, "I lose each of you?" He shook his head as if that were the most intolerable thought in the world. "We have seen the mortal danger of this place, firsthand," he said, coming over to me and touching my chin.

"I swear by my life that Gabriella, and you, sir—your whole family shall—"

"Nay," Dad said, cutting Marcello off as he lifted a finger toward him. "You cannot promise safety. You cannot! A day is coming, Lord Forelli, that no number of men and swords and arrows can guarantee victory."

The plague. He was referring to the Black Plague.

"And then what?" he went on, looking into my eyes. "Then shall I be risking not only my wife and daughters—and son-in-law," he added, brows wide in exasperation, and a dismissive wave toward Marcello, "but also grandchildren?"

"Gabriella," Marcello said slowly, his gaze on Dad, "of what does he speak?"

I shook my head. "We cannot tell of it yet."

"If it concerns your safety, then I must—"

"'Tis…of the future," I said, finally looking at him. "And it is as dire as my father makes it sound. We shall all be in horrific danger here."

Marcello stared back at me. "Then we shall go away for a time."

To where? America had yet to be discovered by Columbus, and all of Europe would suffer as wave after wave of the plague decimated their populations. And as for the Far East…I had no idea if they had suffered too, or when.

"A journey would not spare us," Marcello said, reading the expression in my eyes.

"Nay," I said sorrowfully.

"Is it Firenze?" he guessed.

"Please," I said, begging him not to press me. "I cannot say. We are not certain how our presence, let alone what we share, changes the future. We've already seen some evidence that it does."

"But if it is for good that you change it," Luca said, stepping forward, "who would argue with it?"

I rubbed my right temple, feeling a serious headache coming on. "I don't know. Maybe God?" Suddenly I wished that Father Tomas was in on this conversation, that he knew what had happened to us, that he could help us figure it out…

"God is for life," Marcello said, turning to face me and taking both my upper arms in his hands. "Are you telling me that we shall be in danger of losing you and there is nothing you could do to stop it?"

"It's an illness," Luca guessed, walking among us, looking at our faces. In a second he knew he was on the right track. "You wear the same expression that you did when I was so taken by the plague."

He stopped by Lia, and she looked quickly to the ground, as if she could hide the truth from him by not letting him see her face. "'Tis a plague, m'lord," he said.

Marcello frowned and pressed his fingers into my arms. "Gabriella. *Tell* me."

I stared into his big, brown eyes and thought of him taking ill, of saying good-bye to him forever, of seeing him die like Fortino, and a lump formed in my throat. He was not going to let me go, not without knowing. And yet if I told him he might send me far away—

"It shall be one of the worst the world has ever seen," Mom said at last, clearly aching over each word. Telling him what I could not. "Before the decade ends, a third of Siena's population shall die."

His mouth dropped open, and he released me, staring at me as if I had uttered such words, not Mom. "Siena."

"Siena," Mom said, and my eyes confirmed it for him. "Firenze. Venezia. Roma. Germania. Brittania. Few shall escape it. It will roam, far and wide, like a dragon with endless hunger."

We were all silent for a minute.

"A third," Dad said to Marcello. "That means that two of just this group, here, will likely die, if not all of us."

Marcello met his gaze, and I didn't like the man-to-man look they were giving each other. My heart grew heavy, slowed to a dull *thud, pa-thud, pa-thud…*

"And in Normandy," Marcello said. "Your physicians can treat this illness?"

Dad nodded. "It is an old disease. And new medicines seem effective at stopping it."

"So she would be safe there. You all would be safe there."

"Far safer than here."

"No. Dad…Marcello," I began.

Marcello turned toward me, misery in every line of his face. He took my arm with one hand and touched my cheek with the other. "I've long told you that I want nothing but for you to be well, to be safe. How could you not tell me of this threat?"

"Nay, *nay*," I said, feeling him slipping from me emotionally and physically as he dropped his hands and stepped away—as if he were disappearing underwater, growing dim in the darkness even while he was right before me. "There are no guarantees, regardless of where one lives!" I strode over to my father and switched to English. "In our world a *tractor* can end a life in an instant! *Car accidents*…murderers, plane crashes, new *viruses*…" I glommed onto that. "Remember Dr. Jeffries?" I asked him, glancing at Mom, too. "Remember how he was on site, working with you, and then, *boom,* forty-eight hours later he was dead." It had been some weird virus that struck his heart.

I looked at all of them, lapsing back into Italian. "We are attempting to play God, when maybe God put us here in the first place." Father Tomas's words by the stream came back to me. I could see his stick in the river, the water dividing on either side. "We can only move forward with what we have been given. Negotiate the river of life. Of time. And we've been given this," I pleaded, waving at our circle. "Family. Love. Joy. *Life*. Can we not embrace it, for as long as we have it? Isn't it what we all most dearly want, deep down?"

They all stared at me, thinking.

"We could always make the leap back," Lia said, "if we *did* get sick. The tunnel appears to heal."

I nodded. "Yes. Mom, you remember the blood on me?"

She nodded too, looking a little green at the memory.

"But what if a virus is—" Lia began.

I interrupted her. "I almost died that day. Marcello, Luca—they sent us home because they knew it was our last hope. Dad," I said, going over to him and again switching to English, "Marcello *put* my hand on the print. He sent me away in order to try to save me. You have to trust him, Dad. Trust him, as I do. He'll put my life ahead of his, every time. And if you keep pressing him like this, he'll have no choice but to side with you. To send me away without even trying at all."

"*Nella nostra lingua, per favore,*" Marcello said. *In our language, please.*

"He's generous like that," I said, ignoring his request. "Giving. He'll give up on what he wants, for me."

Dad stared back into my eyes, hesitating. Then, "As a husband ought."

I froze. "Are you saying…?"

He turned away from me and walked over to the cold fireplace, staring at it again for a moment, and then turned to Marcello and reverted back to Italian. "It is clear to me, m'lord, that my daughter loves you, and you, her." He glanced at Mom, and she nodded. Then he looked to Lia, and she did the same.

He reached a hand out to Marcello. "Gabriella has rightfully pointed out that life is a risk—that our lives are in God's hands—no matter where you are. And if you two wish to take that risk together, we shall stand beside you. Together we shall face what comes."

Marcello glanced at Dad's hand, then up into his eyes. "And if I wish to send her away, for her own good?"

A slow smile spread across Dad's face, and then he laughed. "You may send them away, but you cannot keep them from returning, can you?" He cocked his head and looked at me, Lia, and Mom with pride shining in his eyes. "The Ladies Betarrini…you have *yet* to see what they can accomplish. 'Tis best to pay attention to their wishes and give it good weight." He stopped and clapped Marcello on the shoulder, like a father to a son. "Learn that quickly, m'lord, and you are destined for a long and happy union."

# Chapter Twenty-four

We rejoined the others, thereafter properly ready to celebrate and dance and toast, to both Fortino's memory and to my future as Marcello's bride. I met up with the men that I had first met in Il Campo—Signores Salvatori, Bastiani, and Bonaduce—there to pay their respects. As I finished my fifth dance with them—a raucous peasant dance that left me breathless—I smiled at Father Tomas and joined him in the outer ring to accept his warm congratulations. We stood side by side, watching the others as they laughed and danced, Lia and Luca and Mom and Dad now at the center, coming together in a skip, hands raised.

*Dad's here, dancing.* I couldn't help it. Time and again, it struck me…that he was alive, that we were together. Maybe it was in visiting Fortino's grave that Dad's resurrection hit me anew.

"'Tis as Fortino wished, this," Tomas said.

I looked over at him, quickly, trying to focus in on his words. "Fortino spoke of…*this?*"

"He neared death several times during his imprisonment in Firenze, when I was attending Lord Greco. Time and again, Lord Greco intervened, and Fortino renewed his hope to return here. To come home. But he talked of you, and of Lord Marcello…He often mused that if he didn't live to return, that he had great hope for the two of you. That you would return to Siena from afar. And that Marcello would take you as his bride. He had such dreams for the house of Forelli."

It made me want to cry, thinking of Fortino dreaming of, hoping for *us*. Me and Marcello. "I miss him," I said simply.

"He was a fine man."

I nodded and forced a smile as Lord Rabellino—one of the Nine I'd met in Siena—came up to us and kissed both my cheeks as he held my hand in his. "M'lady, this night you have not only made Lord Forelli proud, but all of Siena. A wedding between one of the Nine and a She-Wolf? Siena will have never seen what is to come."

"Thank you, m'lord," I murmured. I smiled, but I was thinking about my barefoot-on-the-beach dreams. Simplicity. Intimacy. Quiet. *Guess that'll be impossible.*

Mom and Dad came over then and asked if we could talk. I glanced at Marcello, and he silently nodded, as if to say, *I see you. Go, if you must.*

Father Tomas and Lord Rabellino were already walking away, deep in conversation. I stared after them, curious what one of the Nine would want with the humble priest. I hoped he wasn't going to offer him a job. Or a position. Whatever they called it. I wanted Tomas to stay here, with us.

Mom, Dad, and I climbed the turret, and we exited through the short, rounded door at the top. I knew that this night, with so many of Siena's faithful celebrating, just outside the castle walls, that the guards would overlook my presence. Any approach on Firenze's part

would sound an alarm with plenty of time for us to take shelter. And
I wanted them to see it, the view from the top.

We walked along the edge, toward the back of the castle, looking
down at the people. I glimpsed Father Tomas's face as he talked to
Rabellino, and I hesitated, seeing alarm in his expression. *I'll have to
find out about that later,* I thought. Right now Mom and Dad needed
me fully Present and Accounted For. They deserved that much. After
all, they'd just given their permission for me to marry a fourteenth-
century nobleman. How often was a parent asked to do that?

We paused in the center of the back wall and stared out over the
valley beyond. We could see three massive bonfires and dark figures
dancing past them. I had seen mountains of food exiting the castello
over the last couple of days—Marcello's nod to his people. Now I knew
why. There had been no way to bring them all inside the castle gates.

"I feel as if I've reentered a dream," Mom said, wrapping her arm
around my waist as I leaned against the far wall. Dad came around to
my other side, and I stood there a moment, just absorbing the sensation of both of them being present with me, shoulder to shoulder.

"I don't know how to begin," I said. "How to thank you both for
trusting us with this decision. I know it's a leap."

Dad laughed. "When you jump nearly seven hundred years in
time," he said lowly, putting his hand on my shoulder, "it's not a
whole lot further to do this. It's all a form of madness, really."

"Or ultimate reality," Mom returned with a smile.

We stared into the night for a time. Then Dad said, "We want to
be sure we're clear with you, Gabi. It is our understanding that if we
are here when the plague descends, and either one of you become ill,
we shall take you and Lia home."

I let it sit a moment. I guess I'd heard it as a *possibility,* not a *plan.* "And what of Marcello?"

"He is one of the Nine," Dad said. "He'll be difficult to keep from Siena—"

"Which shall be vital," Mom put in. "The cities suffered the greatest fatalities by far during the plague."

"And if Siena is suffering," Dad said, "he shall consider it his place to stay, will he not?"

I thought about that. "Yes. You're right."

"So we want you to consider it, Gabi," Dad said. "Consider it fully. You may not be saying good-bye to Marcello now, but you may well be saying good-bye to him in the future."

I swallowed, hard, glancing toward the dark silhouette of the hill where Fortino was buried. Where the eerie carved tomb of Marcello's great-grandparents stood, beneath the scrub oak. Death and disease seemed to loom.

"I think the trick to living fully," I said, thinking through each word, "is to appreciate what we have, day by day, regardless of what we know *might* come our way." I took a breath and slowly looked from one of my parents to the other. "If I live in fear of what might be, how can I truly live my life to the full in the present? And if I do not give myself to the day, to hope, to life, what do I miss?" I raised my eyebrows and shook my head. "Life itself, I think. At least the way I wanna live it."

I glanced at Mom, then Dad.

He looked past me, at Mom. "She's ready, Adri. God help me, I think she's actually ready to do this."

Mom smiled at me as she stroked my hair. "They have to grow up fast, here. Gabi has seen far more than I ever would have imagined. And yet…I think it's somehow made her exactly who she was meant to be. We've raised a lady, Ben. The future Lady Forelli d' Toscana."

Dad's arm slipped from my shoulder, and he leaned his forearms against the wall. "So…I've heard that you are more safe as Marcello's wife than you are as his intended."

I frowned. "Who told you that?"

He shrugged. "Tomas, on the way back from Roma. And more than one person has told me so tonight," he said, turning his head to gaze at the celebrants below. "We were wondering…" he started. "What we thought…"

"We wondered if you should marry sooner than later," Mom put in, rescuing him as he tried to find the right words.

"Oh," I said, trying to cover my surprise. "Siena…I think the republic will expect a William-and-Kate kinda thing."

Dad sighed. "But what if…if you were married here, and then later the republic *got* their fairy tale wedding gig?"

I grinned and clasped my hands together. "Seriously? That would be perfect! I've been dreaming of something small—"

"Intimate," Mom said, understanding right off.

"Right," I said with a grin.

"Then later Siena can have her turn," Dad said.

"But legally," Mom said, "in the eyes of the Church—"

"And should anyone try," Dad said, "to nab you again—"

"I'd be Marcello's alone. Already claimed."

"Right," Mom said. "No more kidnappings with political intent. No more *threats*. We've had our fill of that."

"Well then," Dad said. "It's done. I'll speak to Marcello."

When we returned to the courtyard, Dad moved off directly with Marcello, and I hurried over to Lia to fill her in. She gasped, and her eyes widened with surprise. "No. *Way*. They did *not* say that."

"*Way*." I couldn't stop the smile from spreading across my face.

"How…how soon?"

"I don't know," I said. "Dad's talking to Marcello now. Tomorrow? The next day? Soon. Siena will be insane, once word spreads. And I assume Mom and Dad are right—that news of our engagement will just up the ante for people like Lord Barbato to raise their ugly pointy heads…"

Lia blinked. "I can't believe this is happening."

"Neither can I. And yet, Lia, I know I don't want anything *but* this to happen." My eyes trailed across the courtyard, searching for him among the waning crowds. I found him and stared at his handsome profile, the awe in his face as he absorbed what my dad was telling him at that very moment.

He looked quickly across the remaining guests, searching for me, and found me at last.

We smiled at each other, grinning like idiots. Not only were we to be married—we were to be married soon. It felt like I was floating. Like those cartoon characters bobbing from one cloud to the next? Totally me at that moment. Over-the-moon-dorky-in-love.

"Whoa," Lia said. "You are *history*."

"Ancient history," I murmured dreamily, staring at my knight.

"So it's really happening. We're here for good."

I looked at her quickly, trying to read her expression. Was she having second thoughts? "This will be it, Lia. Are you ready for that? To stay here, forever?"

She turned toward me and took my hands in hers. "Gabi, if you're here, I am too. And not just because I can't get back without you or we might lose Dad somehow on the way. Because I wouldn't *want* to go back without you."

I squeezed her hands. "Thank you, Sis."

"Uh, I'm thinking it's me that oughta thank you."

I followed the direction of her gaze and saw Luca walking toward the Great Hall. Then I looked back to my man as Lia and I grinned and hugged.

Marcello turned to Dad then, shook his hand, and strode over to me. It was like a scene from a dream, watching him edge past strumming musicians and three men who had had way too much wine, past women who reached for him, mouthing, "Congratulations, m'lord," and men who patted him on the back. All the while he kept his eyes on me. As if I were the only one in the entire castle.

"Gabriella. May I see you to your quarters?" he asked huskily, as he finally reached us.

"G'night, sis," Lia whispered, edging away.

"I'd like that," I said, barely able to breathe. I wanted to kiss him *so* bad.

Regally he took my arm, and we paraded toward the back of the castle and to the turret stairs. He opened the door and gestured for me to enter before him. I did so and waited for him under the flickering light of the torch. I glanced upward. No one else was within the tower.

And then he was there, crushing me to him, pushing me backward, into the wall, kissing me as hard and with as much passion as I had for him. He raised me up, his hands on my back, at my side, on my neck, his fingers crawling through my hair, as we kissed, as hard as I'd ever kissed anyone in my life. I wanted to be with him. One with him, always and forever.

He paused, even as I went on kissing him.

He stepped away from me at last, uttering a low groan, and put both his hands on my shoulders. "Enough," he groaned in a pant. "I cannot take another moment."

"Let us not wait," I said. "Let us fetch Father Tomas and take our vows this night."

He laughed under his breath and shook his head. "Do not tempt me. God help me, Gabriella, do not tempt me." He took an end-of-his-rope hold of my head in his hands and smiled into my eyes. "Your parents…we have asked much of them this night, and they have offered so much more in return. Let us do this as they see fit."

"And what is that?" I asked flirtatiously, reaching up to touch his face and kiss his lips. "How long until I become yours, forever?"

He looked down at me with such intensity, I knew he totally wanted to kiss me again. "On the morrow," he said.

I smiled. "Truly?"

"Truly."

"Then I think I can wait one more night."

He looked to the side, as if he was really wondering if he could wait too.

"But," I dared in a whisper, "who would know if we didn't?"

He stilled, but his eyes betrayed the weight of struggle that I felt inside. "God. And if it is He who has brought us together, should we not honor Him in this way?"

I considered him. The heat of him. The strength of him. The raw power of him, so close and yet so deliciously forbidden… "We should, m'lord." But I couldn't help it. I lifted my chin again, hoping he'd give in to at least one more kiss.

His mouth was so close to mine, I could feel every cool intake of breath and every hot exhale. He caved then, to my silent begging, kissing me, pulling me as close as he could—before he growled, stepped away, and took my hand, racing me up the stairs and down the hallway to my room.

He set me, dazed, in my doorway, my lips feeling swollen, my head fuzzy. Then he stepped away, hands up as if to fend me off. "On the morrow," he said, almost angrily, as if I were disagreeing with him, "you shall be mine."

I laughed under my breath. "You shall get no arguments from me, m'lord," I said. It took everything in me not to step toward him, to entice him over the edge. I knew it wouldn't be hard. It would only take one small, quiet, gentle kiss, right between his ear and jawline.…

I struggled against it. Against the pull of the power I now knew I wielded over him. Against the desire I felt within me.

But I couldn't do that to him. To either of us. To our future.

We'd made a promise, and I didn't want anything, *anything* to get in the way of that promise. I didn't want our union to be less-than, tarnished, shadowed, robbed of its potential power.

And judging from what I'd just experienced, that was a whole lotta power indeed.

# Chapter Twenty-five

Someone was in my bed.

I took hold of the covers and edged carefully, steadily away, then sprang to my feet, turning to face the intruder. The very last of the embers in the fireplace cast a dim glow over her profile.

Lia sleepily squinted at me through one eye and rose up on one elbow. "Chill, Gabs. It's only me."

"*Lia*," I said, putting a hand over my hammering heart. "You shouldn't do that to me!" I shivered in the frigid air and hopped back under the covers and stared at her. "What are you doing in here?"

"I couldn't sleep," she said, flopping onto her back and lacing her fingers under her head. "Nice ceiling."

"Isn't it? Marcello's dad had it painted for his mother because she loved stars so much."

"Mmm, that's romantic."

"Yes," I agreed, lying down next to her, hands under my head too. It was almost as if we were out on a summer's night, staring upward. Except the room was so cold my nose felt frosty. I tucked it under the covers. "So…you couldn't sleep, so you decided to steal into my room and give me a heart attack."

"Won't have a chance to do it much after tonight, will I?"

*Ahh, so that was what this was about.* She was worried. Feeling separated. Left behind. She hated that. And I understood a part of it, feared it too.

"It's going to change between us, Gabs. With you getting married."

"Maybe a little," I said, glancing over at her. She was so beautiful. I loved the gentle slope of her nose, the tip of her chin. She looked more like a girl than woman when she fretted. "But nothing can ever come between sisters. Not even marriage. Not if we don't let it. It might change a bit, but let's look it as a bend in the river we're riding on together. I'm on that river forever with you, little sis."

She gave me a close-lipped smile and studied my hand. "No ring?"

"No ring," I said. "I'm not even sure if they exchange rings. Have you noticed?"

"Maybe plain bands. Nothing else."

I nodded. "That's all right. I'm not a big rock kind of girl anyway."

"Yes, you are," she teased. "Total gold digger. We come to Toscana, and who'd you go and fall in love with? One of the richest dudes possible."

"Well, there you have it. My secret's out." I paused and then looked over at her. "So, after tomorrow, I assume my life of luxury? Nothing but sitting around, watching on-demand movies and ordering Chinese?"

She giggled. And then stilled, working up to the question she obviously wanted to ask me. "Gabs, how do you know? Know that Marcello is the one?"

I shook my head. Yes, I knew without a doubt. Images flashed through my mind, and I found my voice again. "It helped to be at that altar in St. Peter's, to be looking at Lord Greco, in a way."

"Because you knew he *wasn't* the one."

"And because, just as much, I knew Marcello *was*. At that moment, even if you and the rest hadn't arrived, I knew I would take a stand. Refuse anyone else, no matter how they threatened me. Because it was so wrong—" I shook my head again. "So different from what I know tomorrow will be—a promise, a hope. Life." I looked over at her. "Marcello is far from perfect. I get that. But he's perfect for me. Together we're stronger. We want nothing but the best for each other. And surely, out of that, there has to be some sort of decent marriage."

It was her turn to nod. "I think that's what Mom and Dad have. That desire to do what's right for the other."

"Yes." I decided it was what had kept them so focused on each other for all those years. It wasn't just the romantic love they shared—it was how they lived life as partners, going-the-distance kind of partners. And knowing how I felt about Marcello, how everyone else kind of faded when he was in the room, I had just a taste of what my parents had been feeling for about twenty years.

For the first time I didn't resent what they had together; I understood, appreciated it.

"What about you?" I asked, finding my breath again. "What are you thinking about Luca?"

She shifted, as if embarrassed. "I like him. A lot. But love? I don't know if I'm ready to go there."

"That's all right," I teased. "He'll wait."

She elbowed me in the side. "Stop it."

"What? He's crazy about you. You know that, right?"

"Right," she said. "But what if he's not the right one for me?"

"Then you'll know that in time," I forced myself to say. I couldn't imagine anyone more awesome than him for her, but that was something she had to come to—I couldn't make her see it.

"What if…I want out of here?" she asked. "Later, I mean? It's kinda claustrophobic, like living on an island or something, living in this castle, so close to the border."

I stilled even as my heartbeat picked up its pace. If she didn't agree…If she was having second thoughts, I was sunk. "Lia…I thought…when we were talking…I thought you were sure."

"I was. I am. I'm just…wow, it's a lot to take in, though. Just tell me you wouldn't freak if I wanted to leave Toscana at some point. Maybe head to Venezia, see what it's like in the fourteenth century there. Give me some sort of break."

I breathed a sigh of relief. She was talking about getting out of here. Not getting back to our time. "Yes, *totally*. Maybe I'll even go with you."

"Road trip!" she said with a giggle. "'Cept it will be by horse, and it'll take a whole lot longer."

I giggled with her. "Let's do it. Get the guys to take us up there."

"Mom and Dad would love that."

"Okay, then. It's a promise. We'll convince them. No one can stand between the She-Wolves of Siena and what they want." I raised my hand, and she took it again. "I love you, Lia. Thank you for doing this. For me."

"Oh, Gabs. It's for you. But I can't help feeling like it's for our family. Without this place we'd still be without Dad. And being together…we're whole again. And more. With Luca and Marcello, you know."

"I know." I took a breath. "Now can I get some sleep? I'm supposed to be beautiful tomorrow. Not all white-faced with deep, purple circles under my eyes. You know. Bride material."

"Right. Do you mind? Me staying with you this last night?"

I turned over to my side and rested our entwined hands on the flat of her belly. "Are you kidding?" I said, letting my heavy lids slip closed. "It's perfect."

"Gabs, come on. Something's up," Lia whispered.

I stirred, stretched, and squinted my eyes at her. "What?"

"I don't know. You had better come quick, though. Marcello's having a full-blown argument with Father Tomas in Fortino's den."

I sat up fast, waited for my tunnel vision to fade, then rose. Lia helped me slip on a gown and buttoned me up. I took a few swipes at my hair with a horsehair brush, wound it into a rough knot, and stuck a stick in it, and we raced down the hall, down the turret stairs, and over to the next corridor.

I heard them yelling as soon as we were through the hallway door. Or rather, Marcello yelling. "You cannot! I forbid it!" he said, pacing as we paused in the den door. It took me back a bit, to be in the room. Remembering Fortino in there too. I eyed the chessboard, the lambskin bound copy of Dante's *Divine Comedy,* the swords on the wall.

"'Tis not your place to approve of my journey or not, m'lord," Father Tomas said gently. Neither of them had seen us yet.

"It was my understanding that you would perform the wedding ceremony today," Marcello said, bending toward him. "It was my understanding that you had agreed to assume the chaplaincy here."

I sucked in my breath. Was that what this was all about? We'd be without a priest for the secret ceremony? I couldn't imagine anyone but Tomas being the one to marry us. *But sheesh, talk about your overreaction…Marcello, ease up! This is supposed to be the happiest day of our lives!*

Lia coughed, covering her mouth with a fist to let 'em know we were there.

"Surely we can figure out a solution," I said, stepping forward. I moved to Marcello and took his hands. He distractedly kissed both my cheeks and then released me. Hardly the kind of warm reception I'd expected on the morning of our wedding. I shoved down my feelings of disappointment and tried to not get too angry. Was he so used to getting his own way that he was pouting? Furious at Tomas for thwarting his plans?

I glanced at the priest. "Tomas. What is it? Where are you off to? And must it be this day? Surely you can stay a few more hours…"

He stared at me and then glanced at Marcello, who was pacing back and forth across the floor, head down as if he could figure it out if he only tried hard enough—

It was then I knew that something else was going on. This was more than a little frustration over our plans. I thought back, remembered Tomas speaking to Lord Rabellino last night. "You discovered something," I said softly.

Tomas stared at Marcello, and when Marcello said nothing, turned back to me. "'Tis Lord Greco."

Lia came fully through the door then. "Lord Greco," she repeated. "Rodolfo, yes."

"He's taken the brunt of the blame," Marcello said with a growl, lifting a hand in frustration. "Lord Barbato pinned our whole escape from Roma on him. Said he's been a Sienese sympathizer from the start. Protected you. Protected Fortino. And ultimately let you go." He took a few steps and stared at the high window, hand over his mouth. He looked over his shoulder at us. "He's been stripped of everything. Title. Land. Thrown in prison. They're bringing him here."

"To us?" I asked, bracing.

"Nay, to the border. To Castello Paratore. They want him to be able to see us, the Sienese, and the Sienese to see him, when they impale him."

"Impale him?" I asked numbly. "What does that mean?"

Marcello closed his eyes and rubbed all ten fingers into his forehead, pressing inward. "The worst form of execution, borrowed from the Ottomans. They take a pointed pole…" He shook his head, as if the mere thought of it pained him and he could not bear to tell us more. He threw his hands out, fingers splayed. "It's reserved for traitors, the worst sort of traitors, and has been used recently by our old friend Lord Paratore, who seems to delight in it. But Rodolfo shall suffer for days before he dies."

"But…but," I said, sitting heavily in the closest chair. "'Tis not how the Rossis were executed, right? Were they not accused of similar crimes?"

"Nay, because the Sienese are civil. Not barbarians," he cried, throwing his hands out again. I knew he wasn't angry with me.

"And you—you think you can stop it?" I asked Tomas.

"Nay," he said sadly. "I must go to him to receive his last confession, to be his friend."

"Which is, in effect, signing his own death sentence," Marcello spat out angrily, gesturing toward Tomas. "He knows as well as I that the Fiorentini will tie him to you, to us. Saints above! The last time they saw him in Roma, who was hauling him away? Lady Gabriella Betarrini. They'll impale him beside Rodolfo!"

I stared hard at Tomas. "Why?" I asked in confusion. "Why would you give your life just to see him?"

"Because he has done far more for me," Tomas said steadily. "He is a friend. A brother."

Marcello let out a sound of exasperation. "Show her. Get it over with!"

Tomas sighed and rolled up the brown sleeve of his robe to show me the triangular tattoo at his elbow.

I let out a soft breath. "Oh." Now it made sense. Him leaving Rodolfo, coming after me. Watching out for me—because I was Marcello's intended as well as Rodolfo's friend. Rodolfo protecting him, giving him a job as chaplain, regardless of his status within the church.

"What's that?" Lia whispered.

I ignored her. "How many are there?" I asked. "How many more?"

"A fair number," Marcello hedged.

"Have you called on them before?" I pressed.

"Only Rodolfo. And now Tomas, in a fashion."

"How soon can the rest arrive?" I asked intently. I threw out my hands in exasperation. "I assume they have men they can bring with them. They're not all priests who've sworn to never wield a sword, are they?"

Marcello's eyes met mine. I was asking if their alliance—so strong that a man would go to his death for another, even betray his current allegiances if necessary—was big enough, wide enough, strong enough to do battle with what was coming our way. Siena would ride to our aid. But we needed something more—something stronger, if we were to save Rodolfo. If we were to change the course of our river, once and for all.

"If I send out messengers now," Marcello said, "they might get here in time."

So there *were* enough.

Men in power. Men willing to fight for one other. Men who would come and help us.

"I take it you're not getting married today," Lia said lowly, from my side.

I looked into Marcello's eyes. "Nay. Today we prepare for the war coming to our door."

# Chapter Twenty-six

My family, Marcello's principal knights, Tomas, and Luca all sat in the den, staring at the map that showed the area around Castello Paratore and Castello Forelli. Ten messengers on our fastest horses had been sent out to find the men who'd once made a pledge to Marcello, to Rodolfo, to Tomas. I had no idea if those men were all there were—or if they were merely all who still lived.

"Tomas cannot go alone," I said, pacing back and forth. "We need people inside Castello Paratore's gates, to aid him if he encounters trouble—"

"Which he shall," Marcello interrupted, throwing his hands up in frustration.

"And to help him and Lord Greco escape," I finished. I looked at the priest as Cook edged past with a heavy tray of food. "What if I went with you, disguised as a nun?"

"Nay," Marcello said. "Are you mad? You are far too recognizable, even in a nun's garb. Paratore would know you in a moment." He paced away and then back again, rubbing the back of his neck. "He sneaked his own men into the ranks of Castello Forelli. He'll be wary of us trying to return such trickery."

"He'll be looking for knights in disguise," Cook said, setting the tray between us. She straightened and rested her hands on her ample belly. "But I've heard tell that they're hiring servants across at Castello Paratore now that the despicable man has returned and his men with him. Could you not sneak in a few of your loyalists within their ranks? They might not be able to wield a sword or bow, but could they not unlock a door?"

Marcello's eyes shone with excitement. He rose and rubbed his hands together. "How many, Cook?"

"From what I hear tell, they're seeking a good ten girls for the kitchen, as well as a good number of men for the stables. I heard about it just this morning, down at the market. Most weren't interested, o' course, owing to their loyalties to Siena. But given the cold of winter is upon us and stores in the cellar draw low…"

Marcello bit his lip and shook his head. "I do not know if I can abide by the idea of sending women into harm's way."

"Even if those women asked to do so?" Cook returned. "Beggin' your pardon, m'lord, but your people have just been returned to their rightful homes. They're willing to give anything to help you keep the castello. As well as protect Siena's own."

He studied her. "What good could an unarmed girl do in the face of so many enemy knights? And men, with no more than a pitchfork?"

"More than you might imagine," I said with a slow grin.

"The women would be in the kitchen," Mom added. "Could they not add something to the stew, the bread, to make the men sick, weak, in the face of your attack?"

"Or barricade themselves inside rooms within the castle?" I said. "Mayhap in the armory, effectively shutting the men out?"

"And the men in the stables, could they not do the same?" Dad said. "Weaken saddle straps, set ropes to unraveling, even set herds free, adding to the chaos?"

I laughed in disbelief. Could it be so simple? *Talk about your guerilla warfare tactics...*

"Some could assist in the camps," Cook said. "They wouldn't be inside the castle gates, but they'd be set to foil Firenze's plans in the most surprising places."

"Cook," Marcello said, shaking his head in wonder, "you are ingenious."

"I take offense at your surprise, m'lord," she joked.

But Marcello wasn't paying attention. His brow lowered by the second. "They shall be executed. Killed immediately, if they are found out."

Cook sobered. "You do not force anyone to do this. But if they so wish..."

"If they so wish, and succeed, they shall be rewarded greatly. But they must enter knowing there shall be no rescue, no aid, if they are captured."

"'Twould be an honorable deal, one many shall leap toward," Cook said, then picked up the empty goblets and a pitcher.

"Not a word to anyone," Marcello said.

"Silent as the tomb," she said in a whisper. Then she was gone.

"We cannot send anyone who might be recognized over at Castello Paratore," Lia said.

Marcello nodded, chin in hand, pacing again. "Only our newest recruits."

"So then," Georgii said, clapping Luterius's shoulder, "we resume life as stable boys, when we've only just parted from our squiring days."

"Nay," Marcello said. "They might recognize you from Sansicino. Go and see if there are knights among the ranks, however, with a youthful appearance. There may be room, yet, for a few fighting men in disguise."

"Consider it done, m'lord," Georgii said, setting off with his brother right away.

"And us? How might we be of assistance?" I asked.

"By our side," Marcello said, "the Betarrinis shall inspire our men and distract our enemies. The Fiorentini will be so wild with hope that they might capture you again, they won't think to second-guess the men and women around them."

"So we shall once again be bait to the bear?" Lia said, tensing, remembering.

Marcello was quick to shake his head. "Nothing like last time. That was far too dangerous. You shall be figureheads—escorted to the safety of the castle—not ever at the center of the battle."

I nodded in agreement, the subservient lil' wife-to-be. But inside I was thinking *Yeah, right. We'll see.* Battle had a way of turning in unexpected directions. We'd be prepared, regardless.

For anything. For everything.

Giacinta was first among the servants to volunteer. "'Twould be my distinct honor, m'lady," she said.

"Oh," I protested. "Do you think it's wise, Giacinta? Your daughter is so young—"

"And I want her to grow up to fight for what she believes is right," Giacinta returned. "My mother can see to her, just as she does every other day."

"But what if you don't come home?" I pressed. "This is hardly like any other day and—"

"And I know it's what I am to do, m'lady," she interrupted gently.

"He's ruthless," Lia put in. "Paratore—he'll be a terror if it's discovered that you have infiltrated the castello for our goals."

"Then he shall not find out."

I studied her. She was far more determined than I thought possible. "Marcello will promise no rescue," I said. "'Twill not matter how much I plead on your behalf—"

"Be at ease, m'lady," she said resting a gentle hand on my arm and looking into my eyes. "I know the stakes are grave. I wish to do this. As you and your sister might, if they did not know you on sight."

I bit my lip and nodded. She seemed sure....I glanced toward Mom, wondering what she thought.

"But what am I to do?" Giacinta said. "I know not how to wield a sword as you do, or a bow as Lady Evangelia."

Mom smiled.

"You wield a far greater weapon in the kitchen," I said.

Mom offered her a glass bottle full of liquid. "Slip this into the cauldrons of porridge for the men," she said. "It shall give them stomachaches that will not kill them but will certainly make them wish they *could* die."

Giacinta's eyes grew wide with understanding. "So they cannot fight."

"Right. It needs to go into the morning porridge the day of Lord Greco's execution."

"You'll have to pay close attention to gossip from the keep so that you are apprised of the goings-on," I said. "We'll get a couple of the other girls to assist you in it."

"As soon as it's done you must take your leave," Lia said. "'Twill not take long for them to suspect you."

Giacinta gave us a shy look. "Fear not, m'ladies. I shall be away like a shadow in the night."

Lia and Mom and I shared a surprised look—who knew my hairdressing maid had such strength within her?—but we all smiled back at her. "I do believe you, Giacinta," I said, "shall be our most valuable secret weapon of all."

We found several women willing to try to free any prisoners in Lord Paratore's dungeon—memories of Lia within it sent a shiver down my back—and still others who agreed to unlock doors and barricade the armory. Meanwhile the youngest and most eager knights and squires were brought together and briefed on their task, which was essentially to bring down any able-bodied knight inside Castello Paratore, as well as assist our cause, the moment they had the chance. "If you can take down one or two in preparation for battle, even," Marcello said, pacing before the group of them, hands behind him, "there shall be one fewer dumping flaming oil down on our backs when we charge the castle gates.

"We have but two goals for this battle ahead of us," Marcello continued. "One, to rescue Lord Greco, who has been an aid to us in more ways than one. And two, to capture Castello Paratore. Once it is in our hands, we shall dismantle it, stone by stone, so our enemies may never take up residence in it again.

"We shall press the Fiorentini back. Reestablish a proper boundary for Siena. Their utter and pronounced defeat, and Lord Greco's defection, shall remove any hope they have of retaliation. Our valleys shall enjoy years of peace." He was giving them the pep talk, psyching them up for what was ahead. But he was guessing, hoping. Not promising.

"If you are not willing to die for the cause, do not go. It is most dangerous," he said gravely, looking each of them in the eye. "If caught, you cannot look to us to save you. You are entering the heart of war. But if you die, you shall be heralded as heroes."

They cheered, as if they could not imagine any outcome other than victory. But I swallowed hard, thinking of how many ways I'd seen my own plans fail.

Marcello set them loose, in groups of three or on their own, heading toward Castello Paratore after Father Tomas prayed over them, long and hard. It was a bit overwhelming, really. It was one thing for knights to fight for you—they were paid, trained to do so—but servants? It was a level of loyalty I'd never seen before. They *wanted* this, still smarting from the beating they'd taken a year ago. When Castello Forelli had been taken, when they'd been turned out from their home.

I walked over to the wall and put a hand on the cold, rough-cut stone. Marcello wanted me here, in the center of the old structure.

But did he not remember that no castle—or even city—had yet proven to be a safe haven? No, we could make wise choices, do our best moment by moment. But our lives would end the day God chose to step aside and allow it. And if either Lia or I died, there'd be no going back in time to save us.

"Visitors, m'lord," announced a stable boy to Marcello. The boy gave the group of servants a curious look, but then left us.

I glanced at Marcello. The first of his brothers from afar? He offered his arm to me, and we paraded out to the courtyard, Lia and Luca and my parents right on our heels.

"Conte Lerici," he called, recognizing the man.

The young man, not entirely handsome but reeking of power and money, swept off his horse, his camel-colored cape—with the herald of a hawk embroidered on it—swinging in dramatic fashion. Beyond him were twelve men, exquisitely attired in the same camel color, each with finely wrought bows and elaborately feathered arrows. He greeted Marcello halfway, clasping his arm and sharing a secretive grin. I'd certainly never met him in Siena—and he was the kind of man you'd remember.

"Conte Lerici," Marcello said. "May I present my intended, Lady Gabriella Betarrini?"

Conte Lerici gave me a slow smile, and warmth entered his calculating eyes. "M'lady," he said, bowing over my hand but not kissing it. "'Tis far more an honor than you realize."

I gave him a puzzled look.

"During the Great Battle," he explained, still holding my hand and straightening, "you led the bulk of Firenze's men away from my castello, sparing it that night."

"I confess, Conte Lerici," I said with a regretful smile, glancing over his shoulder at the dozen men, "that I had no idea where I was leading those enemy forces. I only knew I was to lead them away from Marcello. And I was attempting to preserve my own life at the same time."

"Ahh," he said, joining me in my smile. "Such is my fortune." His eyes roamed past me to Lia.

"Uh-uh," Luca said playfully, taking Lerici's arm next in greeting. "That one is *my* lady," he said, grinning into the man's eyes. They were about the same height.

"Seems as if I shouldn't have tarried so long in the West," Conte Lerici said. "'Twas here that I might have found my contessa."

"After the battle we shall focus on nothing but your quest," Luca pledged.

The visitor laughed, a deep, genuine sound, and I liked him better for it. Based on the easy camaraderie among the men, I knew the count had to be one of the ten Marcello had sent for—those in the brotherhood forged so long ago.

Further introductions were made and the men were given food, the horses water and oats. "The finest archers between Roma and Venezia," Marcello said in my ear, gleeful. "Had he brought a hundred men on horses instead, I would have still opted for those twelve."

"We should put Lia with them," I offered. "She has ideas on where to hide archers in preparation."

"Excellent. Let's get them in place soon, far before the battle begins."

I laughed when Mom came toward us, red-faced and with a smudge of soot on her forehead. "How fares the bread baker?" I asked. With the servants so rapidly disappearing, we all had volunteered to do miscellaneous tasks not normally left to us. And Mom had been so keen to try her hand at baking bread again.

"Brutal," she said, wiping her forehead of its sheen of sweat, despite the cool of the winter afternoon. "I would accept the hazards of baking bread at high altitude every time over the hazards of a wood-fired stove."

I smiled. "How many loaves did you manage?"

"Twenty," she said proudly, obviously pleased with herself. She eyed me over her shoulder. "I said it was difficult, not impossible."

"Well done," I said. "Can I be of help in the kitchen?"

"Not yet," she said, "but come supper time, most likely."

We were continuing on our way toward the Great Hall, where Marcello could grab some food and confer with Conte Lerici, when a call went up at the gates. Marcello and I both froze, fearing it might be the scouts, returning far too soon, warning us that Paratore was on the move. But through the gate walked two teenage boys who had been sent to Castello Paratore earlier.

Marcello smiled gently and clapped the first on the shoulder. "Rejected, were we?"

"Not enough experience," the boy said.

"Nay, we needed a couple of young farmers in the mix, willing to give up their fields in order to work inside the castello," Marcello said. He folded his arms. "How many are in?"

The boys eyed each other and then thought about it, naming one after the other they'd seen inside.

"Fifteen," I said in wonder. "That's remarkable."

"We can utilize your skills here," Marcello said in a tone of consolation.

The boys accepted his words and glumly went on to the well to pull up a pail of water. I watched them and gave a Marcello a wry look. "So becoming a stable boy has become a position of glory."

"Indeed," he said. "Fifteen," he added, squeezing my hand in excitement. It was working—far better than we had hoped. We'd only hoped to get ten of our people inside. I thought of Giacinta and said a quick prayer for her.

The gates were just closing when they opened again for three wagons carrying long, heavy loads of timber. They looked to me like a massive set of Lincoln Logs. "Catapult," Marcello said in a tone of utter delight. "Which could only mean—"

"Forelli!" called a small, wide man in nobleman's clothes. Eight men walked in behind him. Another from the brotherhood. The two clasped arms and then embraced. The short man eyed me, but his attention was on Marcello. "Thought you could utilize this old relic," he said, moving toward a wagon and pulling back a long blanket. Was it dismantled because they wished to hide the fact that Castello Forelli was now armed with such a device? Or was it simply to transport it?

"Old relic—I find that highly suspect," Marcello said, running his hand along the finely carved notches. "Was it just completed?"

"A fortnight past," the man said, shrugging his shoulders. "I'd thought it was necessary to provide some sort of protection for our manor, but when I got your message, I knew it had a far greater destiny here."

"I am beyond grateful," Marcello said. I edged closer, and Marcello turned to me. "Sir Mantova," he said, "my bride to be, Lady Gabriella Betarrini."

"Your bride to be?" said the man with a wide grin. He kept slapping Marcello on the shoulder as if he was the luckiest man on the planet, all the while staring at me and hooting with pleasure over the news.

I laughed under my breath, a little embarrassed. I shifted uneasily, but Marcello took my hand in both of his.

"You'd better marry her this night," Sir Mantova said. "She's far safer as your wife than as your intended."

I squirmed. *So we're back to that again?* I wanted to see this through, and *then* see to my wedding. Thinking about both at the same time was enough to put me over the edge.

"Gabriella shall be safely ensconced in Castello Forelli," Marcello said, kissing my hand.

Mantova cocked one brow and pursed his lips as if he was going to argue it, but Marcello turned him and pointed in the direction of the Great Hall. "Come. Eat your fill and see that your men do the same."

Others arrived over the course of the afternoon and early evening. A young lord with thirty-six highly trained knights. Another with eighteen on horseback. Still another with twenty-four more fighting men.

It was sweltering in the kitchen, and feeding so many took hours. By the time supper was over, Lia and I wanted to dip our whole heads in the pails of water.

Marcello leaned against the doorjamb of the kitchen, arms crossed. Luca hovered behind him. "Look, Luca. Are these not the two prettiest kitchen maids you've ever seen in your life?"

I rolled my eyes and wiped my forehead of sweat. "The two *hottest* kitchen maids you've ever seen in your life," I said.

"And she means that literally," Lia said, edging past me with another pile of dirty wooden trenchers to wash. I looked at them and groaned, seriously wishing we could call back all the servants from Castello Paratore.

"Sit," Marcello demanded. "Luca and I shall see to these."

"We shall?" Luca asked.

"We shall," he said firmly. "You two look as if you might faint dead away if you don't find your escape now."

"You don't have to ask me twice," Lia said, moving out the door just as another servant arrived with more dishes and a second left carrying hot soup and a ladle.

"Go, Gabriella," Marcello said, taking my shoulders and moving me toward the door. "You have done your fair share."

"You could stay and accompany me," Luca said to Lia. "I might get lonely in here." He dipped his hands into the hot water.

"Nonsense," she teased. "You have Lord Marcello."

"You think he is a replacement for you?" Luca asked.

"He's the best you'll get this eve," she returned.

He clasped his wet hands to his heart as if she'd wounded him. Laughing, we turned to go.

"Gabriella," Marcello said, "would you kindly change and meet me in the library in an hour's time?"

I blinked. Change? I glanced down at my dress and saw the stains and water marks all down the face of my brown gown. "Oh. Yes, of course."

He smiled. "Excellent. I shall see you in an hour."

I turned with Lia, and we walked to the back turret that led to my quarters. "Will you help me slip on another dress?" I asked. "Apparently my clothes work for the kitchen but not for company."

"I'd say that again," she said with a laugh.

We waited for a group of new knights to pass; they reminded me of a bunch of college boys out on the town, casting us flirty looks and wolfish whistles. The last of them turning full around to check us out—obviously thinking we were just a couple of kitchen maids—and Lia and I laughed.

"They are going to feel *so* bad when they figure out who we are," she said under her breath.

We entered the turret door and climbed the stairs.

I smelled rose petals and beeswax before we hit the second level.

"Uh, Gabi?" Lia asked, staring down the hallway. Twenty fat candles had been lit along the stone walls, and red rose petals were strewn along the walkway. As we drew closer, I could see that my door was open. I frowned. What was this? Slowly I reached down and took out my dagger.

"Really?" Lia asked, laughing at me with her eyes. "What? Someone's come to kill you with romance?"

But I didn't share her laughter. She hadn't been there, in Roma. Experienced the baths, the preparation. There were a lot of strangers in Castello Forelli this night. And hadn't we, ourselves, succeeded in placing our own within our enemy's gates? Was it such a leap to wonder about this?

Lia stepped forward, and I gripped her arm. She shook it off. "Man, Gabs, ease up," she said. "This has Marcello written all over it." She scooted away and moved toward the door.

"*Lia*," I warned.

But she was through it without even a look back at me.

All was silent a moment. Then, "Uh, Gabs, you'd better get in here."

I entered and saw more candles illuminating my room. On my bedroom door was a note:

*My love—*

*I am yours. Shall you be mine?*

*Marcello*

The den, in an hour. Could it be? Had he planned…in the midst of everything else…?

A periwinkle blue gown, exquisitely simple and elegant, shimmered on the bed. Beside it was a pretty, but more basic, green gown. For Lia, I supposed. A tray, with bread and fruit upon it. An hourglass, turned over, the sands patiently whirring through to the bottom. And the tub, with a shallow bath and rose petals floating on it. I reached down. It was barely warm, but the aroma…"Where'd he get roses, this time of year?"

"I don't know," she said. "1-800-FLOWERS?"

I smiled and took half a breath. "It looks like I'm getting married today after all."

"After all," she said, moving behind me and beginning to unbutton my soggy gown in silence. I slipped into the lukewarm waters, hurriedly seeing to my bath while Lia changed into her gown. When I stood up and had toweled off, I buttoned her up the back. After I'd put on a new set of delicately woven underclothes, set out for me in a neat pile, and she'd wrapped my torso in the soft, silk wrap, Lia eyed the remaining sand in the hourglass and combed out my hair. "Want me to try and braid it or something?" she asked.

"No. They like it down on their wedding day," I said. "I just wish I had a blow-dryer and straightener."

"Nah. You look awesome like that. Fresh. Beautiful. He's going to go nuts."

I smiled and rose, lifting the luscious gown in my hands. It was the color of spring flowers, of delicate petals, of the sky at twilight. The entire bodice was embroidered with seed pearls, reminding me of a gown I'd worn in Siena, of those days in which we'd first danced together on the rooftop of Palazzo Rossi, and known. Known we were in love. That it was inevitable. Inescapable. Fated. Perfect, regardless of the complications and the obstacles before us. That somehow we had to find our way to be together. Even if we tried to escape the truth of it, for a while.

And now, here we were. I slipped the dress over my head, and Lia tugged it down into place. The swooping neckline hit just at the shoulder and fabric at the upper arms clung tight then flared out at the elbow. I winced when I saw the green and blue bruise peeking out. "Well, so much for my career as a bridal show model," I said.

She gave me a soft smile. "He'll love you all the more for it. A wound from your escape?"

I nodded. She moved to my back and buttoned me up, making me suck in my breath to get the last of them closed. The skirt flowed outward, with a slight train. Then she reached for a delicate crown on the bed, made of the same seed pearls as those on my gown, woven in three strands of gold, and gathered into five "petals" resembling orange blossoms. She set it on my head and stood back. "My gosh, Gabi. I don't think we could've ever found a better dress for you, even back home. You are beautiful," she said, shaking her head. "Totally beautiful."

I smiled, never feeling more gorgeous than I did in that moment.

A knock sounded at my door, and Lia went to it and peeked out. I glanced at the hourglass and saw that we were out of time. It was our parents, come to collect us.

We embraced, in the center of the room, wrapping our arms around one another until all four of us were a part of it. In the midst of all those candles, flickering, casting a warm glow over it all. Among the scent of roses. We were totally quiet, for once, not saying a word. Just sensing the sacredness of the moment. Dad smiled and gave me a long, tender kiss on the forehead. Mom did the same, from the other side, and I leaned forward to touch my forehead to Lia's.

"It's time," Dad said at last, breaking the silence. "You ready? Really ready, Gabriella, to commit your life to another?" He stared into my eyes.

And I returned his stare. "Yes."

"Because if you want to back out, now's the time to do it."

"No," I said. "This is perfect. Tuscany's version of a small, intimate service. If I'm not getting married on a Hawaiian beach, it may as well be in a castle library."

Mom and Dad shared A Look. Then she wriggled a sapphire ring from her pinkie finger—it had once belonged to her grandmother.

"Something old and something blue. But not borrowed. It's yours. She'd want you to have it."

"Something new," Dad said, slipping a delicate gold chain around my neck, with a massive pearl, in a teardrop shape as its pendant.

"Ooo, and something borrowed," Lia said, slipping the only earrings she had from home out of her ears. She slipped the tiny pearls into mine. "You're good to go now."

*Good to go,* I thought. *To go and get...married.*

# Chapter Twenty-seven

I couldn't believe it was happening.

And yet I didn't want anything else.

We moved down the hallway. Mom tucked my hand around her arm and said, "The crown—do you know why they look like orange blossoms?"

I shook my head.

"The Crusaders brought back the Saracen custom. There, they use real orange blossoms, which are exceedingly expensive. They'll probably give you a small bouquet of herbs when we arrive—they're for fertility. And they might wrap your hands together in a cloth, signifying your union."

I smiled at her. "I thought you were an Etruscan archeologist. How do you know this about medieval custom?"

She grinned. "You know me. Too many late nights watching the History Channel. And I had a college professor with a particular penchant for medieval wedding customs."

"I'm glad for it," I said, touching her hand. We reached the end of the hallway, and I glanced at them. "Thank you," I said, gazing at them all with tears in my eyes. I knew they wanted to remain here, in this time, that it wasn't just for me. But if I hadn't gone and fallen in love with Marcello? Maybe they would have wanted to try and go deeper into history, to Etruscan times. I knew Mom didn't want to go home—didn't want to risk losing Dad again. And I knew why—the thought of losing Marcello left me feeling hollow inside. But Lia—she, out of all of them, was making the greatest sacrifice. I prayed she would find peace, happiness here. With me. That my choice would ultimately be something she would be glad about, again and again.

We went down the stairs and entered the next corridor, which was lit with twenty more candles and strewn with more petals. Lia and Mom went first, and I came next, on Dad's arm. We hovered in the doorway, and the sight I saw inside caused me to bring a hand to my mouth. There were a hundred—maybe more—candles, of various heights and widths, all lit. The effect was mesmerizing. And the strong honey scent...I would've sworn I was in the middle of a beehive.

Marcello stood, grinning, at one end, beside Father Tomas. Luca offered me a small bouquet of herbs, as Mom had guessed. I lifted them to my nose to smell. Rosemary and mint and something else. The scents blended perfectly with the beeswax and rose petals. Luca took Lia's arm and walked to the end, placing her on one side before moving to stand behind Marcello

Mom and Dad were the only others in the room—two knights closed the door behind us. I knew those knights would stand guard, letting us keep our privacy. At least for the moment. I wondered if there were others, outside. In a castle as packed as ours, it was strange to not be meeting others in the hallway. But it had been utterly empty.

Dad eased me toward Marcello, and with each step, I felt some-how more connected to Marcello inside, as if our lives were literally fusing, inch by inch. I still couldn't believe this man had fallen for me. He looked down at me and smiled, shaking his head as if he felt the same wonder I felt for him.

Dad cleared his throat, and Marcello offered his hand. Dad handed Lia my tiny bouquet, then placed my fingers in Marcello's and covered them both with his own. It made my eyes well up with tears, the gesture, the sensation of us both held by him. He looked steadily at Marcello. "You shall take care of her, with everything you have in you, until your last breath?"

"Until my last breath," he promised solemnly.

Dad held his gaze another moment, then bent and kissed my temple. "Take care of him, too, sweetheart," he said. "If you both care for each other more than you care for yourself, your marriage will endure all."

I smiled at him, acknowledging his words, and he moved aside. If there ever was a marriage I wanted my own to look like, it was Mom and Dad's.

Marcello took both of my hands in his and stared into my eyes as if we were alone in the room. His hair was tied at the nape of his neck, as cleanly as his curls would allow, but one coil fell to the side of his right eye, across his cheekbone, and hovered over that strong jaw.

Gradually we felt Father Tomas staring at us. He was waiting, grinning, and when we finally looked his direction, he began his lit-urgy in Latin. I heard Luca laugh quietly under his breath. I wanted to laugh too. I couldn't stop smiling. Nothing, nothing compared to this. To being with him. Taking the oath to bond with him in a way we'd already done with our hearts.

Father Tomas slipped back into Italian after a prolonged period of Latin liturgy. "Marcello Forelli, do you take this woman as your wife? Before the people of Toscana, the republic of Siena, your family, and your God?"

"Before all, I pledge my heart to her and take her as my wife," he said.

"Gabriella Betarrini, do you take this man as your husband? Before the people of Toscana, the republic of Siena, your family, and your God?"

"Before all," I said, my voice cracking with emotion as tears slipped down my face, "I pledge my heart to him and take him as my husband."

The rest unfolded in a fog.

Tomas wrapped our wrists together with the rope that was his belt. Then slowly unwrapped them.

Prayers. Petitions.

Liturgy. More prayers.

And through it all, I could only stare into Marcello's eyes and wonder at the miracle of what was happening.

He was mine. And I was his.

Forever.

What I didn't expect was for them all to see us to the bedroom, Marcello's quarters. But they did, as was apparently the custom. I was only thankful that there weren't a hundred or more people all trying to cram into the room, as most medieval newlyweds might experience, according to Mom's continued History Channel rundown.

And I was particularly glad there weren't four noblemen there to "witness" what was about to transpire between me and Marcello. At least, what I hoped was about to transpire. And yet feared at the same time. I was totally nervous.

The room was even larger than mine, and decidedly masculine, painted darker and with much heavier woods. But Marcello's bed was exactly the same, which I decided was romantic. It made it feel a little less strange being in *his* room, rather than mine.

When my family and Luca finally left, Marcello turned and wrapped me in his arms as I shook my head.

"Okay, that was just weird," I said, lapsing into English.

He cocked his head and squinted his eyes, trying to translate what I might be saying.

"Strange. Odd. To have them all in the room with us, when it should be," I wrapped my arms around him and looked shyly up into his eyes, "just us."

"Ahh, my wife, so beautiful," he said, caressing my cheek and my neck. He kissed me for several long, lingering minutes and then gradually moved around me to begin unbuttoning the back of my dress. His big hands moved down my back, and I remembered the first day we met, when I put my dress on backward and he had to help me button it up in the woods.

Had I known, then, that this was where we would end up? In some surreal way I wondered if I had. It was as if I had always belonged here, in his arms. Been his from the start. He kissed the side of my neck and moved down across my shoulder. There, he paused, maybe seeing my bruise for the first time.

"Where did you get this?" He eased my sleeve off of my shoulder, leaving it bare. The bruise still looked like a green and blue cap sleeve.

"The night I escaped Palazzo Vivaro," I said, "in Roma." I looked at him over my bruised shoulder. "The night I knew I belonged with you and would do anything to avoid what was about to happen…what was about to keep me from you."

He stared at me, brows knitted in frustration, anger at what had happened to me, and then his face softened in gratitude. He bent and gently covered the bruise in sweet kisses, sending delightful shivers down my spine and up my neck. I closed my eyes and gave in to the sensation of being close to him. Gave in to the idea that we were together and never had to be apart. Not this night. Not ever.

It was like being given access to the most perfect tropical beach ever. No one on it. Palm trees arcing over white sand. Warm turquoise waters, lapping at the shore. Freedom. Delicious heat. And yet perfect cool, too.

And in the hours that followed, I discovered what it might be like to be given a piece of quiet paradise.

To be given intimacy. Tenderness. Passion.

*Oneness…*

A knock sounded at our door in what Marcello called "the dark watches of the night." Locked in each other's arms, we stirred sleepily.

I felt the loss of Marcello's body heat and was finally identifying the incessant sound as *knocking,* when I rose to see Marcello half dressed and striding to the door.

He opened the door a crack and spoke in low tones with whoever was outside for several minutes. Then he closed the door and leaned his head against it.

"Marcello," I said quietly.

He turned and padded over the cold tiles to our bed. I pulled the covers higher to my chest, feeling goose bumps roll down my arms.

He sat down and gave me a half smile, then touched my face, my chin, and pulled a long coil of my hair over my bare shoulder, for once not tucking it behind my ear but rather toying with it, pulling it and watching it spring back in the candlelight. He was keeping something from me.

"Marcello," I said again.

His eyes met mine, and he sighed, looked away into the far, dark reaches of the room, then back to me. "They approach. Traveling overnight, I suppose, to avoid our attack. They shall be here by morning."

I licked my lips and swallowed. "And Rodolfo's execution shall then be…"

"'Tis scheduled for sundown, on the morrow. Today," he corrected himself.

"Today." I took a deep breath. I knew it was crazy, but I had hoped for a day to just be, to settle in to this husband-wife thing a little. Ya know, before we were in the middle of *war* again.

"You are safer now, as my bride," he said, laying his warm hand on the side of my neck. "Safer than you've ever been. They cannot take you. Cannot demand you marry another. You are mine. To take you now would be an act so despicable, nobles from other lands would enter the battle to defend you."

"I understand. I'm yours. Taken," I said with a slow grin. *"Per sempre."* I leaned forward and gave him quiet kisses. "Forever."

He kissed me then, longingly, searchingly.

I pulled away, suddenly worried. "Do we have time for this? Should we not be summoning the men? Preparing?"

"Time enough," he said, tossing off his shirt and rejoining me under the warm covers. "First love," he growled, "then war."

"First love, always love," I said, welcoming him back to my arms.

# Chapter Twenty-eight

I awakened belatedly, and ran my hand over Marcello's side of the bed, reaching for him, wanting him to pull me into his arms. Wanting to feel the gentle rise and fall of his bare chest, the steady, strong beat of his heart.

*Cold,* my fingers told me, running across the fabric of our covers. Like he hadn't been there in some time. My eyes sprang open, and I studied the wide, bare expanse of my husband's side of the bed, then the slant of the sun through the cracks of the shuttered windows.

I could tell from the angle that the sun had been up for one, maybe two hours.

Flames crackled over three logs in the corner fireplace, but the room was still frigid. I tossed aside the heavy covers and glanced around the room. Nothing but my wedding gown, in a pile on the floor where we'd left it. My eyes went to the side wall, the one between my room and Marcello's room. There, I spied a doorway, subtly hidden among the woodwork and plaster—a doorway I knew I couldn't see from the other side. I pulled a blanket from the bed, wrapped it around myself and padded over to it, searching for a handle. There was nothing. But on a hunch, I put my palm against it and pressed.

I felt the soft click of an internal mechanism, and the door popped open. I pulled it fully open, grunting at the weight of it, and strode into my room, ditching the blanket and hurrying to my trunks, tossing one gown aside and then another. I needed one that was regal, suitable for the lady of the castle, and yet one that wasn't too fussy, given that the day might very well entail swordplay. A lady...*Lady Gabriella Forelli,* I thought, trying the name out in my mind.

I settled on the amber gown, conscious that the color echoed the Forelli gold. I liked the feel of the weave of its fabric. It wasn't so tight as some of my others, giving me more room to breathe, move.

Which was kinda important when a girl was headin' into battle.

I laughed at my own joke and then donned undergarments and pulled the gown over my head, yanking it into place. Which was the other reason I liked the dress—it was sewn up the back. No buttons. As much as I liked buttons, especially when my husband was undoing them, one after the other, today was not a day for them.

I smiled. I was married. Marcello was mine. Today we undoubtedly had terrible things ahead of us, significant struggles. But I couldn't help feeling somehow stronger, somehow more ready for it, because of our union. I would fight beside him, as long as he allowed it. I knew he wanted me safe, back in the castle, when the time came. But for as long as I could, I wanted to be with him, helping to keep him safe, just as he wished the same for me.

I raced down the stairs and out the turret door, smiling and nodding at the remnant of the kitchen staff, each of whom nodded back at me with shy, knowing smiles. Something had shifted overnight. I could feel it. They could feel it. I was their lady. I mean, I had always been their lady—claimed by all of Siena, really, as one of the She-Wolves—but now, I was this castle's Lady, with a capital L. I almost felt like whistling, I felt so happy. I know, right? Totally dorky. But I couldn't help myself.

When I rounded the Great Hall and entered the castello courtyard, I stopped short. It was a mass of confusion. Horses reared or circled on tight reins, agitated by all the commotion and tension. Men pushed their way forward, carrying heavy supplies on their shoulders—barrels, burlap-wrapped bundles, massive sheaves of wheat. To one side more than fifty men were sparring with swords, most of them stripped to the waist, regardless of the cold. On the other, an equal number were shooting arrows at targets.

Luca was laughing with two men, looking around like he was in his element, when he spied me. He clapped and hollered. "Gentle ladies and humble noblemen," he called, his breath clouding before his face, "I present to you, Lady Gabriella *Forelli!*"

Those within hearing turned and clapped and cheered for me, but the great majority continued in their war preparations. Luca came over to me and kissed my hand. "A good morning to you, cousin-in-law."

"And a good morning to *you*, cousin," I returned. "Have you seen my husband about?"

"Your husband," he said, frowning and tapping his lip as he searched the crowd. "Husband, husband, husband…" He stopped and pointed, smiling at me. "Over yonder is thy husband."

I saw Marcello then, deep in conversation with six knights who were wearing a coat of arms on their capes I had not seen before.

They must've arrived overnight, as had perhaps a hundred more men. I playfully nudged Luca with my hip and moved out, leaving him laughing behind me.

I moved among the men, dodging several horses and the sword-play of still more knights. I glimpsed my dad sparring with a knight, his face lighting up as if he understood some new move. My sister, over with the Lerici archers, examining their unique arrows, while five men considered her unique attributes. Mom was nowhere to be seen—perhaps she was in the kitchen, making even more bread than yesterday. And when I looked again to where Marcello had been before, he was no longer there.

I frowned in confusion, glancing about when I didn't find him, eyeballing every one of the perhaps three hundred people in the courtyard.

"Dare I hope that it's me you seek?" he said lowly in my ear. I jumped and whirled.

"M'lord!"

"M'lady!" he cried back, teasing me. He grinned and grabbed my hand to haul me to the nearest turret staircase, ignoring the many men who called his name and others who shouted in jest. He opened the door, allowed me to enter, then shut it. A guard was just coming down the stairs, but Marcello yelled up. "Good man, might you remain up top for but a moment?"

The knight caught sight of me, smiled, and then trudged back up the stairs and closed the door. But even before it was shut, Marcello had lifted me in his arms, kissing me with joy more than passion. He was all over the place, kissing my eyebrow, my chin, my nose, my ear, my hair. I laughed and kissed him back, my hands on his broad shoulders, the wide width of his strong back, the narrow of his waist.

"Ah, wife," he said, at last still, pulling away. "It took everything in me to leave you in my bed."

"And 'twas a great sorrow to wake without you," I said.

He touched my chin. "I promise, there will be many days when we shall not leave it at all. But not this day. Come, there is much to tell you, so that you are prepared." He took my hand, and we climbed the turret, exiting up top, giving the men outside a new reason to cheer. Although our ceremony had been private, our marriage was very public knowledge, just as Marcello had wanted it. The more widely it was broadcast that Lady Gabriella Betarrini was now Lady Gabriella Forelli, the better.

The knight we'd delayed edged past us. "My most sincere congratulations to you both, m'lady, m'lord."

"Thank you, friend," Marcello said, patting him on the shoulder as he passed. He took my hand and walked me around the perimeter of the castle, keeping me on the inside in case an enemy archer got a crazy idea he'd like to start this battle sooner than later. I could see that not only had more of Marcello's band of brothers arrived, but Siena herself had ridden to our defense.

There weren't the numbers we'd seen the last time full-scale battle had erupted between the cities, but it was a good start. And it was exactly how Marcello wanted it. He didn't want Paratore too agitated, too alarmed. If the battle went on, more would arrive. I couldn't forget the columns of men we'd encountered last time, heading to the front lines. But Marcello hoped we could win this so quickly, so decidedly, that the Fiorentini would not even have the chance to call for more men.

And with our peeps hidden inside Castello Forelli's walls, I thought we might just have that chance. If they'd arrived without Paratore's men understanding who they were, what they were capable of, we just might have what we needed. I shivered, glad that it wasn't me and Lia on the other side of Paratore's gates. It had been there I received the wound that had ultimately sent me home the first time, far from Marcello. And seeing Paratore again, after Sansicino, after my escape…I knew he'd be bent on taking me down. Lia and Marcello, too, if he could.

I shifted, taking a firmer grasp of Marcello's hand. *Please, Lord, keep us together this day. Keep us whole. May this first day of our marriage not be the last.*

Marcello pointed out the two companies of men from Firenze, who camped outside the enemy castle. I could barely see bits of tent and flags below the castle wall. But Marcello had received the reports. They comprised maybe three to four hundred knights. And they had marched all night to arrive.

Surrounding Castello Forelli, we had three hundred men from Siena, many of who had arrived the day before. And inside we had another three hundred. Marcello grinned at me, knowing that I was putting the numbers together with him. Knowing that we outnumbered them two to one.

I stared outward to the crimson flag dancing in the wind and steeled myself to encounter Lord Paratore again. I'd hoped he was out of my life forever. That he'd retired to the relative safety and peace of Firenze and left this disputed border territory for others to haggle over.

But no. He was back. I could almost feel him, just across the valley.

And I knew that if he had the chance, he would do everything he could not to kidnap me, but to kill me. And he wouldn't be the only one.

Marcello was right.

Maybe I had to sit this one mostly out.

Our men combed the woods on our side of the border, trying to roust out any scouts come to spy on us. Once they were assured a section was safe, they sent in groups of men, dressed in camouflage colors of tan and green, to hide themselves and stealthily make their way to the border in order to do their own espionage work—or, if the battle began, to surprise our enemies in pockets.

"Scouts returning, m'lord," called Lutterius, down to Marcello, who was with me in the courtyard. Marcello tensed at my side. It was maybe two in the afternoon. Had it already begun?

The gates opened only three feet wide—we were still attempting to keep our reserve troops a secret from any prying eyes—and two riders came through. Boys, really, a few years younger than I. Middle schoolers. Except they had no such thing in medieval Toscana. Most did not even attend school. Only the very wealthy could afford to hire tutors.

"They have begun, m'lord," said one, sliding off his horse and only slightly bowing to us both in his excitement.

"What did you see?" Marcello asked.

"Timber," said the second, coming up behind the first. They had a similar, gangly, long-nosed look—definitely brothers. "They are erecting a platform outside the castello."

"How many men do they have?"

"By our guess, more than three hundred."

Marcello nodded, chin in hand. "And did you overhear anything? Any word of more en route?"

"One spoke of a hundred more on their way from Firenze," said the first. He smiled mischievously. "We were able to creep quite close."

"Good. Take your fill of food and drink, pack some supplies, and head north to take up a new position. If you see more troops arriving, come and warn us. To do us any good at all, you must arrive at least an hour before they reach Castello Paratore. Understand?"

"It shall be done, m'lord," said the second boy.

"M'lord," said the first. They gave Marcello a short bow and headed toward the stables, walking their horses.

I studied Marcello. He was staring into the sky, frowning. "What is it?" I said.

He shook his head and smiled for me. "Ah, nothing specific. It's only that it seems I've battled Paratore and his men ever since I first picked up a sword. And while he is not the greatest military tactician, he is not the fool. Right now it seems that he is walking directly into our trap. Or is that what he wishes us to think?"

I looped my arm through his, and we started to walk among the men in the courtyard. "He believes he's safe," I said. "Mayhap he even intends to remain holed up in the castle while the execution takes place. Watch it from the parapets."

"Nay," Marcello shook his head, staring at the gates as if he could see through them all the way to Castello Paratore. "He'll wish to wade into the fray, meet me at the front. We've been too long at this, he and I, for him to stand back. He knows as well as I that this is where it comes to an end. That this is the day."

A shiver ran down my back. Once there had been an understanding—if either young lord was hurt, the enemy would back off. Those days were clearly long over. I remembered the first day I'd arrived. When Paratore had been wounded and the battle abruptly ended. Too much had transpired since then, too much blood spilled…My eyes focused on a man in brown.

"Marcello," I said, touching his hand and gesturing toward the gates. Father Tomas was there, pack over one shoulder, talking to the knights who stood by the massive crossbeam.

We set off to intercept him. The knights in position at the cross-beam seemed relieved to see us coming. Father Tomas followed their gaze, looked upward, as if for heavenly support, and then awaited our approach.

"You cannot still intend to approach them," Marcello said.

"I do," he said simply.

"Tomas, you go to your death," Marcello said. "You must remain here."

"Or do I go to life?" he asked. "I do not fear death. I've prayed the night through, seeking my Lord's guidance. And all I can tell you is that He wants me there, with Rodolfo. In case you do not make it in time."

"We shall make it in time," Marcello said. "There is no question. Rodolfo shall not suffer execution this day."

"So you believe."

"Yes, I believe it."

"Every plan has five unseen obstacles. You know it more than I." Tomas reached out and laid a hand on Marcello's shoulder. "Please. By your leave I must go."

Marcello let out a sound of exasperation and put a hand on his head, studying him. "Why, Tomas? Why?"

"Because all but three of our brothers are here," he said, meeting Marcello's stare. "They all shall serve you and Rodolfo this day. This, this is my way to serve you both."

"By dying? Rodolfo would not want that."

"Rodolfo would want me to do as my Lord bid."

"Ahh, I see. So this is a testament of faith?" Marcello asked. "Your walk into the lion's den? The pit of fire?"

"I know not. All I know is that I am to get to Rodolfo. Perhaps, inside, I can also aid the servants sent to help you and the men."

Marcello turned to the guards. "This man is not to exit this castle. Do you understand me?"

"Yes, m'lord," said the first.

"I must go, Marcello," Tomas said carefully.

"You would go over to Castello Paratore, a castle of Firenze, Guelphs, long faithful to the pope who disowned you, and demand entrance?" Marcello asked.

"Nay," he said. "My God calls me to go, and I shall follow. 'Tis he who shall gain me entrance."

"He'll use you, Tomas," I said quietly. "Trust me. Paratore will use anyone he can to get Marcello or me. He put Lia in his dungeon. Threatened unspeakable harm to her. Don't you see? He'd do the same to you. And then Marcello and I would feel compelled to do anything we could to rescue you."

"I ask you not to do that, here and now, with God as my witness. I am not your responsibility."

"Which is one thing to say here in the safety of this castle," Marcello said.

"You do not understand—" I began.

"Nay, nay," Tomas said in anguish, to me, then to Marcello. "'Tis you two who do not understand." He was finally growing angry, turning red at the neck, and he focused that fury on Marcello, brother to brother. "I relinquished my sword, my bow, the day I became a priest. This," he said, plucking at the fabric of his robe, "represents my faith and is *my* armor. The Word of God is *my* sword. This day represents my battle too." He shook his head. "Allow me to take up my portion the way God intends."

Marcello studied him for a long moment, mouth shut. "Go," he said then, quiet frustration in the single, low word.

"No, Marcello," I intervened. "Tomas, see here—"

"But go ready to meet your Maker," Marcello said over me. "I cannot promise protection." He lifted his hand to the guards. "I've changed my mind. The *priest* shall be allowed to leave," he said, then strode away.

"Tomas," I said, begging him to wait, to reconsider. "Nay. *Nay.*"

The knights slid the massive bar back and opened the gates a foot wide for him to slip through. He paused there, took my hand, and then kissed both my cheeks. "Watch over him, Gabriella. Teach him that we are all on the river of life, and that even when the river divides, we are still somehow one."

I frowned over his puzzling words and clung to his hands. "Tomas, please. Stay. Stay *here* and pray for Rodolfo."

He gave me a little smile. "You more than anyone, m'lady, should know the power of a friend's presence when facing dire circumstances. No doubt Rodolfo has already seen a fair amount of torture. I must try to go to him, be with him."

I hesitated, remembering Fortino, how glad I was that he had not been alone through it all, that he wasn't alone at the end.

I released him. "Go with God, Tomas," I mumbled.

"Always, m'lady," he said and turned on his heel and left.

The knights closed the gates and slid the beam back into place before me, a grating, powerful sound of final separation. I reached up and touched it. But my mind was on the man who had just departed, who would ease through the woods and find the path to Castello Paratore and march right up to her gates.

And then what? Would he find Rodolfo weak and injured in a cell? Find some way to bring him comfort, peace, before he died? Memories of Fortino made me clench my eyes shut in pain.

"Hey," Lia said, coming closer and laying a hand on my shoulder. "You okay?"

I glanced at her and then back at the beam. Would one of these slide shut behind Tomas, locking him in? Would our people be able to help him, save him?

Marcello had told him not to look for rescue.

But was...was God asking *me* to do that?

# Chapter Twenty-nine

"Uh-oh, Gabi. No," Lia muttered. "I don't like that look in your eye."

I ignored her and strode through the mass of men and horses toward the armory. But she stayed beside me as I sidestepped two men who were stripped to the waist, sparring, and entered the Great Hall. "What are you doing? What are you planning?"

"Nothing!" I exclaimed, slipping a sheath over my shoulders and finding the kind of broadsword I favored. I tipped it back and forth, then looked down the length of it, making sure it was straight, true. Then I slid it into its case between my shoulder blades and went to the wall of daggers. I wrapped a belt around my waist and slid six daggers into the small loops. Then I put a seventh at my calf.

Lia shooed away the knights who lingered there watching me arm myself, clearly fascinated. *It isn't every day these guys get to see a girl do such a thing,* I mused, as they all reluctantly departed. We were temporarily alone in the armory.

"You 'bout done, GI Jane?" she asked, gesturing toward me. "Or maybe you want to put a few more knives in your hair. And there's still your other leg. Maybe wrap a whip around it?"

"What's with you?" I asked. "I'm just getting ready to ride with Marcello. You know, go stir up the boys, get 'em psyched. Aren't you coming?"

She stared at me, her blue eyes piercing mine. It almost hurt me, physically, to keep it up, to lie to her to her face. I turned and studied the rest of the weapons—fairly picked over by now. But that was when I found what I wanted. The iron claw attached to the length of rope. I'd have to come back for it later, when I wasn't with Lia.

But when I turned, I knew she'd seen me looking at it. "What are you planning, Gabi?"

"*Nothing*," I said insistently. And it was kinda true, at least. I wasn't *planning* anything. I was *preparing*...in case...

She folded her arms and blocked my way.

"Look," I said. "I'm just going with Marcello to get the boys all riled up, ready to win this battle. But you and I know, firsthand, how battles can take a turn you don't expect. I want to be ready for anything. Don't you, She-Wolf?"

The first hint of a smile thawed her icy expression. "I did consider grabbing a quiver full of those Lerici arrows."

"There you go," I encouraged. "And how 'bout a belt full of daggers for good measure?"

Her smile broadened. "The boys would like to get an eyeful of *that*," she said.

"Yeah," I said. "The more weapons we pile on, the hotter we are."

"Too bad you're an old married woman now."

"And that Luca has already stolen your heart," I teased back.

She rolled her eyes, but she blushed and moved over to the lines of quivers. "I'll have to ask the men of Castello Lerici," she said, shouldering a bow, "for some of their arrows."

I moved over to a crossbow. "What about one of these? Are they hard to use?" I was thinking of the claw and how, without some sort of help, I'd never get it to the top of Castello Paratore.

"It's a whole other discipline," she said, taking it from the wall and grunting under its weight. "Other than aim, of course. You hold it like this," she said, letting it settle in her arms, the bow horizontal. "And they're tricky to get loaded right. You have to pull it back to this point," she said, gesturing to a small metal bar.

Luca appeared in the doorway and let out a long, low whistle. "Nothing finer looking than two beautiful women holding weapons."

I laughed and whispered, "What'd I just say?"

Lia smiled and shook her head, placing the crossbow back on the wall.

"I knew something interesting was transpiring," Luca said, "when I saw the men five-deep outside the armory, all trying to catch a peek."

I glanced past him and saw that he was right—we were drawing a crowd. "Oh, brother," I said in English.

"'Tis best you two finish up so the men can resume their tasks," Luca said wryly. "Can I help you find something in particular, m'ladies?"

"Nay," I said. "I think I'm ready now."

He caught my arm as I edged past. "Why do you look as mischievous as you did the night I caught you heading over the castle wall? The night you were determined to go after Lia?"

"Do I?" I said, giving Luca an innocent look. "My sole goal," I said lowly, "is to see this battle through and my husband home so we can resume...*exploring* married life."

Luca laughed at that, as I knew he would. "Ah, you Norman girls. Simply magnificent, I tell you."

I glimpsed a flash of prancing horse, golden cloth, and Marcello's dark hair. "C'mon," I said to Lia in English. "We have to get to the pep rally."

So we did what Marcello wanted. When the drums began to beat over at Castello Paratore, Lia and I rode out alongside him, Luca, the twins, and ten others he trusted most, in front of Castello Forelli.

In the last hours two companies of Sienese knights had moved toward the border of the creek bed, and it was there that we cantered, the twins carrying two golden standards, shimmering cloths of gold, basically giant flags that said, *Oh yeah? We aren't afraid of you!*

Marcello did his thing, revving up the troops. I stared at him, caught for a moment by the sheer *amazingness* of him—my *husband*—looking incredibly fine from the crown of his dark curls down to his boots. He wore a new leather chest plate as armor, as well as plates strapped to his thighs and calves. His muscles bulged beneath his linen shirt as he lifted his sword high into the air. The men cheered, and for a moment, the steady, creepy beat of the Fiorentini drums could not be heard. But then the sound was back, like a bad memory.

Marcello looked to the twins, and they immediately turned to lead us back to Castello Forelli. I frowned as they led us away. We'd not really spoken of how long he'd intended me to be with him, but I thought it would be far longer than this—which hadn't been much more than a trip around the ring. It was like we'd been reduced to show queens, not She-Wolves. *Totally lame.*

"Wait!" Marcello called. He kicked his horse into a gallop and was beside us in a second. "Come with me," he said, dismounting and reaching for me. I took hold of his shoulders and slid down into his arms, but he immediately took my hand and pulled me several paces off, behind a small stand of old oaks. I struggled to find words to express what was boiling up inside. But he was moving too fast, too focused on getting back to the men, as the sun grew lower in the sky. He quickly kissed my hands, then each of my cheeks. "You'll be safe at the castello, Gabriella. I'll be back as soon as I can. I love you. You know this, yes?"

I nodded, not trusting myself to speak, afraid I would say words I'd regret—or utter promises I could not keep. I knew he assumed I would stay in the castle, as was planned. I just didn't know if I could bear to do it. *I guess it depends on how swift and decisive your victory is,* I thought.

"Take close care, m'lord. I'll be anxious for our reunion." Yeah— that I could say honestly.

"As shall I," he said, tucking a strand of hair behind my ear.

An hour later the sun was setting, and a messenger arrived at the castello. He walked up to Georgii with a furrowed brow. I sidled closer, chin up, as if I, as Lady Forelli, expected to know about everything that was transpiring. Georgii eyed me and then gave the scrawny messenger a nod, granting him permission to speak.

"I have sorrowful news, sir. A man and woman, servants of Castello Forelli, have been hanged. Thrown over the castle parapets, a noose about their necks. Eight more are on the wall. It looks as if they, too, shall be hanged at any moment."

I gasped and covered my mouth. *Giacinta,* I thought, first. *Paratore found them out.*

"Have you informed Lord Forelli?" I asked.

The messenger nodded, with a *Well, Duh* look in his eyes, before he remembered his place. "'Tis Lord Forelli who sent me, m'lady."

"Of course," I muttered, walking a few steps away. *We should never have sent the servants in. Never have sent innocent, simple people to do a knight's job!*

"What of Lord Greco's execution?" Georgii asked.

"No one has yet seen Lord Greco. Nor Lord Paratore."

"Do the Fiorentini show any signs of dysentery?" Mom asked, edging in to our gathering.

"Dysentery, m'lady?" the messenger asked, hesitating. "Nay, m'lady."

Mom and I looked at each other. The plan had failed, then. *Giacinta…*

The gates opened wide, and the three wagons bearing the catapult lumbered out. I knew then that Marcello would order them to fire, regardless of who stood on or hung from the wall above the gates. This was our chance, our opportunity to drive the Fiorentini back and establish peace—there was always a cost to peace, right?

Unless I could somehow make my way in and assist those who remained. *Ten discovered,* I thought, *but there are still five of our people inside, still working on our behalf, ready to assist us.*

I ran over to the stairs and up the curving case to the top. I pushed back a guard, who sputtered at me, trying to find the words to order me, his lady, to leave. Then I ran past another who only stared at me, openmouthed. I reached the front wall of the castle and stood beside a small raised portion that would give me some protection, should there be a Fiorentini assassin about.

Vaguely I realized my family had followed. First Lia. Then my parents.

Together we looked out across the valley, across winter-dead trees to the place where great clouds of dust arose, signifying that the battle was underway. We could hear the roar of some men, the cries of others. Beyond it we could see Castello Paratore, one side of it pink in the glow of the setting sun, crimson flags waving. And atop it, barely visible, were the tiny figures of our people standing on the wall. As we watched, a man in a brown robe was pushed to stand at the top, in the center, directly above the gates.

Mom gasped.

"*Tomas,*" I breathed. "They'll all die," I muttered. "Die because they wanted to help." I glanced at Dad. "Marcello will take down those gates, regardless of who is up there. He told them that. This is his one chance."

Dad nodded once, his face gravely serious. "Acceptable losses in an effort to win the greater good. Such are the ways of war."

I focused on Tomas, wishing I could teleport over there, whip out my sword, and show Paratore what it was like to take me on *armed,* again. *Jerk, using women, a priest as some scummy human shield…* At least Rodolfo wasn't there. Had Marcello and his men reached him? Freed him before Paratore's horrific impaling had begun down by the creek?

But that was when a tenth figure was lifted to the top of the wall. It was impossible not to recognize the dark black, wavy hair, the straight shoulders as he forced himself upright after a moment's hesitation. "Rodolfo," I whispered, leaning forward, sudden, angry tears in my eyes.

"Oh no," Lia moaned.

He'd tricked us. Paratore. Pretended to plan to execute Rodolfo down on the platform to draw Marcello and his men out to him. And all the while, he was back at the castle, ready to kill Rodolfo at his leisure. Where he was certain we could see. And where he would remain safe.

It was then I knew. This display was meant for me. This particular form of pain. My people. My friend. Even my priest…since when did I have a priest? But there he was, in the distance, his round, brown-robed form taunting me, making me shiver with fury. And Rodolfo, who'd saved me, freed me—

I could almost hear my enemy whispering in my ear…*You thought you could take my ears without retribution, She-Wolf? Behold, the price…*

We all stood there a minute longer. The temperature was dropping rapidly as the sun slipped over the horizon, sending five rays up in what could've been a Tuscan tourism photo—if you didn't realize that men and women were dying beneath it. I thought about the servants on the far wall, shivering as the chill penetrated their bones.

"So," Lia said. "You need this?" she asked, pulling aside her cape and showing me the claw and rope beneath.

"Or this?" Mom said, letting me peek at the crossbow beneath her cape.

Dad gave me a tender look. "Marcello has a fine network of men, brothers to ride to his aid. But I think it's time we show him just what kind of family he married into, don't you?"

# Chapter Thirty

We went wide, riding hard around the far side of the tumuli hill, to come at Castello Paratore from the back. Of course, there were about eight patrols of twelve continuously jogging the road around the perimeter of the castle. We huddled beneath a cliff, behind some brush, and counted it out. It wasn't like clockwork, but we seemed to have about two minutes between patrols.

Up on the wall were other knights, pacing back and forth, peering down at the forest growing deep with shadows as the last of the sunset faded. My family and I could see them far better than they could see us, given their torches. In time I hoped we'd meet up with some of the Sienese knights or some of Marcello's secret groups of men. But at this point it was best it was just the four of us. It'd be tough to get a larger group up and over the wall.

"Here," Lia said, handing me and Mom two strands of leather each. She bent and gathered her skirts, tying one side, then the other, leaving her calves exposed and her pantaloons showing.

"I see London, I see France..." I muttered.

"Dresses are not the most convenient attire for battle," Mom said, bending to work on her own gown.

"Dresses are not the most convenient, period." I looked up the wall. This side of the castle wall was higher, since it had been built on a small cliff face. "How tall do you think that is, Dad?" I asked, tying the left side of my gown in a knot.

He considered it. "A good forty feet. Think you girls can manage it?"

"Oh, we can manage it," I said. "The question is, can the old man?"

"Bring it," he said with a grunt, lifting his chin.

I smiled. But then I saw the next patrol was coming. "Ten seconds till launch," I warned. "Ready?"

All three of them nodded. Lia pulled back the crossbow until it clicked into place. The massive claw was at the end, making it so heavy that Dad had to help her hold it steady. The group of men passed, chanting some song like a medieval Marine's sound off, and our eyes went to the knight who walked along the top of the wall. "C'mon," I moaned, wanting him to hurry away.

I drew an arrow across a regular bow, intending to hand it to Lia as soon as she was done. Mom stood ready with two more arrows across her arm. If this didn't go perfectly—

I heard the dull clang of metal on metal and glimpsed the claw sail through the air, like a football toward field-goal posts, glinting in the torchlight. Even before it landed, Lia had grabbed the bow and arrow from me and was aiming at the knight who'd just passed, waiting for him to turn, see what the noise was, show the breadth of his back.

Dad held on to our end of the rope as the claw arced and began racing down on the other side, the loops disappearing at our feet. At last it stopped, and I held my breath. We could not hear the noise inside. But the guard obviously did. As soon as he peered over the far edge, Lia let the arrow go.

It sailed faster and surer than I'd ever seen, striking the man in the back. He bent over with the impact, rose, then crumpled out of view.

"Go, Gabi," Mom grunted, handing Lia another arrow.

Dad was madly pulling on the rope, bringing in the excess as if he were hauling in a shark, while I was running to the small cliff face. We had maybe forty seconds until the next patrol rounded the corner. I rammed my toe into the clumpy clay and climbed, pulling myself up and over the six-foot cliff, rolling to my side. I went to the wall and heard another guard cry out above me. Quickly I cut the rope, allowing Dad to pull the rest toward him and out of the path of the next patrol.

Twenty-five seconds. I leaped up on the rope, found my footing against the wall, and began hauling myself up. There was no time to cinch it around my waist or form safety knots. Lia was a far better climber than I, but we needed her down below, picking off the guys who'd try and pick us off from above. *Eighteen seconds, seventeen…* I counted, glancing back. I was still too close to the ground. *No way will they miss you, Gabs!* I put everything I had into it, up fifteen feet, then twenty. But then I was out of time.

I held on with one arm and pulled up the rest of the dangling cord so it was out of their way, so it wouldn't alert them. And then I prayed. That their attention would be out toward the woods. That God would make me invisible. That my family could take down any man who aimed an arrow at my back. I heard them coming, another chant on this group's lips. My legs were shaking as I struggled to stay still in my odd position. I closed my eyes and squinted, unable to watch their approach, just wanting it over with, one way or another. *C'mon, c'mon…*

They rounded the corner, the beat of their boots on the loose gravel a new kind of rhythm in my ears. I braced, listening, trying to detect any variance in the beat, any hint that I'd been spotted, hovering halfway up the wall above them.

First it was one—near the back? Then a second. The dreaded skid and stop. A shout. I turned and began hauling myself upward, aware now that it was a race. A race between me getting to the top and the patrol below aiming the first arrow and letting it fly. My technique was panicked and sloppy, which in turn made me more lame-tastic. I wasn't making better time; I was working against myself—

I heard the *whirr* of oncoming arrows and braced for them to enter my back. Wondered what would hurt worse—the initial strike of an arrow piercing my back, or my fall to the ground beneath me. *Neither close enough to reach the top, nor low enough to survive a fall.* Then I *heard* the sickening sound of arrows entering flesh, the anguish and surprised cries…but they were *not my own*. They were below me. I turned and dared to glance down for the first time and saw all twelve men, dead or dying. On the far hill, above where my family was hidden, I saw the brush move and then become still. Movement beyond it on the rocky slope. The Lerici archers.

They were running northward. Probably to intercept the next patrol before the soldiers turned the corner and spotted all the dead men beneath me. Giving me some time, some space.

*Man, those dudes rock,* I thought, turning and trying to climb again with trembling hands. *I'm gonna give them all kisses when I see them. And all my gold. I seriously love those guys....*

Somehow I made it to the top, saw there were no guards still alive on this portion of parapet, then threw my leg over the edge and rolled over and onto the floor. I lay there, panting, my heart thundering, before I forced myself upright to stare across the courtyard, to where the servants, Rodolfo, and Tomas stood on the far wall.

*Still there,* I saw, closing my eyes in relief and sinking back, trying to catch my breath again, gasping. When I could finally breathe evenly, I peered over the edge, saw Lia coming fast. Her proximity strengthened me. I wouldn't be alone for long. I forced myself to a crouch, hurried over to the first dead knight and bodily lifted him to a standing position, leaning him against one of the small towers and wrapping a rope around his chest to keep him upright. He looked awkward, but at first glance, he might fool anyone into thinking all was well.

Like Paratore.

Lia was doing the same with the next knight, struggling with his bulk, while trying to keep an eye out for Mom and Dad. I stole over to help her, scanning the perimeter for our enemies. So far they all seemed unaware of our presence.

Dad rolled over the edge of the wall then, with a grunt. "Man, glad I haul rock for a living," he quipped between breaths. He peeked over at Mom's progress and then came back. "I'll wait here for her. You two'd better move out."

We nodded at each other and went in opposite directions. Why weren't there more men on guard? Where were they?

Maybe the poison *had* reached a good number of them before they'd figured it out. Or maybe they were all up front with the prisoners, enjoying the spectacle, trusting the safety of the far walls to the patrols below.

Whatever the reason, I was glad for it. Our goal was to get to the prisoners and cut their hands free, if not cut the nooses themselves, before they could be pushed to their deaths.

Or before Marcello began firing the catapult.

# Chapter Thirty-one

All we needed was about five minutes. Five minutes without being seen as we took down a dozen more guards and reached the servants on the far wall. I knew it was a stretch, but a girl could dream. I pressed on and soon saw Dad stealing toward me.

"Duck, Gabs," Dad said, and I instantly obeyed as he threw his dagger.

I turned around and saw the man who had just come up and over a small staircase that crossed a lookout tower. The man gripped the dagger in his chest, as if he intended to pull it out, and then fell to his knees and down to his face. We pressed onward, entering the wider space of the lookout platform, backs to either side of the far entrance as we caught our breath.

I dared a peek over the wall to my right. Across the courtyard, above it, I glimpsed Mom and Lia making their way too. I couldn't believe it. We were getting closer. Paratore's men seemed to be entirely focused on the front wall.

And then I heard it—the drum beat. A Sienese drum beat. The catapult would soon be in place, and rocks and hot oil fired...

*Wait, Marcello,* I said in my mind, willing him to hear me. I edged my cheek around the corner, peeking at the parapet ahead.

Would seeing Rodolfo there, too, make him pause just long enough? Could he truly order the death of his friend along with Tomas and the servants?

*But he warned them, warned them all. Even Rodolfo…He asked him to return with us when he rescued me from Roma. But Rodolfo chose Firenze. Of all the stupid—*

I found the rest of the guards at last. They were here, taunting the servants, trying to startle them so they would fall, laughing at them. Five of our own were spaced out like sentinels watching over the castle wall. The nearest was Giacinta, with tears slipping down her face. Her auburn hair, loosed, blew in the wind. One guard caressed the curve of her buttock, knowing she couldn't move. She cried, choking on her own snot and spit.

I grit my teeth in fury, easing a dagger from my waistband. Being right-handed, I'd have to roll and toss it.

Dad peeked too, then readied his own dagger. He nodded to it, then touched the hilt of his sword. I'd roll as he sent his knife flying, then toss mine. Then we'd take to our feet and attack the nearest men with swords, perhaps before they had a chance to draw their own. If we could take four that quickly, it'd only leave four, on our side of the wall at least.

The Sienese drums came to an ominous stop.

I was counting down, *three, two*—

When I heard him. Paratore.

Laughing.

I dared to peek around the corner again and saw his back. He stood between Rodolfo and Tomas, both with their hands bound behind them. "I knew you'd come, Forelli!" he shouted downward. "I knew you couldn't stand the thought of your precious friends dying within sight of your castle! So predictable, you Sienese! 'Tis one thing to send your loyal servants to battle, but 'tis another to order their deaths!" he taunted. "You do not have it in you, Marcello. You stand there, helpless, unable to accomplish either task—save your brothers *or* conquer my castle."

We all heard the thrum of a cut rope, the drag of a massive stone over wood and then saw the massive stone—a discarded stone from Castello Forelli?—sailing in our direction.

The servants cried out and gasped.

"Stand in position!" Lord Paratore shouted.

"Take cover," I grunted to Dad, rolling to the ground and wrapping my head and neck in my arm.

The first stone struck the top of the gates. They held, but the massive timbers cracked and splintered inward, leaving a six-foot crater.

"Now," I grunted, guessing it'd take our guys a couple minutes to reload.

The first two knights went down, both of them with our daggers in their backs.

Dad ran forward and struck at the first man to draw a sword.

I cut apart the rope at Giacinta's wrists and roughly pulled her down from her perch. I set her, trembling, against the short wall. "Stay down," I cried, moving to back up Dad. But the passageway was too narrow. All I could do was stand behind and watch.

And that was when Paratore lifted his head and saw me across the corner of the wall. His nostrils flared, and his eyes got big as he stared at me with hatred. Then he laughed in delight and strode toward me, pausing only to shove a male servant over the edge, sending him to his death. I saw the rope over the wall grow taut, wriggle, and then still. I gasped in horror, literally lost my breath for a moment.

Rodolfo and Tomas looked over their shoulders at me as Paratore plowed toward us. Seeing their chance, they both jumped down to relative safety, but they were still tied. Guards rushed in their direction.

My eyes returned to my enemy. He was moving toward the next servant, taunting me with his eyes full of threat, glancing toward the next prisoner.

"Nay!" I cried, jumping to the wall and passing Dad, who still battled the third of the five knights remaining between me and Paratore. I flung myself at the next man as he drew his sword, pulling him against me as I rolled, somehow landing on top. He shoved me backward, and I hit the far wall, which left me dazed for a moment. I forced myself up, pulling another servant down from the wall and cutting apart his tied wrists. "The others," I said urgently, handing him my dagger as I drew my sword to face my assailant, who was up on his feet again.

"Down, Gabs," Dad growled. I ducked, hoping he was aiming at the dude coming at me and not some other guy ahead.

He was.

The servant I'd just saved had reached a young woman I recognized as a scullery maid, but the next Paratore guard was struggling with him, trying to take his dagger. Pressing him backward, driving the point toward his throat. I ran and brought down my sword on his attacker's back, hoping the impact wouldn't drive the dagger point into the boy's flesh.

I didn't stop to find out if I'd been successful because the next guard was upon me, swinging his sword in a wide arc. I bent back, feeling the blade pass by my side, then turned and struck him on the arm. The sword sank into the thick leather, probably drew blood, but held. It was almost stuck. As I struggled to pry it out in time to meet my opponent's next blow, I found Paratore again.

Waiting for me to watch him.

He stood next to a servant girl who was pleading with him. I glanced at the knight before me as I finally wrenched my sword from its grip in his shoulder armor and dodged to one side as he thrust his short sword toward my belly, just missing me. I could see her mouthing the words—*Please, m'lord, mercy*—but Paratore was looking at me as he put a hand on the backs of her thighs and shoved.

I winced, ducked, anticipating the knight's next sideways strike, and took out his legs beneath him, then ran onward as he fell.

The next catapult stone struck the front wall, sending a teeth-jarring rumble through the stones beneath us. I reached out to hold on, thinking for a second that it was all coming down.

"That's some kind of friendly fire," Dad grunted, moving past me.

"We gotta let him know we're here," I said.

"On it." He grinned, like he just had to pick up the closest cell and was going to make the call.

"Dad!" I screamed, seeing what was behind him a half second late. My cry seemed to hover in the air, slowing time and action.

The knight—the only remaining one between me and Paratore—with both hands on the hilt of his sword, lifted it still higher, its deadly point a foot from my father's back.

He did not pause. The sword plunged downward.

I gasped and wavered on my feet—as if feeling it myself—as the blade went entirely through, poking out the front of his shoulder.

"*Dad!*" I cried out again, as my father sank to his knees. *No. No, no, no! Not Dad. Please, God, not Dad. We can't lose him again. We can't…we can't…*

Fury displaced my fear again as the knight put a boot to his back to pull the sword out, and I surged forward.

I was wild in that moment. I didn't know what I did or how I did it, but as the man drew back to finish my father off, I took him down, crashing him against the far wall. I was rising, backing away from the knight, whose neck was now at an awkward angle. Looking to Dad, still on his knees, thinking I had to get to him, staunch the blood—

When I felt the blade biting into my neck.

"*Lady Forelli,* I hear it is now," Lord Paratore said in my ear, lifting me bodily backward. "I bid you proper welcome, again, to my castello."

Another massive stone hit the front wall, sending a shudder through us all. Unsteadied, we fell forward, and Paratore used the momentum to strike my hand against the short, outer wall. My fingers opened involuntarily from the pain, and my stomach sank as I watched my sword go clattering over the edge.

I growled and used my knee to force him backward, pushing with everything I had in me. He grunted as we hit the other wall, but he didn't release me as I had hoped.

"Take care, *m'lady.* The knife is sharp," he hissed, pulling the flat of it back against my throat with both of his hands now, choking me.

I gasped, but I couldn't grab it. Every time I did, I cut my hands. My vision was clouding, a tunnel forming, blackness closing in.

Belatedly I wondered if I still had any daggers left.

He laughed, feeling me thrash about, and easily guessed what I was after. He took out the remaining daggers at my waist and tossed them over the edge. Then he dragged me toward the front castle wall, easing the pressure at my throat just enough to keep me from passing out.

"I think I shall cut off your ears," he said, "just before I push you over the edge. You'll die in front of your husband this night, m'lady. And he'll be so shattered, my men shall retake his castle, once and for all."

Another stone hit the wall, this time at the top right, breaking through and sending stones ten feet long and four feet deep to the courtyard below. I glimpsed Lia and Mom on the far wall, doing battle with two remaining knights, and Rodolfo—thankfully free of his ropes—sneaking up on the nearest before Paratore and I fell to our knees from the impact. My enemy hauled me back up after a moment.

But I rose with the dagger from my calf sheath in my hand.

He held me close, too close to see what I'd done, but if I waited for just the right moment…

I clawed at his arm, trying to pry it from my neck as if I were desperate. "Cease your pawing, She-Wolf," he grunted. "There is only one way this ends. With me as victor. You shall go to your death knowing you crossed the wrong man."

He dragged me up beside Father Tomas, who remained on the crosswalk below the wall. I wondered what he was doing, why he hadn't run. But the priest was whispering, praying. He didn't cease when he saw me held against Paratore. But his bushy brow lowered.

My captor leaned me up against the wall, which was shoulder height, and we stared down below. Forty feet didn't look so high before. But from this vantage point, it was horrific. I could see the catapult now, the men scurrying about it, getting the next stone ready to fly toward the castle gates. "Forelli!" Paratore screamed. "Marcello Forelli! Show yourself!"

We stared toward the men, saw others in the brush.

But no Marcello. Was he hurt? Injured? Or worse?

I couldn't see well—even with the rising moon. The men were but dim forms.

My eyes widened as I saw a man go to the lever and release the next stone. Did they not see us? *Marcello! Luca!*

The stone was dragged along its platform, lifted, then arced and sailed toward us. We could see every deeply shadowed crevice as it came right toward us.

"Tomas!" I cried. "Jump!"

Paratore whipped me to the right, and perhaps by instinct, perhaps to protect his prize, he covered me with his body. The stone slammed into the crosswalk, and I felt Paratore's grip loosen.

And then felt the stones drop out from beneath me. I slid and felt the pads of my fingers scrape away, my nails tear as I clawed about. I had no choice; I released the dagger and tried to find any handhold I could as I fell three, then four, then five feet, when my foot abruptly found a crevice. I immediately cast to either side, pushing against either side of my Channel of Death in order to stay put.

But, yeah, it was seriously iffy. I couldn't hold out for long.

"Come, m'lady," Paratore said behind me. "Reach out your hand, and I'll lift you to safety."

I glanced over my shoulder. He was on a small ledge and had but two steps to go to make it to a stable place on the other side. I laughed without humor. "Take your hand so you can push me to my death yourself? I think not."

I heard the metallic slide of his sword from his sheath. "Take my hand, or I shall deal you the same death blow your father received."

My arms were trembling, protesting, begging me to let go.

"Gabriella!" Rodolfo shouted, peering down at me. Mom and Lia looked right over his shoulder. But they were too far away to reach me.

And then I heard the scrape of another stone upon the catapult. *Seriously?* I thought. I wanted to scream. Was Marcello not there to stop it? Could he not see us here, atop the front gates, fighting to stay alive? Did he not see *me?*

I couldn't make it through another impact. I'd already fallen a good eight feet. Below me was a hole…Even if I survived, falling the remaining thirty feet would make me wish I was dead.

There was no choice.

"All right," I ground out, meeting Paratore's gaze. "I'm reaching for your hand on the count of three." He sheathed his sword and reached for me. "One, two, three."

I didn't think about it, couldn't think about it. I turned and grasped for Paratore's hand even as I was again sliding. He grabbed me, and for a moment I hung, suspended, legs dangling over the hole. I felt the draft of cold up my skirts, the distance to the ground like I had some sort of radar-sensors.

"Tempting," he grunted, "but I have use for you yet." He glanced up and over at Rodolfo, his voice strained with the effort of holding me. "Back away! Drop your weapons and back away, or I'll drop her!"

I held my breath, wondering how long he could hold me. If he'd even have the strength to lift me. But he did then, hauling me upward and into his arms, then up the two steps to safety. He deposited me on my knees, clenching my hair in his fist. "Forelli!" he roared, back over the wall. "I demand to see Marcello Forelli! Tell him I have his bride!"

He wound another coil of my hair around his hand and hauled me to my feet, pushing me to the edge of the front wall. "Bring Lord Forelli to the light!" he screamed.

"I am not down there," Marcello growled from behind us, to the left, "but rather in the shadows of your own perch."

Paratore automatically whirled, leaving me behind him, but his hand was still wound in my hair. Ten of the Lerici archers were behind Marcello, on the wall, arrows pointed at Paratore.

"'Tis over, Cosmo," Marcello said. "Release Gabriella and step away from her."

Paratore cried out and turned, ripping me in the opposite direction, throwing me off balance. Tossing me aside. I heard the thrumming sound of arrows released, closed my eyes, once again preparing myself for impact…

I wasn't hit. But I was falling again, now bumping down the opposite side of the crosswalk, toward the hole again—

I saw Marcello dive above me and Rodolfo dive above him. Then Father Tomas. Marcello grabbed my hand, pulling me to an abrupt stop, and when we both began to fall, Tomas grabbed him. Rodolfo fell across the chasm, shoulder first, taking a firm hold on Tomas.

I couldn't breathe. I could feel my legs dangling again. Over way too much space.

Two more faces appeared above the other men, both grunting and gasping for breath, trying to hold on. The archers. Then Luca, eyes wide. "Hold on!" he cried.

I could feel my wrist slipping in Marcello's hand. I looked up at him in horror, and then felt sadness, such sorrow, sorrow that this was the way it was to end.

"Hold on, Gabriella," he grunted, upside-down, pulling with everything he had. But he was in the wrong position to save me. I could see it. He could see it, even if he wouldn't admit it.

"I love you," I gasped, having trouble breathing well, let alone speaking, as I hung there. "I've always loved you."

He cried out in frustration, red-faced, veins bulging from the effort at trying to pull me upward.

"Marcello!" Tomas cried, sounding like he was about to lose his grip. "Don't move!"

"She's slipping!" Marcello yelled, his voice tinged in panic. He looked at me with such extreme grief, it made me want to weep. "Gabriella...*nay*."

"Marcello. I know. My fault. Mine, for being here." I didn't want him to blame himself for what was about to happen.

"Gabriella!" Luca called, tossing down a rope with a loop at the bottom.

I glanced at it, six inches from our hands. If Marcello released me, could I grasp hold of it? Before I fell? Did I have the strength to hold it, or would I slide too far? Miss it altogether?

Marcello could see my dilemma. "Tomas, Rodolfo! Let us go."

"Let you go?" Rodolfo grunted. "Are you mad?"

"'Tis the only way to reach the rope," Marcello coaxed. "Now," he said, his voice suddenly all commando. "*Now!*"

Marcello slid toward me, even as I started to fall, but in the process, he gained a better grip on my wrist, as I did on his. He reached out with his right hand as we gained momentum, and I knew we had one chance—just one chance—and felt a grief pierce me that I hadn't felt since Fortino, since Dad...

I was not only falling to my death. I was taking my husband with me.

I felt a tug again and swung toward the wall, my feet touching the splintered wood of the gate, and then moving outward. I looked up and let out a breath of total wonder as we swung. Together. Alive.

Marcello held me anew. In a grip that said *I. Shall. Not. Let. Go.*

The men lowered us down to the ground, and when my feet were on it, Marcello released me. I knelt and inhaled the scent of dirt and stone, so glad to be on it. In reality I didn't think my shaky knees could hold me upright. Marcello leaned down and covered me with his body, hugging me, sheltering me. "Ahh, Gabriella," he moaned.

Trembling, I rose up to my knees, and he pulled me into his arms for a brief hug, then lifted me to my feet. With one arm around me, holding me up, he moved toward the men down below. Behind us I could hear shouts and cries and gradually remembered that a battle was still taking place.

When my knees gave way, Marcello bent and swept me into his arms. He turned and looked to the parapets high above us—so high, I could barely look at them, too close to my Near Death Experience. But above, two flaming arrows crossed in the sky, a signal. And then I saw the long ropes, the last of the Lerici knights making their way down, and on the ground, my mother, sister, Rodolfo, Tomas—

"Our people are safe!" Marcello cried, a couple of minutes later. "Take down those gates, once and for all!"

A hundred feet away the Sienese cheered and launched the next stone missile directly at Castello Paratore's splintered gates.

At last I dared to say, "My…my father's body. Marcello—"

"His body?" he said with a frown, turning me toward him. "Gabriella, he is not dead." He shook his head, but he was smiling. "He suffered a terrible wound, yes. But he will recover."

I stared at him, trying to make sense of his words. "In truth?" I asked.

"In truth."

But I was already moving away from him.

Toward my mother, my sister, and the group of men carrying the man in a blanket between them. *Dad*.

# Chapter Thirty-two

"Dad. *Dad*," I said, falling to my knees beside him. The men, satisfied that we were far enough away from Castello Paratore's gates, set him down.

"Gabi," he said, reaching out to touch my face. He smiled weakly and looked over at Mom and Lia on the other side. "All my girls, safe," he breathed.

"Oh, Dad. I—I—you're okay? You're really okay?"

"He'll be okay, Gabs," Mom said. "A good cleaning, some sutures…" She reached across him to hold my hand. "He'll be all right."

I looked to Lia, and with one glance to her baby blues puddling in tears, I lost it. They were all here. All safe. Whole. Or almost.

*Thank You, God. Thank You. Thank You thank You thank You thank You…*

I cried like I was weeping for Dad the first time he died. For all of us, like we'd just died and come back to life. From fear, from exhaustion, from relief, from gratitude. Sheer gratitude. And Mom and Lia cried too, hugging each other, then coming around to wrap me in their embrace as well.

Marcello edged in and wrapped his arm around my shoulders. After a moment he said, "Gabriella, let them take him now, no? Back to the castello, where your mother and the others can see to him?"

"Yes," I said through my tears, wiping my nose with the back of my hand. "Yes," I repeated, now feeling foolish for keeping him from their care at all.

The men lifted him immediately and hurried off, a regiment of soldiers closing in to flank them, protect them on the way back to Castello Forelli. Mom and Lia were right behind Dad. I started after them but then hesitated and looked back.

Marcello stood there, Rodolfo and Luca behind him, in the flickering torchlight. He lifted his chin and grinned. "Go on, wife. Your part in this battle is done. See to your father. And we shall see this through."

Luca and Rodolfo nodded, hands on their belts. I knew Marcello was in safe hands. And I…well, I had had it.

I was scary tired. Hurting. Barely able to stand.

Bleary-eyed, I saw Marcello motion to some men, and in a minute they brought horses over for us. He lifted me up to a mare's broad, bare back and wrapped my hand in her mane. "Go home, beloved," he said. "I will meet you there."

I wanted to stay. With him. To help.

But deep inside I knew I'd serve us all best if, this time, I just did as he asked.

I awakened stiff and freezing cold on the stone floor of the castle. Squinching my eyes, I pushed myself up, hit my head on the crossbeam of a bed, and gingerly made my way upright.

"That had to hurt," Dad mumbled, peeking at me for a sec from one eye, then closing it again as if it pained him. He was under the covers. Mom was asleep in a chair in the corner, Lia by her side.

"Uh, yeah," I said, rubbing my head. But it was the least of my worries. "How are you?"

"Just great, thanks," he said, opening his big, brown eyes again. He was pale, but looking good, considering. "Pretty much like any other morning of my life. Except, oh, right"—he raised his brows— "I watched my daughters and wife take on knight after knight at an enemy castle—and survive. And oh, save a bunch of people too. That was cool. The only downer was that I took a sword through the back and my wife had to stitch me up. And we had to leave my son-in-law behind to—"

His eyes moved from me to the doorway behind me, and in that instant I knew Marcello was there. I turned and smiled. He was dirty—seriously covered in filth and sweat—but I swear I'd never seen a more handsome man in my life. He reached out and helped me to my feet. I groaned, feeling every pulled muscle and fresh bruise in my body. But I forgot all of that as Marcello wrapped me in his arms and pulled me close, kissing my temple and hair and holding me as if he never wanted to let me go.

I could hear Mom and Lia rustling behind me, and I saw Rodolfo and Tomas and Luca behind Marcello. They were all back. Safe. I pulled back. "It's over?"

"It is over," Marcello said gently, pushing a coil of hair behind my ear. "The Fiorentini are now five miles beyond Castello Paratore. My men shall see they stay there." Leaving an arm around my shoulders, he stepped toward Dad. "Sir, I am glad to see you on the mend."

Dad gripped his outstretched hand. "As am I," he said with a grin.

"Well, if you encounter further trouble, I am aware of a certain tunnel that has certain healing powers—"

"Impossible," I said. "Dad shall have to be at death's door in order for me to leave you again."

"A suitable threshold," Dad said.

"Death is always nearby." I paused and looked around the room, at Mom and Lia and Marcello and Luca and Rodolfo and Tomas. "Let's embrace this life we've been given. *Life*, Marcello," I said, squeezing him tight and then drawing back to stare into his eyes. "Let us live like we're celebrating, every day."

"Together," he said, tucking the strand of hair behind my ear again and cradling my cheek. He looked at me with such love it brought tears to my eyes. He bent his forehead to touch mine. "*Together*."

"Together," I whispered.

## ... a little more ...

When a delightful concert comes to an end,

the orchestra might offer an encore.

When a fine meal comes to an end,

it's always nice to savor a bit of dessert.

When a great story comes to an end,

we think you may want to linger.

And so, we offer ...

**AfterWords**—just a little something more after you

have finished a David C Cook novel.

We invite you to stay awhile in the story.

Thanks for reading!

Turn the page for ...

- **Discussion Questions**
- **Historical Notes**
- **A Letter from Lisa**
- **Facebook and Mobile Page**

# Discussion Questions

1. On their way to San Galgano, the family discusses the legend of Excalibur and the sword in the stone. Gabi comments that in her society, people are taught to regard things with suspicion until proven. Do you see that in people you know? What do people believe in without "proof"? Is that a good or bad thing?

2. How old do you think you want to be when you get married? Why?

3. Two-thirds of medieval women were married by the age of nineteen. Some very wealthy noblewomen were as old as twenty-four when they married, but they were a rarity. What do you think marriages would be like today, in contemporary society, if we married earlier rather than later? Would it help or hurt?

4. How did you respond to Gabi's growing attraction to Rodolfo Greco—and her confusion? Could you understand it? What would you have done in that situation?

5. From the beginning of *Waterfall* to the end of *Torrent,* significant changes happen in the Betarrini family dynamics. In the beginning, the girls feel very separate from their parents. Then they feel the loss of their dad, connect with their mom, and in the end, really become one again. Has your family suffered through a time of disunity and

come out better for it? Are you in the midst of it now? What made or would make it better?

6. Tomas has a unique perspective on God, given his time and place. He's serving as a priest, even when he's no longer representing the Church. What's your thought on how we should share our beliefs with others?

7. Once again, Gabi has to do things she never thought possible—jumping to another building, cauterizing a wound, risking her life, etc.—what's the hardest thing you've ever had to do (even if it wasn't life threatening!)? How'd you feel afterward?

8. In one passage, the book titles for the series are somewhat explained: "My eyes shifted to the trickling river. Come spring, it would be ten times as wide and just as deep. On and on it went, rushing toward the distant horizon. Like time. Like life. Sometimes gently falling from one pool into the other, other times fast and cascading, and still other times narrowing into a funnel, a torrent of knots and waves." Have you experienced life like that? Identify three times in your life that feel like a *Waterfall,* a *Cascade,* and a *Torrent.* Which one describes your life right now?

# Historical Notes

The events desscribed herein are entirely fictional. While the story is representative of the volatility of medieval Tuscany, it is merely that…representative. A couple of details in regard to *Torrent:*

The town of Sansicino is based on a Rick Steves show I saw once. In it, he described a hilltop town named Civita di Bagnoregio, which could only be accessed by a bridge. It was founded by the Etruscans and survived two world wars. Today it has a population of ten most of the year and one hundred in the summer. And, yeah, I totally want to visit it someday. How could you not?

We stopped by San Galgano while touring Tuscany—truly one of my favorite excursions of all time (you can read about it on our travel blog, www.TheWorldIsCalling.com), but it was off-season and we could do little more than tour the ghostly, roofless abbey. Up on the hill is the chapel that houses the sword in the stone, but it was closed the day we were there. It's still on my Must-See list. The potential birthplace of the whole Arthurian legend? C'mon! How could you resist? And I took some liberties with the frescoes described within, because they've found alternative drawings beneath the frescoes you can see now. Like the artist changed his mind and just went with what he saw fit for the final version, regardless of what the "rough draft" might've been. As an author, I think that's really wonderful, especially when you can't change it again with but an easy draft from a computer. It was truly a gamble with frescoes.

I didn't do a ton of research into medieval Rome, but there really was a barbershop underneath one of the triumphal arches of the Forum—half buried by this time period. Pretty amazing to think about. The Vatican really was in Avignon at the time—and the Romans did have such a command of their plumbing that they could create elaborate bathhouses with radiant heat, saunas, cold pools, and their versions of hot tubs. When I get to Rome this fall, I look forward to touring Caracalla's public bathhouse (which was closed, last time I went).

Ahh, history. Such rich fodder for a novelist!

—LTB

Dear Torrent Tribe,

Wow, I've loved this ride with you—and Gabi and Lia—in medieval Italy. Thank you for so enthusiastically embracing their story and making it your own. From your comments and emails, I know you've gathered what I'd hoped you'd get out of it. Not only enjoying the entertainment factor, but also investing in the passion, drive, enthusiasm, interest, power, sacrifice, and Great Questions of life that make life, *life*. That's how, for me, this became more of a River of *Life* series than a River of *Time*. Regardless of when you're born, I believe you experience life at a whole different level if you break out of "survival" mode and invest in the plowing/seeding/weeding process, as Gabi and Lia found themselves doing. Then, whether your crop is failing or flourishing, you're *in* it...*living*.

I've already heard from many of you, wondering if there will be more River of Time books. I'd truly love to come back and hang out with the Betarrini clan and write Lia and Luca's love story, but we have to see how these first three books do. In the meantime, I'm writing a series called The Grand Tour, about a group of well-to-do young people in 1914, traveling from England to France to Switzerland, and...wait for it...Italy! (You're totally shocked, right?) Somehow, Italia has captured my heart like few other places, and I'll be eager to return—in my imagination, or in person. The Grand Tour books are titled *From This Day Forward, To Have and To Hold,* and *As Long as We Both Shall Live.* Look for them to be released June 2012–January 2013 (again, in a short time span, thanks to David C Cook—they know readers agonize as they wait).

I'm heading to Rome soon with my second daughter, off to do research for *As Long as We Both Shall Live.* But I'll be holding

River of Time close in my heart as I go. Please don't lose touch with me—find me on Facebook ("River of Time Series" and "Lisa Tawn Bergren") and on Twitter (@LisaTBergren) and on my own site (www.LisaBergren.com) if you want to follow along with my travels, writing, contests, and such.

I'm so happy you're one of my readers…which I see is an investment in *me* and, truly, makes *you* one of my friends. Contact me at any time via Facebook, Twitter, or email. I look forward to hearing from you.

Every good thing,

*Lisa T. Bergren*

*Join other readers and Lisa on the "River of Time Series" Facebook page. There, you'll find information about the books, discussion with other fans, and contest and prize information.*

*Use this QR code to visit the River of Time.mobi page.*

*QR codes link to sites via your mobile phone. If your phone can take a picture, it can read QR codes. Check the web on how to download the software (if it's not there already).*

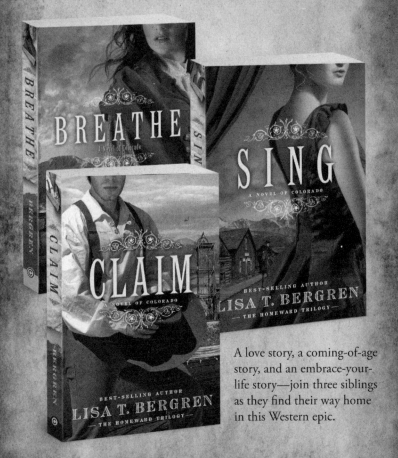